Reader Re

'Once I'd digested the first chapter, I ke
more..." until I ran out of time.'

'I liked the detail and pacing and the gentle way you introduced and
fleshed-out the characters.'

'The very first time I have encountered an author writing about coming
into high speed contact with interstellar debris with any level of accuracy.
I can't tell you how refreshing that is.'

'Nice to see a novel in which the characters clearly aren't the standard
Caucasians.'

'More sex than usual for this type of story. Wonderful.'

'Very much looking forward to your next books.'

'The characters are well drawn and engaging.'

'When can I get the next one?'

'The level of attention to detail here is excellent.'

Also by William John Graham

RIVAL ARRIVAL

Choosing a destination (and other trouble) on arrival in Alpha Centauri

Part 2 of the Alpha System series

(Available Spring 2021)

FUN & GAMES

Engine (and other) trouble on the way to Alpha Centauri

WILLIAM JOHN GRAHAM

SUSURRUS

SUSURRUS

First published by Susurrus 2020
An imprint of Montrose House
Montrose House, Duck Street
Steeple Langford, Salisbury
Wiltshire, U.K.

A CIP catalogue record for this book is available from the British Library

ISBN 978-1-8383305-0-7

Set in
Text: Palatino Linotype
Titles: Bahnschrift SemiBold Condensed

1 3 5 7 9 8 6 4 2

www.williamjohngraham.com

K100 Crew at Departure

NAME / PRIMARY DUTY / BACKUP DUTY

Sahko / Captain / Medical, Navigation

Minogue / Science / Second Officer, Personnel

Yingluq / Medical / Science, Bioengineering & Food

Bita / Communications, Personnel / Safety

Ibo / Engines / Analytics, Payload

Hyun / Printers, Robotics / Environmental Services

Agyei / Chemistry & Materials / Engineering

Bjorn / Safety, Payload / Mimics & EVA

Avalos / Navigation, Mimics & EVA / Communications

Gunadi / Analytics / Robotics, Printers

Massoud / Bioengineering & Food, Environmental
Services / Chemistry & Materials

Menem / Engineering / Engines

K100 Basic Layout

Deceleration Configuration

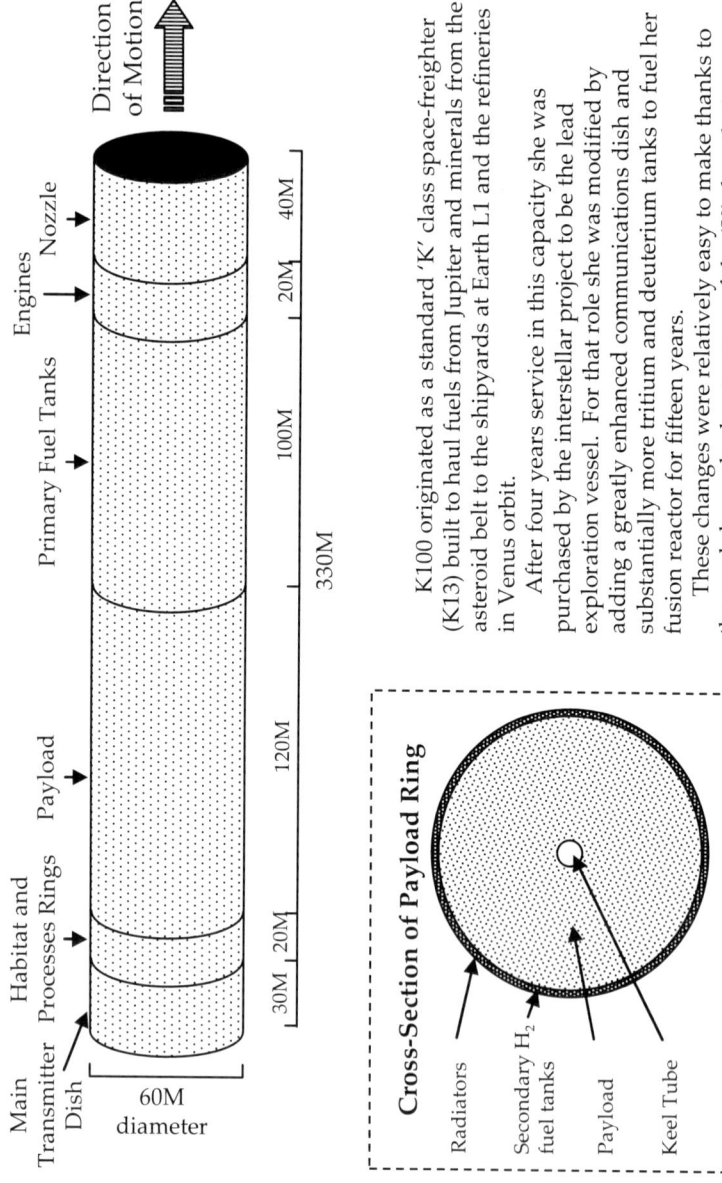

K100 originated as a standard 'K' class space-freighter (K13) built to haul fuels from Jupiter and minerals from the asteroid belt to the shipyards at Earth L1 and the refineries in Venus orbit.

After four years service in this capacity she was purchased by the interstellar project to be the lead exploration vessel. For that role she was modified by adding a greatly enhanced communications dish and substantially more tritium and deuterium tanks to fuel her fusion reactor for fifteen years.

These changes were relatively easy to make thanks to the modular and robust nature of the 'K' class design.

Cross-Section of Payload Ring

Radiators

Secondary H$_2$ fuel tanks

Payload

Keel Tube

K100 Habitat Ring Cross Section
Deceleration Configuration

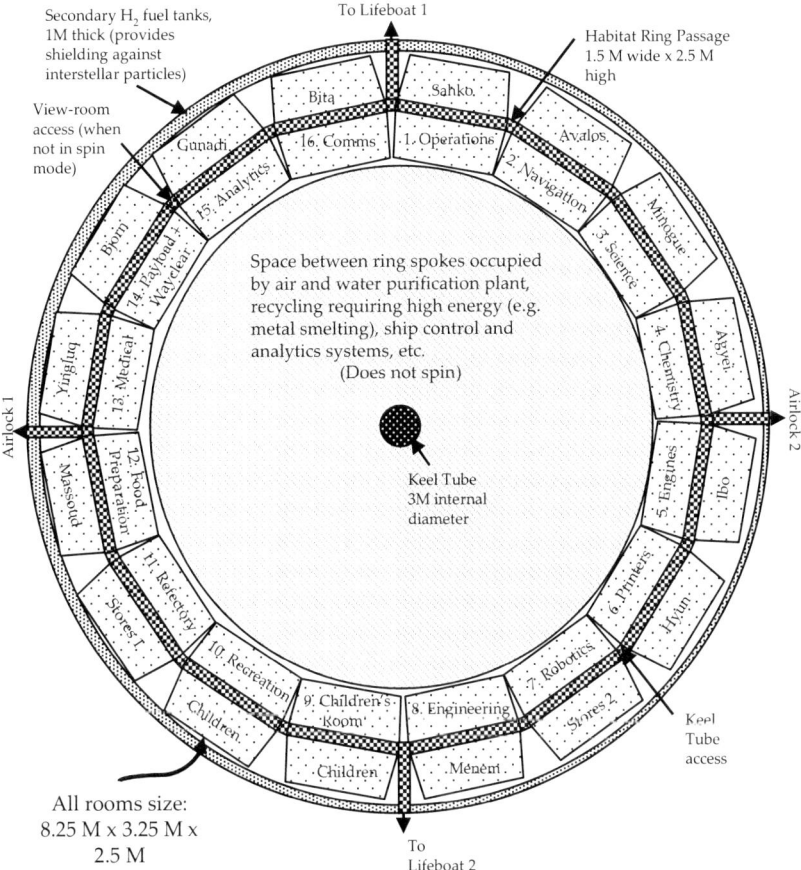

Secondary H₂ fuel tanks, 1M thick (provides shielding against interstellar particles)

View-room access (when not in spin mode)

To Lifeboat 1

Habitat Ring Passage 1.5 M wide x 2.5 M high

Space between ring spokes occupied by air and water purification plant, recycling requiring high energy (e.g. metal smelting), ship control and analytics systems, etc.
(Does not spin)

Keel Tube 3M internal diameter

Airlock 1

Airlock 2

Keel Tube access

All rooms size: 8.25 M x 3.25 M x 2.5 M

To Lifeboat 2

Rooms (clockwise from top): Sahko, 1. Operations, Avalos, 2. Navigation, Mpodgue, 3. Science, Abyei, 4. Chemistry, Ilbo, 5. Engines, Hyun, 6. Printers, 7. Robotics, Stores 2, 8. Engineering, Menem, Children, 9. Children's Room, Children, 10. Recreation, Stores 1, 11. Refectory, Massoud, 12. Food Preparation, 13. Medical, Jingjing, Bjorn, 14. Flayhoul + Wayekar, 15. Analytics, Gunani, 16. Comms, Bita

The K-100 Habitat and Processes Rings were adapted from a standard 'K' class personnel carrier module. These were used either to carry tourists (64 per ring in standard two person cabin occupancy, 16 in first-class configuration) or colonists and industry workers (128 in short-haul, colonisation mode.)

K100 Habitat Ring Profile
Deceleration Configuration

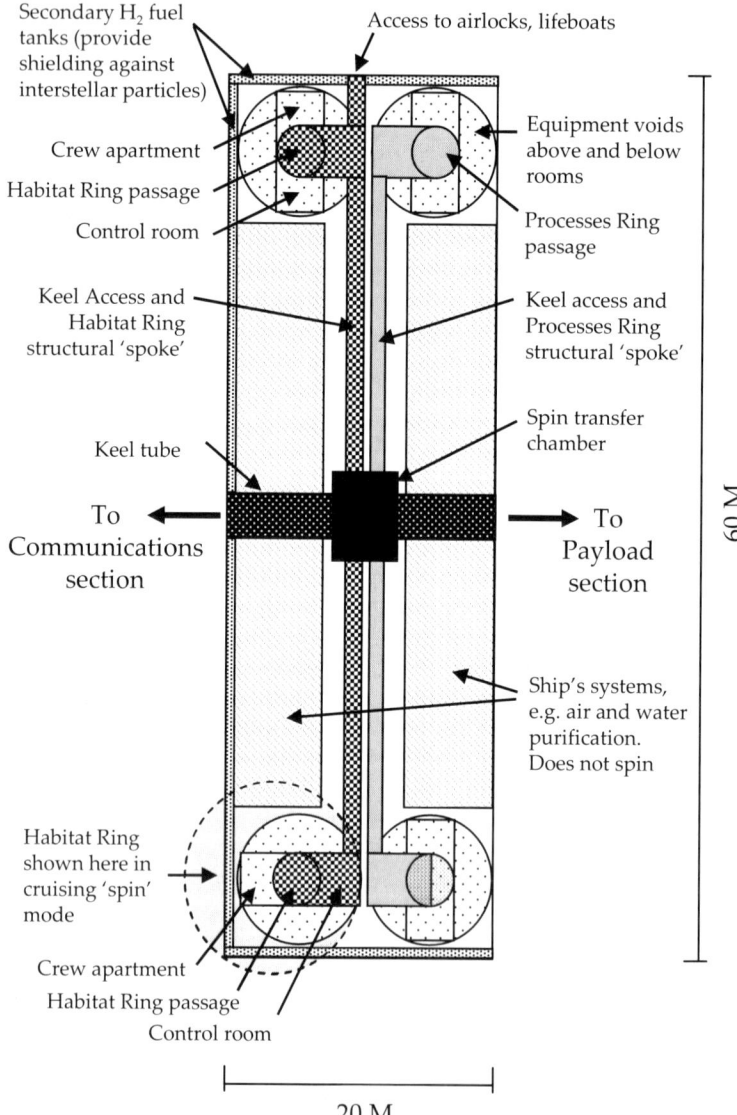

Secondary H$_2$ fuel tanks (provide shielding against interstellar particles)

Access to airlocks, lifeboats

Crew apartment

Habitat Ring passage

Control room

Equipment voids above and below rooms

Processes Ring passage

Keel Access and Habitat Ring structural 'spoke'

Keel access and Processes Ring structural 'spoke'

Keel tube

Spin transfer chamber

To Communications section

To Payload section

60 M

Ship's systems, e.g. air and water purification. Does not spin

Habitat Ring shown here in cruising 'spin' mode

Crew apartment

Habitat Ring passage

Control room

20 M

Mission Day 4018

4018, 04:50

Up ahead, through the window in the door, the air was hazy. Status's report of fire in Engine Control might actually be real and not the result of the increasingly common problem of sensor malfunction. Although the ship had shaken and alarms had started that hadn't necessarily meant fire. Nevertheless I had rushed to investigate before the Captain, my former great love, was on my neck.

'Menem, what the hell is going on?' Sahko's voice demanded in my ear.

'I'm checking out section five,' I replied. 'It could be a sensor fault,'

'Not with all the vibration we felt.'

'Those might have been caused by the sudden shut down of Main: unstable fuel flow or something. Possibly a pump failed. Maybe the trouble in Engine Control triggered an emergency stop. Also there are reports of multiple objects directly in our path and something wrong with Wayclear, but that might be more sensor trouble.'

It seemed unlikely that a fuel pump failure had resulted in the whole ship shaking, and a single failure wouldn't have shut the engine down. Sahko would have the same information from Status that I had so my adding some guesswork was to suggest that I was on top of things.

I pushed through the fire door into five and found the whole section at an angle: it had only half rotated. I stood with one foot on the floor and the other on what should have been a wall. Smoke hung in the air and a smell of something like burning plastic caused me to gag.

'Definitely a malfunction and signs of fire,' I wheezed. 'Is Ibo or anyone else in her apartment, because section five hasn't rotated completely?'

Sahko switched to her Captain's voice. 'All crew, possible category-four emergency in progress. Bjorn, go fast to section five to join Menem and get that fire out. Everyone else to Lifeboat One and prepare for possible launch. No non-emergency related comms. This is not a test. I repeat: this is not a test. Ibo, are you or anyone else in your apartment?'

Ibo replied immediately: 'No, I'm next door in Hyun's.'

Grabbing a full fire suit with head mask and air tank from a wall unit, I tried to make sense of what Status was telling me. The data didn't seem to be coherent so sensor failure was very likely to be at least one of the troubles.

Automatic fire suppression was in progress in Engine Control: the oxygen-rich atmosphere being rapidly replaced with pure nitrogen and all the section fluid, air and power connections closed off. Engine Control up in flames and Main shut down was bad enough, but why was Status reporting that it had no information on the amount of fuel remaining? There had been enough for the remainder of the journey when I had gone to bed. Losing a significant amount of our primary fuel would be catastrophic. On top of that, the shut down of a Wayclear laser was leaving our defences compromised, right at the moment its radars were detecting a succession of objects in our path.

No doubt the captain and the rest of the crew had, like me, been brought instantly awake only a couple of minutes earlier when the ship had lurched suddenly. A moment later an alarm had begun wailing and all the lights had come on. A series of harsh vibrations had followed, objects had started floating and the crash of doors closing had added to the cacophony. A second alarm had joined the first. The usually ever-present hiss of air circulation had stopped.

The floating objects had begun to sink back down in curving arcs while I sat on the edge of my bed in a cold sweat, feeling the apartment moving. The main engine must have shut down and Control had automatically started spin-up and rotation to restore the feeling of gravity.

The vibrations had stopped as suddenly as they had started. My stomach had lurched when I had tried to stand, so I had sat again and it settled. Detachedly I had observed my hands shaking.

'Engineering status,' I had called out.

Status had summarised the faults it knew about and brought up what was supposed to be the video feed from Engine Control but from which nothing could be seen. Either the camera had failed or it was blanked by dense smoke. After a glance at the apparently contented sleeping form of Jazz, I had hastily pulled on a clean ship-suit and shoes and rushed out. The passage was curving upwards for spin mode, rather than left or right for deceleration, as it should have been. All the fire doors between sections had shut.

Bjorn joined me in the tilted corridor, carrying a fire suit and accompanied by an extinguisher bot. He peered through the control room view port and indicated that we needed to suit-up, pulling his over his big frame with practiced ease. He set up a fire-control tent over us and the door to Engine Control, gave a thumbs-up, which, once I had finished struggling into my fire suit and sealing my breathing mask, I reciprocated.

Triggering the manual control, he slid open the door. Immediately vile, yellow smoke billowed out and visibility dropped to almost zero. The extinguisher bot clambered through and disappeared. Bjorn opened an emergency ladder, lowered it down the sloping floor, and cautiously led the way into the gloom below.

Sizzling and grinding noises came from one corner and we could hear the extinguisher bot announcing that it had found where it thought the trouble lay. Bjorn took manual control before it hacked its way through a wall panel to get at the seat of the fire. I felt my way to the main control panel which was all shut down. So why was there a motor still active behind the panel? I used my remote to manually isolate all the external power feeds to the room. Eventually I hit the right circuit and the grinding stopped, leaving us with the urgent cry of distant alarms.

Bjorn guided me to the area the bot had identified as the seat of the fire. The smoke poured from around the edges of some access panels covering a machinery bay. While he readied the bot, I manually released a panel and pulled it aside allowing a dense cloud to billow out. The bot immediately sprayed the interior with fire suppressant, effectively cutting off the supply of smoke. It had been a long time, if ever, that I had looked behind that panel. Archive gave me the schematics for the bay which showed it contained the motor and gearbox for rotating the section. Probably the motor had become overloaded as a result of the section jamming somehow. An overload would have caused rapid heat build-up, resulting in fire in electrical insulation and composite structural materials, generating all the smoke. A sensor should have detected overheating and cut the power to the motor, as should have the fire suppression system. All would need investigating later. However, that little fire definitely wasn't the source of all the other trouble, more likely a consequence.

Sahko's voice, still in full command mode, came over the all-ship channel. 'Faster to the lifeboat. This is a serious category-four emergency: get moving. Full emergency procedures. Ready to stand off in one minute.'

Crew being slow probably meant that some had stopped to grab personal items. The lifeboats would be hell anyway, with us all packed together without privacy. If Bjorn and I had to join them we would use the second lifeboat. Linking up the two wouldn't be fun either, particularly in the catastrophic event that the lifeboats had to un-tether.

The lifeboats were hardly more than a psychological prop out here. No one else was around to rescue us and the lifeboats had little protection from interstellar radiation and limited supplies. Whatever the trouble, if we had to use them, we must stay tethered, re-board the ship as soon as the immediate emergency was over and get Main restarted.

An air-cleaner bot that Bjorn had summoned arrived and plugged itself into the containment tent. It soon began to have an impact: visibility improving as the smoke cleared. Bjorn removed other access panels and conducted a thermal search for hotspots. Status wasn't indicating any cascading failures but the integrity of its sensors was still in doubt.

An alarm was sounding from trouble elsewhere, most likely Wayclear, but it might be another failure or an engine shut down warning. With the drive suddenly stopped, the fusion reactor would be producing a massive surplus of power which would be being dumped as heat into space. The fusion system would be forced to power down soon as the capacity of the ship to radiate away its heat was limited. Lots of relatively unused systems were swinging into action, ramping up the risk levels.

Status was flagging a whole series of warnings but lowering the emergency level, which seemed contradictory. Presumably it was regaining connection to some of the sensors it had lost contact with, consequently improving its understanding of what was going on. Encouragingly, the hiss of air circulation restarted.

Bjorn signalled that he hadn't found any more hotspots. The seat of the fire was cooling rapidly as the thermally conducting foam pulled heat away.

Bjorn reported to Sahko: 'Primary fire suppressed and no secondaries identified. De-tox in section five is underway.'

'Engineering?' Sahko demanded.

'Section five rotation motor is the probable source of the fire. The cause of that is unknown as yet. The fusion engine is likely to go into low power mode soon from lack of demand from Main and the risk of overheating. Other warnings still outstanding are confusing.'

'Fuel status?'

'Unverified as yet.'

'The motor fire can't be the source of the vibrations or possible fuel loss.'

'Agreed. The vibrations might have been caused by some kind of failure in the antimatter fuel feed, which would also have shut down Main. The Wayclear trouble is yet to be confirmed but these failures may

4

all be linked, possibly to an object strike, but we don't have sufficient information yet to tell.'

'What's your assessment of the risk to ship and crew?'

'Status is not detecting any other sources of immediate risk, apart from more objects in our path. At least part of Wayclear is still in action. It would be helpful to have more crew to investigate all the signals.'

'How about Ibo to find out what has happened to Main and Hyun to organise a bot-net external check?'

'Both would be good. I'll investigate the Wayclear problem.'

Sahko went back on to the all-ship. 'Immediate source of emergency identified as the section five rotation motor fire, which has been extinguished. Lifeboat to remain attached for now but prepared to detach and stay tethered at one-'k'. Hyun and Ibo: go back aboard and liaise with Menem and Bjorn for further investigations.'

Sahko called me again. 'Archive shows that Wayclear has been detecting incoming objects for some hours. Status is now showing some structural failure in the area between Main and an anti-matter tank.'

I scrolled through the Status reports. 'The structural failure is particularly concerning, although Status shows it as not immediately life threatening. I'm investigating.'

'I don't like the sound of Wayclear in trouble, with the possibility of further object strikes, if that's what has already happened. Where one object got through, another might follow.'

'We don't know yet if we've been struck. Ibo, can you check over Main to see if the alarms are consistent with an object strike?' I asked.

'I'll see if there was some instability in Main, the secondary engines or the fuel system,' Ibo replied. 'Any of those could have caused the vibrations and shutdown. I'll have to do that from Operations, and also see how quickly I can get Main restarted from there.'

'Thanks, Ibo. The sooner we can get the alarms off the better. Hyun, can you get a bot-net team to check over the exterior and search for strike trouble, possibly a breach in a fuel tank or fuel line?'

'OK.'

'Bjorn, are you all right on your own now?'

'Yes. There are no further signs of trouble in here. I'll call you if something else breaks out.'

I left Bjorn sucking up every last drop of fire suppressant, ready for recycling. Nothing could be allowed to go to waste.

The failed motor would have to come out to be rebuilt as well as determine the extent of the damage to the ship and the cause of the fault. Isolating the electrical and control feeds would do for now.

I clambered up out of Engine Control and used the containment tent airlock to get into the corridor, stripped off my fire suit and hurried around the Habitat Ring to section fourteen, Wayclear Control.

A mass of red warnings on the Wayclear status screen indicated that the system had been overwhelmed by numerous objects in our path. One of the four lasers was offline, and all the radar detectors were still reporting a cloud of unidentifiable objects directly ahead. Wayclear could only do so much in terms of detecting and deflecting objects, even tiny particles would do immense damage if they hit us while we were travelling so fast. Wayclear could see a hundred kilometres out and detect objects smaller than a grain of dust in our direct line of flight. It would direct its lasers to ionise the objects, leaving the ship's electromagnetic field to deflect them around us. But Wayclear had only microseconds to react. Even though we had already slowed to a fraction over thirty-percent of light-speed, the cloud of objects had overwhelmed it. Quite possibly the offline laser itself had been hit by an unlucky strike.

I called Ibo. 'Wayclear is reporting that we're in some kind of object field and it extends ahead as far as it can see. We must keep Fuse powered up.'

'It's borderline without power demand from Main. Even if Wayclear can be kept running at maximum that's not enough to keep Fuse operating indefinitely, even at its lowest output.'

'One of Wayclear's lasers is out, so three-quarters of maximum is the most it can take. What else can we dump power in to?'

'The ion thrusters can take a lot, but that means burning our limited supply of propellant. That might prove to be a problem later when we're in-system.'

'Let me know if you come up with any other ideas. Would the fission reactor on its own be able to provide enough power?'

'Only for a short time, and then almost nothing else, nothing except emergency systems.'

'OK, Ibo. I'll discuss with Sahko. We may need a brainstorm on this.' I clicked channels to Sahko's.

'Sahko, update.'

'Go ahead.'

I summarised my conversation with Ibo and concluded: 'Without Fuse our magnetosphere is limited, radiation counts will start to rise and we'll be at greater risk of object strikes.'

Sahko paused before replying. 'Any word from Hyun yet on external damage and Ibo on what the problem is with Main?'

'Not yet from either.'

'Chase please. I'll get Minogue to run power options and then get back to you. I'm going on to Science.' Sahko disconnected.

'Hyun, Menem here. Wayclear is showing one laser not functioning. Can you see anything from the bot-net?'

'It's been checking over the fuel tanks, which all look intact. The sensors for the hydrogen tanks aren't reporting any problem but those from some of the antimatter tanks have failed and one tank has some torn insulation. There's significant damage to an anti-hydrogen fuel line, between the trap-tanks and the main drive, consistent with pipe rupture and consequent fuel blast. In that area the bots have observed some substantial structural damage and discolouration, as well as severed pipes and cables. The energy produced from a small anti-hydrogen leak, subsequent explosion and the resulting structural damage seem likely to be the cause of the vibration we experienced before automatic fuel-flow stops cut in. I'll now divert part of the bot-net to investigate the Wayclear lasers.'

'Thanks, Hyun. I'll view the images of the anti-hydrogen feed damage. By the way, any ideas on dumping or using excess power from Fuse while Main is offline? We need to keep Wayclear functioning, but to do so we urgently need to dump excess power to prevent overheating.'

'Is there anything in the payload that could take power or could be deployed to radiate more heat away?'

'An interesting idea, but probably not a quick solution. I'll flag it to Bjorn and add it to ideas on a collaboration page for Minogue and Sahko. If you think of anything else, add it too.'

I called Ibo again. 'Any update?'

'The engine management system shows that massive instability occurred in the anti-hydrogen feed, resulting in emergency engine shutdown. Supply of anti-hydrogen appears to be cut. Fuse is starting to show warnings. If the plasma becomes unstable, it too will shut down. Can we ramp up our magnetosphere any more? That would reduce radiation risk as well, which is vital with Main out and the continuing threat from incoming objects. Do we know if the objects are susceptible to electromagnetic field deflection without being ionised?'

'The ship's field should already be at maximum. How about powering the engine nozzle field back up?'

'I'll do what I can there, but it too will create heat.'

'We might also be able to use power in the main transmitter: sending white noise or something; I'll add that. Thanks, Ibo, keep us updated on Fuse status.'

'How about spinning up and spinning down? That uses a lot of power.' Ibo added.

I groaned. 'And makes us all sick, notably me. Most of the crew are sub-par for a while as we get used to a single change. But if we have to....'

Hyun came on the comms again. 'The bots are showing one of the Wayclear lasers swinging in the breeze. Either it was hit by something or it came loose during the vibration. I'll investigating further and see if the bot-net can fix the problem. A printer is on warm-up and will be available as needed to make replacement parts. No other damage has been seen so far. The bot-net is continuing to check over the whole exterior.'

'Get a second printer on warm-up too. We'll need parts for the antimatter feed presumably.'

I instructed Control to isolate the damaged laser but found that it had already been done by Hyun. He wouldn't have wanted one of his bots fried while doing an inspection.

Status showed no new urgent problems so I went over to Science where Sahko had joined Minogue. The main display was lit up with Archive data, schematics, ship-status sensor reports, Hyun's inspection bot images, star maps, power maps and a whole host of other information. The two were in deep discussion: trying to piece together the story of what had happened and to decide on action priorities.

Sahko looked up. 'Menem, anything new?'

'You've Ibo's report on the engine and Hyun's latest on the damage to both the antimatter feed pipe and to Wayclear, so no. Do we have any idea how big this object field is?'

'We don't know what we've encountered yet,' said Minogue. 'The rate of detections has now started to decline. We don't know how close we are to the centre of the cloud, or its shape, so we don't know if we've mostly got through it, and the danger has largely passed, or if it's perhaps like a hurricane or an eggshell, and we're now in the eye, and we'll therefore pass back into a dense region of objects again. We're reconfiguring the main antenna to search for anomalies. We don't know how well it will work in detecting distortions of the star-field: it depends on the size and distribution of objects in the cloud. We may miss its centre of mass anyway, with the main antenna unable to sweep the sky. Gunadi is analysing all our deep-space sensor data to try to detect any recent electromagnetic or gravitational field anomalies.'

Sahko cut in. 'So our priority must be to keep Wayclear fully operational as far as possible and maximise our deflection field. Fuse must be kept running. Minogue agrees that we should keep diverting as much power as possible to our magnetosphere. The nozzle magnets are back on to take more power and add to our field. The heat radiation system can handle a higher load, now Main has cooled somewhat, which buys us time. Additionally we're putting power into the primary and secondary transmitters: as much as they can handle.'

'At the speed we're going, it must be a massive field if we're still in it,' I said.

'Yup.' Minogue paused a moment. 'Like a comet's tail or an entire ring system centred on a cold brown dwarf.' The cold object: one of the nightmares of deep-space travel.

Sahko brought the discussion to an end. 'Menem, I want you to work with Hyun to get Wayclear fixed. Use whatever resources you need. Perhaps Bjorn can help as he's already aboard. Minogue, liaise with Ibo to keep Fuse powered up and then your second priority is to get Main restarted. I'll get the rest of the crew back on board. It seems unlikely that we're in imminent danger of being annihilated in an antimatter explosion, and the lifeboats are probably more vulnerable than the ship to object strikes. Agreed?'

Minogue and I nodded. Maybe we were both thinking that if it was a ring, and we were just passing out of its densest part, then we could be approaching its centre. A lifeboat would be just as useless as the ship if a planet or dead star lay there.

4018, 05:30

Disconcerted again by the change in corridor geometry on leaving, I called Hyun. 'Anything new?'

'Currently part of the bot-net is swarming around Wayclear three. Substantial damage to the laser's casing and support pylon is visible. We'll have to deploy a couple of mimics because it's too big for the bot-net to attempt to fix. Also, one of the radiators over the engine section, directly behind the broken laser has holes in it. Otherwise no other damage has been detected yet. The back of the ship all looks intact but I haven't yet checked the payload section. '

'OK. We may be in this object field for some time according to Minogue. I'll see if Bjorn is able to drive one of the mimics, I can take the other, and I trust you can provide support with the bot-net.'

I called up Bjorn. 'Is the fire definitely out? Can you divert to running a mimic to fix one of Wayclear's lasers?'

'The fire appears to be fully suppressed. The fire extinguisher bot can be left to monitor the area for any possible flare-ups. I'll come down now to Robotics. It's been a while since I ran one of those things; I may be a bit rusty.'

'Me too, but Hyun will be there to keep an eye on us.'

'I'm on my way.'

Bjorn arrived before I did. They were already in discussion about the proposed mission. Hyun directed us. 'Bjorn take number one and Menem, you take two. I'll use the bot-net to monitor proceedings and advise.'

'I'm out of practice with these things as is Bjorn, so keep a watch out for us.'

Bjorn and I strapped ourselves in the control "chairs" which supported us in harnesses, allowing complete freedom of movement. We had done a lot of training before we had set out, but had only used them intermittently in the intervening eleven years. I hoped that, like riding a bicycle, my muscle memory would quickly kick back in.

I called up Ibo. 'Two mimics about to EVA down to Main to inspect and retrieve damaged Wayclear equipment. I want to make sure nothing moves while we're down there. Can you voice-print maintenance keys for us?'

Ibo called back. 'OK, keys activated. Let me know what you find. Clear the keys as soon as you can. I want to continue running a series of engine tests and keep as much active as possible. It'll speed up restart when all the trouble is fixed.'

Hyun was nervous about our lack of recent training. Somehow it came across as though he was more concerned about us damaging his machines than about us. 'OK, slowly to start with. Bjorn, you first.'

'I'm ready,' said Bjorn, with a lot more confidence than I felt.

On pulling down the control helmet visor my view changed to the mimic hold. Bjorn grunted in the chair next to me as he started up his mimic. Slowly it came into view, shuffling with small steps as Bjorn got used to the strange sticky-feet walk. The mimic had a weird, anthropomorphic look, with two arms and two legs. However, its feet were far from human: large, flat and round with highly flexible soles that could grip like a fly on smooth surfaces but had a prehensile ability to fold around a bar or hook around shaped objects. We had been told that there was nothing they couldn't stick to, and that one foot wouldn't let go until it was sure the other was securely attached to some part of the ship. It was possible to make the mimic float free, but supposedly only with at least one tether attached to the ship and preferably several.

Bjorn's mimic gradually disappeared into the airlock. Hyun gave me the signal to go. I picked up one foot and moved it forward and down, lifted my other foot and pulled the first back towards me. I tried to remember the correct actions and the lesson about how the mimic interpreted, but didn't directly replicate, the movements we made.

My mimic walked towards the airlock and manoeuvred in. The lock's inner door closed behind me, sealing me between its elastic layers. The space was hardly bigger than the mimic itself, taking very little time to evacuate and for the outer door to open. I emerged upside down relative to the ship. The airlock automatically rotated my mimic until I could walk out, my sticky feet preventing me from being hurled off the spinning ring.

With the incredible clarity of deep space, pricks of light from billions of stars and galaxies peppered the dome above. The plane of the Milky-Way, a brilliant, ragged, smudged line, stretched from horizon to horizon. The stars ahead significantly bluer than the reddened colour of those behind. We had been the first humans to see the Starbow for real as we had accelerated slowly up to forty-percent of the speed of light, and it never failed to impress, even if it wasn't quite the rainbow as some had theorised.

As I watched, standing on the spinning Habitat Ring, the star-field appeared to be rotating around the ship. I looked left and found the horizon swinging which made me feel queasy. I quickly looked down at the surface. 'Small movements only,' I kept repeating to myself. Looking right, my mimic's head started to rotate right, bringing Bjorn's mimic into view. Head centre, and my view fixed on Bjorn. My ability to control the machine was coming back.

Hyun's voice came over the comms. 'Bjorn, go straight towards the front until you get to the edge of the Habitat Ring. A group of bot-net elements will be there to assist you. Menem, get the tool-pack and follow.'

The mimic airlock opened again and presented me with a tool-pack that was hopefully carrying the right tools for our intended task. Slowly I manoeuvred my mimic around and reached out an arm. The mimic interpreted my intentions correctly, taking hold of the pack and automatically attaching it to its back. I turned again and saw Bjorn walking up the Habitat Ring towards the payload section. I followed; gradually improving my walking technique and keeping my view down at the ship to avoid looking at the unsettling rotating stars.

Bjorn walked his mimic onto the transfer deck which was parked stationary relative to the Habitat Ring. Once both his feet were firmly placed, the deck started to move around the ring, changing speed until it became stationary relative to the payload section, which, like the rest of the ship, wasn't spinning. Bjorn stepped off the deck which then accelerated again until its speed matched that of the Habitat Ring. I stepped my mimic onto it and repeated the transfer Bjorn had made, wobbling alarmingly as the forces on my mimic changed.

As the ship was supposed to be decelerating, the main engine faced our direction of travel. Wayclear's four masts were arrayed around the engine's nozzle to give them a clear field of view ahead, but a little back from the line of fire of intense gamma radiation created by the engine when running.

It was a long walk to the front: a hundred and twenty metres for the payload section, a hundred metres of fuel tanks, and then sixty for the engine section and its nozzle. Nearly all the ship's skin ahead of us was covered in liquid droplet panels, radiating away into space the surplus heat the ship generated. Between the radiators were narrow walkways, and it was up one of these we laboriously trudged.

I concentrated my gaze on the path itself as my mimic plodded along. Although the star-field was stable relative to this part of the ship, my brain was still having trouble reconciling the apparent gravitational force I was experiencing in the control chair and the gravity-free environment the mimic was now operating in.

One step at a time: foot down, grip, pull back on foot to move the mimic forward. Release other foot and swing leg forward. Repeat.

Hyun's bot-net had attached a tether to a rail alongside the walkway preventing the mimic floating away if somehow both feet lost grip at the same time. I didn't fancy the feeling of hanging by a tether in deep space, even if it was the mimic and not physically me. The sensation was real enough.

As we crossed onto the main-engine section I saw the damaged coolant radiator that Hyun had mentioned. It had several cuts sliced through it; another item that would need fixing in due course.

Finally we arrived at the damaged Wayclear station. The radar, a two metre square flat panel, looked undamaged. At first it appeared as though nothing was wrong with the laser, but as we came up close we could see that it wasn't pointing straight forward, and a big chunk of the two metre high support structure had been torn out and was missing. There was a neat hole out of the back of the laser itself and what looked like an oil leak but was probably coolant. Given the extent of the damage, it seemed unlikely that the laser was going to be fixable in place. It would have to be dismounted and carried back to the Habitat Ring for repair.

Bjorn extracted a containment tent from the tool-pack I was carrying, popped it open, and together we placed it over the Wayclear station and us. Assisted by bot-net elements, it automatically moulded and sealed itself around the surface of the ship. Reaching up to the laser, I tried springing its case open, but it wouldn't budge. Instead, I marked some lines on both it and its support. Bjorn changed the hands on his mimic to tool holders, attached a fixed-depth vibration saw and cut through the composite fibre casings along the marked lines.

Once opened, it was clear that a very small object had penetrated completely through the laser, fractionally off-centre from its axis. The physical damage to the laser itself appeared to be minimal but the support was in a bad way. On its way through, the object must have severed a high pressure coolant pipe which released a jet strong enough to blast off the side of the support. The object must also have caused a lot of internal damage that we couldn't see. We would also have to work out if any of the parts that had been blown off had caused further damage elsewhere or been lost to the void. At least one piece had most likely sliced through the broken radiator and ruptured the anti-hydrogen feed pipe somewhere below.

'Hyun, are you seeing this?' I called.

'It looks like it's going to be a complex print job. I'm already on to identifying the more obvious parts needed and will get the printer-weaver started on the structural elements.'

'We're not going to be able to repair the laser out here. We'll have to get it back to Engineering for rebuilding and realignment.'

'Agreed. I'll send a trolley for it.'

'Bjorn, once we've disassembled the laser, can you and the bot-net handle the trolley and take all the damaged parts back? I want to have a look around to see if some of the splinters from the laser mount have caused the main fuel supply problem.'

At least we didn't have to worry about the weight of the laser, with no gravity out here. However, its three-metre long tube was massive and its momentum would need to be carefully controlled. The trolley should prevent it floating away or drifting into something, causing further damage. However, the last part of the journey back, on the spinning Habitat Ring, would be particularly problematic.

The bot-net attached a tether from the laser to the ship's structure and Bjorn cut it from its mount while I disconnected the power, coolant and control lines. We lifted it down, gathered up all the tools and loose parts and opened the containment tent, collapsing it back into its pack just as the trolley arrived.

Bjorn lashed the laser down, and, following behind, set the trolley on its way back towards the Habitat Ring, slowly trundling along the walkway rails. He had become adept at walking the mimic by now and could move faster than before, but while accompanying the loaded trolley, he was still being cautious.

I walked back down to the end of the engine section, looking around for the best way to get to the damaged fuel system. The broken radiator was there, its composite surface slashed as though a huge, sharp knife had been repeatedly plunged into it. The panel would be a simple patch-up job, a priority, once the laser was back in action, with our need for all the coolant capacity we could get.

Identifying an access point that led below the coolant panels, I opened it and descended into a maze of pipes, tanks, cables, structural components, actuators and sensors: a combination of chemical plant and heavy electrical and mechanical engineering. Down here in the belly of the engine everything was precisely optimised to its function: maximum power with minimum mass. The apparent chaos was made sinister as the lights from the mimic's head cast dancing shadows. My display gave me the most direct routing to where the damage lay, but occasionally I deviated from its suggestions when the routings it gave required a contortionist's ability to work around the machinery.

14

Magnetic pipes guided the flow of antimatter fuel from tanks to engine, and it was one of these that had been struck. The fuel tank itself should have instantly sealed the moment leak was detected. But once the pipe had been breached, the small amount of anti-hydrogen in that section would have come in to contact with normal matter, and the two would have annihilated each other, instantly converted into almost pure energy.

I worked my mimic around to where the trouble lay, and, as the bot-net images had shown, the fuel pipe damage was obvious, with a large part of one side of a section torn away. There were broken cables and coolant pipes nearby, twisted into a tangled mess. A massive structural beam had taken the force of the blast and been peeled back like a banana. This was almost certainly the cause of the first shock we had felt. Without that beam, and with Main still running on the last of the fuel in the pipes, the casing and keel of the ship would have rung like a bell: the continuing vibration we had experienced, stopping only when the fuel in the remaining pipe had run out.

I examined the area in detail, adding to the data Hyun had collected. It was going to be another difficult repair job.

'Agyei, has Sahko let you back on board ship yet?' I said, opening a coms link.

'I'm in Engineering, and reviewing the logs.'

'Have you got something urgent on, or can you help out?'

'I came here to see what I could do.'

'Can you take a look at my recent imaging and start making a plan for fixing the damage in the area of the fuel pipe? Ask Hyun to send an inspection and test bot here for you to use, when he has a moment. He's busy helping us with the bot-net and he's also continuing to examine the rest of the ship. I'm searching around for the rest of the Wayclear structure that probably caused the damage.'

'Will do. I'll message Hyun for the inspection bot. Let me know if you spot any other damage in the area.'

I manoeuvred my mimic around but couldn't see anything obvious. Small high speed projectiles might not leave much in the way of visible traces. Ibo was going to have to run a lot of diagnostics before Main could be safely restarted. I finally found a spear of torn off structure embedded in a tank insulation blanket. I wasn't going to remove it until the area was X-rayed to avoid the risk of doing further damage when pulling it out. Images and my suggestions went into the file for Agyei. There was nothing else I could see here so I worked my way back up to the outside.

As my mimic wasn't needed again until the laser was repaired, I climbed into an equipment recess, locked the mimic to the ship's structure, and put it in standby mode.

I was cautious about getting up from the control chair while readjusting to my own body's movements. Too sudden a change from the mimic VR to the real world could also easily make me giddy and there was quite a risk of hurting myself from the different way of moving. I took off the helmet and unbuckled my arms and legs, but remained seated for a minute.

Hyun asked: 'OK?'

'Yes, fine. I haven't done that for a while. It's disorienting.'

'Hmm, sounds as though we need to up the training.'

'How's Bjorn doing?'

'He's in the process of transferring the laser from the payload section to the Habitat Ring.'

Bjorn came on the comms. 'I've tied the transport cart to the transfer deck. I'm going to get on at the same time.'

'I'll open the outer door of Airlock Two,' Hyun said.

We could see from the bot-net feed that Bjorn's mimic was now guiding the cart holding the laser towards the airlock. The movement of both cart and mimic rather different now they were on the spinning ring. Bjorn went down the ramp to the door, spent a bit of time fiddling to get the cart lined up so it would fit in. The airlock entrance slowly inverted the trolley so that it now rested against the ring's apparent gravity, and its outer door closed. Bjorn walked his mimic back to the mimic store airlock, and we watched as it disappeared and the door shut, folding back flush with the ship's surface.

Once he had parked his mimic, Bjorn released himself from his control chair's restraints and carefully reoriented himself back inside the ship. I messaged Ibo to let her know that both the mimics were clear, and we were cancelling the maintenance keys and she could resume engine testing. Bjorn confirmed his key cancellation.

Hyun arranged for the bot-net elements to return to their garage for parking and recharge. I climbed out of my control chair, stretched and shook out my limbs, taking care to remember that I was working with a normal human body once again. When steady on my feet, I went around to the airlock where the laser had been placed and, using a crane trolley, lifted it from the exterior cart and had it carried to Engineering.

The dull black tube of the laser lay suspended from the hoist. Turning it around revealed the damage: the torn mounting, the penetration and exit holes, and all the smashed components in between. The holes themselves were small and tidy as though cleanly drilled. We began by un-seaming the casing and dismantling the laser's components. As I had guessed, the major structural damage had been done by the high pressure coolant escaping after its pipe had been shot through, but now it was clear that the jet of coolant had caused the laser's charging system to disintegrate, a large chunk of which had smashed into the support, its reaction forces twisting the whole structure. There were a lot of ruined parts to be rebuilt.

As we identified each one, Hyun called up the schematics from Archive, loaded the part specifications into the printers and set them to work. We discussed how to repair the structure, devising a sleeve to fit over what remained of the support still fixed to the ship and to which the laser could be mounted. Hyun and I worked up the idea into something that could be quickly printed and easily installed.

A food cart appeared which Massoud must have thoughtfully sent over. It made me feel hungry. I stretched and suggested we take a break.

'I'll take the opportunity to review the bot-net log to see if they've come across any more damage,' said Hyun.

The food was tempting as always. Today I had something like a rich mushroom soup, soft Nan-like bread and what seemed to be salad leaves but couldn't be. All had been constructed from a panoply of amino acids, formed into proteins, extruded, spun or printed into appropriate structures and combined with culinary alchemy. Massoud was always experimenting with new flavours, textures, smells and methods of presentation. To keep us healthy over the long haul he also had to balance our individual nutritional needs and preferences.

Sahko's voice came over the comms. 'All crew meeting in an hour for a situation review.'

Hyun and I exchanged glances: we didn't need the interruption. However, making sure everyone understood what was going on might save arguments later. Maybe it would generate some good ideas to get ourselves out of the mess we were in.

'Hyun, let's finish this strip-down and get all the parts requests loaded into the printers. We're going to have to wait for them to be finished anyway.'

'They're being scheduled in the order needed for reassembly. This was supposed to be our number one priority.'

'I know, I know. Communications...' are vital for the optimal running of the ship, as Sahko so often said. 'Let's get all the printer requests loaded as best we can. Could you review the feedstock and also check all the bots, which Sahko is bound to want to know about. I need to get the latest engineering status of the ship's systems and liaise with Ibo and Agyei.'

We finished stripping out all the parts from the laser that were most likely to have been damaged and I left Hyun to schedule the printers.

I called Ibo. 'How is Fuse doing, Ibo?'

'It's holding at present with the power being dumped all over the place. It's got down to cruise-mode without melting anything, although one coolant panel seems to be out of action. Minogue pulled up the test schedule for the payload deployment system and we were able to absorb some power there. The payload is probably warm by now, but it's big enough to cope, and we can radiate the heat away later. Most importantly, we're able to keep what's left of Wayclear operational.'

'That at least is good news. While I was out in the mimic I saw the damaged coolant panel. It has some big slashes in it but that should be an easy patch-up job. On another point, how quickly could Fuse be ramped up to full power if needed in a hurry?'

'About ten seconds. Why, what have you in mind?'

'If, say, we needed to make a sudden manoeuvre by using the thrusters.'

'Why on earth should we want to do that?'

'Who knows? Maybe to avoid a big object.'

'We wouldn't know about it before we hit it.'

'You're probably right, but maybe Minogue will work out if something is out there. If it's big enough it will have a detectable gravitational field.'

'I'm not sure if that makes you a pessimist or an optimist.'

'Me neither. You answered my question anyway, in case someone asks you or me in the meeting. Now, what about Main: will it take a lot to restart?'

'Once the fuel pipe and everything damaged in that area is fixed, we'll have to purge the fuel pipes, do a full systems test, and then we can go from a cold start. All that would take about six hours. However, I should like the hot-bot to take a look inside the nozzle first to check for surface damage.'

'Let's hold off on that until the Sit-Rep meeting and see what the risk of further incoming is. We may have to wait for the storm to pass before we can take the risk of putting the hot-bot in the nozzle. Could you liaise with Hyun to get an inspection set up, ready to go as soon as possible after we're given the all clear? If there's any damage, it will take time to fix.'

'Time, time, time.'

'Yeah, I know: we ain't got enough. Did you discuss the repairs required in the area of the broken fuel pipe with Agyei?'

'She has a possible plan, but that will take time too. It's mostly simple stuff: replacing coolant pipes, power and control cables, and repairing the structural damage. The fuel pipe itself will be much more difficult. You know those things: lots of complex precision components, magnetic and electric field generators, vacuum tubes. We don't want another big bang. More time I suppose.'

'Sahko will decide: that's what she's paid for.'

'Is she being paid? What about me? I'll have to talk to the union.'

'Get off the comms, Ibo, and get back to work. See you at Sahko's place in half an hour.'

'It's a date.' Ibo cut off.

Next I called Agyei. 'Ibo tells me you've sorted the repair.'

'April the first every day. I've suggestions for next steps that may lead to a plan which may lead to a fix. There are still huge uncertainties.'

'Good start. Sahko and Minogue will want a heads-up at least.'

'I'll say what I know.'

'Good. Any other engineering issues?'

'Well there's the rotation motor that caught fire to fault-find and fix. If it looks potentially systemic, we should run a test on all similar motors. Then there's the list of the usual things to fix and routine maintenance tasks that were on our schedule for today, before the trouble started.'

'Anything stand out as a 'can't wait'?'

'The captain's refresher for one. Not really, but the longer maintenance is neglected…'

'The captain can remain dirty for a while longer, or use someone else's refresher.' Perhaps mine, I thought. 'The routine can wait for the urgent for a bit. I'll see you in the meeting, but I need to talk with Bjorn first about our little EVA.'

'OK, see you there.'

I cut the link and made another call. 'Bjorn, I need to review the EVA with you, and anything else relevant.'

'Fine,' he replied. 'I thought the EVA went all right, given that we were both out of practice. We achieved our objectives in a reasonable length of time, and without damaging anything else.'

'I agree. I was very slow with the mimic at first, but it came back to me. I never like the transition between the rotating ring and the fixed, but the system is good, and I never felt unsafe.'

'The equipment works and we did the job. Did you find any of the missing bits from the laser?'

'Some of it. Almost certainly one part severed the A-M fuel pipe and there's a part embedded in insulation around one of the trap-tanks. We'll need to X-ray that before attempting recovery. The fuel line is a mess, as is some of the structure and equipment in that area. Agyei has some sort of plan to fix it, all except the fuel pipe.'

'More EVA I suppose, for that as well as reinstalling the Wayclear laser. Has someone worked out how we're going to reattach it to the broken support while we're on the front edge of the ship being shot at by unknown objects?'

'Hyun and I think we can fabricate a coupler that will fit over the remains of the support, and into which the new laser leg will slot and be glued in place.'

'Durability? Extra weight? Material consumption?'

'Good questions. We only need to have it hold the laser for the duration of the storm. The reaction forces are minimal once the laser is powered on.'

'An engineering solution then?'

'Yes, an engineering solution, as you so politely call it, to keep us alive a bit longer.'

'Fine by me. My priority is staying alive over purity. Minogue won't like it though: upsetting the ship dynamics. '

'Anything else? What about the fire suppression? Any toxicity issues in Engine Control?'

'All cleaned up well. Ninety-eight percent fire suppressant recovery and we may get a bit more out of the air cleaner in due course. A tiny bit may have leaked somewhere where it couldn't be recovered, but no doubt engineering will find it eventually.'

'Thanks. That means I'm probably going to step in something nasty at some point and have to be rushed to decontamination.'

'It's not that bad, but it is kind-of sticky.'

'So I'm going to become glued to some bit of machinery and remorselessly sucked into a cog wheel. How about the air quality? Am I or Ibo going to be gassed next time we go in to Engine Control?'

'Unfortunately not. It's back to a normal oxygen-rich atmosphere in there. The ship's air conditioner is reconnected, and it has even recovered some useful chemicals to add to our stocks.'

'Tiny amounts, I hope.'

'Tiny amounts of some quite nasty stuff: quite a bit of carbonised insulation and resins that had become smoke. Engine Control is now quite within acceptable tolerances and even I would be happy to breathe in there.'

'OK, Bjorn, see you at Sahko's meeting.'

'Clothes pressed, I trust.'

'Engineering has to live down to its reputation. Menem out.'

I reviewed Status to see if there was anything else to be aware of, and also that no new disasters were in progress that would take priority over Sahko's heads-up. Status had managed to reconfigure its network and had regained connection to most of the sensors, including those for the A-M fuel tanks which hadn't suffered any measurable loss. It was reporting that all readings were now within normal operational bounds. However, during the vibrations a number of indicators had got close to their risk warning limits. These seemed to be primarily in parts of the power system and might have been the result of the sudden excess produced by Fuse when Main suddenly shut down.

It was a lot more concerning that Status had been unable to regain communications with Engine Control. Perhaps the fire had severed the links. I needed time to investigate and fix that, as well as examine the odd non-standard controller for that section's rotation motor and work out why the overheat sensor had failed to shut the motor down. It looked as though someone had messed up in there.

I made my way to the refectory, the only space in the ring clear enough to accommodate the eleven of us. I encountered Massoud on the way there and he looked cheerful.

'Trouble, Engineer? Think of it as spice, we always need some of that in our life, eh? Maybe things had become a bit routine. You should get out more, take some fresh air.' With that he gave his deep rumbling laugh, clapped a meaty arm round my shoulder and guided me into the refectory.

Most of the others were already there, clustered around Minogue who had set up a holographic of the ship. All the known areas of damage were identified and linked to fact panels. Another information screen displayed our route, showing where we were between home and target, and the position of the pursuing ships

Agyei and Ibo arrived together and joined the group. 'No change in Fleet formation then?' asked Agyei.

'Not according to the last position reports,' said Bita.

Hyun arrived breathless at the last minute and was immediately followed by Sahko, timing her entry on the dot and looking immaculate as usual. Her small neat frame was clothed in black: a beautifully-tailored, severe suit with buckled and strapped ankle-boots which had quite a heel on them, her straight, black hair cut in a bob. Pale skin and hazel eyes the only exceptions to the monotone. She was still hot, although she had turned cold on me long ago, and, after the two deaths, become increasingly detached from the day-to-day.

Voices immediately quietened as she looked around to check that everyone was present. This meeting was going to be one of the serious ones, without any preliminaries. Everyone had some idea of the trouble we had encountered from their visit to the lifeboat, and they would all have been monitoring Status. The change of direction of apparent gravity was a constant reminder that things weren't right.

Sahko used her quiet commanding voice. 'Situation summary please, Minogue.'

Why had Sahko asked Minogue to summarise? Surely the one closest to the problem would be best placed to do that, i.e. the number one engineer: me. Perhaps she didn't want it to be wholly my show, and she would call on me next to fill in the important details.

Minogue began. 'Starting at three-thirty this morning, while I was on watch, Wayclear reported identifying an object directly in our line of travel. A laser successfully struck the object and our magnetosphere deflected it. Twenty-five minutes later a second object was detected and deflected. That second detection triggered the transmission of an automatic report to Fleet. The comms system becoming active alerted Bita who was preparing to relieve me on watch anyway. Ten minutes later there was a third strike. Bita and I watched as the number of strikes rose slowly. At that time Wayclear was having no trouble deflecting the objects. Analysis suggested these were no bigger than grains of fine sand: around a tenth of a millimetre in diameter. At about four-fifty there was a rapid build up in object detections and Bita and I were about to alert everyone when the ship shook and the alarms went off.'

Minogue went on to make quite a good summary of the events of the day, similar to something I might have said. He concluded by saying: 'Correct orbital insertion becomes more problematic with every passing hour.'

There was silence for a moment as that sank in. Sahko looked around at the crew and then looked at Bjorn. 'Any lessons from the fire and its suppression?'

'The motor should have cut out automatically on overheating, before anything caught fire. We don't yet know why it didn't. Fire suppression worked as planned, with no equipment problems. The fire was small, accessible and relatively non-toxic. I'll maintain close monitoring of the area for the next twenty-four hours to ensure nothing is still smouldering which could reignite. Engineering will no doubt review the causes and measures to be taken to prevent a future occurrence.'

Thanks Bjorn, now I'm being lined up for failing to prevent the ship from falling apart.

Sahko turned to Hyun next, who immediately dropped his pad, stylus and earpiece and had to scrabble around on the floor for them. 'Hyun, how is the Wayclear laser rebuild going?'

'It will take a long time: a lot of complex parts have to be printed. The object penetrated the laser along the edge of the liquid steering block, distorting it. The object then passed through the coolant inlet manifold, releasing a very high pressure jet which caused the laser's charging system to disintegrate. This shattered the laser's mount sending high velocity fragments everywhere: including through a coolant panel and almost certainly into the antimatter feed pipe.'

Hyun might have gone on for a lot longer, giving us a complete technical breakdown of the laser and its damage, but Sahko headed him off: 'Only the time to print and rebuild please at the moment, Hyun.'

'Uh, yes, uh, sorry, uh printing will take about five hours if we use all the printers. Engineering will report on the rebuild time. Also we lost some high pressure coolant and the chemical plant will have to make it up, if we have the components.'

'The loss was small and we have the components,' cut in Agyei, who was responsible for chemistry.

Agyei looked at Massoud, who gave a confirmatory nod and he added: 'The cut-off kicked in as soon as it detected the pressure drop. I checked

23

how much coolant we lost and there's no problem making up what the laser needs. Please don't go losing a whole lot more or we're going to have to do some serious molecular rearranging. That will use other stores, and you won't enjoy that.'

No one would want our food supply compromised and favourite foods to become unavailable for the remainder of time, or at least until we could reload with organic molecules from somewhere.

Sahko looked like stone, completely unreadable. She summarised: 'So when the laser is fixed we'll need an EVA to reinstall it, connect it up, and tune it in. A total of perhaps ten hours before Wayclear is fully back. Agreed, Minogue?'

'Control confirms the critical path to be a little under ten hours from now.'

'What plans are there to get further information on the object field that we seem to be in, and on how much of it still lies ahead?'

Minogue looked around. 'We haven't been able to detect any distortions to the star-field. It's far too risky to turn the ship to have the big aerial forward facing to assess it. We're relying on information from the Wayclear radars which have a very limited field of view and only directly ahead. Given the speed we're still going, they cannot see far. Without better data our ability to model the field is very limited, so all we can really say is that, at present, the rate of object encounters is declining slowly but steadily.'

Bita put up a hand and Sahko invited her to speak.

'An idea on that,' Bita said. 'We're dumping power by transmitting unfocused white noise from the main antenna right now. We could insert a pulse signal and see what reflections we get from the part of the field that we've already passed. It might enable us to get a feel for the spatial distribution of the objects and make some inference on the size and shape of the field.'

Judging by his reaction, Minogue and Bita hadn't discussed this ahead of the meeting. Perhaps the idea had occurred to her only a moment ago.

As always, Minogue jumped in to support Bita. 'Great idea, let's work that up. Perhaps Gunadi could help with the analysis.'

Sahko took back control. 'Fine. Bita lead on that with help as required from Minogue and Gunadi. Everyone is to remain on high alert and with a clear path to the lifeboats. All personal position locators to remain on until I give the all clear. Keep an eye out for the children: no doubt they'll sense continuing trouble. Next: Ibo, what about Main?'

'Main itself is fine: it shut down without damage. The problem is with the antimatter feed from the tanks to the injectors. The broken fuel pipe is a precision electromagnetic containment tube and at least one section will need almost total rebuilding. There are other damaged parts in the area, most of which are easily-replaced ordinary pipes and cables. There's also substantial damage to one of the main struts which convey the thrust from the engine to the rest of the ship.

Parts will be needed from the printers, including the complex mag-pipe parts. The book print time for that alone is estimated to be a minimum of twenty-four hours but, until we're able to do a strip down in the fuel feed area, we won't know for sure. We've seen a piece of the laser mount embedded in fuel tank insulation and are preparing to X-ray before attempting to remove it and repair any damage. In addition, with all the incoming objects we've encountered already and the fact that at least one hit the ship, a thorough inspection of the hot-side of the engine nozzle is required. If the nozzle surface has been damaged restarting the engine could well blow a hole in it.'

'What might surface damage take to fix?'

'If repair is limited to a single tile it could be replaced in a couple of hours. We carry three spares, but they're only suitable for the outer edges, the ones most likely to be hit. Any damaged inner tiles will need to be extracted, reformed and reinstalled. That would take a lot longer of course. The repair would be hot-side working, and we've never run the hot-bot to perform such an operation before, other than in tests before we departed.

'A further problem is that Engine Control is no longer communicating with the rest of the ship. That may have been caused by the fire, possibly fibres got caught in the rotation system or burnt through, who knows? Running the engines from Operations is less than ideal.'

'Once everything is repaired, there's nothing to prevent a straight warm-up and ignition sequence then?'

'It should be as book, around twelve hours.'

Ibo seemed to be giving herself some leeway compared to the time that she had told me earlier.

'Fizz and Fuse OK?' Sahko asked.

'Both functioning normally,' Ibo replied. 'Earlier we had a problem with dumping the excess power Fuse was producing, with Main suddenly going offline and while having to keep output up for Wayclear. That has now been resolved thanks to help from all round. Fizz is normal and remains quiescent.'

Sahko looked about. 'Yingluq, any medical issues we need to know about?'

'Air quality problems in Engine Control have cleared. There are no other known new physical hazards at present, but we need to watch each other for stress.'

Sahko looked at Bita. 'Anything to add?'

'No personnel issues to publicly air at present.'

I could imagine Bita hiding a multitude of private issues behind those quietly spoken words.

'Good. Keep on top of things everyone, and we have every chance of fixing everything and getting back on mission track within forty-eight hours. Any questions?'

Massoud raised his hand. 'What are the implications for our mission, with Main off for a couple of days? I thought that we needed to be decelerating continuously until arrival.'

Sahko answered calmly: 'The loss of two days at this stage means that we'll have to decelerate a little harder when the engine restarts. We're about a hundred days out, assuming one-'g' deceleration. To come to rest at our target we'll have to decelerate two-percent faster for the remaining days. The engine is quite capable of that because we've already burnt fuel equal to about half the ship's total launch mass. The engine has the power to decelerate us at two-'g' now if needed. Not that we'd want to do that for long.'

Sahko looked around. 'Anybody want to add anything?' Silence. 'Any further questions?' Silence.

No one had any further questions, it seemed. Sahko turned on her heels in good military fashion and marched out. Minogue went across to Bita, and Gunadi joined them, presumably to work out how to use the comms system as an object field mapping device. Ibo and Hyun huddled together deep in discussion, whether on business or personal matters I couldn't tell.

Bjorn called out, 'Hyun, I'm teacher for the next couple of hours. Give me a call if you need me for an EVA.'

Hyun lifted a hand in acknowledgement but continued in close conversation with Ibo. Bjorn caught up with Yingluq as she was going out and asked her about the children's health, and they went off together in the direction of the children's room.

26

Massoud put his arm round my shoulder and gave me a little squeeze. I had got used to his tactile nature over the years and appreciated his sympathy. Presumably he had noticed that Sahko hadn't called for a contribution from me. It was petty I knew, but pinpricks hurt too. Massoud then went over to Agyei and they left together, having a loud and friendly argument about coolant chemistry.

I was left on my own, free to slink out and make my lonely way back to Engineering. Why had Sahko ignored me? OK, I hadn't fixed her refresher yet, but other, rather more vital things, had taken priority. We had history of course. Mostly very good memories and I still wanted to add to them. The pain would never completely go away, but that was shared too. I mustn't think about those things now, I needed to focus on the integrity of the ship. My personal problems would have to wait.

4018, 12:30

I activated a comms link. 'Hyun, how is the printing going?'

'All running smoothly at present. First parts for the Wayclear laser will be coming off soon.'

At least something was working. Next call. 'Ibo, do you need Engine Control fully functioning for main engine restart?'

'It's not absolutely essential but it would be hugely helpful. Also I would quite like my apartment the right way up.'

'OK, there are similar motors in each section of the Habitat Ring. The one in eleven is definitely not mission–critical at present, that section doesn't have anyone's apartment, and it's easily accessible. It will save a bunch of time if we don't have to print another motor to get Engine Control oriented correctly.'

'Massoud won't be happy, but Engine Control has to be the priority.'

'Sahko won't like swapping good parts around either. I'll try to get the other motor fixed and back in section eleven before engine restart, when it will be needed again.'

'And get the comms links back working.'

'That too. It seems odd, the failures there.'

'It does. I'd like to know who messed up.'

'Me too, and why. On another thing, were you and Hyun able to sort out the nozzle hot-side inspection?'

'Control has a process already worked out, so it takes minimal input from Hyun to get it going. We'll almost certainly require someone else to help out if we need to replace any tiles.'

'Agyei would be the obvious person. If we have to make any new tiles we'll need chemistry.'

'If she can help out with that, I can manage the X-ray inspection of the fuel-tank and pipe area and start dismantling and recovering broken parts.'

'Thanks, Ibo. I can help you if Agyei gets overloaded. If needed, we can get Bjorn out of school duty and back into a mimic.'

'I would like Yingluq or Minogue to have a look if there's any damage to the nozzle and to check over the repair processes. I don't want any mistakes.'

'You've obviously thought this through. Let me know if you need my support on any of that.'

I was second on engines, but clearly wasn't needed for now. My paranoia was starting to grow again, which reminded me that we had been told to watch for that, both in ourselves and in others. It was a known risk in our confined environment. We were supposed to keep up our de-stress routines but it looked as though I wasn't going to be able to do that for a while.

I took down a toolbox and went back to the refectory, summoning a crane trolley to join me there. Before starting work, it occurred to me that there may be similar motors in payload, possibly including a spare. I should check with Bjorn first, in his role as payload lead.

'Bjorn, can you talk for a moment?'

I heard Bjorn's voice saying 'Well done Sky, that's right.' Sky was Yingluq and Minogue's eight-year-old daughter. Bjorn was a surprisingly natural teacher, and the children loved and feared him in equal measure. 'OK kids, got to talk with Menem for a moment.' Groans filled the background. 'Sorry about that, Menem. Go ahead.'

'I need to replace the burnt-out motor in five to get Engine Control upright for Main restart. All the printers will be busy with Wayclear laser parts for a while, so I've decided to replace it with a similar motor that's not being used.'

'So you thought of the payload.'

'Do you know if there is one there we could borrow?'

'There might be. I would have to check, but it would almost certainly be very difficult to get at. It might mean unpacking a whole load of stuff and dismantling something. There isn't a box of spares just sitting there. How about borrowing one of the other rotation motors?'

'That's my next choice, but it has to be from section eleven because it doesn't have an apartment. The only other section like that is seven and I don't want to risk Robotics being disoriented.'

'You aren't going to be popular if the refectory ends up on its side for any length of time.'

'I'll have to take that risk. I expect I can fix the burnt-out one during the engine start-up sequence, and get it back in place before it's required. I'm in section eleven now and will extract the motor from here.'

I made a verbal note on Status of my plan and marked it for the general log. Archive gave me the schematic of the wall panels that hid the rotation machinery and identified the motor. It was positioned identically to the one in section five. A wall panel and several equipment racks had to come out to gain access to the motor at the back. Great: going to have to crawl around in a tight space that hadn't been accessed since it was built. I could already see Status reporting the disturbance I had made. It was about to get a lot more excited when the motor driving the rotation gearbox was removed.

The equipment racks showed finger marks where I had touched them. Everything seemed to be covered in a fine grey dust. That didn't seem right: this was conditioned space and the air was supposed to be super-clean. This bay hadn't been touched in ten years so perhaps even the tiny residual amount of dust in the air was enough to coat everything over that time. There was also the possibility that some piece of equipment in the area was breaking down. An electrostatic charge might have built up on the racks, although it seemed unlikely that the whole bay had become charged. The earth bonding that was supposed to prevent static electricity accumulating in one part of the ship relative to another would need checking. I decided to ignore the dust problem for now, making a note to investigate later and also to ask Agyei to run some chemical analysis checks on it.

Extracting the motor was more trouble than expected: somehow the mounting had become distorted and the bolts were all binding. My joints were aching as I reached into the recess while lying on the floor and trying to lever the heavy motor off its mount and get it to where the crane trolley could pick it up. I backed out of the hole, banging my head as I sat up. I was a mess from the dust and started to sneeze, hoping that whatever it was wasn't toxic. The crane trolley lifted the motor and extracted it. I relaxed a bit as step-one was complete.

The refectory systems Status screen was now lit up with lots of reds, indicating that at least some sensors were working properly. I pushed back the equipment racks and locked the wall access panel into place.

Minogue called: 'Menem, don't we have a spare motor available? Aren't we going to need the refectory rotated when Main restarts?'

'Cannibalising the ship isn't great,' I replied, 'but we won't be getting Main relit until Engine Control is back upright. I did check, and we don't have any spares of this type of motor. Once a suitable printer is free, I'll get Hyun to fabricate new parts for the one from Engine Control and fit it back here.'

'I saw your note about the dust in the equipment bay. You seemed concerned.'

That was quick: he had actually picked up the detail in my note.

'It's something unexpected. That bay has never been opened since we started so there could be a host of explanations, mostly non-lethal. We do need to determine the source of the dust though: it may be symptomatic of some underlying trouble that may affect more than just that bay.' Time for a subject diversion, so I added: 'Any luck with using the main comms array to map the object field?'

'We've been able to get a reflection off part of the field and Gunadi is trying to come up with a way of processing the data to produce a visualisation. Wayclear is still reporting a steady stream of incoming, but at a level that its reduced capacity seems to be able to handle. I would really like to take a look with the big telescope to see if there's a large object in the centre of the field.'

'Wayclear couldn't protect the telescope if we deployed it at this speed.'

'So you keep saying.'

We still didn't know if we were through most of the object field or there was worse ahead. Speed kills, they used to say, and we were going fast.

I followed the crane trolley round to Engineering and had the motor placed on the workbench. It would have to be stripped down and tested in detail before it could be trusted; there might be a problem with all these motors and it just happened to be five that overheated. I called up the test processes and set the assembler to work on taking the motor apart and performing a battery of mechanical, electrical and thermal checks.

The machine extracted the stator and immediately flagged up a problem. The tiny wires connected to each coil had become brittle, and the thermal image showed that several were out of spec. I halted the test, withdrew the assembler arms and brought a microscope camera up to one of the worst wires. I couldn't see anything wrong, but they were going to have to be altered in some way to make them last.

I went digging through the engineering database in Archive to see if anyone had encountered the problem before with this type of motor. There was one obscure note reporting a similar problem due to a manufacturing fault: it was thought that the wires connecting the coils had been made too short and that the material used wasn't able to cope with the vibration of a piece of mining equipment. The manufacturer had commented that this had been detected early on in production and fixed. A slight modification had been made to the material to increase its durability and a longer length of wire used. Perhaps this motor was from the first batch, and no one had picked up the issue. No details were given of model numbers affected or the specification of the revised connector wires. So it was going to a Menem special botch job: a quick hunt for some stock wire that was probably suitable, adjust the virtual model on an engineering screen with the proposed change, and then running a simulation of the modification through the performance envelope of the motor to check for any problems. The simulation passed, so the assembler got to work: rewiring the coils, putting the motor back together again, and testing it.

Status gave me an update on the printing of the laser parts showing that they were coming along on schedule. I browsed Status for Ibo's findings on the problems in the fuel pipe area. The first of the X-rays she had arranged were in and showed that the part of the laser's mount I had seen, plus a couple of other smaller fragments that she had detected, were not embedded deeply in the tank shielding and had missed penetrating the superconductor magnets around the fuel. Ibo was having the bot-net recover the pieces and patch the damage. She and Agyei had designed a repair for the structural beam and had determined what replacement parts were needed for the broken service pipes and cables. The bot-net was starting work on all those things, leaving only the fuel pipe without a repair plan. It looked as though between us we were fixing faults faster than they were appearing. Progress.

Out of curiosity I checked the Status logs on the object field project. Gunadi was still working with Minogue and Bita on mapping the field, so no news there. Not much more I could do for the moment, and suddenly I felt exhausted and that it was time for a break. After stopping briefly in my apartment for a refresh and change of clothes, I went back to the refectory. I wanted something to eat but also to try to gauge the mood of the ship, and particularly that of Sahko, from whoever was around. Even the spirit of the children could sometimes be revealing.

Massoud was the only one there when I arrived and he seemed cheerful. 'Hi, Menem. Good that you're able to drop in. Can I tempt you with something new?'

'Comforting and filling would be good.'

'Tell me what you think of this.'

He placed a plate in front of me which held some strange brown and green lumps in a thick sauce, surrounded by what looked like a bed of grass. It smelt appetising so I cautiously sampled it. It was certainly tasty and felt comforting too.

'That's what I needed: food to reinvigorate. I feel better already. There's nothing mind bending in it is there?'

'All food is to some extent. This should be soul-enhancing but not faculty-impairing. How are things with the ship?'

'We may be getting on top of our most urgent problems. I hope environmental control and bioengineering aren't in the process of collapsing.'

'Nothing to distract you from the mission-critical stuff at present.'

'I need to free up some time to fix some of the little things that niggle and slightly degrade everyone's ability to get on with their jobs, like the captain's refresher for example.'

'She doesn't seem so bothered by it now. She has been using Avalos's. She still looks clean and tidy doesn't she?'

'Always immaculate, the captain. I didn't know she was using Avalos's refresher though. I haven't been in his apartment since he died, and I didn't know anyone else had.'

'Not the sentimental type, the captain, or perhaps she thought it was time to move on. Maybe one of the children will want their own space one day, and it would be better to have that apartment in normal use, rather than being a dark cloud we've all been avoiding for so long.'

'Alice is only ten so I wouldn't expect her to want her own space for a couple of years. I hope we'll be off this crate before then.'

'Yes indeed, a new world to explore. We've come all this way and we still don't seem know much about it. For example: how quickly can we set up on the surface? We're going to have to wait for Fleet to arrive to be able to land at the very least.'

Before I could reply we heard animated voices from the corridor and Minogue came in, followed by Bita and Yingluq.

'That smells good,' said Minogue, 'I'd like some of that and one of your funny beers.' The sever bot prepared plates and glasses for the new arrivals. 'What was that about landing?'

'Visions of the future,' responded Massoud. 'Menem thinks there's a chance we'll live another day, so we were dreaming. I hope you people aren't going to dampen our spirits.'

'Not yet at least,' said Bita. 'We've left Gunadi developing algorithms to try to make sense of the data we've been getting from the comms aerial.'

'That was a great idea, Bita,' said Minogue. 'It worked even better than I expected. But interpreting the data is proving tricky. It's a bit like crystallography, but we don't have the pattern recognition experience to make sense of the dots on the screen. I have every confidence Gunadi will crack the problem soon. She has pulled up some old neural-network tech that may help, although I've no idea how seeing that we've no similar datasets to train it on. More your field, Yingluq, than mine.'

'We might have it cracked soon,' said Yingluq. 'Gunadi is a wiz but sometimes needs to be left alone. Good food, Massoud. You can definitely add this to my list of likes.'

'All nutrition balanced of course, but really devised to pep up Menem, who seems to need it.'

'Lots on his plate,' said Minogue, with a glint in his eye, 'what with the old ship ageing, and now under attack.'

'We need to share the load,' said Bita, conciliating, perhaps in her personnel role.

'Hyun, Ibo and Agyei are all hard at work while I'm scoffing here,' I said. 'I need to get back: the ship won't fix itself.' How many times had they heard me say that? 'Thanks, Massoud for the new dish. Just what I needed.'

The door closed behind me as I left, but then I heard it reopen and saw Bita come out. She came after me. 'Where are you headed, Menem?' she asked.

'Back to Engineering. The assembler is rewiring a motor and should have finished by now. I want to get it installed in Engine Control so that the section can finish its rotation and make relighting Main possible when everything else is ready.'

'Can I come and see?'

'Sure. I didn't know you were interested in engineering.'

Everyone found it easy to talk to Bita, a cheerful extrovert. She was always animated and loved to dress flamboyantly. Her hair was often wild and of frequently changed colours and apparently disorganised styles.

I wondered who counselled the counsellor. Perhaps it was personnel number two, Minogue, or maybe Sahko as captain. Massoud was another possibility as he was usually very good at listening and giving reassurance and comfort but perhaps not with giving the more direct 'get-over-it' kick when needed, which Bita did with good grace.

'Sometimes I regret not knowing more about the nuts and bolts of how things work,' Bita said. 'I might have thought up the notion of using the main comms as a sort of radar sooner if I had. Seeing Minogue and Yingluq run with the idea and convert it into an implementable solution was impressive. But much as we all need to be multitalented and cover all the bases, we also need to remain focussed on our main priorities.' Was that aimed at me? Hard to avoid that thought with counsellor Bita. It got in the way of a relaxed conversation with her.

'Do you know where your counselling begins and ends?' I asked.

'Not really and it doesn't matter. I don't compartmentalise myself like that. Every communication has a function doesn't it? I want the crew to be as effective as possible and that means remaining well-adjusted human beings. It's very hard for all of us with such a small crew, confined together for so long.'

I sighed in acknowledgment. Now I was thinking about Bita, who was perched on the end of a desk, casually swinging a long slender leg. A disloyal thought. How could I be thinking about Bita and her short skirt when I was supposed to be pining for Sahko? I tried to concentrate on the motor test results.

'We need you, Menem. We all need you. Sahko needs you, I need you. We're all frightened that things will fall apart before we get there and we know you're the one to keep the ship together, so we need you to keep your shit together.' She gave a cheerful laugh.

'You would survive without me. There's nothing that I can fix that Agyei couldn't. Ibo manages the engines much better than I. Hyun gets stuff out of those printers that I never could.'

'But you've a feel for the ship that none of the rest of us does, not Agyei, Ibo, Hyun or anyone else. Between us we could fix things, but they would take longer, be harder, more wasteful, and all the time more problems would pile up. They would get away from us.' She stood up and came over to me, rested a hand on my shoulder and looked me in the eye. She was a toucher like Massoud. I felt the warmth of her hand through my shirt. 'We need you, Menem.'

'We're all needed. Although we have survived without Avalos for quite a while.'

'We haven't needed Avalos's special sauce recently. Once he'd set us on our way, his skills weren't going to be really missed until close to arrival.' She paused and then quietly added: 'Soon we might miss him very much.'

'I think about that too. I also miss his philosophising, his stories and his even some of his schoolboy pranks.'

Bita put her arms around me and gave me a hug. 'Of course, Sahko feels it too, the missing, very deeply. She thinks that as captain she's responsible for everything that goes wrong. Either she should have seen it coming and prevented it, or somehow have an immediate solution. Good as she is, she's human too.'

'And you as well?' I asked, 'Do you feel responsible? Do you think that you should have foreseen every conflict that has arisen, or been able to apply exactly the right balm to every wound?'

'I was used to being amongst the best at what I do, but the more I see, the more I know I don't know. We're all floating here, buffeted by our own and other's emotions, actions and reactions. I too am trying to keep the ship together in my own way. I do know that talking is better than not talking, even if we sometimes say things we don't fully mean, to test the waters or to stir things up.' She stopped, perhaps realising she wasn't helping any more, and stood up. 'I'm going to talk to you again soon, Menem.' She smiled and turned to go.

'Thanks, Bita.'

I'm not sure what she had done, but I did feel better: more together, more resolute. The door closed behind her, and the image of those long legs and soft warm hands came back.

4018, 15:00

The assembler had finished putting the motor back together. All the tests had been carried out successfully apart from a long-term reliability test for which there was no time. The crane trolley picked up the motor and wheeled it out and around towards section five, stopping in the connector just before the tilted section. Opening the section door, I eased myself down the sloping floor into Engine Control. The air had cleared but the extinguisher bot remained standing by, still on guard. Ibo had returned, sitting at a crazy angle in front of the control desk. The big screen remained blank. She looked to be engaged in some tricky process using her remote, waving as I came in without looking up.

'Is it OK if I swap the rotation motor now, Ibo?'

'Please go ahead. I'm looking at all the tests needed before I restart Main. It looks doable, dangerous, but doable. Yes, definitely doable, doable definitely.' She seemed to have started a chant on that theme and was making a song. 'Do-able, definitely do-able.' She had a sweet voice, and liked to make use of it. Sometimes someone would switch on a microphone and she could be heard around the ship, the corridor echoing in chorus.

Section five was similar to most of the control sections: a big major screen and an array of subsidiary displays, control panels and a holographic table display. All the screens and displays were blank. Total communications cut-off.

The blackened mouth of the equipment bay was still open. I got back down on my knees and crawled inside. The heat detection sensor, although scorched, was still properly attached to the motor. I released it, unplugged the motor's power cables, disconnected the gearbox and undid the motor's mountings. One bolt was tight, perhaps distorted by the fire, and I struggled with it for a bit. Suddenly it gave and I scraped my knuckles and then banged my head, which brought out a curse.

Ibo's singing stopped suddenly. 'You OK in there? Ooh, there's a pair of man's legs in one of my bays. Call the police.'

'Shut up, Ibo. The human species that made this ship must have been a lot smaller than me, or they never intended it to be taken apart.'

'Ooh, it's a dirty man crawling out of my bay.'

'Well it was a lot cleaner in there than in the refectory one. Perhaps you've been having Bjorn do a real special clean up job for you.'

'Well someone set my bay on fire, didn't they?'

'Perhaps it was Hyun.'

Ibo burst into laughter. 'Been a while since Hyun set my bay on fire. Perhaps I should arrange that. If not, maybe I see if Bjorn couldn't oblige, or maybe you fancy that role for yer'self. You been casting your dirty male gaze over my fine form, you sinful creature?' Ibo ratcheted up her accent.

'That would really set Hyun on fire. I wouldn't want to be the one to get between him and his woman.'

'Sure would, Hyun can be a real jealous man. Tee hee. Him jealous for me, tee-hee.' I was afraid she was about to burst in to song on that theme, but instead she said: 'Now I know you ain't got nothing better to do, but you stop distracting a lady from her work or we're going to shoot right past that pretty star we is pointed at, and only be able to wave as we sail by.' She went back to her screen and starting tapping and gesturing away at it.

I assessed the burnt racks, pipes and cables to determine what had to be replaced, and ordered up stock spares. The pipes would have been automatically isolated as soon as leaks were detected. Any liquid in them would have drained out and been recovered by Bjorn's bot.

After attaching a strap to the ruined motor, I dragged it to a position where the crane could winch it up and out.

The motor's control box had become somewhat melted but was still recognisable. However, round the back it had a pair of quad-core, high-capacity, optical fibre links that didn't feature on Archive's schematics. I was disconnecting what remained of the box when the connection to the motor's heat detection sensor fell out, almost as though it had never been properly connected. The odd fibres were neatly clipped in place and went up onto a cable tray at the back of the void. I followed them and found each had a coupler into fibres running in opposite directions along the tray. It looked as though it was some kind of system signal intercept-bypass. Maybe it was a test device left behind by the shipyard. I unplugged the two tail fibres and joined up the two ends of the main cable just to see what effect that would have.

Ibo yelped, gasped, cried out and then shouted: 'What did you do?'

'What happened?' I asked.

'The main screen suddenly came on. Whatever you did seems to have restored communications in here.'

'That's good, isn't it?'

'Absolutely marvellous. You're a genius. What did you do?'

'I just plugged the ends of some fibres back together. There was some kind of device inserted, probably a piece of test gear that got left behind by someone. Presumably it got damaged in the fire, cutting off the link.'

'Leave it like that. I will give it a thorough check out. Status seems very happy with what you've done. What was the test box thing for?'

'I don't know. I'll try and take it apart later, but it got quite damaged in the fire. The case melted.'

'Ah well. Now just get the place oriented correctly and we'll be back in business.'

I used the crane on the cart to get the repaired motor to the door of Engine Control and to restrain its slide down the floor inside until I could pull it across and into the bay. Another awkward crawl, some more cursing as I shifted it into position, reconnected the gearbox, carefully realigned the power train and bolted it down. The retained nuts in the floor that held the motor seem to have been forced but they held it securely enough for now.

By that time the replacement stock parts had arrived. I fitted the new power and control cables, including a new overheat power control box, and glue-welded in new sections to replace the damaged fluid pipes.

After attaching some test gear, I cautiously activated the fluid lines and electrical connections and then, after warning Ibo, instructed the motor to start rotating the section. There was an immediate hum as it sprang to life and I felt the floor moving under me. The test equipment didn't detect any heat build up. It all seemed to be functioning and soon the section was fully rotated. The wall panel surprisingly still fitted back over the bay despite being badly scorched by the fire and discoloured by the smoke.

'All done ma'am.'

'Thank you my man. You're a marvel. It's so nice to be back on an even keel again. Show yourself out and send the maid in to clean up that panel and the dirty floor where you been messin'.'

'Will do, ma'am.' I touched my forelock, and followed the crane trolley back to Engineering, calling up a service bot for the clean up as I did so. Repairing the fire damaged motor and exploring the odd control box would have to wait: more urgent now was the laser repair.

I called Hyun. 'Hi, how are the laser's parts coming on? Is it worth my while coming by to collect anything and get started on the rebuild?'

'Sure. It's going better than expected.'

I went round to Printing in section six and Hyun continued with his update. 'With a bit of fiddling about, a lot of the old parts were salvageable. They simply needed some filling where they were pierced. Most of the holes were completely clean, the material presumably vaporised as the object passed through. You can certainly get started on the rebuild. All the remaining internal components should be finished in another hour. The structural support is the longest job and the big printer-weaver is well along with it. Two hours at most for that. You were quicker than I expected with the rotation motor, assuming you've finished.'

'I took the motor from the refectory. It needed some marginal components replacing, which didn't take long. That one went into Engine Control and I've brought the burnt-out one back to Engineering for repair. I also had to replace some burnt pipes and cables in the equipment bay in five. The motor control box was odd: it looked as though the overheat sensor wasn't connected and the Engine Control main systems fibres were linked through it. I took the box out and joined up the ends of the fibres. Now everything is back working in there.'

'Ibo will be pleased that her section is now aligned and the connection restored. It will make getting Main back alight rather easier.'

'Definitely. Ibo seemed in a jolly, jokey and singing mood when I left.'

'Any ideas about that control box?'

'It might be a bit of shipyard test kit that got left behind. Although why that would have looked like a normal control box, I have no idea. Also, the fibres connected into it were neatly fixed and hidden as though it was permanent. Unfortunately it got rather melted, but I will have a go at opening it up at some point to see what its function was.'

'Odd, as you say. Could it be a sabotage device?'

'Good grief. That's a theory I might have concocted: a way to seize control of the engine perhaps?'

'Anyway, I hope you have time to get the motor back in the refectory before Main restarts.'

'Minogue noticed that I was cannibalising the motor from the refectory. Not sure why he was particularly concerned. He also mentioned again deploying the big telescope, wanting to see if he can spot anything related to the object field. You know my view that the telescope would be vulnerable, sticking out from the side of the ship at this speed. Regardless of all that, I need to focus on repairing Wayclear.'

'The printed parts are in that crate. They'll need some finishing and you should check the laser structure to see if it got distorted by the impact.'

'I'll get going. Can I call on you for help?'

'If I can. I have to keep an eye on the printers though, and help Ibo with deploying the hot-bot for the nozzle inspection. Also, I need to be printing parts and directing the bot-net fixing all the damage near the fuel pipe for Agyei.'

'OK, I get the picture. I'll see if Yingluq can contribute. I seem to remember she has expertise in optics.'

'It would be helpful if she can assist, but do call me if you need an extra hand. I'll do what I can.'

'Thanks, Hyun. Let me try to spread the load a little wider.' I picked up the crate of finished parts and went back to Engineering.

I wasn't sure how to tackle Yingluq: she could be quite prickly, particularly when being asked to do jobs outside her designated areas. Still, optics was once one of her things and I needed help. I called her and asked if she could guide me in setting up the laser.

'That should be possible. I'm on classroom duty at the moment but I can probably duck out for a bit, provided someone is around to stop them killing each other.' Yells in the background suggested the children were having a go. 'Perhaps Massoud can look in if he's not at a delicate stage of boiling up a witches brew, or maybe there's someone else around who is not too busy.'

That seemed unlikely at the moment. Possibly Sahko? Good luck with that. No, that wasn't fair: she took her turns in looking after them as much as the rest of us did. But maybe now, in the midst of a crisis, was not a good time. She would need to be in Ops, in touch everything that was going on and deploying resources in the best way possible. Supposedly.

'Thanks, hope you can make it,' I said, and the link cut.

The printed laser components went into a parts rack and the machines set to work. The finisher carried out all the necessary machining to bring each part within its design tolerances. It also cleaned the parts, heat-treatment them and applied coatings as required. Within a couple of minutes the first parts were coming back out.

While that was happening, I ordered some stock items from Stores, mostly electrical components for the damaged charging system. The laser's chassis was stripped of its remaining parts, mounted on the assembler and tested for any distortion. A bit of judicious bending and clamping fixed some minor trouble. The assembler began piecing all the components together, including the delicate optical system, much of which was made from what looked like fragile glass. It added the usual collection of electrical sub-systems, coolant assemblies, seals and mechanical elements to provide support. Assembling some items proved to be beyond the machine's capability because of the sheer size of the laser and it had to let me take over. The assembly station monitored what I was doing, prompted me for the next action, and warned me of any mistakes.

I thought I was getting near the end of the assembly when Hyun dropped by with another crate of parts.

'These are the alignment system components and should be the last printed parts for the internals. You should be able to finish the guts of it now and start testing. Please don't try it on full power in here: it will burn a hole through that wall and I'm right next door.'

'I'll endeavour not to drill a hole in you. Yingluq said she would try to get here to help out. It's her turn in the classroom at present. It sounded as though she was having a bit of a hard time and welcomed a task that would take priority, allowing her to pass responsibility for the children onto someone else. Usually she seems to be organising competitive games for them as she does for the rest of the crew. No doubt she wins most of the children's games as well. She may be the mother of Sky, but she isn't really the motherly type.'

'The kids usually have fun and expend a lot of energy in her classes. Alice often chats about them later. I must be getting back.'

Before the door closed I heard him say: 'Hi, Yingluq. Menem said you might be able to come down and help. Alice not giving you a hard time I hope?'

'Those children are exhausting, especially Alice,' Yingluq replied. 'So many questions.' The door opened and she came in. 'Hi, Menem. Show me this laser.'

'Most of the assembly is done. The next step in the manual is optical alignment, but we don't have all the equipment required. Let me get these last few parts that Hyun has just delivered loaded in to the assembler and then perhaps you can give me some guidance on how we might get it tuned up.'

Yingluq was all efficiency and self-control: super-fit, super-toned. Like a true sportswoman, she had her hair tied back in a neat plait from the top of her head to her shoulders. She took off her bomber jacket and underneath she wore a tight fitting sports top. From the back, I could see the muscles in her neck and shoulders as she bent over the laser. Along with the strappy top she wore loose trousers and heavy kick-ass boots, much favoured by the female members of the crew. A woman not to be messed with.

'Been a while since I looked inside something like this. It's much heavier than those I use in surgery. I have worked on, and used, very similar ones to this in the past, some much bigger.'

Presumably in the military, I guessed. I didn't know a whole lot about our good doctor's past, and she never offered anything. Most of what I knew about her had come by way of others, and might not all be true. Funny how you can live in close proximity to someone for years and know so little about them. In the early days Yingluq had been lively, always up for a party. But since the deaths she had also become more withdrawn and focussed. Perhaps she felt responsible too, although neither death was due to her negligence: both were beyond revival before she could do anything. We were all sure that there had been nothing else she could have done, particularly given our limited resources. But even given the finest facilities and a team of doctors, almost certainly both would have died anyway.

'Tell me what you know,' Yingluq said.

'Well, the laser's beam is steered and focused in the fluid chamber on the front. The chamber is surrounded by intense electric and magnetic fields which are driven straight from the planar radar: there's no time for computation. This thing can steer by a fraction of a degree in nanoseconds. That's all the time it has got to hit an object closing with the ship at forty percent of light speed. The beam is supposed to ionise objects in our path, allowing them to be deflected by the ship's magnetosphere. To identify objects in time, the radar needs to be continuously monitoring the area a hundred kilometres directly ahead. The laser remains permanently powered up, ready to strike.'

'To achieve that the laser's optics must be very precisely aligned and focused,' said Yingluq. 'It must have been set up on a sophisticated optical bench at the factory before it was installed.'

'Great. We know the structure got distorted and I've had to rebuild most of the interior of the laser. Any ideas on how are we going to achieve any kind of alignment?' I asked.

'The way we used to do this in the field was to shine another laser beam back down the optical path and use diffraction gratings to fine-tune it. I have a laser in medical that should be suitable. Can you find a pair of identical silicon memory chips and etch a square millimetre in the centre of each? This should be done from the back and it needs to leave about five nanometres remaining thickness of the grid of memory cells. We can use a pair of those as diffraction gratings.'

Yingluq stood up and turned to me. Her top left nothing to the imagination, delineating a pair of high firm breasts with small nipples, perfectly placed.

'Get your head out of my chest, Menem. Concentrate on the job in hand.'

I felt sweat on the back of my neck and wrenched my gaze away, mumbling something stupid like: 'Not usually such beauty in Engineering.' Got to remember this woman could probably kill me with one blow. Perhaps that was what she had been teaching the kids: how to kill each other more effectively. Once I had walked by the classroom and it sounded as though she was teaching them how to scream.

Yingluq seemed to smirk, marched out the door and I heard her jogging away towards Medical. I messaged Gunadi to see if she had a pair of dud memory chips amongst her piles of junk. I also messaged Agyei for suggestions on how to etch them.

With this being ship priority-one both replied almost immediately. Gunadi was sure she had some spare memory chips and would dig a couple out and send them down. Agyei suggested etching with hydrochloric acid, which she volunteered to do. Using fine temperature control and the ultrasonic stirrer facilities in Chemistry would allow precision work. She said it wouldn't take long, perhaps fifteen minutes. I asked Gunadi to send the parts directly to Agyei in Chemistry.

I heard Yingluq's footfall as she jogged back. She appeared with an instrument case from which she extracted one of the surgery lasers and its power supply. The assembler had finished and moved out of the way, allowing her to set up the medical device in front of the Wayclear laser, clamping the two together. Her movements were calm and precise, as though operating on a patient.

'How are you getting on with the gratings?' she asked.

'Gunadi says she has the parts and is sending then to Agyei for etching. They should be ready in ten minutes or so.'

'Good that we can still co-operate when we need to after all these years. I'll start doing some initial tests of the optical paths.' Yingluq began examining the inside of the reassembled big laser, making measurements and comparing them with its specifications. 'It doesn't seem to be structurally distorted now, which is good news.' She described her actions as she worked, and I passed her tools and tried to make sense of the process. 'Flare and colour seem to be within tolerances.' She ran through some more tests. 'It all seems to be functioning. As long as we can get the optics aligned, we should be able to get it back to working condition.'

Agyei came in with a small box and looked surprised to see Yingluq. She said: 'I didn't know you were here. Welcome to Engineering. It's good that we're attracting such able recruits.'

I wasn't sure if she was upset that Yingluq was helping in Engineering when she hadn't known or been asked. Agyei was hard to read sometimes. Normally these two seemed to get on well, on the surface at least. Agyei's son Kent and Yingluq's daughter Sky were about the same age. Perhaps it was only a momentary resentment of being out of the loop, or maybe there was something else going on that I didn't know about. Agyei handed me the box with the gratings.

'Thanks for getting on with these so quickly, Agyei,' I said. 'Hyun suggested that Yingluq's expertise in optics might help get the laser sorted and he was right. She clearly has skills in this area way beyond mine.'

I handed Yingluq the gratings and she said: 'I've seen similar lasers before and had to fix them in the field. I was also glad to have an excuse to take a break from the children for a bit.'

Agyei looked a bit stiff as she left. I was going to have to do some smoothing there later.

Yingluq was bent over the laser again. 'Quiet now and be still, the less vibration the better. You need to tune those four levelling screws at the back end on my instruction. I'll let you know what and when to adjust, and by how much.'

She pulled up a high stool and sat at the bench. I watched as she slid the pair of gratings in position and explained how the tuning would work. Her surgical laser shone a beam through a splitter, one half of the beam going straight down the optics of the big laser and the other through one of the gratings and then across the room to a camera sensor which produced an image on a monitor screen in Yingluq's field of view. The beam down the main laser went through the excitation crystal and was reflected off the main mirror, back up through the crystal again, through the half mirror at the front and then deflected by another mirror that Yingluq had placed in its path. That beam passed through the second grating, was further reflected and, combined with the first, ended up at the camera sensor. By careful positioning of the gratings and mirrors, a diffraction pattern was supposed to emerge on the screen as the laser came in to tune.

Yingluq started calling out a series of instructions: 'Top, quarter turn, anticlockwise. No, the other way, yes, that's better. Left, half turn, clockwise. No, you idiot, left, not right.' Left, right: it depended on which direction you were looking.

My actions were adjusting the main mirror at the back of the laser. Yingluq was making similar adjustments to the half-mirror and lenses at the front. At first I couldn't see what effect we were having, but gradually a pattern began to take shape on the screen. Sometimes it would jump out of focus, but with the next adjustment it would be a little clearer. It seemed sharp to me but Yingluq continued to tune it, taking increasingly long pauses between steps. Finally she stopped and stood up.

'That looks good, probably as good as the original setting. Lock in the adjusters without nudging anything and it will be ready.'

She packed up her surgical kit and I sneaked a last peek at the fine hairs on the nape of her neck and at other parts of her anatomy before she put her jacket back on. She gave me a smile and hit me on the shoulder with her fist, slightly harder than strictly necessary.

'That was kind of fun. It's been a while since I fixed any complicated machines,' she said. 'It's usually people I work on and they're somewhat less predictable. You never know if they're really fixed and sooner or later they'll be back for repairs again, regardless.'

'Machines often seem to come back for fixing again too, entropy gets everything in the end. Thanks for your help, Yingluq. You've saved me a lot of time. At the very least I would have had to do a load of research in Archive to get close to that.'

'OK, Menem. Got to go.'

'Perhaps I could call by when things are quieter. I feel as though I need fixing too.'

'Dream on, Menem,' she said with a grin as she left. I heard her jogging away down the passage.

I turned back to the laser, locked the adjusters in place and closed up its new casing. Just the support structure to attach and then it could be put back in to action.

4018, 17:00

I called Hyun. 'Yingluq was a wiz with the optics and the laser is fixed. How's the support coming on?'

'Getting there. The casting and weaving is complete and it's currently in the autoclave for curing. Should be cooked in about fifteen minutes, then we're all set.'

'I'll alert Bjorn for another mimic session. I also have to consult Agyei on the appropriate adhesives to lock the structure in place.'

'OK, I'll let you know when it's done. Agyei shouldn't have any problem with an adhesive: it should be a stock item because the structure is normal materials. I've posted the material specs on the collaboration page.'

I called Bjorn. 'The laser is fixed and its support is nearly ready. Can you do another mimic job with me to reinstall, starting in about fifteen minutes?'

'I'll be there. Yingluq returned and said the laser was about ready, which seemed quick. I was standing in for her with the children, and she has now taken over again. I'm having a meal which may not have been the best thing to do before a mimic trip, but I didn't know when I would be able to eat again.'

'I've never known your stomach not to be able to hold its food, unlike mine.'

Bjorn laughed and said 'I'm usually OK, but I have lost it before now. The mimics can be a bitch. Do you want me to bring you anything?'

'That would be kind. Please ask Massoud for something my stomach can hold on to, a protein bar or something. See you soon in Robotics.'

Next I called Agyei. 'How are the repairs going around the fuel pipe? Very tricky I imagine, trying to avoid sending us all to kingdom come.'

'Ibo and I have worked out what needs to be done and we've started on the repair to the structure. It's all in a job file in Status. If you've any suggestions, let us know.'

I couldn't detect any resentment in her voice over Yingluq helping me. It was probably going to be cool professionalism from Agyei for a while, rather than warm banter. No time now for smoothing.

'I doubt I'll be able to add anything. At the moment I'm working on the repairs to the Wayclear laser, and we need an adhesive to fix the new support to the remains of the old one that's still attached to the ship. Can you check Status, where Hyun has posted the materials spec, and sort something out for us? Bjorn and I hope to start mimic work in about ten minutes.'

'Will do. I'll bring it around to Robotics.'

'Thanks Agyei. Can you send it to Airlock Two? We'll take everything out through there.'

Agyei had a rather aristocratic bearing and sometimes appeared to be a caricature of the cold chemistry and materials specialist, but then she would suddenly switch on a glorious smile that would transform her face with radiance. Massoud often said what a cheerful soul she was. He was deputy in chemistry and materials as Agyei was deputy in engineering and I was deputy in engines and so on. I usually found her a calm and reassuring presence and we worked well together, most of the time.

The crew-alert klaxon gave a brief wail and Sahko spoke urgently on the general comms channel: 'All crew listen up. The simulation is indicating a high probability that we'll start to re-enter the densest part of the object field in about five minutes from now. We need Wayclear fixed as soon as possible. Bjorn, Hyun and Menem will reinstall the laser, once it's repaired. All other personnel to Lifeboat One now as a precaution. Ibo, continue monitoring Fuse remotely from there; we can't afford to lose power now. Gunadi and Bita, keep updating the object field simulation from the lifeboat. Bita, retract the secondary antenna sufficiently so that it's shielded by the body of the ship. Menem, how is the laser repair coming along?'

'The laser has been repaired and realigned. Bjorn is already on the way to Robotics. Agyei is preparing the adhesive we need and will deliver it in a few minutes to the airlock for us to collect. The printer will require another five minutes to finish the support which will then also be taken to the airlock and I'm about to load the laser and take it there too. Hyun will then be standing by with the bot-net as required and I'll join Bjorn in the mimics.'

'Good. Agyei: deliver the adhesive and then make your way as quickly as possible to the lifeboat. We really need to get that laser back in action. However, if we see the risk level rising too high, Menem, Hyun and Bjorn, you're to evacuate to Lifeboat Two.' Sahko cut off.

I pulled over the crane trolley, hoisted the laser and carefully manoeuvred it out the door and round to the airlock, transferring it to the exterior trolley inside. Hyun appeared with another trolley with the support structure which we offloaded and fixed beside the laser. As we were finishing, Agyei came running up with the adhesive, ready loaded in an applicator gun. We fixed that to the trolley too, closing and sealing the inner door. The airlock started the air evacuation sequence and a stray thought about the possibility of air trapped in the laser blowing it apart made me shudder.

'Thanks, Agyei, your captain awaits,' I said, trying to appear calm.

'Good luck you guys, see you later.'

Don't we all hope? I thought, as Agyei turned and ran. I watched her trim figure go.

Hyun and I ran round to section seven and found Bjorn had arrived. He thrust a food bar into my hand, gave me a grim smile and said: 'Could have done without the extra pressure from the captain.'

I took a couple of quick bites of the bar and stuck the rest in a pocket.

'The parts are loaded in Airlock Two and it's evacuating,' I told Bjorn. 'They should be ready to collect when you arrive outside. My mimic is still in the engine section. I'll come down and give you a hand with the trolley.'

The process was going to be a mirror image of the retrieval that we had carried out earlier. Bjorn and I strapped ourselves into our mimic controllers. Thumbs up from Hyun and Bjorn, and I put on my VR helmet.

I was back in my mimic, still clinging to a support in an equipment recess up in the engine section. I clambered out of the bay and began walking down the long fuel tank and payload rings, quickly getting back into the mimic stride.

Bjorn came into view, pushing the trolley loaded with laser parts onto the transfer deck, but I lost sight of him again as the Habitat Ring spun away. He came over the comms. 'I'll stop next to the track you're coming down. It's not heavy but the load was a bit of a brute to keep steady against the spin.'

Bjorn came back into view and the transfer deck stopped by me. 'Phew. I don't think it hit anything. Can you go in front and I'll walk behind down to the engine?'

We got in rhythm with the sliding walk along the narrow track between the radiator panels. All the time Hyun had the bot-net scurrying around, part of it keeping our tethers attached and part keeping an eye out for hazards and to warn us if the load was looking like shifting.

Sahko came over the comms. 'Wayclear is reporting an increase in objects in our path. Not yet saturated, but rising fast.'

She would also be picking up a view from either the bot-net or a mimic camera. Even if an object had flown right past us we wouldn't notice it:

our perception was nowhere near fast enough, and there were no sounds or shock waves in the vast, supposed emptiness, of space.

We arrived at the front of the ship, close to the end of the engine nozzle. The broken laser mount, with the planar radar still attached, stood out oddly against the star-field. Lights carried by some of the bot-net elements illuminated the scene.

Hyun must have done some work with the bot-net to clean up the broken section and prepare it for the repair, fortunately, because I had forgotten to ask. There was no time for a containment tent. Bjorn got the new strut out of the bag and held it while I smeared a heavy bead of adhesive in a groove formed on its inside. Bjorn lifted the strut over the remains of the old support and slid it into place. Together we lifted the laser and positioned it over the mount, threading the pipes and cables into it, fixing them inside. Hyun told us that the bot-net had checked and confirmed that we had positioned the structure correctly. I worked an ultrasonic fixer round the new join, fluidising the adhesive and causing it to drawn by capillary action into the joint between the old and new parts. Once the fixer had moved on, the adhesive would bond with both surfaces, locking everything in place permanently.

I climbed up the support to look down into the laser, reconnected the coolant pipes and felt around for the power and control cables coming up through the strut. At that moment my vision went blank: I couldn't see the laser, and when I looked around the star-field had gone.

Blind, near to panic and trying to keep my voice neutral, I said: 'Hyun, my vision is out, can you reset it?'

'Wow, oh shit,' cried out Bjorn. 'The back of your head, I mean your mimic's head, has gone. Rotate you head. Jeez, there's a hole in the front of your mimic's visor. I don't think a reset is going to fix that.'

'Damn, damn, damn. I had so nearly finished, but the power and control cables still need to be plugged in and I can't do that by touch alone. You'll have to do it, Bjorn.'

'OK, I'll guide you down and you can park your mimic in a recess. I'll plug the cables in; you tell me what to do.'

I felt Bjorn's mimic guiding my hands onto the laser support as I eased myself down onto the skin of the ship. Bjorn gave me step-by-step instructions to walk towards the equipment recess where he got me into a sitting position. Sliding the mimic's legs over the edge of the recess, I lowered myself into it, lay down and grasped a retaining hook with each of the mimic's hands and feet. At least my mimic was out of the way and protected to some extent by the engine nozzle. It would have to be recovered later when things were quieter, assuming we survived.

I unclasped the mimic controls from my arms and legs and took off the VR helmet. The control room sprang back in to view and I immediately bent over and threw up.

'Shit, sorry Hyun.'

'It happens. You need to recover and guide Bjorn with connecting the cables.'

'Yes, yes.' I spat some vomit out of my mouth. Climbing out of the mimic chair my hands were shaking. I sat at a work-screen and pulled up feeds from Bjorn's mimic's eyes and a more general view of the scene from a bot-net camera. Bjorn had climbed up to the laser where I had been.

'Bjorn, you see the big black cables coming up from the strut? One has a brown plug, the other blue.'

'Yeah, got those.'

'The brown one goes in a brown socket that's inside the laser, towards the back.'

'Ah yes, I see that, it goes in pretty easily. Presumably the blue one goes in the blue socket towards the front.'

'Yes, amazingly it does. Once the plugs are inserted, rotate the knurled ring on each to lock them in place.'

Pause. 'OK, done that. Now the control link: I see a cable that divides and is terminated by several plugs of different sizes.'

'That's the one. The sockets are all along the top of the box at the back. Colour coded and of different sizes so you can't plug them into the wrong place or the wrong way round. There's one plug on a longer lead that goes up to the front of the laser to the steering unit: that's the odd shaped box on the front of the laser.'

Bjorn methodically worked his way around, making all the connections.

'OK. Found all the ones on the back and they seem to have a clip that swings over to hold them in place. Now the front one. Where is that? Hiding under that pipe perhaps? No. Ah, there it is, at the back of the front bit. I'm sure that's the right terminology. Good they're all done. What next, boss?'

'Close the internal cover and then climb down and shelter behind the support. I'll pull up Wayclear Control, run some quick checks and then you'll have to set the laser's aim before we're done. I'll check first with Ibo that Fuse is ready to ramp up another notch.' Opening another section of screen, I accessed Wayclear Control, calling up Ibo as I did so.

'Ibo, we're about to warm up Wayclear's fourth laser. Is Fuse good for the juice?'

'Fuse standing by, ready to ramp up to meet demand. The sooner the better.' She sounded tense.

Wayclear Control showed that the three operating lasers were in almost continuous fire. Their target screens a mass of detected objects, flickering in and out. The diagnostic for the fourth laser came up and it ran through the test sequence: coolant flow, power connection, control cycle. Good so far.

'Bjorn, ready for alignment? You need to stand at the back to do the adjustments. There are two large silver coloured knurled knobs, one on the underside, one on the right-hand side as you face towards the front.'

'OK, Menem. I see the knobs and am ready to make adjustments.'

'I'm directing a visual from the setup sequence to project in front of your headset so you can get direct commands. I'll monitor for instability or any other problems as the power to the laser is ramped up. We don't want to lose another mimic.'

'OK, I see the screen. Looks clear what I have to do to start the sequence.'

I confirmed 'go' and the performance dials started to edge up. Coolant flow looked good and the laser ignition went smoothly. The radar was up and running, feeding back targeting information. I watched the laser sights come in to alignment as Bjorn made adjustments to its aim.

'That looks good to me: the operational performance is well within spec. Close up the outer casing, Bjorn, and stand your mimic back. I'll ramp the laser up to full power.'

'OK, closed up, and standing clear. Let her rip.'

I put the laser online. The power surged into it and the targeting screen lit up with objects. It was immediately in action, relieving the other three lasers of some of the work. At least our defences were now as good as they were ever going to be.

I called up Sahko. 'Wayclear fourth laser online, Captain.' She probably knew that anyway if she was looking at Status.

Sahko was abrupt. 'The modelling suggests we're going to be in this dense object area for another half-hour, and then it will quickly tail off. Bjorn, Hyun and Menem, get to Lifeboat Two until we're through it. Thanks for fixing the laser. There's nothing more you can do.'

I left Robotics and walked quickly round to where the second lifeboat was held. Hyun came up as I was opening the hatch and we dropped in and buckled up.

Bjorn came on the comms: 'I'm not far behind. I've parked my mimic in the equipment recess near yours and I'm unbuckling from the control chair.'

We waited a half minute and then Bjorn came tumbling through the hatch, pulling it closed behind him. He quickly sat and buckled himself in. Lifeboat launch would be very violent and come without warning if it happened. At least I had already lost the contents of my stomach.

We were all silent for a while, exhausted as the adrenalin started to drain away. Bjorn looked up, his eyes still glowing with the buzz. 'That was something wasn't it?'

Hyun was still looking at his feet. 'Sure was. We did something there. Whether we survive in this shooting gallery or not, at least we tried.'

I looked straight ahead. 'We did, along with Yingluq, Gunadi and Agyei too when they were needed.'

Bjorn added: 'And Ibo has managed to keep Fuse alight.'

Hyun sighed. 'Yeah. But when we get through this we still have a mess to clear up.'

'Sorry about that,' I mumbled.

'Not the vomit, Menem, the cleaner will handle that. I meant Main.'

'Oh, hell, we need both mimics to do that, and one of them I trashed.'

'Hardly your fault, Menem,' said Bjorn. 'It's a lottery out there. Anything could be hit at anytime.'

'It was one of the worst experiences I've ever had: suddenly being blinded like that. Those mimics are too damn real, total immersion.'

'Aren't they just?' said Bjorn. 'I'm that machine, that machine is me, in a moment, superman, super-powers.'

Hyun looked up. 'Don't get too carried away, we have to stay grounded. Work on the next problem.'

'Sorry about the damage to the mimic head, Hyun. I don't suppose we carry a spare?' I asked.

'No, and it will take quite a lot to fix. We'll have to bring it back inside and probably fabricate a lot of parts. They're seriously complicated, full of all sorts of special stuff: optics and other sensors. From what we could see from the bot-net and Bjorn's view, the damage was pretty severe. It's not going to be a five minute job.'

'Could we use the bot-net to provide the vision for the mimic somehow, at least temporarily?'

'Maybe. We would only need a small array of bots from the net, comprising a pair of specialised camera units, with a small collection of others to hold them to the head, steer as required and transmit the pictures. Integrating the array with the mimic to allow you to control it would be a challenge: any signal delay would be disorienting. The elements could tap into the mimic's power grid so they wouldn't need separate recharging. Gunadi could probably help if she's not on other urgent tasks. I'll communicate with her.'

Bjorn's eyes were closed and he seemed to have fallen asleep. He had the ability to take naps easily and be fully awake and functioning in a moment. I suddenly felt tired too. It would be a good idea to rest because the next EVA was also going to require intense concentration. I hoped that Gunadi and Hyun could work out a solution for the mimic without my input.

What a day. Normally life on the ship consisted of long, very dull periods when nothing much changed and we had to manufacture our own excitement, like Yingluq's tournaments or Minogue's brain teasers. Today we'd had plenty of unplanned excitement and I had experienced surprising mood swings. That didn't usually happen, which led me back to thinking that Massoud might have been fiddling with hormones in my food. Either that or I was just frustrated. After lunch, I had been thinking far too much about all the women on board. Ah, all except Gunadi, easy to overlook. In the lull, I fell to thinking about her.

Gunadi had always been self-effacing and had got noticeably quieter after Avalos had died. She hid her femininity, wearing loose black ship-suits and her shoulders were usually hunched forward as though to de-emphasise her breasts. Her head was often down with her un-styled hair limply hiding her eyes. It was hard to tell what she looked like most of the time. I remembered that she had a rather cute button nose and that she was slim hipped, but that was about it. Only once I'd had a glimpse of her body shape. I had gone to the recreation room and she was there after a workout, which she didn't often seem to do, or did at times when I wasn't, it being a necessary part of staying alive in space. She had been facing away from the door when I came in and was towelling her hair. She'd had her arms raised and her loose exercise top had ridden up slightly, exposing a band of skin around her waist. In that brief moment I saw her as a woman: slender waist broadening to slim but definitely female hips.

She had glanced shyly at me, mumbled an apology, gathered up her things and left before I could stop her. She seemed to avoid me for a few days after that.

She was never chatty, at least with me, and not often the subject of gossip. There had been some male banter when Avalos was alive, but that had applied to all the women when the handsome and dashing Avalos's favour was being speculated upon. Linking Avalos and the goth-mousy Gunadi usually brought laughter and hoots of derision. That was about it. She was the only woman aboard not to have been pregnant during the trip, so that was unusual. Pregnancy, childbirth and bringing up children were the main elements keeping a small crew like ours sane over the long, very uneventful years. We were investing the prime of our lives in this journey, and our children would be our legacy.

Maybe I should get to know Gunadi better. It may be late in the day, but it would be useful professionally to improve my understanding of the analytics systems, or at least be in-tune with Gunadi's thinking: help the team and all that. It might become especially important when everything had to be reconfigured after our arrival. I tried to hold that worthy thought, but my mind wandered to the moment in the gym and to that rather cute nose. I drifted off to sleep.

4018, 18:50

Bjorn talking excitedly with Hyun brought me awake. 'There's a definite slackening in the density of things in our way. Wayclear is having a much easier time of it now, targeting and deflecting objects.'

Hyun was more cautious. 'Seems to be, if we can trust the data. It could be that there's some degradation of the sensors.'

'Unlikely: it would have to have affected all four simultaneously.'

'Unless there was some change in the structure of the field that blanketed the whole array.'

'That also seems very unlikely. We should ask if the others are able to check the shape of the object field from the main aerial. Yup, take a look at Status: they're feeding real-time data into it. Switching the aerial between radar mode and transmit mode to tell Fleet about what we're experiencing.'

At that moment Sahko came on the comms. 'The density of the object field has dropped away. The risk of strike is diminishing rapidly. Unless anything changes in the meanwhile, those directly needed for Main fix should move back aboard. Those not involved with that should remain in the lifeboats for a while longer. Simulations show that we can expect to be substantially out of the field in a little over fifteen minutes from now, assuming it's symmetrical. If that's the case, then there are likely to be only a few residual objects in our path, fading out completely over the next two hours or so.

'To be sure everyone is up to speed, I'll summarise what's been done recently and what needs to be done next. The nozzle has to be checked: Ibo and Hyun, set that going first. Gunadi, assist Ibo and Hyun with setting the hot-bot's inspection path. If needed, go back to Analytics to work on that. Once that's going, Hyun and Gunadi fix the mimic vision as you have proposed. Ibo and Agyei have defined a process for the structural repairs in the fuel-pipe area using the bot-net. We need parts made for that, so printing is a critical-path item. Agyei, manage the remaining work on the structure repair and replacement of other components in the damaged area. Hyun, once you're free, get the printing underway for the repairs. Bjorn and Menem, prepare for another EVA to recover the damaged fuel pipe.'

Bjorn was fully alert and clearly eager to go. 'I'm ready.'

I was less enthusiastic. 'Very difficult to use the mimic without visuals. How long will it take to get the workaround online?'

'Gunadi thinks about ten minutes to set up the programme. Hyun has the bot-net ready to receive orders and enough elements are already near the mimic.'

'OK, I'll be ready. Any chance of some food?'

'Is that a joke, Menem?' asked Sahko.

'I can give you a bloodstream protein injection which will bypass your stomach,' put in Yingluq.

'Maybe not,' I mumbled.

'I'll have something truly satisfying for you when you're done, Menem,' added Massoud.

'Can someone watch him prepare it?' I said. 'I'm suspicious that he put something in my last meal.' I heard giggling in the background and noticed Bjorn and Hyun smiling. Were they all in on the game, or was it my paranoia returning? 'Nothing funny,' I snapped. More muffled laughter.

'Focus team,' said Sahko. Even her voice seemed to have a smirk in it.

Hyun hurried out first. Bjorn waited for me to un-strap and stand. I felt stiff from sitting and woozy from the sleep I'd had. I could still taste and smell vomit, not even having had time to wash my mouth out. Perhaps the relief from being out of the object field was also reducing my pep. 'Go ahead, Bjorn. I had a kip while we were waiting and it always takes me a bit to recover.'

'Sure, old boy. I'll help you back to your chair.'

'Very funny. I'm recovered now. Lead on.'

I wasn't going to be 'old boy'. Bjorn and I were practically the same age. Maybe I hadn't been spending as much time in the gym as I should have, and certainly not as much as Bjorn or Yingluq. There was so much to fix on the ship these days. The repair list never seemed to grow shorter, and low priority items, like Sahko's refresher, never got done. Well maybe that was really because I was reluctant to go into her apartment, and had been ever since she had cooled towards me. How I wish my thoughts wouldn't keep going round and round like this. You need to focus, Menem: you've a difficult task ahead. Yes, in that vomit machine, great.

I followed Bjorn back to Robotics. As we went Bjorn said 'How about we split this mission into two? We can recover your mimic, and set up and test the bot-net camera. It might take some getting used to. After that, we can both go down to the pipe area, do whatever disassembly is required, and bring the broken part back here. It'll surely take some time to make whatever new parts are needed and test them. We can take a break while that's going on, and perhaps have something to eat then.'

I wondered if he was making a joke with that last part. I decided to ignore it.

'Good plan, except we'll need to test the pipe for radioactivity. If it's hot we won't be able to bring it inside, although working on it outside is a nightmare prospect. Before any of that, I need to wash my mouth out.' I took a pouch of water from the chiller station and went over to a wash-drain.

Bjorn and I spent some time going over all the video footage of the broken fuel pipe, examining the connectors for damage, and working up a process of who was going to do what and when, and what tools we would need. Eventually we had everything pinned down and had word from Hyun that the bot-net elements were in place in the head of my mimic. They were able to act as its eyes quite well, he said, but he'd had to add some lights to maintain visibility in shadow. I went over to Engineering to select some specialist tools, sent them round for loading into a mimic pack, and returned to Robotics.

Bjorn was strapping in to his mimic, looking up when I came in. 'Are you good for this one, Menem? We need to be on-game.'

'Yes, yes, I'm good, I'm fine now.' That was mostly true. EVAs usually gave me a buzz, and I was starting to get it as I sat in my control chair and strapped in.

'All crew, all crew.' Sahko came on the broadcast comms channel again. 'We've a new problem and hence a change of priority. The first data from the hot-bot shows serious damage to the nozzle coating. All crew to the refectory for a brainstorm on how to fix this. This is a mission-critical problem: five minutes everyone.'

Bjorn and I looked at each other and then started un-strapping ourselves. 'What do you think is the problem, Menem?'

'My guess is that repairs to the nozzle on any scale aren't going to be easy. Perhaps Agyei and Massoud can't cook up the right materials for the tiles. Someone should have thought of this risk, but who knows, perhaps they did.'

'Ah well, let's go and find out.'

As we came out of Robotics and were about to set off for the refectory we saw Hyun coming out of Printing. We waited for him to join us and, as he came up, Bjorn asked 'Know what this is all about, Hyun?'

'Big repair job, not enough time it seems.'

'Shit.'

'Yeah, doesn't look good.'

Most of the others were already in the refectory when we arrived. Ibo followed a moment behind us. There was a buzz of discussion going on which immediately quietened as Sahko came in, still looking stylish and severe in her black outfit and finely made ankle boots.

'OK everyone, we've a problem and we need a solution. Minogue, give us a brief.'

Minogue brought up an image on the screen. It was hard to make out what we were looking at. 'This is an Archive picture taken years ago by the hot-bot inside the nozzle. The image shows a portion of one tile's surface and you'll notice that it looks completely uniform.' He brought up a new image onto the screen, placing it beside the first. 'This is a picture taken of the same spot about ten minutes ago.' The picture had the same matt grey tones as the first only now there was a lighter coloured splotch in the centre.

'We presume the marks that you see are the result of an impact. It's unlikely that it was caused by one of the cloud objects that Wayclear didn't hit because an object of that size would have penetrated right through. It was most likely caused by micron-size particles etched off an object hit by a Wayclear laser as it was ionising it. However the damage was caused, it now needs fixing. The plan for repairing a broken tile is simply to cut it out, fit a new one, and re-fuse the surface. As Agyei said, we only have three spares. A new tile can be made from an old one by cutting out a damaged tile, breaking it down and separating out any radioactive atoms and impurities. The remaining pure material is brought back to Chemistry and formed into a new tile using a sputtering technique. The whole process takes about twenty hours from starting extracting an old tile, through forming a new tile, to finishing reinserting the replacement into the nozzle. The cursory inspection of the nozzle that we've done so far indicates that about a hundred tiles are likely to need replacing.'

Minogue paused. The room had become completely silent. I was beginning to see why this was a mission critical problem.

Minogue continued. 'As you've no doubt worked out, the repair using the prescribed process will take eighty-three days, assuming we're right about the extent of the damage. At one-'g' deceleration we had expected to arrive in about one hundred and nine days' time. Eighty-three days without Main means we wouldn't have enough time to slow down: the engine is not capable of decelerating us fast enough, despite our current reduced mass, and even if it could, we humans couldn't survive over four-'g' deceleration for that long and the ship wasn't built to withstand it either.'

Minogue's words hung in the air. Everyone seemed stunned, looking at either the floor or ceiling and not at each other. This was it: game over, reset not available. The ship would drift endlessly in the void and we would die when the fuel for the power systems finally ran out or some other catastrophe put us out of our misery more quickly.

Sahko stood again and spoke quietly into the silence. 'It is not quite fatal though. When we've repaired the nozzle and got Main restarted we'll come to a halt on the far side of our target, the distance depending on how much deceleration we can withstand. We'll then accelerate back again, rotate the ship once more to decelerate and bring us to a halt at our target. We can only do those extra two stages very slowly because our fuel will largely be out by then. Although we can make it back we'll be well out of time to complete our mission, unless Fleet slows its arrival too.'

The crew look slightly happier as though the death sentence had been commuted to life. I noticed that Sahko had said 'when' rather than 'if' we repaired the nozzle. The equipment we had wasn't intended to replace anything like a hundred tiles.

Sahko continued 'We're not going to let the repair take that long. We need to come up with a much faster fix. We can rack up the deceleration somewhat once the engine is back online, we'll have to work out how much the ship and crew can stand. Also, we might be able somehow to use the Alpha stars and planets to slow us in the final stages. It may take us longer to slow than we had planned but we'll find a way. However, we can't rely on that until we have much more precise data about all the major objects in the system.'

Looks as though we might really miss Avalos on the run in, I thought, with his amazing feel for orbital mechanics. Sahko is a very good navigator, but by-the-book. She would never take the risks that Avalos had been capable of turning in his favour. Still, all that was whistling in the dark. No fly-by was going to have a significant impact on our speed and direction, given how fast we were coming in.

'Agyei,' Sahko continued. 'Please outline the current tile manufacturing process, focusing on why it takes so long and what can be done to speed it up?'

Agyei looked around at us and speaking in a quiet, calm voice, which we strained to hear, outlined the problem. 'There are two main constraints: one is capacity, the other is the chemistry used to make the tiles. The equipment we have can only rebuild one tile at a time. The machine to form the tiles is a sputterer, somewhat like the three-dimensional printers that deposit layers of material on to a surface. The sputterer builds up a crystal structure that's carefully set to ensure that the gamma rays from the engine are deflected in a controlled beam by the outer layers of the tile and the neutrinos deflected by a deeper layer. It has to be this very precisely structured material because the efficiency of the engine depends on the quantum mechanical properties of the tile crystal to deflect the subatomic particles the engine generates. The crystal structure has to be flawless or the tile would explode when the engine is running. Each layer of atoms has to be deposited in precisely controlled conditions and the material has to be perfectly pure. Each tile also has to be very carefully shaped during manufacture so that they interlock without gaps and cover the complex geometry of the nozzle.

'We don't carry extensive stocks of tile raw material, so we have to breakdown and reuse the old tiles. However, we can never reuse all the old material because some has become radioactive. Additionally, we may have lost some tile material, broken away by impacts. We can fabricate some extra tile material by scavenging our stocks of the basic elements required but I don't know if we have enough to repair that many tiles. We may never be able to repair the nozzle fully.'

Oh boy, I thought, this gets worse.

Sahko looked around. 'Ibo, could the engine work without some of the tiles?'

'It's possible,' said Ibo, somewhat to everyone's surprise. 'However, only from the outer ring. They could be used as raw material for tiles lower down. That would be more work of course, and the engine would be less efficient as a result.

Sahko stood again. 'Hyun, can you outline the hot-bot's capabilities and limitations.'

Hyun spoke up, his voice stiff but firmly emphasising his points: 'The hot-bot is the only machine we have that's hardened to withstand working in the residual-radiation environment of the engine-exhaust side of the nozzle. It can only work on one tile at a time and has to be very precise. Extracting a tile takes on average thirty minutes. The bot has limited energy on board from a battery which has to be recharged after each tile is extracted. Recharging takes two hours. The batteries are special and we've no spares. Cutting out the tiles uses a unique vibration saw which doesn't contact the material it's working on and so won't wear out.'

Well that's a relief, I thought.

Hyun continued: 'Re-fixing a new tile requires a laser bonding process which fuses the new tile with its neighbours. The bot is equipped to do that but it takes about an hour to fuse in a single tile.'

Minogue cut in. 'The bot is cutting out a damaged tile as we speak. We would like to get a good look at the impact to see if there's another way the tile can be repaired: it may be that not all the damage is critical and some of the tiles can be repaired in situ, rather than replaced.'

Yingluq asked. 'As these tiles have become radioactive, how are they broken down and radioactive elements separated out, so that the remainder can be brought into the ship and reused?'

'This was one thing that was thought through, although there is some residual risk,' Minogue replied. 'The hot-bot places the extracted tile into a radiation shielded container. That's brought back to the cold-side and placed in a dedicated recycling machine, located in an equipment recess near the edge of the nozzle. The machine breaks down the tile by grinding it into a fine powder which is disassociated into its constituent atoms.

That's done by ultrasonic heating in an inert-gas environment to prevent re-bonding. The atoms are ionised and separated using a mass-spectrometer type device, and the radioactive particles removed. The remaining material has below-background residual radiation and can be safely handled inside the ship.'

Bjorn intervened, his voice agitated. 'As a non-scientist, I can state the obvious: we haven't got time to use the accepted process. We have to come up with another solution or we're fucked. I don't know what, perhaps like fixing all the tiles in place by resurfacing them or something. Unless we get very lucky with the navigation, and take some massive risks, we have to fix this problem and get Main alight in not much more than twenty days, and at that limit we've used up most of our leeway.'

'Exactly,' Sahko cut in. 'And that's what we want some blue-sky ideas on.'

'I shouldn't be here,' said Bita quietly. 'I can't add anything. I've hardly understood anything you guys have said so far.'

'There are three reasons I want you here,' said Sahko in her calm commanding voice. 'Firstly we're all in this together. Secondly we're going to need to communicate to Fleet at some point, before they notice we're off mission. At the very least that allows them to adjust their flight paths. The third reason is precisely because you're not technical. You or one of the others here who aren't specialists in this area, and I'm one, don't have thinking constrained by what the book or training has told us is possible and what's not. We know what the defined solution is, and it doesn't work for the mission.

'Minogue, get us close ups of the damage and chemical analysis, as soon as it's available. Gunadi, set up a model of the nozzle on the holograph to help us focus on this problem. Everyone, take ten minutes in free discussion. Walk around and ask questions of each other and make notes. At the end, I'll ask each of you for ideas, any ideas. Go.' With that Sahko marched out of the room.

We all looked at each other in silence. I noticed Gunadi and Massoud looking down at their personal screens and presumably starting to search for information, either that or to compose their last words. Yingluq and Minogue began conferring and Agyei joined them. Ibo and Hyun were talking and they left the room. I wondered what they were thinking regarding Alice.

Bjorn said 'I'll go and check up on the children,' and he too left.

Bita was staring at the hologram of the nozzle which Gunadi had activated, walking around it, as though in meditation.

I was alone for a moment, making notes of all the ideas, crazy or not that I could think of. It was a short list as I quickly ran out of the obvious. I walked over to the scientists and listened in. It seemed as though they had decided to start with the basic physics: how the nozzle tiles and electromagnetic fields performed their function of deflecting the pions, gamma rays and neutrinos to maximise thrust and to protect the rest of the ship from being torn apart by their energy. The conversation was into quantum mechanical spin, crystal structures and electromagnetic fields. Quantum mechanics had never been my thing. The answer to our problem could well lie in that mathematical construct, but I wasn't going to be the one to find it there. Perhaps Minogue, Yingluq or Agyei would.

Bita had stopped walking round the hologram and was getting herself a water pouch. I joined her and asked: 'Bita, what were the images like that came back from the main aerial transmissions you sent?'

She looked up, surprised by my question. 'What do you mean by that? They were reflection patterns and I sent the data on to Gunadi.'

'Tell me about the patterns. How would the artist in you describe them? They weren't simply random noise, were they? Gunadi managed to process them into a useful image.'

Gunadi, who had been standing near me, stopped interrogating her screen and began listening.

'Well yes, there seemed to be a pattern in the raw signal,' Bita said. 'It did appear to be random at first, but then it brought to mind an image of a complex musical scale. I know it seems a funny way to describe it: an image of a musical scale, but I did think that. There were many layers to the image, as though it was polyphonic. That may not be the right way to describe it either, but for a moment I experienced a harmony in the noise. At the time I dismissed it as most likely a creation of my own imagination, stimulated by the stochastic noise we were getting. The human brain is great at spotting patterns, even when they don't exist.'

'Did you see anything in Gunadi's simulation of the object field that reinforced your impression of harmony?'

'No, wait, yes. Perhaps I did, but I may be projecting a dream onto reality, a sort of déjà vu.'

Gunadi was fully engaged now. 'Where are you going with this, Menem? It sounds a bit metaphysical, and we thought you were the grounded one. Aren't we supposed to be fixing a load of broken tiles?'

'We presume that the tiles have been damaged by atoms of material blasted off the objects by the Wayclear lasers. We don't know very much about the object field itself. We didn't know it was here until we slammed in to it. We don't know what it's made of. We don't know its proper motion - how it's moving relative to the rest of the galaxy or to the Alpha System. We don't know how it was formed, what's holding it together, or how the shell-like structure we've apparently experienced was created. We do know something about the distribution of the objects in at least the part of the field we passed through. We've some idea of the rough size of the field from the time we spent in it: about twenty billion kilometres across or two light hours, staggeringly big on a human scale but tiny in galactic terms. Hopefully soon we'll have analysis of the composition of the material blasted off the objects and embedded in the tiles, and maybe the solution to our problem lies there. But maybe the solution lies elsewhere, in a greater understanding of the object field. At the very least, the more we know about it the more we, and Fleet, can avoid it and any others like it, if they exist.'

Gunadi and Bita both looked at me, but said nothing. Was I losing it, getting too metaphysical, as Gunadi had said, when I was supposed to be Mr Practical, who fixed stuff?

Sahko came back in with Hyun, Ibo and Bjorn. 'OK, let's get the ideas out there.' She put one of the screens into transcribe mode. 'How about we classify the ideas into three: A: Speed up tile replacement, B: Fix in situ, and C: Other.'

Everyone shuffled back and looked anywhere but at Sahko. I was the only one staring at her. 'Menem, why don't you start?'

Everyone looked at me. Thanks Sahko, I've got no ideas at all. It looks like this mission is done for, and the best we can hope for is to wander on round the galaxy. I didn't say that of course, what I said instead was bullshit.

'A: The simplest solution would be to print one or more additional tile manufacturing machines. Alternatively, repurpose one of the big printers with a new head and finer controls to speed up tile production. Move manufacturing outside so we don't have to remove radioactivity. Switch to a continuous manufacturing process where the hot-bot is fitted with a grinder head, feeds the dust straight into the printer. Cut the tiles out from the emerging continuous strip of material in the precise shapes required, and then the hot-bot re-fixes them. Make a second hot-bot.'

Hyun, Minogue, Yingluq, Agyei were all bursting to point out flaws in these ideas, but Sahko had the meeting under her steely-gaze control. No idea is a bad idea and all that. So I pressed on:

'B: Develop the process, which is currently used to join the tile seams into a single crystal, to the point where it can be used to heal any cracks in the tiles where they were impacted. We might also look for a way of filling any divots in the tiles, and adding a new layer on top of the existing tiles to ensure the integrity of the finished surface. We could make a more powerful hot-bot to speed up the fusing process.'

Sahko was unreadable as usual, but, given her extensive scientific and engineering understanding, I had a pretty good idea where she would mark her card in the event of a vote. I was toast, so went for three out of three:

'C: The answer lies in understanding the object field: by doing that we understand the source of the problem. I was starting an interesting discussion with Bita and Gunadi on this subject before we reconvened.'

Bita and Gunadi both looked at their feet and edged away from me.

Sahko quelled murmurs in the room. 'Good start. We can put together resource estimates and work on process designs once we've selected the most promising ideas, so hold you comments until later. Who wants to go next?'

Bjorn stood which surprised most of us. 'I'm leaning towards A: The only certainty is the current process, so let's get on with it. While it's going we can work on each step incrementally to speed it up. In addition, we can look at other ways to slow us down, or give us a longer flight-path. As we get closer we can refine our navigation. Maybe there's some way we could deploy the payload that would help us slow down without compromising the mission.' In the silence that followed Sahko posted the ideas on the list.

Minogue spoke next, his deep voice was penetrating, rather like Avalos's had been, although the accent was different: Australian rather than Caribbean. 'Yingluq, Agyei and I were in discussion about ideas that may fall under B. We'll need to do a lot more research,' there speaks a true scientist, 'but it centres on the interaction of the gamma rays and neutrino beams and the structure of the tiles at the quantum level. There's a theoretical possibility that we can use the gamma rays themselves to heal the surface of the tiles.'

Sahko looked at Yingluq and Agyei. 'Anything to add?'

Yingluq put in 'Quantum chemistry has moved on since those tiles were designed. We've seen research coming from Earth recently in this field that looks exciting, but we've limited capability here to experiment.'

'So might a different design be quicker to make?' Sahko asked.

'It might,' said Yingluq. 'But we would need to dig into the reports in more detail.'

Sahko added "New Tile Design" to the list, and there was a buzz in the room.

Sahko cut in. 'Hold the concerns at the moment. Agyei anything?'

'I'll take a look at the tile fabricating process and see if the time can be shortened somehow. I am not hugely optimistic because crystals take time to form – fundamental chemistry.'

'Thanks, Agyei,' said Sahko. 'Hyun?'

'It must be worthwhile looking at the tile rebuilding process. No-one envisaged a situation where we would suffer such extensive damage to the tiles, and particularly at this critical point of our mission: during deceleration, while the nozzle is facing our direction of travel, and when we must continue to decelerate to come to a halt in the system. I can look at the tile rebuilding process and see if we can adapt some of the robotics and printers to the task, either to speed it up or to make a second tile manufacturing unit.'

'Massoud?'

'Bioengineering is not the solution in a gamma-ray environment. I do have extensive experience with crystal formation though. If I can help with speeding up tile repair or rebuilding, I will. I can also look at the repair process with bioengineering thinking.' Sahko added "crystal formation" to the list under A.

'Ibo' called Sahko.

'Well, I don't want any of you messin' wi' my engine.' That brought laughter. 'Seriously, good people, this is bad shit and we need it fixed quick. Don't change the shape of the inner surface of the nozzle: it's optimised for power and safety. If time wasn't a constraint I would be urging sticking with the tested process because that engine is a very dangerous beast. I ain't got any anything else to add to our list for now.'

'OK Ibo, sorry we got to mess with your engine. It ain't running so good at the moment and we are about to miss our target and head on round the galaxy.' Sahko sensed that we were through with our most obvious and sensible ideas and we had to get loose to get creative. 'Gunadi?'

'Nothing to add,' said Gunadi, almost inaudibly and while studying the floor. 'I can help with process re-design and any analytic resources required for that or quantum-chemistry modelling. I would also like to spend some time studying the object field data. Menem had interesting thoughts on that.' She looked up and gave me a brief smile.

'Bita?'

'There do seem to be patterns in the object field that we've no explanation for. They may not exist in reality, and may have no relevance to finding a solution to our immediate problem. I'm no scientist or engineer but I'll do what I can to help with whatever we go with.'

'Thanks everyone,' said Sahko. 'Here's my current thinking. Our first priority is to get going on the normal tile repair process. Agyei, take the lead on that and call on anyone else you need to help. Secondly, Menem and Bjorn, go through the rest of the process step-by-step looking for ways to speed it up, call in help from whoever you need. Hyun and Massoud, see if you can apply any of your ideas to speed up tile production, possibly by making more manufacturing units. Thirdly, Minogue and Yingluq, research and work up your ideas on tile repair and a new tile design that would be faster to fabricate. Liaise with Ibo and Agyei as needed. Fourthly, Gunadi, your priority is to support the others as required and Bita, yours is ensuring prompt communications of any information back to Fleet. When you're not doing those things, Bita and Gunadi, work on the object field data in any way you want.

'We also need to keep the ship running and children in order so don't take your eyes off the basics. We will reconvene here tomorrow evening at six to review and reallocate resources. Any questions?' There were none. 'Right, it has been a tough day, and the outlook appears grim but by applying ourselves we'll find a way through. Everyone should take a break now and try to get a good night's rest. I'll handle the children for the rest of the evening. Menem, perhaps it's a good time for you to have something to eat now.' Which brought a few smiles as the meeting broke up.

4018, 20:45

Massoud came over to me. 'I'll cook you up something real special to keep you perky for a while and then relax you ready for sleep.'

There was no way to avoid Massoud's cooking. I had to trust the man not to mess with me too much. He, as much as anyone, surely needed me to keep fixing things, so I went along with him.

Half the crew were ahead of us, clustered around the servery to see what food and drinks were on offer. Gunadi and Bita had disappeared. Sahko had departed for the children's room and Hyun and Ibo had left with her, perhaps to spend some time with Alice before her bedtime.

Massoud fiddled with his control pad and, in a moment, a server-bot started distributing bowls of soup to each of us. Drinks were poured and we settled down to eat. The atmosphere remained tense.

Minogue remarked: 'Sahko certainly knows how to run a meeting.'

'She does,' said Yingluq. 'There's not much time wasted, everyone gets a chance to speak, and she makes a decision.'

'Text book,' said Minogue. 'Suits me.'

'Text book is good in many ways, but we're in deep here,' said Bjorn. 'We need imagination and a leap in thinking.'

'I didn't think she shut down any of the more speculative ideas,' said Massoud. 'She has encouraged us to run with all of them for the next twenty-four hours. It seemed very sensible to me: a fine balance between risk and potential.' Massoud was nearly always emollient, smoothing disturbed waters.

Bjorn seemed to want to make a point. 'But we may need to take more risks. If we run down the clock resolving this, we'll fail to complete our mission. By-the-book may not do it.'

Minogue looked up. 'What kind of risks are you thinking of?'

'I'm thinking of system entry. We know quite a lot about the major objects in the system, even if we don't know enough to exactly optimise our trajectory. Maybe we could slow down a lot more using sling-shot manoeuvres. Surely we know enough about the stars and big planets.'

'It doesn't work at the speed we're going.' said Minogue. 'The planets are practically stationary relative to us and we're not coming in on the ecliptic plane. Our plan was to go straight to our target, and if our plan is good, we will have slowed down enough to enter orbit around it. I don't think Sahko ruled out some manoeuvring at the final stages, when we've slowed enough, but we're still far too far out, and travelling too fast, to fine tune navigation right now.'

'I accept that,' continued Bjorn. 'But when it comes to it, will Sahko, as our navigator, take sufficient risks?'

'Sahko wants to complete the mission as much or more than any of us,' cut in Agyei, perhaps wanting to restrain Bjorn before he got too over excited. 'She's the captain after all and her place in history would be mud if Fleet had to jettison all their cargo or swing around Alpha to head straight back home. It also wouldn't look good if we ploughed into a gas giant because she had misjudged a turn.'

'Well we can't bring Avalos back,' I put in, voicing everyone's unspoken thought. 'Sahko is the best navigator we have left. Ultimately we have to leave it to her.'

'She doesn't seem to want to learn from Avalos's flair. The way he swung us by Jupiter on our exit manoeuvre, that was so fine, to get this space truck in so close. It saved us a month and a ton of fuel.' Bjorn rehashed the old ship's legend of Avalos's manoeuvre.

'Debatable at most,' I said, 'but we were all absolutely terrified when we realised how close in he was taking us. It was crazy, insane, suicidal. Sahko hadn't checked his detailed plan beforehand, and it was too late when she realised what was up.' I was leaping to Sahko's defence as usual. 'She never really trusted Avalos after that.'

'But such a beautiful manoeuvre. He was a genius. I don't know why his old outfit let him go, or why he wanted to join such a solid lump as this freighter.'

Bjorn had for ever after been an admirer of Avalos's flair. This was old ground and we had rehearsed this bit of the conversation many times, so it died there.

Yingluq was looking away, waiting for the subject to change. When we first came together as a crew, there had been scuttlebutt that linked Yingluq and Avalos. He was very good looking, charismatic and charming; very much the ladies man it seemed. She was always super-fit, also very good looking and outgoing, and as highly skilled at her job as he was at his. Yet after about a week or so together his charm didn't seem to work on her any more as far as the rest of us could tell, and there was plenty of curiosity.

Why had Avalos joined us? Perhaps Sahko and Bita knew, but for the rest of us it was pure speculation. As navigator, he was central to our mission only as we exited the Solar System, and then he was supposed to be vital again as we entered the Alpha System. In between there was the long, ten-year gap, where his primary skills weren't required. It was a rare occasion when the ship needed his secondary role as EVA master. There was also little outlet for his gregarious nature, with such a small crew. Ah well, we all had our reasons for ending up where we were. AT least for some of us it was a way of rescuing the glorious careers we had envisaged when we had first started out in life. It did have its attractions: we would, if all went well, be the first humans to travel to another planetary system and, with luck, to set foot somewhere there. It was going to be our place in history, but the risk was high and there would be no return. Avalos had voiced all these sentiments, but he didn't seem to fit the pattern of the rest of the crew, solid achievers all. Avalos seemed to be a dilettante when he first came aboard, but surprisingly he had settled in. His death had been a bombshell, although the cause was mundane enough: an electrical shock and he was too far gone when he was found for Yingluq to revive. That was the official version anyway.

Yingluq had been very down after Avalos's death, seeming to avoid the rest of us for a while and then came the second death and another black period. But gradually she had recovered and started to spend more time with Minogue, who eventually became the father of her daughter. Sky had been born at almost the same time as Kent, Agyei and Bjorn's boy. The births of Sky and Kent had transformed the mood of the ship, which had got rather dark after the two deaths. We had new life aboard, new responsibilities, renewed purpose. The children worked their magic on us. Later Bita gave birth to her and Minogue's daughter, Joko. Yingluq didn't seem bothered by Minogue fathering a child with another woman. She and Bita seemed to get on just as well, if not better, than before. They both bossed Minogue around, which he enjoyed.

The conversation moved on from Avalos. I finished my soup and reverie. A second course appeared. Massoud had concocted another plate of unusual looking, but great smelling and tasting food. He smiled benignly as we ate, at first with caution, and then relish. The talk moved on to the latest news from Earth. We were keenly following the Olympic Games, cheering on our home countries' modest showings. It was slightly odd to think that another Olympics had nearly finished back on Earth while we were learning the results of this earlier one, the information racing across four years to catch up with us.

The others started to drift away as Hyun and Ibo reappeared. I finished and left as well.

I called Gunadi up and asked if I could drop by for a moment and she invited me round. The door to Analytics slid open but didn't close behind me. Gunadi must have set it to stay open. Sitting in a high-backed chair, raised up slightly on a platform, she was surrounded on three sides by a huge curved screen, almost immersed within it. How could she make use of so much screen space, I wondered? She took off her control gloves as I came in and rotated her chair around, pulling her knees up to her chest and clutching them as if to hide in a ball. She didn't look directly at me. There were piles of what looked like the guts of electrical and optical digital equipment scattered over boxes and cabinets. I looked around for another chair but could only see a strange, soft-looking stool with odd bumps on it. I perched on the corner of a cabinet.

'Wow, looks as though things got a bit stirred up in here,' I said.

'If you want an explanation for the décor,' she answered in her quiet, defensive, little-girl voice, 'a lot of stuff that's waiting to be fixed was around loose when the gravity went off, and things drifted. I haven't had time to tidy up, and I don't want a service bot in here because it would break stuff and put it where I'd never be able to find it again.'

'I came around to thank you for finding those memory ICs. It was great that you were able to deliver them so quickly.' I looked around at the mess again.

'They came from a cabinet where I keep old parts. I know were that stuff is.' She paused. 'I should really send most of it to recycling for component recovery but it can sometimes be useful as it is.' She looked up briefly from under the hair that had been hiding her face.

'Also, I wanted to ask you about the meeting this evening,' I continued. 'I'm not sure I should have involved you in that. It was a crazy idea anyway. When Bita started talking about music patterns I realised that it was something I have no feel for, and, similarly, I've no idea how you constructed the field model out of the data. I should like to understand more about the algorithms, but you've always been here to do this type of work and I've had other priorities.' We were both silent for a while. 'Anyway, thank you Gunadi. I don't know if you were pleased to be involved or not.'

Silence. Eventually she spoke. 'There may not be anything useful there in the patterns but, yes, I was glad you asked me: you wanted my help. Minogue wasn't so happy though, nor Yingluq.'

'How do you mean?'

'You had an idea that hadn't occurred to them. You're not usually the one who comes up with weird new ideas. You're supposed to be the practical one, holding the ship together, fixing things. They're supposed to be the scientists: open to new thinking, spotting patterns where others haven't.'

'Sounds as though I've stepped in something there.'

'Yeah.'

'You see a lot, oh quiet one, don't you?'

I looked at all that space on the screen around her chair. What did she see there? We were supposed to have our privacy, but every part of the ship was sensored-up in case of trouble, so privacy was limited. Gunadi was the one who was in charge of all that. From what little I knew of her she could almost certainly get past any security restrictions, and she had probably devised those restrictions in the first place. Only Ibo, her number two in analytics, would be likely to have any idea of what Gunadi could see and do.

Gunadi said nothing, got up off her chair and came and sat on the edge of the platform, so that she was now below me. She again drew up her legs against herself in that protective gesture, but shook back her hair and looked up at me. I was disconcerted by her gaze and had the impression that she wanted to ask me something but didn't know how best to phrase it.

'Tell me something about yourself, Gunadi,' I said. 'It would help us communicate if we knew each other better.'

She smiled shyly at me. 'What sort of things?'

'Well, I'm not sure. We've been together on this ship for a long time and I only know the basics about why you're here. Like the rest of us, you come from a non-aligned country, and I seem to remember from your introductory CV that you come from Bali, joined the Indonesian military, got into the cyber unit, then University, at first in Jakarta, then Tsinghua and finally IIS in Bengaluru, before going back to the Indonesian military, if I've got all that right. Then you worked in the Non-Aligned Systems Group, had a few space trips, and therefore were a natural for this posting. Those are supposed to be the facts that I'm aware of, but, like the rest of us, there would be hidden currents that swept you here. How did you get into the military for example? That doesn't seem to obviously fit with what I see.'

She was staring intently up at me, her dark eyes wide. She flicked her hair again. She began in a quiet, controlled voice: 'I had an uncle in the military, my mother's brother. He was always popular in the family: a big jolly presence, when he came home on leave. As small children we loved playing with him. He was quite physical, swinging us around, which made us shriek and laugh.

'My parents both worked in the hotel industry, as many always have in Bali. My mother was an accountant, my father a stores manager. They had met in a hotel where they both worked. They were not well paid, but we didn't starve. They probably expected my brother, sister and I to go into the hotel industry too. Sometimes I used to go with my mother to the office. When I was a small child she would stick me in front of a screen. Child care, I suppose. Analytics clicked with me, and soon I was fiddling with the software, getting into the code, learning to hack so we could play games we couldn't afford. I started fixing neighbours' tech.'

Gunadi was staring into the middle distance now, absorbed in her own story.

'One weekend, when I was a teenager, I was home alone fixing a phone, illegal of course. My parents were both out at work and my uncle dropped by unexpectedly. He asked what I was up to and so I showed him. He enquired what I wanted to do in life and I said that I wanted to do something with analytics, but that hotel reservation systems and such were pretty boring. He said that the military had far more exciting analytics stuff and they were always looking for people with my sort of skills. He painted a picture of them sponsoring me through university, which my parents wouldn't have been able to afford. My uncle asked me to sit on his knee, although I was too old for that by then, but he had always been so jolly and friendly.'

'Oh no,' I said quietly.

'I paid a full price for my escape from a small life. Under the jollity he was a violent man. However, he was true to his word about introducing me to the cyber-warfare unit, and, once I joined up, I got away from him and mostly had a great time. But there were plenty of other bullies around.'

'Shit. I'm sorry, I'm so sorry. I shouldn't have stirred this up.'

She sighed and glanced at me. 'The military was a long time ago now. We should talk about ourselves more. Maybe we could help each other, get us out of our own heads. Anyway you can see why I jumped at the chance when this mission was proposed. I thought I would be able to leave all that behind.'

'But you couldn't?'

She paused and then softly added: 'I couldn't leave my head behind.'

'Is that why you've effaced yourself all this time? Avoiding the risk involved in human entanglements?' I spoke slowly, picking words. 'Did you not want a family of your own? Space has proven to be an aphrodisiac for most of us. There's only a short menu to choose from, but it's a very carefully selected one. You seem to have chosen not to join in, the pairing-up I mean.'

'Oh, at the beginning I competed all right, and I thought I had won. But it didn't turn out that way.'

I couldn't see what she meant at first. Then it dawned on me. 'Avalos?'

'He was so beautiful: powerfully muscular, big strong hands.' Gunadi's voice became dreamy for a moment. 'He paid no attention to me in public, but in fleeting moments, when no one else was around, he would stare at me, eating me up. His stare, like that, made me go weak. It was a long time before he came to me. It was the night after we had done that dive into Jupiter that flung us on our way. He was still high on it.'

She was silent for a while, and I thought I had already heard enough, perhaps too much. I stood to go but the door closed before I could leave. Somehow she had triggered it. She knelt in front of me, looking up, her hair fallen away from her face. Her eyes were moist, perhaps with tears. Her lips were dark against her ash-pale skin, her button nose turned up, appealingly. 'Don't go yet, Menem. There's more.'

'I don't know, Gunadi. I don't think this is good for either of us.' She reached around my legs, pulling herself into me, pressing her cheek against my thigh. 'Please, Menem, I've watched you for a long time. You are kind to me. I need help, help me, Menem, help me.' She buried her face against me and then pulled herself up. 'I need you, Menem. It has been so long since a man touched me. I'll do what you want. You can have what you want.' She reached up and tugged at the waist band of my trousers, dragging them down. 'Show me what you want. Make me.'

'I don't want that, Gunadi. I didn't come here for that,' I said pathetically, looking at the ceiling.

Her voice was below me, panting and breathy. She let go and moved away. 'I've been bad, Menem, I've been very bad.' When I tuned back she was bent over the strange stool, her trousers off, her shirt drawn up, her legs parted. I longed to place my hand there, and I did. She shuddered at my touch. Fascination drew me on, that lightening feeling of touching a real woman's flesh after so long. She groaned and pressed back against me. 'Yes,' she hissed. 'Bad girl. Go on, do it, punish me, beat me, do what you want with me, hit me, hit me, hit me, Avalos, hit me.'

Her words finally cut through to my conscience and I leaped back in horror. 'I'm not Avalos,' I screamed. Suddenly she was still and I heard her sobbing, catching big breathless gulps of air between cries. She rolled sideways off the stool and curled into a ball.

'No you're not, are you? No fucking use,' she spat out in frustration, then softly. 'No you're not.' She cried quietly for a while as I pulled up my trousers and stood with my back to the door, frozen in horror. Eventually she stilled and collected herself, adjusting her clothing. 'I'm so sorry, Menem. I don't know what came over me. You reminded me of Avalos for a moment, brought back memories of him paying attention to me. I shouldn't have dragged you down, sweet, kind Menem, who knows how to fix everything. Well how do we fix this? Can you fix me?'

She seemed to be calm now. 'What did he do to you?' I asked. 'Did he hurt you? Yes, I see that he did. Did he hit you?' She said nothing but began crying quietly again.

I could see her now in those early days, when Avalos was still around. She had often been curled up, her hair hanging over her face, which could have hidden bruises or even black eyes. Now I came to think about it she had suffered from quite a lot of accidents back then. I had thought that she was just careless, unused to the space environment. There had been a bent finger, a crushed toe, even a broken arm once. If I had been blind, had anyone else known what was going on? The injuries would have been impossible to hide from Yingluq, who must have patched Gunadi up. Yingluq had probably guessed, even if she hadn't been told the truth directly. Perhaps Sahko had known too as the second doctor, although she had never given a hint to me when we had been so close. But Sahko too was good at concealing things, as I had later found out. Bita might have learned what was going on from one of her regular counselling sessions with Gunadi. Who else?

What could anyone have done if they had known? We were a small crew, dependent on each other. But then Avalos died. My thoughts tumbled over each other. Had his death really been an accident? Yingluq had tried to revive him, Sahko too. Yingluq had signed his death certificate as well. Someone could easily have tampered with the machinery, although it looked as though he had simply gone to the wrong cabinet at the wrong time. Who had initiated the transmission at that precise moment? Was it Bita? But then again, any member of the crew could have misdirected him and fixed his accident if they had been determined and careful enough, and, after all, we had no police aboard with forensics expertise or equipment. Had anyone even asked where each of us was at the time? Had we all accepted the accident story because we were afraid of what might emerge?

I knelt on the floor and put my arms around Gunadi. She lent in to me and cried a bit more until she became quiet again. 'I'm sorry, Menem. I shouldn't have got so, I don't know, wound up. I don't want to drag you down with me. You've troubles enough of your own, not only with the ship.' I wondered how much she knew about me, although some of my 'troubles' were public knowledge. 'It has been so long since a man took any notice of me. Time is passing for me too. I don't want to die alone. I want a child to send in to the new world. Maybe we can help each other.' She looked up, appealing to me. 'I don't know how, but maybe, somehow.' It seemed as though she might know something about me.

'Don't get involved in my problems, Gunadi. Sahko is dangerous and you've enough troubles of your own.'

'Oh, Menem, how little you know. Sahko has human needs too. Like you, she's stubborn and she puts on a cool, professional front. You two need to move on, it would help all of us. Sahko was more relaxed when she was in a settled relationship. Maybe it's time for you to look elsewhere.'

I thought about that for a while. Surely Gunadi was wrong about Sahko. She didn't know her the way I did: the temper, the need for control, the absolute focus on the mission. Sahko had pushed me aside because I had failed her. There was no going back, I was sure of that. I tried to put Sahko out of my thoughts, and looked down at Gunadi sitting on the floor, in the soft light of the glowing screen. If I got involved any further with her it would absolutely end any chance I had with Sahko. I thought about our child and tears came to my eyes. Gunadi wants a child and there was no reason she couldn't have one, it might help all of us.

'Gunadi, talk to Yingluq or Bita about a child, if you really want one. You have choices, and you know how the whole crew welcomes new life. You seemed to have welcomed others' children. You're good with Alice and you could make a good mother.'

'I once dreamed of having a happy family, like my father and mother, my brother, sister and I, when we were young. That was my picture, but all the good men seem to have been taken.'

'Oh, Gunadi. There are lots of types of happy family.'

'Yes, but it's too late. We're on the brink of disaster, despite Sahko's fine words. And even if we do, by some miracle, manage to fix the ship, the voyage will be over in a few months and this happy family will break up too. What then?'

'We'll fix the ship and then we'll have a new world to build. We may have more room but no more people for quite a while. We'll still be dependent on each other for many years yet. We'll have our role to play even after Fleet arrives.'

'Maybe you're right. I'll think it over.' Gunadi stood up. 'It's getting late. Can we talk again sometime? It's OK if you don't want to, after tonight… I understand you've important work to do, things to fix to allow us to complete our journey. The mission may be legacy enough for both of us, whatever the outcome.' She moved away from me and stood up. 'You have helped me, Menem. Thank you.'

I stood too, brushed away a strand of hair from her face, looked into her eyes and then looked away, looked back and kissed her briefly on the cheek. I turned and went out of the door without saying anything.

The passage lights had been dimmed to indicate night. I felt weary, and trudged round the corridor towards my apartment on the other side of the ring. Yingluq was running the passage, doing some late evening exercise. She looked up as I came past, gave me a smile and a wave, but didn't slow her pace. There was a warm hum from the ship's machinery, mostly aircon and other life support systems, all the normal sounds.

Jazz was sitting by the bed but got up as I came in. The place was tidy and clean, so at least the service bots were still functioning. Jazz touched my hand, smiled, and then went back to her seat. One touch and a look was enough for her to guess my mood and likely need for companionship. She put on some soft mellow music and, as I stripped off my ship-suit, I looked at her. She still looked like Sahko, with the same body shape. I was worried that she might have become more like Gunadi, but I didn't think she had. Yes, still like Sahko, but with a different hair cut, a style from my student days that I favoured. My fantasy women usually wore it.

My old suit carried the marks of the day: streaks from the crawl in the motor bay in Engine Control, lubricant from somewhere, coolant stains from the laser. I hoped that one of the other marks was a food spill and not vomit. I dropped the suit and shoes in the laundry box and stepped into the refresher. I stood for a while in its reviving sprays, emerging cleansed, dried, teeth cleaned and hair brushed. A last enquiry to Status told me that Wayclear hadn't detected any incoming objects for some time.

I felt sleepy as I climbed into bed. Jazz untied her robe and slipped in beside me. I felt her warmth as she snuggled up, her cheek pressed against my back. One of her arms came over my side and a delicate hand rested on my shoulder: warm and companionable. We lay like that for a while, and then I turned over to face her. Our heads were very close together and I smelt the dusky rose of her skin perfume. I looked into her eyes and we smiled at each other. Then she turned over and pushed herself against me. I embraced her and she took my hand and placed it over a breast. I looked at the fine hairs on the back of her neck, closed my eyes, drew my arm tight around her, prayed that the ship and crew would hold together, at least overnight, and fell asleep.

Mission Day 4019

4019, 07:45

Jazz was gently shaking me awake, but I kept my eyes closed and pretended to be asleep. She lent over me, blew a kiss in my ear and said: 'Time to get up my love. The ship and crew need you.'

Memories of yesterday started to crowd back into my consciousness. I looked at Jazz and tried to ignore them. She was leaning over me, checking that I was awake and no doubt assessing my immediate needs. Her robe was loose and I looked down her fantasy cleavage. She let me look for a moment then closed up her lapels whispering 'bad boy' in my ear. I smiled at her, but she drew back. Pulling off the cover, I sat on the edge of the bed for a moment, slowly got up and went to the refresher.

Jazz had gone by the time I emerged washed, shaved and brushed. A clean ship-suit waited on a hanger which I pulled on, seamed shut, coupled it into my communicator, checked the diagnostics which said it was all functioning and activated Status which gave me a headline report of no new emergencies. A pair of grip shoes enclosed my feet and I was ready.

Unlike yesterday, I planned to have breakfast in the refectory to catch up with whoever was around. If no one else was there, I would review Status for all the ship's details and see what had broken in the night and was going to kill us if I didn't fix it soon.

As usual, I planned to limber up with a gentle couple of circuits around the corridor but that did entail going past Sahko's door. As I was feeling fresh and strong I decided to do a whole circuit. The door to her apartment was closed so I trod quietly in passing and made it to the refectory after a couple of laps without encountering anyone. However, as I opened the door and started through, there was a shout behind me. 'Menem, when are you going to fix my useless refresher?'

Quickly shutting the door, I was faced with six of the crew seated round the table, all staring at me, trying to contain their laughter.

'Lovely weather for the time of year, don't you think?' I enquired nonchalantly.

'Come on Menem,' said Yingluq. 'You know that's just her way of showing she cares.' I tried not to notice the tittering going on in the background.

'What are you conspirators up to at this time of the morning?' I asked.

'Yingluq was about to give us a quantum mechanics and rocket science teach-in' said Bjorn. 'She and Minogue think they may be on to something.'

I moved over to the table and noticed, somewhat to my surprise, that Gunadi was there as well, and she made space beside her. She looked quite rested and relaxed, rather more at ease than I had seen her in a while although she was still wearing a rather shapeless black ship-suit, a size too big, and her hair still covered her face.

'Thanks, Gunadi, at least someone cares. Don't let me interrupt the seminar.'

I sat down, made a quick choice on the menu pad and right away the server bot brought me black coffee and porridge. Ibo and Bjorn looked at what I had chosen and grimaced. I tucked in with relish and listened as Yingluq recapped for those of us who had missed the beginning. They included not only me, but Massoud, who came out from the servery, and Bita, who had arrived a moment earlier, looking as though she had recently fallen out of bed after a heavy night.

'At the heart of the engine is a strike-point where the hydrogen and anti-hydrogen fuels meet and instantly annihilate each other to form high energy particles, mostly gamma rays and neutrinos,' began Yingluq. 'On Earth, neutrinos don't usually interact with anything, but gamma rays can be absorbed by a screen of either a very heavy element like lead...

Ibo looked bored: she knew all this stuff.

'The solution our engine uses is to surround the strike-point with a nozzle that's lined with...'

Hyun was fidgeting. I was paying full attention, having a rather good profile view of Yingluq.

'The properties of the crystal material allow it to absorb the gamma rays and reflect them back without...'

I noticed Bjorn looking rather stunned, his eyes glazed over.

'In the case of gamma rays, we can't use an ordinary ceramic-metal reflector because their frequency...'

Massoud and Gunadi were looking at their personal screens.

'Neutrinos, on the other hand are leptons, and not electromagnetic waves...'

Bita was doodling. Agyei was being polite and still looking up.

'The sub-quark components: dark halls and wind pools, interact...'

Ibo looked up and scratched her head. Perhaps this was something she was unclear about.

'The deeper layer of the crystal tiles are again oriented...'

Yingluq removed her sweat-jacket and I sat up straight, paying full attention. I noticed Bjorn becoming more alert too. Agyei glanced at him and Bjorn moved as though shocked, winced a little, and looked down at the table again.

'The momentum of the neutrino emission causes the daughter atom to recoil...'

Bita had sketched a rather beautiful abstract bird impression of Yingluq.

'Those particles that fly out towards the front of the engine...'

My mind was gradually closing down, although the view was still good. I ceased to understand what Yingluq was saying, only picking up odd words now and again.

'...Fresnel's equations...'

'...Feynman diagram...'

'...quantum-spin energy...'

'...Xi thought.'

'Eh?' said Ibo, who suddenly sat up.

'I was checking to see if anyone was still awake.' Yingluq looked around but then continued, oblivious to the rest of us. Perhaps she wanted to order the theory in her own mind. 'The tiles are so difficult to make because they must have flawless structure: each layer of atoms precisely laid down to form concentric, multi-layered surfaces, curved in three-dimensions.'

Gunadi pumped her fist under the table as though she had just won some game. I noticed Massoud grimacing at something.

'Last night Minogue, Sahko and I were working on the idea of growing a new layer of crystal over the inside of the nozzle. However, we ran in to many problems: for example, our lack of enough additional suitable material and the difficulty of achieving crystal level perfection while the underlying surface was flawed, even if it was patched up in some way. We were also unable to overcome the problem that Ibo had raised, of not changing the shape of the nozzle. Adding an extra inner layer would seriously affect the performance of the engine.'

Ibo had looked up again at the mention of her name.

'We even considered repositioning the fuel strike-point to compensate for changes in nozzle shape but that presented a whole new set of challenges.' Ibo nodded her head.

The door opened and Minogue arrived, Yingluq paused as he sat down and chose some food.

'As Minogue mentioned in the meeting, he and I were aware of work done back on Earth, after this ship was built, that improves our ability to model the crystal structure at the quantum level.' That was being kind: actually she had said it in the meeting. 'This work shows that it would be possible to use a much thinner crystal and be equally as effective. The work also suggests that we can use a slightly different design of crystal structure which would make it much easier to precipitate, be self-seeding and require no catalyst. We reviewed that new work last night, and, this morning, Minogue thinks he has cracked the conditions necessary to make the new structure. Theoretically, the time to form the critical crystal layer can be got down from twenty hours per tile to something close to seventeen minutes.'

Agyei was nodding her head now and I assumed that she had been involved in this part.

'To retain the shape of the nozzle, we would have to use a backer to bring the new tiles up to the thickness of the old. The backer is made of the same material, to prevent it distorting the magnetic field, but it doesn't have to be flawless. The grains would be microscopic, but form very quickly, and hence the whole backer can be created in seconds if we get the process conditions right. We can also add a filler to the lowest layers of the backer if we need to cover any short-fall in tile material.

'We would like you, Gunadi,' who, startled, looked up, 'with Ibo, if needed,' who shook her head, 'to build a quantum level simulation of the nozzle and its interaction with the engine particles, based on this design. We need to check it works through the whole operating envelope. Agyei has started looking at the crystal formation process. Hyun and Massoud, can you work with her and see if you can come up with a practical way to make the tiles? We need to lay down the atoms of the upper layers of the crystal flawlessly. Massoud has suggested using a form, like a two dimensional sheet of DNA, but with a single base, that could be used to assemble the atoms of the crystal and lay them down. This would remove the problem of random fluctuations in chemical density because only when the form was completely filled would the next layer of the lattice be added. We think we might be able to print a whole series of these forms, one for each layer of atoms in the crystal, each of which has to be different to create the three-dimensional curved structure. These forms might be linked together and run like an ancient film projector, laying down a single atomic layer with each frame.' Yingluq sat down.

'Phew, impressive,' I said. After a pause, I added: 'It doesn't seem possible to do any practical testing of the new tiles, so the simulations will need to be perfect.'

'I'm starting to think about that,' said Minogue. 'The risk is real and so we need a set of tests, short of engine ignition, that shows these ideas will work. We should be able to get low power beams of gamma rays out of Fizz and neutrinos from Fuse, possibly. Can we run stuff by you, as we design the tests, to check that they can be carried out? We'll need to be further down the road before the meeting tonight.'

'Is Sahko aware of this idea, of changing the nozzle crystal design?' I asked.

'I talked with her earlier, and she suggested the workload breakdown. We were wondering if you, Menem and Bjorn, could work on speeding up the processes of cutting out the broken tiles, disassembling them to the atomic level and getting that material ready as feedstock for forming into new tiles. Also, can you look at the process for reinstalling the tiles? We would like to cut down the time to do each of those, if at all possible.'

'OK.' I looked over at Bjorn to check he agreed. 'We'll do what we can. If the tile extraction and material processing can be got close to your theoretical timescale for crystal formation then we could be back on track for the mission. That would be good, very good.'

The gathering started to break up, and I went over to Bjorn to discuss our job. 'Could we meet in Engineering in about half-an-hour to work on this? I have routine checks and maintenance stuff to do to keep the rest of the ship functioning, but should be done by then.'

'Sure. I'll take a look at the current process schematics and resource requirements. We're likely to have a few questions for Hyun, Massoud and possibly Agyei as well.'

4019, 08:30

I was about to leave when Massoud caught my eye and came over. 'Can I have a quick word, Menem? Perhaps I can walk with you towards Engineering.' He guided me out the door.

'Something up?'

Massoud didn't say anything as we walked around the ring. Once we were well clear of the refectory he continued. 'I wondered if you could take a look at the water system sensors. They're not showing any faults but the pressure seemed slightly reduced this morning in Food Prep. Status hasn't reported any loss of water, but when I tapped the clean tank it definitely sounded less than full. It may be that the problem is more in where the water is rather than any loss to the system.' Massoud had never raised a false alarm before and as he was primary on environmental services he knew what he was talking about.

'I presume you've checked the filters and purifiers?'

'Yes, they all look fine. The grey and black water tanks aren't full so there shouldn't be any backup in the pipe work. It worries me because normally the pure water tank is full at this time of day. I was wondering if there might be a sensor fault and a loss was not showing up.'

'Could yesterday's sudden gravity stop and spin-up have upset things?'

'It had crossed my mind, but no one has reported any sudden leaks and I've been suspicious for some days now that something was not right. If a level sensor was defective then there could be a leak into some sealed part of the ship, one that hasn't yet made itself visible.'

He left unsaid that a leak could be out into space, which we also might not have noticed. We couldn't afford much loss of water: another mission-critical element.

'Just what we need,' I said. 'OK, I'll take a look at the sensor logs and see if I can spot any anomalies. It will be hell to find if we have bad sensor data.'

We had reached Engineering and went inside.

Massoud continued. 'I'll get out the leak tracer and see if I can find anything in the environmental-services system, but its range and sensitivity is limited. I wanted to run it by you first, partly because you may have a simple explanation or some previous experience with this type of issue, and partly in case it's a real problem and could be serious. Sorry to have to burden you with this.'

'Regrettably I don't have an immediate flash of genius. I'll take a look at the logs and you have a go with the probe. Do you think the leak is slow?'

'Most likely it's only a tiny drip that has been going on for a while, but I suspect it got worse yesterday. I estimate the loss to be around two hundred litres so far. However, it may be a symptom of something that could become much worse, very quickly.'

I groaned and said: 'We'll have to flag it up to Sahko. Can you do that, and let's talk again in ten minutes? All the tanks have pressure drop cut-offs, don't they?'

'Yes. They should prevent a sudden catastrophic loss, but it has been a long time since they were last tested and there's a lot of water in some sections of the pipe work that wouldn't necessarily be isolated.'

'I get the picture: risky to let this one ride.'

Bad, bad, bad. I hated lifting floor panels on the old ship, and this problem might require a lot of that to trace a small leak. There was always trouble below the floor and behind access panels. That was what they were there for: to hide the slow but inevitable deterioration: the wood-worm, the moth and rust, the rot. Old buildings, sailing boats, spacecraft: the processes of decay were remorseless.

I called up Gunadi. 'Hi, finished your breakfast yet? I've a quick question for you.'

'Menem, yes, I'm back in Analytics. Look, I'm sorry about last night, I shouldn't have involved you…'

'This isn't about last night, although we do need to talk about that again sometime soon to get things a little straighter between us. I'm calling about a ship systems issue. I need you to have a quick look at the environment systems.'

'OK, business first. What part of the environment systems?'

'The water system, specifically the clean water tank sensors. Can you spot any reason for an anomaly, perhaps indications of a failed sensor?'

'Sure, that won't take long, I can get in to that now. Let me pull it up from Control… find the right part… sensor control settings… Yup, here it is, clean water tank sensors, ten tanks. All sensors off while awaiting recalibration. Is that what you wanted? Menem? You still there?'

I had gone cold. Everything moved very slowly. My eyes had narrowed their focus to a spot on the floor. Sound had faded out except Gunadi's breathing in my ear.

'All sensors off while awaiting recalibration?' I repeated slowly.

'That's what Control says. You weren't expecting that?'

'No, I was not expecting that. When were they switched off?'

'Err, let me look in Archive, calling up more depth, date stamps. Funny, there are no date stamps. It's almost as though those sensors were never switched on. Either that or the date stamp file has become corrupted.'

'Or deleted?'

'Tricky to do that without leaving a fingerprint, and why would anyone want to?'

'Indeed, as we're all in this ship together, dependent on each other, no reason for anyone to do that. But the sensors are off now, and there's no indication of when that happened?'

'It seems most likely that they were never switched on.'

'But they must have been tested, by me, and others: Massoud, Agyei, anyone. Surely we ran a water loss test during shake-down?'

'Long time ago. Who knows? Perhaps the shipyard turned them off after the shake-down and reset the time-stamp file. It looks as though none of you have touched them. Perhaps each of you thought they were someone else's responsibility. They're off, so do you want me to turn them on?'

'Yes. Please turn them on.'

The ship exploded around me in a sudden cacophony of noise as alarms started and intense yellow warning lights flashed. 'Off, Gunadi, turn them off.' The alarms died away as quickly as they had started.

'Engineering, what just happened?'

Oh no: Sahko. Sounding pissed off again and on the general comms link too so everyone could hear.

'Captain, we've detected a problem with the water system controls. Sorry about the alarm everyone, it looks like a sensor malfunction.'

'Thank you engineering, let us know beforehand if you're about to trigger the alarms again.'

'Will do, captain. Sorry everyone.'

Sahko then spoke on a one-to-one link. 'Menem, I'm coming down right now to Engineering. I want you to tell me what the hell is going on. I don't like unexpected alarms on my ship, and this is the second day in a row.'

To look busy, I activated as many sections of screen as possible, pulling up miscellaneous data, most of which unfortunately looked bad. I heard Sahko kicking the door as she came in. Wow, she looked good: fierce, mad, tense in every muscle. She was wearing black as usual but had a bright red scarf around her neck. Her eyes scanned like lasers, she shifted her weight from foot to foot, wound up, ready to spring. Her tail, if she had had one (interesting thought that) would have been straight up, twitching at the tip. She was about to breathe fire, magnificent creature.

Through clenched teeth she said 'Menem, I don't know about you, but I want to stay alive a while longer. Why are you trying to kill us?'

She came towards me, a finger out ready to poke me in the chest. I backed out of strike range.

Sahko continued: 'Yesterday we had a fire in Engine Control, an emergency shut down of Main resulting in a gravity direction switch, we sustained serious damage to a Wayclear laser and one of the mimics, and we found that the nozzle is so badly damaged that we may not be able to restart the engine for six months, by which time we'll have passed the Alpha System and be halfway to the next star, with Fleet hot on our tail. If we're very unlucky, we'll make it back home to a hero's welcome, and be torn very slowly limb from limb for blowing ten-percent of Earth's GDP on a failed venture. Why? Because engineering couldn't fix this ship.'

I gulped air and in a quiet voice, quavering, but as calm as I could manage, said 'I want you to live, Sahko, you know I do. What can I do to convince you that I'm trying my hardest?'

'Stop that, Menem, you know it doesn't work. Let's find out what the problem is today.' She had turned on a dime, the anger gone and was now all cool and collected, the professional captain. 'Massoud told me last night, after the meeting, that he was concerned about the water system. He didn't think it was a big problem at that time, and we agreed not to put it to you because you'd had a tough day and we need you to be in good shape. This morning, Massoud told me that he's increasingly worried about the possible water loss. Without water there's no life; we all know that. I agreed that you should be told. So what happened?'

'Massoud did discuss it with me and I agreed that it was serious. Massoud is not usually wrong about such things. We decided that he would start leak testing, and I would look at the sensors to see why they weren't reporting any loss. They're designed to be foolproof, failsafe, networked, with no moving parts and with backups, but Massoud knows the environmental system, and if he thinks there's a problem, at the very least I had to check it out. I asked Gunadi to have a look at the sensor status and she immediately found that the clean water tank sensors were offline. They had been put into some kind of maintenance mode. There are no date stamps in the log, so we can't tell when they were switched off or by whom, or indeed whether they had ever been switched on.'

'When did you last do maintenance on the water system?'

'I don't recall ever having done maintenance on the water system sensors. Apart from changing the filters, which I do, Massoud looks after the purification plant, but that wouldn't have required checking the sensors either. There's no regular maintenance protocol for the sensors which are all linked to Status. As I said, the sensors are failsafe and fault detecting, and an alarm should have been triggered if even a tiny leak had developed. Most likely, the sensors were switched off in the shipyard after shake-down, for some reason, and never turned back on. We left in a hurry, I recall.'

'The wretched Fleet build arms-race needing us to get away as soon as possible. No point in unleashing the hounds until the hare has a good lead. So for ten years we've been blissfully unaware that a critical system was not being monitored.'

'That's a distinct possibility.'

'Makes one think that there might be other critical systems unmonitored on this ship.'

'I've been trying not to, but when things are calmer I'll draw up a list of systems to check, and get everyone to contribute for their areas. Time to fix things will be limited when we get in close and components could become more stressed as we manoeuvre. We don't want the ship to be falling apart as we make our approach to the planet.'

'No we don't. Once we're out of our current mess, we need to get on with tightening up the ship. We need confidence in it, especially if we come in faster than we would like and have to get closer than ideal to a planet or a star.' She paused. 'So what triggered the alarm this morning? We haven't got to that bit.'

'I asked Gunadi to turn on the sensors.'

'And that made all hell break loose?'

'Seems like it. The alarms stopped after I asked her to switch the sensors off again. Archive will have a log and tell us what triggered the alarm.'

'OK, Menem, here's what we do now: pull up the Archive log.'

I switched one of the displays to the environmental system, Archive data, water sub-system, tank sensors. It showed that they'd only been on briefly, but in that time they had self-calibrated and then detected out of spec water levels in the pure water tanks, triggering the alarm. Some of the other water system sensors were indicating borderline conditions, but none were over the line, none reported water build-up in other parts of the system.

'Massoud was right about the water loss,' said Sahko.

'So it would seem,' I mumbled quietly.

'We need to find the leak, stop any further loss, and find where the lost water has gone. This has become priority two. Massoud reckons that at the moment the leak is not large. However, loose water could get into and damage the ship's systems, or it could be lost to space. We need to stop the leak sooner rather than later. How easy is that leak detector thing to use?'

'It's easy to operate: you simply strap a sensor on a pipe or tank and another sensor somewhere else, and it tells you if there's a leak between or near the sensors. It's pretty good at giving an exact location, marking it on the ship's plans. The problem is that its range is limited to about ten metres and we have an awful lot of water piping on the ship. We may have to pull up a lot of floors and take off a lot of wall panels.'

'So all the crew could use the detector?'

'Yes, anyone could. Alice probably could, or maybe even Kent and Sky. We would need to be thorough in our search though: a very small leak would be easy to miss. Even if we happened on a drip, water can move a long way from the source of a leak before becoming apparent, particularly given the change of orientation two nights ago.'

'That may have caused the leak in the first place.'

'It could have, but Massoud thinks it probably started earlier. Anyway, we need to be smart about this. Begin with the most likely places, such as pipes in the Habitat Ring that would have been flexed in the change of operating mode. We also need to be methodical, not to miss anything or duplicate too much.'

'I'll put Yingluq on it because I need you to focus on the tile rebuild process. She should be good with plumbing.'

'Aren't bodies a bit different from ships? Both mostly pipes though,' I mused. 'But isn't she tied up with quantum mechanics and redesigning the tiles?'

'I want to draw her back a bit from that. Minogue can do all the detailed stuff and he knows the physics best. I would rather Yingluq was a little more distanced from the detail and not so vested in a particular solution. She's the only other one here who really understands that stuff, so having her critique Minogue's work is preferable to succumbing to group-think.'

Once again I could see why Sahko was the captain. Yingluq was the only one capable of questioning Minogue. She could stand up to his scientific battering, however close they were personally, and I was never sure about that.

'Can you show Yingluq how to access the water system?'

'Yes, but she probably knows already. She could also call on Agyei, Bjorn or Massoud, who all know how to access the ship's guts.'

'I'll talk to Massoud, get him to show her how the leak detector works and its limitations. Perhaps we can get Bita to do some of it too; she's looking for a way to help. Maybe at least some of the children can be involved somehow, if we can find a way of doing that without slowing things down.'

'Child labour? Great.'

'Shut up, Menem. It was your idea anyway: that will be in my report.' She smiled at me briefly and then headed for the door.

'I'll get the sensors on without triggering the alarm, and then at least we'll know how much water we're looking for, or have lost. I'll set up a work log for us all to access.'

'Do that. No more alarms, please. The crew are jumpy enough as it is.'

'Oh, and that ten-percent of Earth's GDP was a bit of an exaggeration,' I added, trying to delay her departure.

'Maybe, but ten-percent of one-year's GDP is not so far off, if the total expenditure over the past thirty years on the whole programme for all the countries involved is included. Think of the cost of the design, build and operation of each of the Fleet ships, plus ours.'

She walked out, those boots clicking commandingly as she went.

I turned back to the engineering control station. 'Get a grip on yourself, you need to fix stuff,' I said to myself. I reset the sensors to diagnostics-mode, to avoid triggering the alarms again. A screen filled with data and I called Massoud. 'I've just had Sahko down here in Engineering.'

'Ah-ha. The alarm?'

'Yes, indeed. You were right about the loss of water. The sensors are now showing there's about two hundred and fifty litres missing.'

'Out of twelve thousand, so we're a little over two percent down. The seriousness depends on how fast it's being lost.'

'Any luck with the leak detector?'

'Not so far. I've checked the immediate area around the tanks in Food Prep, but the pipe work runs everywhere.'

'It really does. By the way, Sahko is going to ask Yingluq to organise a search party.'

'Yingluq?'

'An expert on plumbing apparently. It seemed sensible the way Sahko explained it. Can you show Yingluq how to use the detector? Ah, sounds as if Sahko has arrived with you. She can explain better than I.' Massoud clicked out.

I pulled up the schematics for the clean water system and studied it. I marked the locations that would have been flexed when the gravity changed, added a few other notes and suggestions, and appended them all to a new work log. I forwarded a note and a link to the log to Massoud, Sahko and Yingluq, and also copied in Gunadi. Best if we were all working off the same hymn-sheet.

The other parts of the water system, the grey-water, black-water, coolant and heating, all needed checking. All those sensors seemed to have full logs, going back to the shipyard when they were first activated. I had Status manipulate the data into some more meaningful graphics, but couldn't spot any anomalies. I appended those to the work log anyway.

4019, 10:25

What next? Problem number one should be next I suppose, so I called Bjorn: 'Hi, made any progress with our little problem yet?'

'Just getting started. I've been clearing housekeeping on fire systems. After yesterday's bit of fun I want to make sure everything is up to date and all the kit in the right place and working.'

'At least one of us is on top of their day job.'

'You've been distracted by that alarm presumably. Is it serious?'

'Two percent of our water is missing somewhere, so not fatal yet. Unfortunately, we don't know where it's leaking from or where it has gone.'

'Do you have to deal with that?'

'Sahko has delegated it to others for now. Can we get together and sort out what we're going to do about the tile processes?'

'Definitely. There's a load of technical stuff which is out of my area of competence, but the process stuff I can do. Shall I come round to Engineering?'

'Unless you're already on your way, why don't I come to you in Payload? It's a bit of a mess here.'

'OK, come on over.'

On my way I looked in Printing to see Hyun, who I found bent over a machine I hadn't noticed before.

'Have you seen this tile printer, Menem? Agyei asked me to check it over and I've had it dug out from the Processes Ring stores. It's quite different from the usual 3D printers. It's not what I would call a printer really, more like a crystal puller. It uses a laser to scan the surface, enabling the catalytic reaction that precipitates the material completely uniformly. It's halfway between Agyei's province and mine. A long time ago I had some training on its use. I'm now refreshing my memory and looking up any more recent literature on the subject. As usual, there have been some advances since this was designed.'

'Have you been able to talk to Massoud to get more detail on his proposal?'

'Not yet. He messaged me that he was tied up with some other problem that had arisen, presumably to do with that alarm. I'm not sure we can do any useful modifications yet, at least until Minogue has got somewhat further with his tile redesign. But I do want to be up to speed and ready to go when he's got close.'

'We must keep a dialog going between all of us. We don't want him coming up with the perfect tile that we can't make with the equipment we have. Anyway, I'm on my way to discuss the tile extraction and replacement processes with Bjorn, so we may call on you.'

'Whatever I can do.'

'Thanks, Hyun.' I scooted on.

Bjorn was studying ship diagrams on one part of his screen and had some process designs up on a couple of others.

'Took your time, and you didn't even bring me a coffee,' was Bjorn's greeting.

'I dropped in on Hyun to see how he's doing. He thinks there have been advances in tile printing since our unit was made. He was getting buried in the details.'

'Sounds like Hyun.'

'By way of amends, let me order you a coffee and I'll have one too. We need all the help we can get on this one.' I ordered the drinks. 'I see you've started looking at our bit. Any thoughts so far?'

'In my role as safety officer, I decided to look at the risk assessments for the processes. I've started skimming through and they look super-cautious. Given our predicament, we might dial down the caution in areas that would make a significant difference to end-to-end process time.'

'Hmm,' I hesitated. 'We would need to run that by Sahko, and possibly the whole crew, if we departed too far from approved risk levels.' Bjorn and I seemed to have swapped roles here: he was usually reining me in on risk.

'Sure, but we're way off mission plan already, we're doing an engine refit while we should be running it at max. I've no doubt that Sahko and the crew would approve a notch up in risk.'

'Very likely, but it'll depend on what type of risk we're talking about. Blowing ourselves to smithereens is one thing, but upping the radiation hazard tends to be one of the things the crew are quite cautious about.'

'Yeah, fertility.'

'It's not only me,' I said defensively.

'No, all our counts are down, even more than they should be in ten years.'

'Does it bother you?'

'Yes. I would like more children. Kent is great.' Bjorn looked a bit shifty.

'There's also Avalos: a risk too far.'

'Avalos? What has he got to do with this? That was an accident which was most likely his own fault.'

'Presumably he was taking a risk, looking inside that high power cabinet. It didn't work out too well for him, assuming his death really was an accident.'

'Sure it was an accident. It was far too late when Yingluq got to him.'

'So we've thought. How come he was there, fiddling in the wrong cabinet, just as the transmitter came on?'

'Come on, Menem, there was no one else there. He was second for comms and generally dealt with that equipment. No one could have fixed him. Sheer bad luck.'

'Avalos had his faults.'

'Sure he was a cocky bastard sometimes but he was a damn good navigator.'

'He took risks.'

'This is a risky mission.'

'So speaks our safety officer.'

'It's about correctly assessing risks and having mitigations ready for when you end up on the bad side.'

'Sorry Bjorn, I wasn't attacking your professionalism. A major factor in our still being alive today is down to you: loading the dice a bit in our favour. But Avalos was cavalier: no-one knew we were going in so close to Jupiter on that pass.'

'Sahko approved his flight plan.'

'Sahko was distracted and she was appalled when she worked out what he was doing, but by then it was too late.'

'It bought us a big advantage.'

'A small advantage for a big risk. It could have torn the ship apart.'

'Anything else on your mind about Avalos?'

'He wasn't always nice to women.'

'Come on, he was the best looking bloke around; the girls were all gagging for him. He did tell me once that he liked rough stuff but I heard no complaints.'

'Neither did I at the time.'

'But you have since? So now you think they, presumably a she, did him in? Leave it, Menem. It was a long time ago and people play games around here; it's all there is to do for a lot of the time. Ever thought you might be being played?'

'No, I hadn't, I hadn't thought of that. Sorry Bjorn, I guess I need to keep my eyes wider open.'

'Yeah, well. Back to work or we'll have the boss on our necks.'

'Please no. I've already had that once today.'

'You and Sahko still not patched up your differences? It's been far too long. You're both so uptight. It might help everyone if you could simply sort each other out. Things might be more relaxed around here.'

'I wish.'

'Sorry, Menem. Perhaps that's a problem the rest of us can try to help you with, as you haven't been able to.'

'No, please. I don't need help. I… oh dear, Bjorn, leave it please.'

'OK, sorry, man. Let's get back to a simple problem like how to speed up this tile replacement process by a factor of twenty.'

'Let's do that thing.'

We settled into it, looking in turn at each step on the critical path, running scenarios. What if we had an extra hot-bot? What if we could develop a faster cutter by using more power or a revised design? What if we accepted a higher level of radiation? What if we could move tile fabrication to the outside, near the nozzle? What if we could speed up the breakdown of the old tiles? What if we upgraded the separator? What if we could speed up the fusing process when fitting the new tiles? We laid out our assumptions for each step. We would need approval from the relevant experts for each possible change: Hyun for robotics, Agyei for chemistry, Minogue for tile design and probably installation. Ibo and

Yingluq could provide ideas and additional input. Sahko too would have suggestions, and she would have the final say on risk, after checking with all the crew.

After a couple of hours, Bjorn and I were still not very pleased with what we had come up with. We were struggling to find significant hard time savings. We had lots of gaps and questions and now needed to talk these through with others. If we could convert some of these vague ideas into real changes, using some reasonable assumptions and a modest increase in risk, we could probably halve the process time. An additional bot would halve the time again. Promising, but the real critical-path element was fabricating the tiles. That was down to Minogue and Agyei at this stage.

'That's about as far as we can go for the moment. How about we take a break and catch up with the rest of our duties?' I asked.

'I need a stretch at the very least,' said Bjorn. 'I'll write a summary note to go on the front of our proposed model and post it, so everyone can start reviewing and commenting on it.'

'Thanks, that would be good. I need to see how the water-loss problem is coming along. Could you drop in on Hyun, see how busy he is, and see if we can get him to start thinking about this stuff, or at least to have reviewed it ahead of the meeting this evening?'

'Sure.'

'It would be good if Agyei could give it some attention too. How are you guys getting on these days, by the way?'

'Well, very well, thank you. As you know, our relationship has had some rough patches, but recently it's going very well.' This seemed unusually fulsome for Bjorn. He was rocking forward on his chair, smiling. It seemed as though he was not sure whether to say more so I waited, expectantly. 'Yes, look, we're going to say something tonight, but Agyei wanted you to be prepared for it. She suggested that if I had the opportunity, I should tell you.'

I sat still. A couple of possibilities started to spring to mind. Was she going to die? We couldn't do without our chemistry number one, and I certainly would miss our engineering number two.

'Go on then.'

'Ah yes, well, umm, Agyei is pregnant.' I felt a flush rush up my face, gripping my jaw.

'Fantastic,' I managed to get out. 'Good news, that's great news, and, err, you're the father?'

'Yes, I've been told so. I did make a donation and Yingluq did all the refining and so on.'

'Congratulations. The hell with everything else, this is what the mission is really about: the future, seeding the galaxy.'

'Well thanks, Menem. We, especially Agyei, were a bit worried how you would take the news.'

'Thanks for that kind thought. I'm worried about my engineering number two having morning sickness or whatever.'

'We were thinking of other things, history, you know.'

'Yeah, history, as you say. Can't change the past, can change the future. Tell Agyei that I'm really pleased, especially for you two, but also for the ship, and that includes me. More precious cargo we need to safely deliver to our new home.'

'Thanks again.' He looked really happy.

'Let's talk some more later. Got to get on with solving our problems, redouble my efforts.'

I got up and went over to Bjorn, took his hand and shook it. I looked him in the eye, and then clasped his shoulder in a manly way. I then turned and went out the door before he could see my eyes starting to water.

The corridor was noisy back the way I had come, so I went the other way and ducked into Stores so that I could order my thoughts and get a grip. When I came out, I went back to find out what all the noise was about. Kent and Sky seemed to be racing in opposite directions and Joko was shouting and cheering. There were taped marks at regular intervals on the floor. I walked around, narrowly avoiding Kent, and saw Alice standing by a hole where a number of the floor panels had been lifted. She was studying a little portable screen.

'Nothing here,' she shouted. Then she saw me. 'Oh, hi Menem, we're looking for the missing water.'

'Any luck?'

'Not yet, but Yingluq thinks we're close. She has worked out it's most likely around this area somewhere.'

That meant somewhere between section fifteen, Analytics, and section three, Science. That narrowed things a lot and was likely to be much less of a danger than it could have been. I had feared it might be somewhere in the engine room.

'Do you know how Yingluq has worked that out?' I asked Alice.

'Yingluq and Bita thought that if water was escaping somewhere, it must be leaving a trace, even if we couldn't see it. So they got this humidity sensor thing, and we're sniffing the air under each floor section. It reduces the number of places where we have to use that other machine that Massoud has for tracing leaks to find where the water is escaping. The humidity is higher here than elsewhere, but there are a lot of pipes and wires and stuff under the floor, and it's really dark.'

'The ship's all very complicated, which makes faults difficult to find and fix. Keep at it: you're doing a very important job. We can't do without water.'

'Ah no, no refreshers, yuk, we would all smell really bad.'

'We would very quickly. You carry on with what you're doing, and I'll go and find the others and see if I can help.'

As I left, Alice called for Sky and Kent to put back one floor panel and lift another. They came running. Alice seemed to be in charge of operations.

Through another section, I found Yingluq and Bita. They were standing right outside Sahko's apartment door in section one.

'Hi, Menem. Just in time for the final pinning down of the leak,' called Bita. 'We've narrowed it to somewhere around here, probably under Sahko's apartment.'

'Well done, it will be a great relief if we can track it down. Is Sahko inside?' I asked. She wouldn't be happy with an invasion of her apartment or with us tearing it apart.

'Sahko is in Science with Minogue,' said Yingluq. 'It's about time we called her. The leak will be easier to find from inside her apartment if it's under her floor.'

A troubling thought occurred to me: Sahko's refresher. The one I was supposed to have fixed ages ago, but had put off because I always had higher priorities.

'Ah, Menem, I see that look,' said Yingluq. 'You have an idea and it's not good.'

'I get it,' said Bita. 'Oh, you're in deep, deep trouble Menem, very, very deep. You're going to have to think up something really, really good to get out of this one or she's going to have you tossed into space.' Bita was starting to laugh.

'What do you mean?' Yingluq looked puzzled for a moment then it dawned on her too. 'Oh, wait a minute. Sahko's refresher, the one you were supposed to have fixed, how long ago was it? Let's get Sahko over here. I want a ringside seat when Menem tells her.' Bita and Yingluq were laughing like mad.

'Ladies, please. I, umm, I, err...' My voice had stopped working for a moment as my mouth went dry. I managed to rasp out: 'I've urgent business back on Earth. Please give my regards to Sahko.' But I was trapped between Yingluq and Bita who seemed to be closing in on me, a pair of Amazon warriors about to make a human sacrifice, but who were having difficulty owing to their giggling.

I was saved by Alice's shout: 'Something here.'

I was frogmarched around to where Alice was. We found her kneeling, peering into the void where a panel had been lifted. Kent and Sky were looking in too, and Joko was trying to squeeze in as well.

'Alice, what have you found?' called out Bita.

Alice looked up. 'A drip. We found the humidity was highest in this part, and when it was quiet, I heard water dripping.'

'Could this be a stay of execution, Menem?' breathed Bita in my ear.

'Why are you and Yingluq holding Menem like that?' asked Kent.

'He's their prisoner, I think,' suggested Sky.

'What have you done, Menem?' asked Alice.

'It's what he hasn't done that's the problem, and he's in deep trouble,' Bita told them.

'I'll help you,' said Kent.

Well done, I thought, us men have to stick together. 'It's a very fierce dragon that I may have upset,' I said.

'I don't mind. I'll kill the fierce dragon for you.' Kent started to wave an imaginary sword around.

'Thanks for your support, Kent. I appreciate it.'

'I'll help too,' added Sky. 'I can fight dragons as well.' She and Kent started pushing each other.

'I can too,' put in Joko. 'I like dragons.'

'Yes, Joko, I usually like dragons, well some dragons.' I looked at Yingluq and Bita. 'But sometimes they get very fiery, and it's better to avoid them until they've cooled down.'

'This is not helping.' Yingluq tried to restore some sense. 'Alice, show us what you found.'

'If you stick your head in here, you can hear dripping noises.'

Yingluq knelt down and looked in the void. I manoeuvred myself around behind Yingluq and took a look. We were all quiet. Yingluq leaned further into the space, her head to one side to hear better.

'You're right Alice. There's definitely a dripping sound in here.' She sat back. 'But how did the water get to here from under Sahko's apartment?'

'Why don't you have a listen, Bita?' I suggested.

Bita glared at me. 'I think you've seen enough for the time being. Why don't you take a look?'

'Yeah, well thank you very much everyone,' I said. 'You've found the source of the leak, and judging by that sound this is where a lot of the water has ended up. It probably migrated here when we went through that gravity shift. It's now down to me to fix it, unless I can persuade Agyei to do it.'

Yingluq looked at me fiercely. 'You need to sort out this mess, Menem. Don't get Agyei involved. Besides, she's working with Minogue on the tiles.'

'Mmm, perhaps I need bigger protection, I mean help. Massoud will need to know what's going on, and this is an environmental systems problem. Bjorn could be useful, with his fire-fighting skills. He should have some good ideas on recovering the water.'

'Coward,' laughed Bita. 'OK, children. I think we've done all we can for now. Time for lunch, don't you think?'

'Can I help Menem?' asked Joko.

'Well thanks, Joko,' I replied. 'I think we all need lunch first. Let's go to the refectory and see what Massoud can cook up for us.'

Kent and Sky raced off. I picked up Joko and carried her on my shoulders, ducking as we went through doorways. Yingluq, Bita and Alice followed us.

'Found the problem?' asked Massoud, as our troop arrived.

'We think we've found the leak and at least some of the lost water,' replied Yingluq.

'I found the lost water,' said Alice proudly.

'Well done everyone. Fine food for the conquering heroes coming right up.'

'A certain member of our party needs fortifying, and has suggested asking for your help with his protection squad,' said Yingluq.

'Really? Who does he need protecting from?' ask Massoud.

'A dragon,' said Sky.

'A very fierce dragon,' said Kent.

'I think I can guess who the dragon is. Oh no, it isn't Sahko's refresher is it?'

'The very same,' answered Yingluq.

Massoud laughed out loud. 'Oops. Fortifying food coming right up.'

A server bot appeared with plates and cups. My mouth was a bit dry and I wasn't sure I was all that hungry. However, the food smelt good, so I lifted a fork and found I could eat after all, although the hollow in my stomach remained unfilled.

After lunch I felt a trifle stronger and decided it was time to face the dragon. I called Sahko. 'Hi, if you are going to be in Science for a while, would it be OK if I could get into your apartment and fix the refresher?' Yingluq, Bita and Massoud were all ears, but fortunately could only hear one side of the conversation.

'What?' asked Sahko. 'Don't you have anything better to do at the moment? I thought we had two existential crises on our hands and you want to fix my refresher now? Doesn't fixing the nozzle and solving our water loss problem require your immediate attention, chief engineer?'

'Yes, well sometimes I find that doing something else can clear the mind for the big items.' That sounded desperate even to me. Bita and Yingluq were nodding sagely and smirking.

'Wait a minute, chief engineering genius. Could it possibly be that the problem with my refresher, that you've failed to fix for weeks, is in a tiny way connected to the potentially life threatening loss of water that the ship is experiencing?'

I hastened to turn down the volume on my communicator, but I think the others had got the drift. The dragon was about to breathe fire.

'Your refresher has only been out for a few days.'

'Twelve, thirteen including today.' I wasn't arguing. 'So I'm right aren't I? It's the refresher in my apartment that's leaking.' I mumbled something non-committal. She put on her razor-sharp steel voice and I could feel its cuts as she spoke through gritted teeth. 'Menem, get in that apartment if you need to. Stop the fucking leak, recover the water, and then get back to fixing the engine will you?'

'OK, thanks Sahko, I'm on it. Shouldn't take long.'

She interrupted: 'It had better not, Menem, it had better not.'

Sahko cut the link. Should I start walking back to Earth now?

'Wow,' said Bita after a pause. 'I've heard the expression 'deathly pale' before, but I don't think I've seen such an extreme example.'

'Fascinating,' said Yingluq. 'The only time I've seen that colour on a face before was on a corpse. Went well then, Menem, your little chat with Sahko?'

'Careful ladies,' said Massoud. 'I don't want him to waste any more of my fine food.'

I stood up, and in silence, with all the little dignity I could muster, marched to the door.

'They love each other really,' I heard Massoud saying over Bita and Yingluq's howls of laughter. I went to see if there was a knife in my tool bag that I could slit my wrists with.

4019, 13:15

I almost ran in to Bjorn who was heading to the refectory. 'Oh hi, Menem. I was going for something to eat and then I would like to get back together with you to work on the nozzle rebuild. I've had talks with Hyun and Agyei and we should be able to move our ideas on before the meeting this evening. Hold on a minute, are you all right? You look a bit pale.'

'Yes, sorry. I've had a bit of a run-in with Sahko. It seems as though the problem with her refresher has resulted in a little water loss into the service ducts.'

'Ah, oh dear. I can see that that might be bad. She has been going on for weeks about how inconvenient it is that you haven't fixed her refresher.'

'Only been out a few days.'

'Really? Seems like weeks. Anyway, I can't see how that could have happened. A leak should have been detected almost immediately.'

'It should have been. It's a long story. Bjorn, could you help, once you've had your lunch? There's quite a lot of water in a service void in section fifteen.'

'Say, no more. I'll have a quick eat and then get one of the fire bots with a liquid recovery unit to work.'

'Great, thanks. Once the leak is stopped, which I'm going to do now, and the water recovery is underway, we can get back to the nozzle repair.'

'Sure, see you in about fifteen minutes. Around here?'

'I'll either be in Sahko's apartment, in or under the refresher, or inspecting the service duct under the corridor floor between Sahko's and fifteen where Alice found water dripping.'

Bjorn disappeared towards the refectory. I pressed the access to Sahko's apartment. She had allowed me in which hadn't happened in quite a long time, years.

It looked about the same as the last time I had seen it: sophisticated use of elements of bright colour against a soft background. The lighting made it look upbeat and invigorating during the day and mellow and comforting at night. Being there brought back a host of memories, many wonderful memories from our early days together, and some very painful memories from our shared tragedy and rupture.

A service bot had clearly done its work and all was ordered. I noticed a fresh set of clothing on a hanger: another simple yet sophisticated black ship suit, and also fresh underwear on a table. I went over and looked down at it. A flush of warmth rose up my neck. Slowly I reached down to touch.

'Don't touch my clothes,' Sahko's voice screamed in my ear and I jumped back.

'Err, I wasn't...' but she had cut the connection. Heavens, was she watching me? Had she bugged her own apartment? Or had she guessed, knowing me only too well? Perhaps she had set up an automated warning that sensed my movements: not beyond her capabilities.

I went back to the refresher and looked at it. It too brought back its share of very pleasant memories. It was a standard model, the same as all the others on the ship. No special version for the captain. It looked like an off-the-shelf, mid-range, space-hotel issue, but it had been reengineered to reduce weight and behind-the-scenes space.

Kneeling down, I clicked the hidden latches on the floor access panel. The seals released and there was an immediate smell of damp: getting close. Shining a light inside showed a mass of pipes, cables and controls. Superficially it looked dry. Thanks to the space-saving, it was going to be awkward to find and fix the trouble, one of the reasons that I had been putting it off. After a lot of faffing around, thanks to the space-saving cramming together of all the pipe work, I eventually tracked the fault down to a corroded steam pipe. The leak from that had trashed the refresher control box.

The quickest way to get Sahko's refresher back in operation would be to replace the parts with some from one of the unused refreshers in the ship. Avalos's apartment seemed like the best place to ransack. When I got there the door was locked. I called Minogue because it was only either he or Sahko who could give me access.

'Hi, Minogue. How are you getting on with the tiles?'

'We think we're on to something which would be significantly faster to manufacture. I gave Bjorn a quick update a while ago, and we should all get together, including you and Hyun, before the meeting to ensure there are no surprises. Can you do about four?'

'I hope so. I'm fixing the water leak problem. You probably heard about that.'

'I was with Sahko when you told her. Gave me a good chuckle.'

'Thanks, Minogue. As a reward can you do me a favour? I could ask Sahko but you can understand why I'm not keen on overburdening her at present.'

'Coward. What do you need that I can do?'

'I need access to Avalos's apartment. I want to ransack his refresher for a part to replace the faulty one in Sahko's.'

'Sure. Is the apartment locked?'

'Yes. I had heard that Sahko was using the refresher there while hers was out of action, so presumably she would lock it.'

'To keep you from wandering in at an inconvenient moment?'

'Something like that.'

'I know she's not there now because she's back in Ops. You'd better get her refresher fixed quickly, particularly if you're going to disassemble Avalos's.'

'I'm confident that I can get hers working with parts from there. After all, if she has been using his, it must be fully functional.'

'I'm sure she would have told you if it wasn't. Anyway I've authorised access for you.'

'Thanks. Oh, by the way, before I go in there, do you know if his apartment has been cleaned up?'

'Worried about being spooked?'

'Yeah, a bit.'

'Well I think it has. I seem to remember that all Avalos's personal stuff was put in a sealed box in the baggage lockers. All the rest would have gone for recycling. It should be clean as a whistle.'

'Good, thanks.'

'Let me know if you see the ghost of Avalos.' Minogue gave one of his big laughs and cut the link.

I pressed the access panel and the door to Avalos's apartment slid open. Cautiously I went in, securing the door lock with a little fixture so that I could regain access when I needed without having to bother anyone. At first glance it looked entirely impersonal, as though no-one had ever lived there. It had an almost neutral, clean smell; the service bots had been doing their work. I looked in the refresher and picked up a slight smell of

Sahko, her favourite cleanser perfume, just a hint. It presumably hadn't worried her to use Avalos's refresher. Sahko and Avalos flashed through my mind. That was a bad thought, which I tried to ignore but it came back. I didn't want it at all. I wanted to un-think that thought.

Quickly I went to work, unclipping the access panels. Behind, it looked identical to Sahko's. I went through the same process as I had with Sahko's: services off, cut pipes and unplug cables in front of the control unit, lift the unit out. Then off with more panels, disconnect and take out the steam pipe that matched the corroded one in Sahko's refresher. This one looked good. I now had all the parts I needed. I left the panels off, ready for when I came back later to restore the refresher.

Before going back to Sahko's apartment, I went to the section of floor where Alice had first found the water. The floor was still lifted and Bjorn had set up one of his bots to pump the water out of the void and into a black-water drain, from where it would be cleaned and recycled. The bot was also drying the air in the void.

At Sahko's, I tentatively opened the door. She wasn't there and it didn't look as though she had been in. Again I glanced briefly at her clothes laid out on a table, then hurried back to the refresher. I hesitated as I was about to install Avalos's control unit and decided to have a look inside to check that nothing was loose, corroded, or in some other way suspect. At least that was what I tried to tell myself. There was nothing obviously wrong in the interior and there were no hidden secret messages, weapons or clues. It was a foolish search; no one could have got at it to place anything in there, short of cutting pipes as I had done. Either that or a massive disassembly of the refresher, which would be beyond the capability of the crew, except myself and Agyei. Mind you, Yingluq was pretty handy, and Sahko too, when she wanted. Actually, Sahko could have fixed her own refresher. A disloyal thought. Of course Hyun and Ibo were both very practical, as was Minogue, perhaps Massoud too, and who knew about Gunadi's capabilities? That only left Bita, who would be last on my suspect list, had I found anything. Avalos himself had also never displayed any practical aptitude for disassembly that I could recall, apart from risking disassembling the entire ship in Jupiter's atmosphere on our way out.

I got the control unit back in place, but before refitting the pipes and cables had a quick look around in the void. The tiny inspection camera bot looked behind and under everything it could access. Nothing: no hidden supplies of chemicals or drugs, nothing suspicious at all. What was I thinking? That Sahko had somehow done away with Avalos, or that someone else had, and planted the means in Sahko's refresher? Seriously?

The replacement steam pipe went in easily enough and diagnostics showed that it was leak free. After refitting the other parts that I'd had to remove, the refresher cycled through its functions. It was all working. Sahko could now clean herself in her own apartment. Sahko could stand naked here, caressed by cleansers, scrubbed all over, dried and polished, emerging like Botticelli's Venus. This run around inside my head had to stop.

After checking around to make sure that everything was back where it should have been, I called a service bot to do a final clean up. My tools went back to Engineering on a cart and Sahko's door closed one last time.

I called Bjorn. 'Thanks for setting up the bot to recover the missing water. It must be spread all around there, from Sahko's apartment to where most of it ended up. It smelt damp under Sahko's floor.'

'We should be able to recover all of it in time. The last bit will come out of the air as the humidity levels drop back to standard in all those ducts. I'll leave the bot running to ensure the air is circulating down in the voids for a few hours more.' Bjorn paused. 'Did you find the leak, and manage to stop it?'

'Yes, and it's all functioning now so I'll head over. You're back in Payload I see. Be there in a minute.'

'How did you get on?' I asked Bjorn as I arrived. He was running scenarios on the tile replacement process.

'I've made quite a lot of progress and been in touch with Minogue to keep up to speed with how they're getting on.'

'How are they doing?'

'Well Minogue was all excitement.'

'As usual.'

'He believes they're on to something. That research he talked about seems to be useful, to do with all the crazy stuff which Yingluq explained to us this morning, which I still don't understand. He and Agyei have cooked something up. They've got Gunadi doing simulations, and Yingluq is back reviewing their ideas. As far as I can tell, if it works, then the tiles would take less than an hour each to make.'

'So if we have to do a hundred, then a hundred hours or about four days. Better, much better. What about our side? Can we keep up with that pace?'

'Good and bad. Hyun has made it clear that we can't have another bot that can operate on the hot-side. We don't have enough material to make one, with all the radiation hardening it needs. He did think that the existing bot might be upgraded with a more powerful motor, if we can find one to fit in its casing. That would allow quicker cutting out of the broken tiles and possibly also fixing in the new ones. It would also allow the bot to move faster, which would save some time, particularly when the tiles are on the far side or deep inside the nozzle.'

'Makes sense. I'll have a look at the hot-bot schematics and see if we can find a more powerful motor to fit. What do the timings look like?'

'I've made a load of assumptions about the upgrade and run a range of scenarios. The hot-bot could do the cutting out in about fifteen minutes, less with a more powerful cutter head, and the refitting in something between twenty and forty minutes. It also needs to trundle around the nozzle with the old tile to the transfer station and back with the new tile, about another five minutes in total, on average.'

'Fifty minutes per tile. Not much room for trouble. Without a lot of spare tiles, we're dependent on the whole remaining in sequence.'

'The hot-bot is a big risk factor. It assumes you can deliver the upgrade. Any breakdown there and it's all delay.'

'What if it breaks down out on the far side of the nozzle?'

'Fortunately someone thought of that, and it's on a tether. As long as it hasn't welded itself to the nozzle it can be made to let go of the pyramid and be reeled in for repair.'

'So how far off a recommendation on process redesign are we?' I asked.

'We're pretty well there in everything except any final impacts the tile design might have on the process, for example in terms of handling the tiles and attaching and seaming them.' Bjorn paused. 'There's one more thing.'

'Yes?'

'The process requires a lot of time to bring the tiles from the engine room all the way to Chemistry for processing, and then back again. The estimate is a minimum of eight minutes each way, and there will be a lot of movements. It seems like we need to rethink it.'

'Like moving the tile fabrication closer to the engine room, or indeed into the engine room.'

'That would help a lot.'

'We'll need to check out whether the fabrication process can be made to work there.'

'Maybe it's not a good idea.'

'We should float it. What else needs to be done? The tile refiner? Risk assessment?' I asked.

'I haven't yet looked at the tile refiner to see if it could be speeded up. Perhaps you could do something there? Maybe we could make a second machine. I've identified key risks, evaluated them and given some alternatives with the impact they would have. Of course we don't have everything buttoned down as yet, and probably never will. However, I am sufficiently confident to put this proposal to Sahko and the rest of the crew.'

'Great, I can use confidence today. What else can we usefully do before the meeting?'

'We need to continue to keep tabs on how Minogue and that group are doing in case it impacts our proposal in a major way. Other than that, I would like to continue working on the risk factors and minor options. No sense in wasting much more time on our bit until the tile design is finalised, and Sahko and the others give the nod to our risk assessment and outline proposal.'

'That seems about right,' I said. 'I'll have a think about the tile refiner. Otherwise you seem to have done our bit. Minogue asked me to look in to make sure we're aligned. If there isn't much to discuss I might make a trip up to the engine, to see if there's any room for setting up a tile factory.'

'We'll need to check with Ibo before we make any modifications in there.'

'Definitely. The engine queen won't want us messin' with her stuff.'

'There will be hell to pay if she can't get the engine to restart because of anything we've done. Oh, and we'll have to think about zero-'g' working up there. That's something we haven't yet factored in. The original process wasn't designed for that because it was expected to be done in the Habitat Ring.'

'Take a look for any impacts from our point of view, and I'll ask Minogue and Agyei if it's possible from the tile fabrication angle. Give me a call if you want anything.'

'Take care up there. None of us has worked in zero-'g' for a while, at least since deceleration began.'

The door to Comms was open as I passed by. Bita was there, studying what looked like an abstract pattern on a huge screen. She was perched on a high stool, swinging a long slender leg gently back and forth. We gave each other a wave and it was tempting to go in, but I resisted and hurried on to Science, where the door was open too and there was a chatter of voices inside.

'Come in Menem,' called out Minogue, waving a hand. 'Help me persuade Yingluq that this idea is really good.'

Yingluq raised her eyes heavenwards and said forcefully: 'It won't work for us, the electron field won't remain entangled long enough for crystallisation to be pure.'

Minogue appealed to me but I shrugged my shoulders. 'Sorry I haven't a clue. Agyei, what about you?'

Agyei said quietly: 'It could be done, but we don't have the equipment on the ship to do it. Yes, outside is cold enough, but no, we couldn't make a high enough frequency electromagnetic field over a big enough area to form a whole tile. We don't have the resources on board to make the required superconducting magnets.'

'See, I was right,' said Minogue. 'It could be done.'

'In theory,' replied Yingluq. 'But we need in-practice, and we need it tomorrow.'

'It's a beautiful idea. When I've more time I'll pursue it. It only needs a bit more thinking to make it work. Perhaps I'll write it up sometime. So we're back to our first idea.'

'We're all sure that will work, well as sure as we can be without actually doing it. It may not be the most elegant solution but we can certainly make tiles this way.'

Agyei added: 'And we have all the kit to try it out.'

'Can we make it work in a zero-'g' environment?' I put in. They all turned to me and stared.

Agyei said quietly: 'Zero-'g'? That would be very helpful, very helpful to the fluid distribution.'

'Much more uniform,' said Minogue.

'We would have to watch the heat transfer,' said Yingluq.

'Up the pressure a bit,' said Minogue.

'Add magnetic stirring,' said Agyei

'Need some peristaltic pumps with no 'g' on return flows,' said Yingluq.

'All quite doable,' said Agyei.

'What had you in mind, Menem?' asked Minogue.

'Bjorn and I are proposing that we shift the tile manufacturing to the engine room to shorten material transfer paths.'

'Genius. I should have thought of that: the engine room being in zero-'g' at the moment.'

'Ibo is not going to like us setting up a cobbled-together factory in her engine room,' said Agyei.

'How about we ask her to set it up?' suggested Yingluq.

'Somehow we need to make it her idea,' I said.

'Could we ask Hyun to ask her,' suggested Minogue.

'Dangerous waters.'

'Maybe. It could go either way: divorce or happy families.'

As I started to turn and go I said: 'I'll take a look to see if it's feasible to do the manufacturing down there. Initially I'll tell Ibo that we're looking at how the original process proposed transferring the tile powder from outside to up here in the Habitat Ring.'

'Transport bot, I imagine,' said Yingluq.

'I will point out that we're now talking about at least a hundred tiles in and out, not just one or two.'

'We'll leave Ibo to you. We need to think through all the details of the tile design,' said Minogue.

'And how they're going to be made,' said Agyei.

4019, 16:50

I left them to it and went around to one of the connectors from the ring to the keel. As I arrived at the access door, I opened a comms link.

'Hi, Ibo. I'm on my way to the engine room. I want to check out the path the tiles have to take from the nozzle to where they're going to be re-formed. I wanted to let you know what I'm up to.'

'Thanks. Can I join you? I've been running routine engine checks from up here and would like to have a look around the engine room to make sure nothing is amiss. I haven't been there to do a visual since the shutdown.'

'Sure, it would be good to have you along. I may have some questions, and we can discuss how to make things flow easily. We're going to have to deal with many more tiles than the process envisaged. I don't want anything to get in your way or risk damaging anything.'

'Mmm, I think you're up to something, you bad man, always causing me trouble. I don't like the idea of so many trips by transport bot near the engine.'

'Let's see if we can arrange things so they work for all our needs. When can you make it?'

'I'll be right behind you, keeping a close eye on that cute ass of yours.'

'Whatever would Hyun say?'

'He know me well enough by now. Sure do.' She burst into deep throated laughter.

I cut the link before she could say anything else. I began climbing up the ladder inside the spoke, a weird sensation when we were in spin-gravity mode. The centrifugal force reduced as I got closer to the spin axis making my body seem lighter. Climbing 'up' was also rather subjective because I was heading towards the ship's core.

By the time I had reached the keel, I was floating in zero-'g'. I went through the access door into the spin-changer and activated spin-down. The process was like being on a fun-fair ride and made me feel nauseous. I tried to quell my stomach by studying the graphic on the door, put there for that purpose. As the spin slowed, my inner ears began giving me the same information as my eyes and my motion sickness subsided. After about ten seconds, the access door opened into the keel tube, and I glided in.

The bulkhead door to the payload section opened and the lights all down the tube up to the next bulkhead came on. Had Main been functioning, I would have had to use either a platform to carry me down the keel or the ladder all along the wall. For now, I launched myself gently from the door and floated steadily down the tube. I made slight course corrections with my fingers as I came close to its side, careful not to get entangled in all the attached pipes and cables. Occasionally I had to grab the ladder and pull to compensate for slowing due to air resistance.

The door behind me opened and I twisted around to see Ibo entering. That proved to be a mistake as the reaction forces caused my body to twist and I crashed slowly but inelegantly into the wall and had to turn back to reset my motion to the slow glide down the tube.

Ibo soon caught up with me. She was far more practised than I, usually making a daily inspection of the engines as well as occasional longer operation-and-maintenance visits. All the engine systems could be remotely monitored through Status, but Ibo was a believer in hands-on listening and feeling. It was probably her vigilance that was the reason I had had so little occasion to come down here: typically to replace an odd pump seal or bearing. Mostly she brought anything that needed my attention back to Engineering where I could work on it more easily, with my tools to hand and gravity to keep parts where they had been placed.

Ibo slowed her pace to match mine and remained a respectful distance back, avoiding my flailing boots. The long payload section had only a few access points which led to airlocks and the cold dark. The payload itself was mostly outside the controlled environment of the ship where it was going to have to survive anyway when deployed.

At the end of the payload we passed through the double bulkhead doors into the fuel tank section. We glided up that and reached the next set of bulkhead doors that led into the engine room. These doors were more elaborate than the others, consisting of three consecutive cone shapes, each formed of an iris of interlocking petals, with the cone peaks facing towards the engines. The doors were carefully designed to deflect any blast out through the side of the ship, preventing it travelling down the keel and into the inhabited section. Only one cone door could be opened at a time and so Ibo and I went together through the intermediate compartments, with each door behind closing before the one ahead would open. Finally we left the keel and entered the engine room.

This section was quite different. It was like coming out of a tunnel and into a chemical factory. A deep throbbing sound came from the fusion reactor, Fuse, as we had named it, which was currently supplying all our electrical power. The reactor vessel itself, along with its deuterium and tritium fuel tanks, was outside the conditioned environment we were in, taking advantage of the cold of space for the superconducting magnets that contained its plasma. All its controls and ancillary systems, however, were here in the conditioned engine room.

The fission reactor, Fizz, was silent apart from a gentle hum of coolant pumps. At present it was in standby mode. Its reactor vessel was also outside and in a heavily shielded chamber to protect the rest of the ship from its radiation. It was a small device, intended only to power vital life support systems if Fuse failed and also to supply the necessary power to charge the capacitor banks used to get Fuse reignited, if it ever shut down.

Ibo listened to the sounds of the room and ran her hands over various machines, feeling for unusual vibrations or hotspots. This part of the engine room was packed, with little spare space and certainly not enough to set up any kind of tile manufacturing facility. The ship's schematics showed there was more space beyond, where the main drive lay.

'Looking good, Ibo. Fortunately no debris seems to have penetrated in here.'

'Well let us all give thanks for that.'

'All neat and clean.'

'I like to keep things tidy.'

'Indeed you do.'

We worked our way forward, around an array of structural elements, and came to the back of the antimatter drive, Main. The space opened out here, with the centre occupied by the core of the engine. Substantial beams carried its force to the keel and to the outer structure of the ship. A host of fibres came from the back of the core, carrying sensor information from the engine and control signals into it. They snaked towards cabinets that held the data processing and management systems. A massive tube came into the engine from one side which had a bundle of large cables and pipes feeding in to it. It fed the antimatter into the engine from the tanks outside, also held in the cold of space to still the fuel. Power cables energised the magnets that kept the antimatter from touching the walls of their tubes and the electric fields that injected precise quantities of fuel, anti-atom by anti-atom, into the strike point that lay at the engine's heart. A relatively modest tube on the other side fed similarly precisely metered hydrogen atoms into the machine. Where the two fuels met the matter and antimatter annihilated each other, turning their mass into high energy subatomic particles: pions, gamma rays and neutrinos. The magnetic field and tiles surrounding the nozzle directed these particles into a beam, travelling at light-speed. It was the reaction to that beam, felt by the nozzle, which provided the thrust we needed. At least that was what was supposed to happen, when nothing was broken.

'My beautiful engine, silent,' said Ibo, laying a hand on the casing.

'Everyone is working to bring it back to life, Ibo.'

'I appreciate that.' I could almost hear the tears in her voice. She stiffened. 'So what do you want to see here?'

'Where the tiles come in and out. The schematics showed a small airlock, somewhere high up, right near the edge of the nozzle. Outside, nearby, in an equipment recess, there's the unit that breaks down the tiles and separates its elements.'

'I know where the airlock is. It's only for materials transfer.'

She led the way around one side of the engine. We emerged into a vast space that reached right out to the ship's sides. Floating ourselves along, we used rungs set in the wall to control our motion until we had reached the outer edge. From there we looked down on the monster, swelling from the ignition chamber to the full diameter of the ship, in a parabolic

111

curve that matched the nozzle which lay beyond. Field generators filled the space between the wall structure and the nozzle itself. The generators helped the tiles contain and shape the thrust from the annihilated fuel. All we could see on the inside were a host of fibres that came from sensors and led off to cabinets that held the field control circuits. The superconducting cables from Fuse's electricity generators, which supplied power to the electromagnets of the nozzle, were all outside in the cold.

Ibo floated along to a far corner, where the curve of the engine's nozzle ended close to the skin of the ship. Beyond lay the outer structure and a host of support equipment, including the Wayclear lasers. Near the corner was a small airlock, bulging into the engine room.

'This is it,' said Ibo. 'You didn't really need to come all this way just to take a look at it.'

'Like you, I find it helps to see things firsthand. It makes it easier to spot any potential problems. It's not only the airlock, it's the whole issue of moving so many tiles in and out, round past the engine, through all the doors, all along the fuel tank and payload sections and then into the spin-changer and up into the gravity environment of the workshop. I'm not sure we've really got the space up there to set up an efficient production line for what Minogue and Agyei are proposing anyway.'

'Plenty of space here,' noted Ibo and then she paused and I could see her thinking. 'It would also save moving all the material back and forth.' She paused again and looked at me knowingly, a gleam in her eye. 'Could the tiles be made in zero-'g'?'

'Agyei thought that would be helpful.'

'So you want to do it here.'

'That seems like a great idea.'

'OK, Menem. Well done, you got what you came for.'

'Thanks, Ibo.'

'We need to get that nozzle fixed and we need to do it quickly, or all this is so much junk and we'll never stop in system. Neither the ship nor crew would make it back to Earth.'

'Almost certainly not.'

'But don't think I'm giving you a free hand down here. I'm going to be keeping a very close eye on things. No good fixing the tiles if you careless boys and girls damage anything.'

'That would be good, Ibo. I want the engine to run again as soon as possible. You protect what isn't broken.'

'Have you seen all you want to see, or do you want to measure up or something?'

'The ship schematics have all the measurements we need. There are lots of struts and structure around here that we can fix things to without making holes in anything.'

'No holes.'

'Not if we can possible help it. Unless Minogue and Agyei have changed anything drastically since I saw them a little while ago, there should be no problems with excessive torques twisting the structure or stray fields interfering with anything.'

'You'll set up a containment perimeter around the whole tile factory. No stray dust to float around and cause trouble later.'

'Good idea, can you help with that?'

'Now he wants me to do his job for him.' Ibo rolled her eyes theatrically. 'Yeah, if I'm keeping a beady eye on things, I might as well help out.'

'We'll need power and coolant lines and clean water supply and black-water drain connections too.'

'I should have known that demands were not going to stop at "can we use a little of your space?", sure all those things are available near the back of the engine, so we can run what you need by way of services up here. Give me a list and I'll get it done.'

'You're a marvel and a truly wonderful person.'

'Yeah, yeah, keep the compliments flowing, honey. Are we done here? I need a drink and to do a couple of checks before we head back. Care to join me?'

'I'm in no hurry now we've sorted a solution here. We will, of course, have to get captain and crew approval for our plans, at the meeting later on.'

Ibo propelled herself in a carefully controlled and choreographed manoeuvre back down to the area near the back of Main. This was really her space and she moved through it with complete ease. I followed rather more clumsily, keeping a hand gripped on something at all times. Round the back of a pair of control cabinets there was a drinks pouch dispenser and some couches. These used a gentle negative air pressure to keep the occupant in place, allowing longer working in zero-'g' which could become quickly tiring if one was not used to it. We sat and sucked on our pouches in silence for a time.

'Well how's life, Menem? These problems we've been having can't help, but ship problems don't usually seem to bother you too much. You been having woman trouble again? Sahko treating you mean?'

'Nothing new there.'

'Well maybe there is. Tension been rising all around since we started decelerating. Last phase of our voyage and all that. Can we hold it together long enough? Sahko feels that particularly. She feels that she should be doing a better job, that somehow if she did something different we would have less problems with both the ship and crew. You ain't helpin'.'

I sat up a bit. 'How do you mean? I want to help her. I've been trying, I thought.'

'She doesn't want just a nice guy trying to please her. She can get that from her companion. You must be more of a man and stop moping around her.'

'I haven't been moping.'

'You have, and it's not attractive. She's a sharp, intelligent person and she wants someone to debate with, someone who will defend their corner, someone who knows what they want, as well as some idea of what she wants. She wants an equal, not a poodle.'

'She certainly likes an argument. I don't find that easy.'

'Good relationships aren't easy. You used to be more assertive, expressed your views more.'

'Did I? I wonder when I lost it.'

'Well the rot set in a long time ago.'

'Maybe there were reasons.'

'Of course. Mo's death was a tragedy, a terrible, terrible tragedy.'

She had said it. I hadn't heard anyone use Mo's name in a very long time, most likely never, after the first month following her death. Poor thing, she never really lived, was never able to live. Genetic, Yingluq had said, but who really knew? No one's fault everyone said.

After a pause I said quietly· 'Yes. Yes, it was. I wanted to give Sahko some space, but that space has become a chasm.'

'It has, and it's affecting this ship, maybe endangering all of us. You two are both so wound up. We need you to be on top of your game to stop the ship from falling to pieces under us, and we need Sahko to keep making sensible decisions and to be fully functioning as navigator now we are in the outer reaches of the Alpha System.'

'We might miss Avalos soon.'

'Avalos is no loss. As long as Sahko keeps it together she's as good or maybe even a better navigator than Avalos ever was.' Ibo almost never expressed such strong views.

'Avalos was supposed to be a brilliant navigator. Didn't he save us a load of fuel on our way out?'

'He saved us a relatively small amount of fuel by taking a huge gamble that might have killed us all. We didn't need to save fuel: we had plenty. Avalos was a risk taker. He loved the high of taking us in close. Sahko wouldn't have taken that risk, wouldn't have let him take that risk, had she realised in time. It was not the approved plan.'

'I didn't know you had doubts about Avalos.'

'From early on, when he suddenly joined the crew after, who was it? Yes, Frousch, who supposedly decided our mission wasn't for him.'

'All those last minute changes. Avalos joining after all the training and the shake-down trip, still we thought we were lucky to get him: he was a star navigator, been on several racing ships that had won big prizes.'

'I thought so too at first, and he was a very good looking and charming fellow. I was delighted when I first heard he was to be Frousch's replacement. Quite an upgrade, I thought. I quite fancied him myself. Twelve years on a small ship with Mr Handsome, not bad, I thought. Then I got a message from a friend, who had been on a ship with Avalos, who told me to watch out because he had a nasty side. Did you ever wonder why he wanted to come with us? It seemed a bit odd that here was the great navigator, winner of sports trophies and all, and he was joining a stodgy old freighter on a very long and probably very dull voyage to an uncertain destination with almost certainly no return. Did you ever look at his history? Did you notice that he had never done more than one trip on any of his ships?'

'Well, that could have been because each ship was a step up. He rose fast up the ranks from a modest background.'

'Not so modest, not at all modest for a non-aligned. His parents were very rich. They had built a massive tourist business, one of the few running excursions to the outer planets: billionaire stuff.'

'I didn't know that. But now you mention it, he did have that confident air of someone from a privileged background.'

'My friend said that he took whatever he could and had some nasty habits.'

'So you knew about him from the beginning?'

'I had been warned so I kept a little distance and kept an eye out. Sometimes these things get exaggerated, you know, little jealousies. Perhaps my friend had heard a rumour from someone who had got hurt and was trying to muddy the waters for him. I wasn't rushing to judgement.'

'So you didn't tell anyone? Sahko, Bita?'

'No, not based on what little I had heard, and anyway we were stuck with him by then and I didn't want to poison the atmosphere. Sometimes these things can be self-fulfilling: you treat someone in a certain way and soon enough they start acting like that, fitting into the role you've placed them in. Besides he was always charming in public, always helpful, he seemed to be fitting in. Fortunately for me, Hyun and I somehow hit it off from the first, before Avalos was around, and pretty soon Alice came along, so Avalos didn't bother me. You and Sahko had teamed up, and soon it was happy families all round: Bjorn and Agyei, Minogue and Bita. I think Yingluq toyed with Avalos for a bit, but not for long. Initially they seemed to get on well enough, but after the first couple of weeks I got the impression she was off him, and ever-after rather resistant to his charms. She's physically strong as well, so he probably decided not to pursue her, not his type.'

'So that leaves Gunadi and Massoud.'

'Yes, Avalos tried his luck with both of them.'

'Wow, you noticed a lot, far more than I did. He didn't try both at the same time?'

'Not a threesome, if that's what you mean,' Ibo laughed. 'But yes, I believe so. I think Massoud wised up after a while. He was taken with Avalos, but I guess they had different tastes. So like Yingluq, Massoud moved back and created a barrier between himself and Avalos.'

'I heard only recently that Gunadi was not so lucky.'

'No.'

'So you knew what he did to her?'

'Some of it. Sometimes I caught her crying and I provided a good shoulder. I had her do more work down here than was strictly necessary, to give her a break. But she kept going back, couldn't stay away for long. Usual story, hoped to change him, blaa, blaa.'

'Why do you think he signed up for this mission?'

'I really don't know, maybe to escape from something. My friend hinted at that, but I never did work out why or if he was forced in to it. There were hints of family rifts. One bit of scuttlebutt said that he tried playing around with his brother's wife but my friend thought that was a smokescreen for something much deeper.'

'Good grief. Any ideas what that might have been?'

'Not really. Did you ever look at the list of ship's he had been navigator on?'

'I assumed they were all rich people's racers, but I never looked at the list.'

'Not only rich people. Corporations. Corporations that do a lot of business with governments. All sides: American, Chinese, Indian, European.'

'All of them?'

'All. Some might not have liked that. Some might have found it useful: access to high places, apparently innocent. Maybe he got caught in some bit of dodgy dealing and decided he needed to make himself scarce very quickly.'

'So he escaped with us. At least he was free of that here.'

'Possibly not. Fleet ships all following. Looking for an edge. Might be useful for one if they had a placeman aboard.'

'Come on, that's fantastic. What could he have done? All our comms are public to the whole Fleet.'

'The only evidence of anything he did that was underhand while he was aboard that I know of was that he was in Engine Control while I was giving birth to Alice.'

'How do you know that?'

'I keep a tight grip on my area of responsibility. I never did find what he was up to in there and I checked everything very thoroughly afterwards. He hadn't messed with the engine software, sensors or control feeds as far as I could tell. It may have been part of one of his practical jokes.'

'And then he died.'

'He did.'

'And you were relieved?' I asked.

'Not liking to speak ill, but yes, I was. If he had messed with anything it would be of no further use to him. And at least Gunadi would be left in peace.' Except from her own demons, I thought. 'Wait a minute, are you playing detective? Am I a suspect in the death of Avalos? Oh boy, you need to get laid; you think way too much. Avalos died in an accident, we all know that.'

'Yingluq tried to treat him and signed the death certificate.'

117

'It was far too late by the time Yingluq got to him and actually Sahko signed the death certificate as number two doctor and captain.'

I looked at Ibo and she looked at me. She seemed untroubled. If her conscience was bad she was very good at masking it. 'I apologise for grilling you on this. I should get out more.'

'Like I said, you need to get laid, with a real human. Perhaps you need to look elsewhere and maybe that will make Sahko think on you a little more.'

'Yeah, maybe.' I reflected on that too for a moment: nice idea but it wouldn't work, more likely to consign me to the outer darkness of Sahko's world, and it probably wasn't a good time to rock that boat. I had another thought and smiled. 'Well, are you offering dear lady? I wouldn't mind a piece of what you've got there. No one else around.'

Ibo squawked: 'You keep your dirty mind off me, filthy creature. That's better, Menem. Cheered me up too when we were getting a bit gloomy. However, me and Hyun are a happy family. We agreed that we'll be exclusive, which has worked well for us for a long time now. We have our ups and downs, but we work things out. We're very lucky with Alice, who seems to be coming on well so far. No doubt she will start being irritated with her old folks pretty soon. Maybe we'll have another when we put our feet on some ground.'

'You should, Alice is great, don't wait.'

'Not supposed to have more than one while on ship, and we would probably need Yingluq's help in making a bit of a selection for us: been in space too long.'

'We've room enough and journey's end is not so far away.'

'Provided we fix the damn nozzle.' Ibo got up. 'We need to be getting back. Lots to do.'

'The time, yes, much to do. I must catch up with the others working on the tile problem, and let them know about your gracious offer, the one about setting up the tile factory down here.'

'Best we keep the rest to ourselves, oh?'

'You're a bad woman.'

'I hope so.'

We floated together and had a quick hug. 'Thanks, Ibo, you've helped me a lot. I've some thinking to do and some things to straighten out.'

'You straighten them out and we'll be a happier ship.' She pushed off, heading back though the engine room to the access doors into the keel. I followed close behind.

From the keel, we made that weird transit up the shaft to the Habitat Ring: gravity getting steadily stronger as we moved along, what felt like down, the ladder. There was a real danger of misjudging things and falling dangerously to the end. Safety lines were required.

I staggered a bit as we regained normal gravity and emerged into the passage, waved Ibo goodbye, and hurried round to Science.

4019, 17:45

Minogue and Agyei looked up as I came in, Yingluq had left.

'How did it go with Ibo?' Minogue asked.

'She helpfully offered us space to locate the tile factory down there, near the tile airlock. She'll set up the necessary services and a separation barrier to keep all our stuff from polluting her engines.'

'That's great, well done. We're pretty well ready. The meeting is in fifteen minutes.'

'OK, see you there. I must check in with Bjorn before then.'

Bjorn wasn't in Engineering when I arrived, but had left the plans and tests open for me to review. He had a clear story to tell with recommendations and some alternatives where things were not clear cut. I had about got the picture when Bjorn came back in with a drink pouch.

'Hi, Menem, how did it go with Ibo?' Exactly the same question Minogue asked, so I gave him the same answer and added: 'You seem to have tidied things up well here. I haven't got anything to add at the moment. The option of working in zero-'g' in the engine room is a bonus according to Agyei, and your figures show considerable time saving in operation, even if it takes a little longer to set up.'

'I talked with Agyei while you were out and she definitely prefers zero-'g' manufacturing to reduce the risk of defects, so it's great that Ibo is supportive. That'll help a lot.'

'I think Ibo will be very helpful. She is, of course, very keen to get the engine relit. By the way, she and Hyun are thinking of expanding their family too. They were planning to wait until our arrival, so they may be jealous of your news.'

'I suspect that Ibo has guessed.'

'Not much gets past her. Can you give the briefing on our bit in the meeting?'

'Sure, if you want. Sahko may ask you to do it.'

'That I doubt.'

Bjorn said nothing in reply. He tidied up his work on the screen and made sure it was accessible on the shared file. As we left Engineering, we caught up with Minogue and Agyei, who were coming out of Science. Hyun followed, and I spoke to him.

'Hyun, about the hot-bot: would you be all right with my taking a look at upgrading it by putting a bigger motor in it?'

Hyun looked anguished and scratched his head. 'Well, Menem, that bot is working at the moment. If you increase the power of the motor then you're going to be stressing it a lot more. It's the only one we have, so why mess with it?'

'Assuming the new tile manufacturing process works, the hot-bot becomes the critical-path. Speeding up the bot speeds up the whole process.'

'What if it breaks down?'

'I can fix it: its internals are straightforward. With extra power any breakdown is likely to be in the transmission: simply swap it out. All the guts are shielded by the casing and aren't radiation hardened. They can be replaced with standard parts.'

'What if it breaks down on the far side of the nozzle? How are we going to recover it? We can't send another bot to collect it. Nothing would last long enough before it was fried.'

'It's on a tether. It can be instructed to release the grip of its feet and it will float off, then we can reel it in.'

'As long as it hasn't become jammed and can't release its feet, which is a plausible failure mode, particularly with a more powerful motor driving it.'

'We could unhook the pyramid and fold it back over to bring everything to the cool-side. Then the mimics could release it.'

'Overheating could be a problem too. Look, sorry Menem, I want to get the nozzle fixed as soon as possible, but I don't want to make a bad situation worse.'

'You're right; it does need thinking about very carefully. How about we work on this together? You're very good at thinking of the risks. If together we can find a way to speed up the bot without significantly increasing overall risk that would be good wouldn't it?'

'OK,' Hyun sighed, 'we can take a look at it. If I can watch over your shoulder and scream every time you try to wing it that would be acceptable. After all you did break one of the bots yesterday.'

'It was hardly my fault that a space rock took off my, its, head, and it wasn't technically a bot, it was a mimic.'

Hyun laughed. 'You're so easy to wind up these days. Relax man.'

We had arrived at the refectory and found that most of the others were already there. We were followed in by Yingluq. A minute later Minogue came in with Sahko. That was a bit odd because I had thought that Minogue was with Agyei, but I had lost sight of him during my discussion with Hyun. Presumably he had dropped in to see Sahko to get her up to speed. She liked to be briefed in advance, and not be surprised in meetings. Perhaps I should have briefed her too, but then she wasn't inclined to listen to me much these days and she could read the workbook which was up to date with everything Bjorn and I had done. Only my conversation with Hyun wasn't there.

Sahko held up a hand for quiet. 'Before we get on to the main reason for our meeting, I want to talk briefly about the other potentially very serious problem we faced today. Fortunately this turned out not to be so serious and is largely resolved. I expect you all know about it, and you can't fail to have heard the alarm that briefly went off this morning.' I cringed. 'There was a water leak. Sensors should have quickly detected this, but it appears that they were never switched on out of the shipyard. Fortunately Massoud noticed something was wrong with the water tanks, and alerted us. There are two points here: firstly we cannot completely rely on automated systems, secondly it's by vigilance and intimate understanding of our areas of responsibility that we can spot failures before they become life threatening. We cannot afford to let even minor faults fester because they may result in catastrophe down the road. As well as Massoud, I would also like to thank Yingluq for stepping in to take charge of tracking down the leak and the location of the lost water. Thanks too to Alice who, I understand, first discovered where the water had gone.'

No thanks to me then, the one who discovered that the sensors weren't functioning and who later fixed the problem.

'Now to the main business of the meeting: Minogue, please summarise where we've got to.'

'On the negative side, the damage to the nozzle tiles is more extensive than we thought yesterday,' Minogue began. 'The detailed survey Hyun has carried out using the hot-bot shows a hundred and twenty three damaged tiles.

'On the positive side, a group of us have developed a new design of tile that's much quicker to fabricate than the original. We believe they'll also perform better. The new tiles are made from the material of the old tiles but the crystal structure is slightly rearranged and the way it's laid down much improved. This means that the critical face layers can be much thinner than in the old tiles and these layers can be built on an amorphous structure which is very quick to form: it precipitates in seconds, as experiments Agyei has done prove. Adding the face layers should take no longer than twenty-three minutes per tile on average. We estimate that the total time to make a tile will be thirty minutes. We expect some rejects, particularly at the start of manufacture, but with a conservatively estimated failure rate of fifty percent, we hope that all the tiles could be made in five days.'

There were smiles of relief amongst some of the crew. Our mission was back in the achievable range again. However, they had heard only half the story so far.

Minogue continued. 'Bjorn and others,' that would be me then, 'have been looking at the processes required for tile replacement, from stripping out the old tiles to bonding in the new. The book processes are very slow and cautious for two reasons: firstly it was never envisaged that a large number of tiles would need to be replaced, particularly at such a critical stage of our journey, and secondly because the manufacturing was designed to be carried out in the Habitat Ring. Bjorn's proposal is to move the tile manufacturing to the engine room, which eliminates a lot of transport time and is a long way from the inhabited sections of the ship, lessening the risk from radiation. The engine room is after all the place where radiation risk is highest inside the ship. This change saves about sixteen minutes in transport time there and back for each tile.'

This bit brought more smiles from the crew. There was a sense of rising optimism.

Minogue continued. 'This switches the critical path to the hot-bot. At the very least we need to find a solution to the battery problem to get the total repair time down. We only have one hot-bot, which is a significant risk itself, and we don't have the materials to make another.

'The current tile breakdown process has not yet been reviewed. The book-time is ninety minutes per tile, so it would be on the critical path if the hot-bot battery problem can be resolved. All three elements, hot-bot, tile refiner and tile fabrication can be run in parallel once everything is rolling.'

'There may be other improvements we can make. For example, the process of bonding in the new tiles is the same as that required for the old tiles, except where two new tiles touch, when the bonding time is much shorter because the bonded layer is so much thinner.'

Hyun raised a hand to interrupt and Minogue gave way to him.

'Menem and I talked just before the meeting and we think it may be possible to upgrade the hot-bot with a more powerful motor. This would have two benefits: it could cut out the old tiles faster, and it could move back and forth across the nozzle much more quickly. We haven't yet done any simulations on this, so these are preliminary ideas.' No kidding. 'If these changes can be successfully made, we can meet the average good tile manufacturing time of one hour to extract the old tiles and fit the new.' Cripes, Hyun, that's a bit of a hostage to fortune.

Even Sahko was looking less grim and she quelled the room. 'Thank you Minogue, Hyun and everyone else. All of us have contributed to the progress that has been made, either directly or indirectly. Yesterday we were looking at a catastrophic eighty-three days to perform the repairs to the nozzle, today it looks as though we may be able to get it done in fifteen days if we can solve the hot-bot battery problem and maybe less when more work has been done on the hot-bot upgrade and on the tile refiner. This is still not ideal, but inside our mission envelope, necessitating a tolerable increase in the rate of deceleration once the engine is functioning again.

'Now, has anyone any suggestions for how we might improve things further? Please confine your comments to this.'

The room was quiet, so after a few seconds I raised my hand. Sahko pointed to me so I began. 'Minogue has told us that it's much quicker to fuse two new tiles together than to fuse a new one to an old one. The diagram showing the location of the damaged tiles suggests they are randomly scattered across the nozzle, and it seems that there are some areas with lots of damage and some with none. Could we simulate the impact on process times of removing some of the unbroken tiles, in areas where most are damaged, to make a whole new area, most of whose seams would be new tile to new tile and therefore much more quickly bonded?'

Yingluq asked: 'How would that help? If the process time for manufacturing new tiles is the same as the hot-side working, all you are doing is reducing one to extend the other. Overall it would take longer.'

'Minogue used an estimated failure rate of tile manufacture of fifty percent. It would be normal to assume that the percentage might be large to start with but decline over time with experience. It seems highly likely that, with focussed effort, we can drive down the experience curve so that our failure rate goes down to say ten percent. Then tile manufacture would be way off the critical path, and it's all down to the hot-bot. We only have one of those and we're proposing to upgrade it, which makes the risk of breakdown in that area more likely. Anything that can re-balance work away from the hot-bot would be good.'

'Cutting out more tiles requires more work for the hot-bot not less,' pointed out Yingluq.

Gunadi raised her hand and Sahko signalled to her. 'I have the tile locations modelled with all the damaged tiles marked. I could run simulations that play around with hot-bot work depending on a range of process times. We'll need to do most of that anyway, to optimise the bot's path around the nozzle, minimising its travel time and to balance that against the changes in tile manufacturing time. I can add a section to the model that explores scenarios based on tile manufacturing time and bot working time, including the different seaming times for new to new and new to old tiles. As we get to know the manufacturing times, and our rate of progress in improving reliability, we can keep running simulations on the model to determine the optimum tile replacement strategy.'

'Excellent idea, can you work on that?' Sahko asked Gunadi, and then added: 'Anyone have any other suggestions?' The room remained silent. 'Risk: anyone concerned about any of the risks in what's being proposed? Ibo?'

Ibo looked up. 'Sure I'm concerned about the risk. You should be all aware that setting up a tile factory in the engine room carries risk. There's a lot of delicate and sensitive machinery down there. However, we're in a situation where we have to take risks. I'll do everything I can to ensure the engines don't get damaged and that we can fix the nozzle as soon as possible.'

'Thanks, Ibo. Anyone else?'

Bita moved forward. 'I haven't been able to contribute to solving this problem, but I want to say that we all benefit, especially the children, from keeping the risky stuff away from the inhabited sections of the ship.' There were quite a few nods at this.

'Thank you all for making such good progress,' said Sahko. 'Lots to do still, but at least now we've a good chance of being able to get Main relit in sufficient time.' The meeting started to fragment but Sahko raised her voice again. 'Quiet please. I have one more thing that I would like us to discuss. Agyei.'

Agyei stood and everyone looked at her. She said simply: 'I'm pregnant.'

A moments silence was followed by claps, loud applause and shouts of congratulations. Someone called out: 'And who's the daddy?'

'Bjorn,' Agyei said.

Everyone turned to look at him and he smiled bashfully and went and stood beside Agyei, placing an arm around her shoulder. There were more cries and congratulations.

After a short while, Sahko called for silence. 'My congratulations to you both and we all look forward to welcoming a new crew member in due course.'

She looked genuinely delighted and went over and gave them both a hug and a handshake. I was wondering what she was feeling inside. We always think a little of ourselves in such moments, however well we hide it. I hung back from the crowd around Agyei and Bjorn, who were both beaming and flushed with joy.

In a moment of madness I raised my voice. 'Captain, I have a concern.' The room quietened with a few giggles. 'As you all know, ship's regulations allow for only one child per couple on a voyage. This rule is in place because of the limited room and resources on the ship. It appears as though there has been a breach of ship's regulations in this case.'

The room was completely silent. Sahko turned to look at me, trying to work out if I was serious or not. I could see the fire of fight in her eyes.

'Come on, Menem, this is not the time or place to discuss ship's regulations. If you want to, we can do that later.'

'With respect, Captain, this is the right time because this is the first time the crew have been made aware of this breach and the sooner it is dealt with the better. It is the place because we're all here.'

Sahko's tone darkened. 'Go on, Menem. You've more to say.'

'It seems likely that this breach of ship's regulations was almost certainly known to others and they may have abetted it. Which if they did, they should have brought the matter to the crew's attention at the first possible opportunity.'

'What are you implying, Menem?'

'Bjorn and Agyei almost certainly sought assistance with this pregnancy.'

Yingluq stiffened and took a step towards me. 'Yes, Menem, I gave assistance. I'm definitely in breach of regulations. What do you propose?'

Bita came over and stood beside Yingluq. 'I too gave assistance. As personnel officer, they sought my advice and I encouraged them. I'm also in breach of regulations.'

'I am too,' called out Massoud. 'They wanted me to know so that I could provide the right nutrition. Entirely sensible, Menem.'

I looked at each in turn and then said: 'You should all have informed the Captain of this matter immediately you knew.'

A smile had returned to Sahko's face. 'Bjorn and Agyei came to me before they got started and had talked with anyone else. I suggested they talk it over with Yingluq, Bita and Massoud as a sensible way of facilitating and managing the pregnancy.'

I put on my stiffest voice. 'Regulations are there for a reason. We can't ignore them because we feel like it. That would place all of us and the mission at risk.'

'I agree,' said Sahko, her voice level and calm. 'That's why I asked Agyei and Bjorn to talk with those I did before approving any action. That group constitutes a majority of the crew.'

'Regulations cannot be altered simply because a majority of the crew approve the change. When we signed up to this mission we signed up to a set of regulations. They're in force for the duration of our contracts. Otherwise we don't know how to conduct ourselves. The minority could be walked over without being consulted.' I sensed the hole beneath me getting deeper, but I was already a long way down so I might as well keep going. Maybe I could dig out the other side.

Hyun joined in. 'Ibo and I've discussed a similar matter with Sahko. We've no problem with the majority position.'

Well I was snookered, only Minogue and Gunadi to go. Minogue was nominally second in command and might be able to swing things, so I appealed to him: 'What about you Minogue, are you happy to see ad hoc breaches of regulations?'

'Yeah, well, I'm in a slightly awkward position here. Technically one could say I've been in breach of this rule for at least four years, seeing that I'm the father of two of the children already born on the ship. So I won't be voting for maximum punishment in this case.'

That brought laughter from all around. Deeper and deeper. One more shot.

'Well Gunadi, what about you?'

Gunadi never liked to talk in company so it was unfair of me to appeal to her, however she spoke calmly: 'Never given a fuck for regulations.'

There was a cheer. Even Sahko smiled. I studied the ceiling, calling on higher powers.

Sahko waited for calm and then said: 'Menem is right that ship's regulations must govern our behaviour. However, I will point out that the regulations are entirely at the captain's pleasure. That was also in the contract you all signed up to. The captain considered the matter as follows: it was clear that the action proposed was not in accordance with regulations. However, this ship has the capacity for six children, and we only currently have four. We're also less than four months from the end of our planned voyage, and it seems unlikely that we'll therefore exceed our child carrying capacity, even if the regulation be relaxed equally for everyone. Indeed, one might say that the rule will not be breeched because the birth will not take place before our scheduled arrival. Until now I hadn't heard a single objection to this proposed action. The exact definition of the end of our voyage is not clear. We expect to remain aboard for a considerable time after our arrival, although some of us are likely to be working away from the ship for long periods. I therefore decided on an amendment to the ship's regulations to allow a second child per couple. Does anyone, apart from Menem, have any objections to amending ship's regulations in this way?' There was absolute silence in the room. We could hear one of the children screeching down the corridor.

'Good. I'll amend the regulations and backdate the amendment. Congratulations Agyei and Bjorn.' There was a cheer.

I said stiffly: 'My apologies Agyei and Bjorn. I take the regulations seriously but, in spite of that, I'm delighted for you. New life is very important to all of us. It's that, more than anything else, which keeps me motivated to do my bit to keep the ship running.' Pompous to the last, I turned away. No one wanted to speak to me; I was the spectre at the feast, so I left.

4019, 18:35

I went straight back to my apartment, shut the door and sat on the bed. I tried to organise my thoughts. Why had I done it: spoiled Agyei and Bjorn's moment? Was it my conversation with Ibo that prompted me to contest Sahko? Deep down, I knew why. I opened a drawer and pulled out a private notebook. Automatically I pulled in a picture, the only one I had of Sahko and Mo. I stared at it for a long time and then put it away. I got up and went across to Engineering. There was work to be done and it might help still my trembling.

I started on the planned list of the resources we would need, listing all the items required to set up the structure and services for the factory in the engine room and all those for modifying the hot-bot. I added detail to Bjorn's action plan, refining the order of activities and allocating responsibilities. It took a while before that awful meeting stopped dominating my thoughts. Eventually I got back in the groove. Engineering, the thing I was good at.

After a while I began to lose concentration and became aware of being hungry. I ordered a meal and a service bot soon delivered it. Eating alone, I worked on, getting stuck into the parts that were my responsibility.

The structure for the tile fabrication facility in the engine room should come first. I prepared a preliminary design, using standard components, which I sent off to Ibo, Bjorn, Agyei and Hyun with a list of questions. What equipment did they need for their parts of the process? Did they have the right kit on hand, or could we find it somewhere else? What would need to be fabricated or printed? Did we have the raw materials? If not, what could be cannibalised? Questions, questions, answers leading to more questions. Gradually the details were filled in. Time, the great healer, ticked away.

While I was waiting for answers, I turned to the next item on my list. Archive had all the details of the hot-bot, including a full virtual model of the machine showing how all its components fitted and worked together. The bot used a plug-and-play design inside its hardened casing. A new chassis could be inserted with a more powerful motor and connected up to its arms and legs. The limbs were highly specialised for this application: two arms, handling its unique tools, and four long legs, allowing it to move over and grip the maintenance pyramid inside the engine nozzle.

The pyramid consisted of four latticed towers, all hinged together at one end. The towers were normally stored folded up in a bundle in a long equipment recess on the outside of the engine section. When required, the bundle was pivoted around the end of the ship, rotating right over until its far end was deep inside the nozzle. The four towers then unfolded and latched around the nozzle's lip. The result was a rigid pyramid pointing into the centre of the bell, close to, but not touching it. This allowed the hot-bot to climb on the pyramid and reach anywhere on the nozzle's glassy tiled surface without having to walk on it. It was vital that the pyramid structure and the bot were extremely rigid when cutting out or inserting tiles to avoid creating surface imperfections.

An electric motor inside the bot powered a hydraulic pump to create the pressure used to operate its limbs. My plan was to use a more powerful motor and hydraulic system, but it still had to fit in the bot's hardened casing. There didn't seem to be a functional reason for the special battery used in the current bot. It must have come from the nuclear industry, working to different standards to those used in space-freighters. In our hurried departure there hadn't been time to change it for one of the standard type we used in other equipment. We had probably hoped to never have to use it.

A different motor could use a smaller, more powerful, standard battery, of which we had plenty. That change would free up some space, but the battery would run still down quickly. At the very least it would have to be changed with each tile, swapped over for a recharged one. Maybe a slightly larger battery could be squeezed in to ensure the bot could complete both a tile refitting and a cut-out on each battery cycle. A different battery would require a new recharging station and that would have to be set up near where the bot brought in the old tiles and picked up the new.

Cooling was likely to be a problem with a more powerful motor. A thermal pack inside the bot's body would be needed to absorb the heat. It would have to be changed over at the same time as the battery.

I compiled a list of parts, checking what was available in Stores: batteries, electric motors, pumps, hydraulic pipe and fittings, power circuitry, and cooling packs. All went in to a virtual model of the proposed design, allowing the whole to be tested under realistic, in-use conditions before anything physical was assembled.

Around eleven in the evening, as my eyes were starting to droop and I was losing concentration, I ordered a Stay-Awake. It would flag up on Yingluq's medical system but, as this was an emergency, it would surely be approved automatically. A service bot delivered it, along with a water pouch. I swallowed the pill and took a draught of the water. Within a minute I was feeling sharp again.

Back and forth the work went, between making design tweaks and running simulations. There was a substantially more powerful motor in Stores that would fit inside the casing, but the heat load was proving a problem as I had feared. It was possible to absorb it into a cooling-pack if the pack was placed around the motor, but then the pack couldn't be simply swapped out. The guts of the bot would have to be removed from its casing after each tile operation, which would be both complicated and time-consuming. Ideally the cooling-pack and batteries would slide out together, using the battery access panel already built into the bot's casing. However, if the pack was placed there it wouldn't pick up the heat effectively. I played around with heat pipes to move the heat, but they added a lot of complexity and used up too much space.

Upgrading the hydraulic actuators in each of the bot's legs was also a problem. They too would also cause overheating, potentially distorting the joints. Fins could be added on the outside of the legs to radiate heat away but they would become a snag hazard and it would be difficult to get the heat transferred to them. The heat problem looked intractable, although the rest of the design looked good, delivering the desired uplift in speed.

It was time to work on something else and hope that a solution to the overheating problem would come to me. I looked through the Status logs for what others were up to. Minogue was awake, on watch and still working. Agyei had recently stopped. Hyun, Ibo and Bjorn had all worked on their parts after the meeting but stopped at a reasonable hour. It would be all go again in the early morning.

Mission Day 4020

4020, 00:05

I was feeling restless and strangely energetic. Perhaps the Stay-Awake had been a bit more powerful than I was used to. I needed to burn off some of that energy. Ring-running would help distract me, freeing my mind.

Slipping out of Engineering, I began a slow jog round the Habitat passage, upping the pace after a couple of circuits. All the apartment doors were closed. Everyone except Minogue and I was most likely asleep. Occasionally it felt good to be on a lonely vigil at night: a feeling of freedom and lack of distractions as our little world slept. I ran a fast circuit but then slowed as a light appeared from an open door up ahead that hadn't been there on my last lap. It was from Yingluq's apartment, and she was leaning casually back against the door frame, one leg bent with her foot resting against the door. She was wearing some silky shorts and a loose, cut-off top. The clothes shimmered slightly in the half-light and it was hard to tell whether they were blue or gold.

Coming towards her, I raised my hand in greeting, not intending to stop. She called out in a stage whisper: 'Hello, Menem. I wondered who was pacing the corridor at this hour.'

I slowed to a walk and stopped by her: 'Sorry to have woken you. I thought these doors were soundproof.'

She leaned back and looked at me, appraising. Her eyes seemed bright but slightly sleepy. There was a sheen on her shoulders and her skin was clear and firm over her toned midriff. Her top hung loosely from her breasts. The light from the room behind her haloed her head.

'You didn't wake me. I was expecting you to need to burn off some of that Stay-Awake.' She raised a hand and casually brushed it through her hair which, unusually, was loose and drawn away from her face by two sweeps held in a clasp at the top of her head.

As I turned to go she said: 'Interesting meeting this evening.'

'One might say so. I'm surprised anyone wants to talk to me at the moment. I apologise for what I said.'

'Come on, Menem. We all know you. Actually I quite admired you: taking an unpopular but principled position and sticking with it. You were quite forceful for once.'

'Maybe, but it wasn't a good choice of time and place.'

'Definitely not. But you stood up for something you believed in, which made us all think. Sometimes it gets all a bit easy going around here, too accommodating, a bit too nice. Sometimes we need to be more direct, say what we want, take what we need. Don't you think so?'

She looked me up and down, measuring. She looked away and then back, almost coyly. She played with her hair again, invitingly.

I came closer and we locked eyes. She reached over to me and casually adjusted the neck of my shirt. My fingers pushed her hair back, feeling her warmth. Her hand went behind my neck and up into the hair at the base of my head. I felt pressure from the softness of her hand and the sharpness of her nails. She brushed my chin with the back of a hand, feeling the coarse stubble. We closed up and I bent down towards her, although she wasn't much shorter than me. She tilted her head back and pressed mine forward until our lips met gently, and I felt warmth and softness. My mouth locked with hers and I inhaled her scent: warm, musky, infinitely exciting. Her hands were on either side of my head, holding me steadily for a while before pushing me away. We studied each other, calculating, guessing. There was hunger in her eyes. She took my hand and, freeing herself, led me in to the apartment and shut the door behind us.

Immediately I closed with her, pressing her up against a wall. Bringing my mouth over hers, we began again with kisses long and soft, short and urgent. Exploring and caressing, we stripped each other. I knelt down in front of her and she leaned over me, pressing her breasts to my face. I kissed them and then all down her front. She climbed on me, one leg over my shoulder, opening herself to me and pressing my head into her. Her nails were in my scalp, her scent of musky flesh filled my nostrils and she tasted of the ocean. She took her time and her pleasure.

A large soft couch stood on smooth rug and a table was placed slightly away from a wall with a large mirror behind it. She walked over to the table, stopped, turned and pulled me close for a full throated kiss. Inflamed, I grasped her hips and turned her around. While watching me in the mirror, she lent forward over the table, taking hold of its far edge. Her legs were slightly apart, and she twitched in anticipation. I absorbed her with my eyes, trying to lock her into my memory, relishing the certainty of what lay ahead. Now I was the beast and she my prey. She gasped and started moving, pushing herself back on me, watching me in the mirror. Slowly at first, and then with urgency, I took what I wanted and at last felt the heat rising until it overwhelmed and I lost control.

Shaking from head to toe I lay over her, shattered, exhausted, spent. I kissed the nape of her neck and studied her in the mirror. She looked up and met my gaze. We were both smiling languidly. She reached a hand back and caressed my side. We stayed like that for a while, slowly cooling.

Afterwards we stood and kissed delicately. She whispered in my ear: 'Well that was a nice surprise.'

Looking in her eyes, I said: 'Yes, it was, very, very nice. Thank you, Yingluq.'

'I hope it has done you some good. I rather enjoyed it.'

'I'm glad, very glad.'

'Now I think that you have work to do elsewhere.'

'Yes, but…'

'Time to go, Menem.'

'Perhaps so. I wish we had more time,' I sighed.

'Never enough of that for the things we like best,' she said. I looked around and found my trousers crumpled on the floor. I pulled them on. 'Your shirt is near the door,' she added.

'Yes, yes.' Finding the shirt, I seamed it up, turned around and watched her standing, one knee bent, a foot resting against the wall, one arm raised, a hand lifting her hair away from her damp neck, still completely naked, watching me.

'Sahko has perhaps forgotten what she's missing, so lucky me. That was good.'

I wished she hadn't mentioned Sahko's name. It sent waves through me, mostly of guilt. I went over to Yingluq, couldn't stop myself from cupping one of her breasts and sliding a hand down behind to caress her bottom. 'Thank you, Yingluq. You're gorgeous, spectacular.' I sighed and gazed at her, torn. She pushed me away, brushing me. 'I suppose I must go.' Sighing again, I walked slowly over to the door and opened it.

Glancing back, she was still standing there smiling, still naked. The door closed behind me and I jogged away round the ring. It was almost as though it hadn't happened, but I knew I was spent, so it must have. I also knew I now had the answer to the hot-bot heat problem.

I hurried back to Engineering and pulled up the model of the bot. All I had to do was turn the power unit around, bringing the hydraulic motor close to the cool-pack. The hydraulic fluid would run through a small heat exchanger pressed against the cool-pack which would extract and store the heat. The pipes from the hydraulic pump could be coiled around the electric motor, gathering its heat, and then divide and pass up each of the four legs of the bot. Larger pipes in the legs would reduce heat generation from friction and improve efficiency. They could be attached with thermally conducting glue inside, allowing the legs themselves to radiate a considerable portion of the heat into space. The larger pipes and cooler fluid also had the great advantage that the hydraulic servos and actuator mechanisms operating each of the bot's joints wouldn't need to be replaced: a huge saving in rebuild effort and resources.

Once I had loaded these changes into the model, the thermal simulation ran again. In the worst case, with the bot working hard, the cool-pack still heated up alarmingly quickly, but with a bit more tweaking its size could be increased. The model now showed that the whole bot would stay within working temperature bounds.

The next step was to check the static and dynamic loads caused by the bot. With a more powerful motor, and with a slight increase in weight, it was going to stress its own legs and the pyramid structure considerably more than the old design. I set up the simulations and started to run tests. Using up rated hydraulic pipes, and gluing them to the inner surfaces of the tubes, actually resulted in stiffer legs. The pyramid flexed a bit more when the bot moved, but the data showed that it had been over rated anyway, so that wasn't a problem. There remained an issue with increased flexing of the bot when operating its tools, operations which required great precision. I looked at the control software and realised I hadn't let it retune to the changed loads. Unlocking the control parameters and having the model go through its complete operating envelope allowed the simulator to tune the control parameters, resulting in a considerable improvement in precision. With dynamic parameter adjustment, the controller could adjust the bot's operations for each phase: flexible and relaxed when moving, rigid and precise when cutting and bonding. It was looking good.

Examining wear characteristic simulations showed there was almost certainly going to be a problem with some of the bearings and seals. The bot would require a major maintenance overhaul no later than halfway through, possibly earlier, and maybe more than one. There wasn't room in the legs for bigger bearings and anyway that would upset the dynamics that I had so carefully tested.

It would be difficult to get at the bearings, integral to the structure of each leg joint. Each leg had three joints, two of which had two directions of movement, each of which had a pair of bearings, meaning that forty bearings would have to be replaced each maintenance cycle, along with all the joint seals. The bot would almost certainly become at least slightly radioactive from the time it spent inside the nozzle, making maintenance problematic. The work would have to be done outside, requiring a mimic, preferably in a shielded suit. Not easy.

4020, 06:15

I was sufficiently confident in the bot redesign to start building, sending an order for the parts not in stock off to the print shop. Immediately Hyun pinged back asking how I was getting on. Already morning, the early birds were getting down to work. I messaged Hyun asking if he would like to review my proposals for the bot. He replied that he would come around in a few minutes. I felt stiff, stood and stretched and then feeling hungry, ordered breakfast.

'Hi, Menem.' Hyun put his head around the door.

'Come in, come in. I want to get your thoughts on this redesign.'

'You sound all right this morning.'

'Wonders of a good night's work.'

'Up on a Stay-Awake?'

'Yes. Made some good progress I think. Firstly, I need to apologise to you and everyone for my outburst in the meeting yesterday.'

'Ha, ha, livened things up somewhat. No need to apologise for standing up for something you believe in.'

That sounded rather similar to the words Yingluq had used. Perhaps they all had had a chat about me, once I had stalked out of the meeting. Poor old Menem, must humour him.

Hyun continued. 'Bad timing perhaps, but we all know you, so we listen and think about what you say and why you said it. You're right that the capacity of the ship to support more children is limited and if we have to live on the ship for a long time...' Hyun paused, beginning again on a different tack. 'If there's anything I can do to ease the situation, you know, with Sahko...'

'Thanks, Hyun. I don't think there's anything anyone can do there. Too much time has passed and, well, positions have fossilised. Appreciate your offer though.'

'OK. Well, umm, err, let's review your proposal for the bot.'

We were both grateful to get back on to safer ground. A service bot came in with my meal. Hyun said that he had already eaten, having been on early watch after taking over from Minogue. He sat down beside me, studying the screen, working his way through my proposed changes, nodding his head and asking questions as we ran through the simulation reports.

When we got to the end he said: 'I like it. The heat gain from the extra power seems to be under control. The design has many good features.'

That was quite encouraging from the robotics master. Despite the praise, I did sense a 'but' coming, being aware of at least one, i.e. the bearing maintenance problem.

'Tricky build because the bot is already hot.' Ah, yes, another 'but', and one I hadn't yet considered. 'The body part is simple because the chassis is designed to be removable from the casing and it's only the casing that's hot. However, re-plumbing the hydraulics in the legs will not be so easy. They'll be hot and working on them wasn't planned for. The easiest solution would be to build new legs but we don't have sufficient raw materials to make shielded components like that. We could break down the old legs, separate any hot atoms out and rebuild the legs, but that would take three or four days to complete. Let me take a look at their schematics.'

Hyun pulled up their engineering drawings on another section of screen and studied the cross-section dimensions and the hydraulic connectors from the pipes to the joint motors. He sat completely still and his eyes seemed to be no longer focused on the screen.

After a minute's silence he spoke again. 'We'll use a bot-net. A column could climb up inside the legs and release the hydraulic connector. It could also feed in and connect the new pipes. There's just enough space for them to feel their way around the knee joint and up the lower limb to the foot. The bot-net could also bond the pipes to the sides of the legs and fill the void with thermal transfer foam as it withdrew. Problem solved, don't you think?'

'Wow, yes, that sounds great. If you can get the bot-net to do that, it would be perfect.'

'Oh yes, the bot-net can do that.' Hyun paused again, but not for long. 'There's then the problem of the short life of the leg joints. The bot-net might be able to open the joint covers and use a bearing puller to remove the bearings and insert new ones. However, the force required would take a lot of bot-net elements and they would be working with hot components. If they could survive long enough in that environment then it might be worth the sacrifice, but there's a strong possibility that they wouldn't.' Hyun stared at the screen, flicking back and forth between various images of the bot's joints and their specification data. He shook his head as though trying to rid himself of something troubling. 'This is not an immediate problem, but one we should be confident that we can resolve before we commit to this design solution. I'll think on this, and perhaps you will too. With so little time we should go ahead and build the new chassis in anticipation of a solution.'

'Good. We can let the new parts order I sent to the printer run. You've worked your magic on solving one problem I hadn't even thought about. It would be great if you can think about the maintenance problem too. I'm sure there's a solution to it somehow. Sawing off the old joints and bonding in new ones is one possibility, but that seems a bit drastic.'

'Drastic I agree, but possible. It is definitely a viable solution. It increases my support for going ahead with the upgrade. Good, good, and in the meanwhile, I'll try to find a more elegant solution.'

Hyun got up and left to check the printers.

Status told me what the other members of the crew were up to. Yingluq was with Minogue in Science, running through a series of test simulations on the new tile design. Not much I could add there and it might be best to avoid Yingluq for the moment or I might get carried away again. Agyei was in Chemistry, working on the tile manufacturing equipment, and Gunadi was helping her with its control system. Massoud was working out how to route the necessary environmental services up to the location we had selected for the factory. Ibo was working in the engine room with Sahko and Bita, setting up the structure that Bjorn and I had designed to support the tile factory equipment. Those three were the most adept at working in zero-'g', particularly Bita, who somehow seemed entirely in her element there: twisting and tumbling with balletic grace and control. Bjorn was on his way back from the engine room to the Habitat Ring to collect some equipment and set up a transfer bot to take it down to where it was needed.

A mass of new hot-bot chassis parts was accumulating on my bench which I set up for the assembler. A few minutes later the door opened and Bjorn came in. He was looking purposeful, wearing a brown and red ship-suit. He rather abruptly asked if I needed anything from Stores because he was rearranging them to get at some kit Agyei needed.

'Not for now, thanks, all the parts required for the hot-bot upgrade are here or being printed, so nothing extra from Stores for a while at least.' I paused and it looked as though he was turning to go so I quickly stood to face him and went on: 'Look Bjorn, I apologise for what I said in the meeting yesterday. It wasn't intended in any way as a criticism of you and Agyei, but well, it didn't come out right.'

'It's OK, Menem. We understand. It was principled of you, I realise that,' he said in a cold voice.

Bjorn strode directly over to me, coming in close so I automatically backed off. He came closer and stared down into my eyes. I felt his steady gaze and could see his muscles tense. He was a big man, and I suddenly felt fear.

He said very calmly directly in my face, his eyes boring into mine: 'But, Menem, if you ever again choose to make Agyei part of your power games with Sahko I shall tear you limb from limb. Do I make myself clear?' I blinked and found my throat dry but the back of my neck wet with sweat. 'Do I make myself clear, Menem?' he repeated.

I nodded weakly and croaked 'Yes, sorry Bjorn. Sorry.' I managed to break from his gaze and looked down at the floor.

'OK, Menem. I've said my piece and I don't want to fall out with you, but you need to know where I stand.' He stepped away and relaxed. 'Right, now we can be friends again.' Back to the old kind, reliable Bjorn. 'Let's get back to work, huh? We all need you to pull this ship back together, that includes me and mine. You may be an idiot sometimes, but if anyone can fix the shit we're in, it's you. Appears as though you're on it,' he said, looking at the workbench with its heaps of parts.

'Err, yes, this is for the upgraded hot-bot. It can be done. Hyun has reviewed the design and made a couple of good suggestions.' The shaking in my hands was dying away.

'Great. Anything I can do to help here?'

'Well I was going to ask you about using the mimic to do maintenance work on the legs. The simulations show that the bearings won't hold up long with the additional loads from the up rated drive. We're going to need to change them at least once during the tile replacement. The big problem is that the legs will be radioactive by then, so we would need a radiation suit for the mimic or a set of disposable long-arms and hands for it to keep its body far enough away. Hyun is trying to think up another way to get around the problem, but if he doesn't, then you're the mimic master, so we'll need your help.'

'Sure. We don't need to sort this immediately?'

'No, it's not an immediate problem; we have a couple of days to think it over. Our default option is to cut each of the joints out and fix in new ones. That's a workable solution but there must be a better method.'

'Fine, I'll give it some thought too. By the way, Ibo has set up a zip-wire in the engine room which makes it much easier to get equipment and people up to the tile factory. We also have a platform bot set up in the keel for the same purpose. You won't have to float around to get there any more.'

'That's very welcome. I'm always clumsy in zero-'g'. Bet Bita won't use them though.'

'No, definitely not. She's really beautiful in zero-'g': flies like a bird and swims like a fish. Don't tell Agyei that I said Bita was beautiful, by the way.'

'I won't cause any more trouble there than I already have. So there's only the vomit inducing 'g'-to-zero-'g' transition to manage.'

'You still have a weak stomach? Take a pill.'

'Been doing that a bit too much recently.'

'Stay-Awake?'

'Yup.'

'Don't overdo it. Not helpful.'

'Work to do.'

'Get others to help. You don't need to do the mimic jobs, and definitely ease off on the meds. Better leave you to it.'

Bjorn seemed to have relaxed as he left. I couldn't remember having physically feared anyone on board before. He was more powerful even than Avalos had been.

I set up the main assembly station and put it to work on the hot-bot chassis. A service bot collected parts from the printer, fed them into the finisher and, when they were ready, placed them within reach of the assembler. The machines would alert me to any problems, so didn't need watching. I had to get around and see the others, deciding to look in on Agyei next.

I cautiously opened the door to Chemistry and looked in. There was a sharp, astringent smell and the lighting was dim. Agyei, wearing an overall and head mask connected to a powered air filter, was bent over a tank that emitted a strange blue glow. She waved me to come in and pointed to hooks that contained similar overalls and head masks. I took a set, put them on and came across.

'What do you think of this?' She pointed to the glowing tank, her voice, although muffled by the mask, registering excitement.

I looked through a clear panel in the top of the vessel and saw, floating in the centre, a large wire frame around a flat, darkly-translucent block, the frame connected to a mechanism above. Below the block was an intense light, which eventually, as my eyes adjusted, I made out to be flashing an image on the block's underside.

'It's working, it's a new tile forming,' said Agyei. 'The frame is being lifted from the fluid, and the light is catalysing the formation of the crystals on its underside using an imaging system, rather as Massoud had proposed. This is so much faster than the old process. The reaction conditions are very sensitive though: lots of variables need to be precisely controlled, which is what all this stuff does.' Agyei waved her arm around to include an array of equipment that surrounded the tank. 'Gunadi was a genius in getting it to stabilise.'

'Wow, so the new tiles can actually be made. Let's hope they work as well as the old ones did, then we might actually be able to repair the nozzle and get back on track. That's great news, Agyei. Is it ready for production?'

'Coming on. I'm working this tile up to the full thickness of the crystal layer and will then try pulling it faster for the structural polycrystalline backer underneath. Assuming that part goes well, and it's supposed to be the less critical bit, it then has to be tested. Strength tests, for example, to see if it can bear being handled, as the simulations show it will be. We'll also have to test the edge bonding. Finally there are tests to make sure that it actually deflects high energy gamma rays and neutrinos. As we keep saying, simulations are one thing, the real world can be another, but my confidence is growing along with that tile. It's looking possible that the process will be ready to go in to production in a couple of hours, maybe a bit longer depending on the testing.'

'Then we can ship this lot down to the engine room and set it up there?'

'Bjorn is standing by to do that. He looks in now and again, checking up on me, I think.'

'Hmm, he looked in on me a little while ago.' I paused. 'Agyei, about last night's meeting, I apologise for what I said. I didn't mean it to be an attack on you and Bjorn. I'm sorry if it came out that way.'

'We've worked together long enough. I know you. You like things clear and open, and maybe we sneaked around a bit about this.'

'That's understandable,' I said. 'We've been isolated as a group out in space a long time now and sensitivities have developed. Bjorn knows how delicate these things can be. He was worried that I might have upset you.'

'He can be quite protective.'

'Yes, he was quite clear with me. Anyway, I'm sorry I got a bit wound up after your announcement.'

'Thanks for your apology, but there's no need. I can understand you being upset.'

I turned away.

Agyei put an arm around me. 'Menem, we all feel for you. I never understood why Sahko didn't want to try again.'

'Me neither. Well perhaps I do. We've both spent too much time in space, I suppose. After what happened I was then keen on getting as much help from Yingluq as possible. We argued about that. Then we started getting problems with the ship and I was busy.'

I didn't understand why I was suddenly unburdening myself to Agyei. She was naturally sympathetic, and once I had started I couldn't stop myself. Somehow articulating my swirling thoughts helped solidify them in to some kind of order, as though rehearsing an argument to be presented to a judge.

'The death of Avalos had previously affected Sahko badly. After Mo, she felt she was losing control and had to get a grip on the mission. I tried to help, but she became cold with me. She saw her personal feelings and desires as impediments to our success. She began to see the mission as her legacy. It was going to write her name into the history books along side Gagarin, Armstrong, Chang and Patel. Maybe the commander of the first mission to another planetary system would be an even greater place in history than first into space or to walk on the Moon, Mars or Enceladus.'

Agyei was silent for a while, looking at me. 'I don't think I've ever heard you talk like that, about that.' She paused again. 'I'm not quite sure you're right about Sahko. Yes, much of it, but I don't think she has suppressed her feelings quite that much, and I don't think she thinks a lot about her place in history. We won't be the first to walk on an extra-solar world, even if we come to a halt in the Alpha System first. We don't have the means to get back, even if we could land on a planet. It will be someone in Fleet, probably from the Indian Federation, seeing that their ship is leading, who will walk there first.'

She paused again. 'Look, Menem, when we're past this immediate crisis and the repair is underway, if you won't talk directly to Sahko you really need to see Bita. You're going to explode if you don't unwind a bit, and none of us wants that, not least because the ship won't hold together without you. Please talk to Sahko or Bita, do it for me, do it for my unborn child.' She looked pleadingly at me, searching my eyes.

I looked back. 'Yeah, you're probably right, Agyei. I do get wound up a bit sometimes. Maybe some meds or some counselling could help.'

'Don't think of it as a problem that can be fixed with a bit of adjustment. And don't overdo the meds. You had a Stay-Awake last night, didn't you?'

'Lots to do. Made good progress last night.'

'Don't overdo the meds, Menem, those things can really mess with you. Talk to Bita, she's a really good listener. She has helped me a lot.'

'Yeah.' It took me a moment to realise what she had said. 'Agyei, I can't believe you've had too many troubles.'

'We all have our share, from time to time. But times are good for me at the moment.'

'I'm glad of that at least. Thanks for listening and for your understanding. Oh, and great work here. Together we're going to get through this.'

'If we can keep it together, yes, we are. By the way, have you ever seen the tile material?'

'Not directly, no. Is it interesting?'

'There's a sample on the bench there. Pick it up. It's quite safe.'

A rectangular grey block, about ten centimetres by five by two, lay on the bench. It looked like a lump of dull steel. I put my hand on it and it was warmer to the touch than a metal would be. I went to pick it up and found it glued to the bench.

Agyei laughed. 'It's amazingly heavy, isn't it? Fortunately the tiles are much thinner than that sample. The crystal is a complex matrix with a lot of Tantalum and Bismuth in it, as well as some Actinides. You can see why we don't carry much spare feedstock.'

She turned back to her tank and her face was illuminated by that ethereal blue glow again. I took off the chemical suit and mask and left.

4020, 08:40

I walked around to Analytics. Gunadi's door signalled that she was in and disturbable so I stuck my head around the door. 'Hi, Gunadi. Can I come in?'

Gunadi was curled up in her high-backed command chair, with her legs tucked under and the huge curved screen encasing her in its glow. She made a few gestures and a portion of the screen flickered. She looked at me and smiled.

'Hi, Menem, come in. I'm tuning some simulations for Minogue. They need to run for a minute or two. Good to see you.'

'Nice of you to say so. I want to apologise for my behaviour in the meeting last night.'

She was the fifth crew member to whom I had apologised. It was a custom of the ship to make a round and apologise individually to everyone when one had screwed up. It was painful, but helped clear the air.

'I found it quite funny really. I hadn't seen you like that before, standing up to Sahko for a change. Usually you're a bit of a wet blanket around her.'

That was a bit surprising from Gunadi who was usually reluctant to say anything personal.

'Well I'm sorry. It put you in the spotlight. I hope I didn't embarrass you.'

'Cool it, Menem. Sorry I wasn't able to help you out. The rulebook isn't my thing: had to follow too many rules when I was in the military and they weren't always the right ones. Anyway if Agyei and Bjorn want another kid, good for them. The children keep the ship lively, less time for introspection. You should have a kid, Menem. It might help you to be a bit less uptight.'

'Yes, well, I tried.'

'That was a long time ago: nine years, isn't it? Things are a bit different now that we're getting closer. It's time to think beyond the mission. You're good with the kids; they're always talking about what you did with them in my sessions.'

Somehow I had never thought of Gunadi with the children. My image of her was as she appeared now, in the high-backed chair with a big screen arrayed around her. I wondered what she taught them: hacking perhaps.

'The children do that to everyone: comparing classes. It seems to be a bit of a game with them, trying to get the adults to compete.' I paused for a moment before continuing. 'I would like to have children, or at least one.'

'You're a nice guy, Menem.'

'Maybe, one day. How about you?'

'Maybe.'

Something flickered on a screen behind her, she half turned, made some gestures and a keypad appeared on which she briefly typed, her fingers long and delicate.

'Looks like you're needed again. Thanks, Gunadi.'

She didn't turn back but raised one hand in acknowledgement and stared intensively from one part of the screen to another, and then started typing and gesturing again.

Status told me that Yingluq had left Minogue and that he was alone. I walked back around the ring to Science. The door was open and Minogue was lying back on a couch staring at the ceiling.

'Hi, Minogue. So this is how scientists work is it: having great thoughts while staring at nothing?'

'These ceiling tiles contain all the knowledge of the universe, if only we look at them in the right way,' he said as he sat up. 'Come in, old man, and tell me how you're getting on.'

'Well, first I want to apologise for my behaviour in the meeting yesterday.'

Minogue cut in. 'Formal apology accepted even if there's no need for formality with me. You know how I like it: free and easy, say what you think, no burdensome obligations. That's one of the reasons I came on this adventure. Despite all your talk of contracts and regulations they are meaningless out here. We have no one to enforce them but ourselves and as we're never going back to Earth there's no long term threat of sanctions. Our rules are what we choose. Ones imposed by outsiders hold no sway here.'

It made me think about Minogue, fathering children with both Yingluq and Bita. I wondered how they all felt about that triangle. Then I felt guilty about my own infidelity, but tried justifying it to myself by thinking that at least I wasn't fathering lots of children like some ancient potentate. Then I felt guilty for thinking about Minogue like that. No one was more open and honest than Minogue and I couldn't recall seeing or hearing him pressurising anyone to do anything.

'The trouble with you, Menem, is that you think too much. You can get caught up in your own arguments. You should relax more.'

Why was everyone telling me to relax more?

'I didn't intend that my statement would put you on the spot,' I said.

'That was very funny. I hadn't thought about it before, that I was in breach of ship's regulations. Like Gunadi, I couldn't give a fuck.

Interesting choice of word that under the circumstances. Sahko was pissed with you though. You were questioning her captaincy and trying to recruit the crew to your side in an open meeting. Not clever. I'm looking forward to seeing how you get out of that one.' He laughed and jumped to his feet.

'Now let me tell you about how your brilliant science team has made another giant leap for mankind. Well, I say team because I shall be claiming some of the credit for the idea in a paper we're going to write, but really it was Yingluq's idea. Never give all the credit to your number two, eh, because it's the leader who sets up the conditions for them to display their brilliance, the leader who asks the right questions to inspire them, yadda, yadda. You've heard that speech from me before, but don't say that I don't give credit where credit is due, blah. Well here's the thing: the intensity of the radiation from the engine is much less at the outer edge of the nozzle than it is down near the annihilation point, and the angle of incidence and reflection of the radiation is much greater as well. We, that is Yingluq, realised that as a result, the pure crystal layer of the tiles near the edge of the nozzle can be much thinner than it has to be for ones much nearer the annihilation point. Gunadi has simulated the tiles and the layer could be one tenth as thick. Agyei can tune the crystal layer thickness accordingly, although we probably wouldn't want to go that thin on the outer tiles because the bonding-in becomes more difficult if the crystal layer is too thin. Gunadi has finished optimising the trade-off and calculated the overall saving. The outer tiles can be made in about ten minutes. So there you have it. It all comes down to how quickly the hot-bot can work. So tell me, how have you got on?'

'We've made some good progress too. Hyun and I are upgrading the hot-bot. It should work as well as we envisaged yesterday, with one exception: we'll need to take at least one break for maintenance, perhaps halfway through replacing the tiles. The leg bearings won't hold up for the whole job, we think. How long their replacement will take depends on how we do the work, and we're still looking for the best way to do that. It could be a twelve-hour job.'

'So sort of good and bad news. Overall that suggests we're getting close to having solid plans to meet our seven-day engine-off target, except for the tile refiner.'

'Looks like that's the best we can achieve and it requires us to start production by tomorrow morning at the latest. The new bot chassis should be finished by midday today and then all the parts have to be taken outside and up to the front for installation. We hope to have the upgrade finished by midnight tonight. I haven't yet had time to think about upgrading the tile breakdown kit. That's next.'

'Well it sounds as though you've come a long way already. Don't overdo it, Menem. I know you were up all night last night, presumably on a Stay-Awake.'

'You too? I noticed you were here late into the night.'

'I was on watch until the middle of the night, and then went to bed. I sleep a bit during the day. Those things aren't good for us. Don't want to use them too often.'

'So everyone keeps saying, but I'm going to have to use one again tonight. When tile replacement is running smoothly I can sleep.'

'Be careful, Menem. Let others take the load when they can. We don't want to try to survive without you, now we've come so far and are getting close.'

'Fortunately, I'm not needed to help install the tile factory in the engine room. I saw that Sahko and Bita were working on getting the infrastructure set up down there and Bjorn and Massoud have been helping with logistics and services. Everyone is working on this.'

'And we have to keep the other ship's functions running and look after the children as well.'

'I've missed a couple of my shifts with them. I have a lot of making up to do.'

'It's OK, Sahko is managing the schedule.'

'I'm in yet deeper with her.'

'Talk to her, Menem. Talking helps.'

'I'll try.'

'Not try, do.'

'Yeah. OK, thanks Minogue. Great work here, genius stuff. That's one big load off anyway.'

'Ha, ha, yes it is, yes it is. Oh, and by the way, I had a look at the tile deconstruction device: it's a fairly general purpose tool. My first thought would be to tune it up for the specific task we're using it for. Talk to Agyei when she's done with the tile fabricator design, also Massoud might be able to help as he's in charge of recycling which is mostly breaking down old molecules.'

'Massoud, there's a thought. I'll talk to him as well as Agyei. She seemed quite busy when I looked in on her, but close to getting the tile fabricator to work. I think she'll have Bjorn start moving the kit, once you and she are happy with the sample tests.'

'I plan to go over there soon.'

'Oh, I wanted to ask: how are you going to test the tiles' performance?'

'Simple. As I suggested: gamma radiation from Fizz, neutrinos from Fuse. I checked, and it can be done. Even Ibo will allow it. We measure the pressure on the tiles.'

'Glad you understand that, well above my pay-grade. So you don't need me to fabricate anything for the testing?'

'No, thanks. Ibo has all the kit we need it seems.'

'Good, I'm glad of that. Must go. See you later. We'll get it fixed, yes we will.'

Minogue was collecting up something as I left. I checked Status and saw that Massoud was back in Food Prep, next door to the refectory. I let him know I was planning to drop in, so he greeted me when I came in his door.

'Hi, Massoud. I've a question for you, actually a couple of questions, but first I want to apologise for my outburst in the meeting yesterday. It was wrong of me.'

Massoud came over and, standing directly in front of me, he placed his hands on my elbows and tilted his head back and looked at me. 'No need to apologise to me, my friend. It was not wise of you, it's true, but we know you've been under a lot of strain recently. The ship gets old and cranky, and maybe the emotional nature of the announcement upset you more than anyone realised. But it was not wise to go against our good captain Sahko in a crew meeting like that. You need to talk to her one-to-one about this and many other things. I doubt that you've apologised to her yet.'

'No, Massoud, I haven't, and I dread doing so.'

'That doesn't surprise me either, but, you know, the longer you leave it...'

'But there's so much I have to do to get the mission back on course.'

'We all want that, but you cannot wait that long. You must apologise to Sahko as soon as possible, or you'll be thinking about it all the time. The thought will grow in you and occupy too much of your mind, when we need you focussed. Go to her after you've finished what you came to say to me. Don't delay any more.'

'I'm not sure I can.'

'You will. Now, what was it that brought you to my door apart from an unnecessary apology?'

'Well, as you know, we have to break down the old tiles once they have been cut out, and we want to speed up that process.'

'Recycling: one of my specialities.'

'We need a faster process.'

'Let us have a look at the specification of the tile material and the machine that's used for this purpose.'

Massoud pulled up the engineering data and drawings of the refining machine and tiles.

'The tile material I know well. It's a complex crystalline ceramic with fairly simple chemistry, effectively a single molecule with known and very pure properties. Interestingly made from all heavy elements to maximise quark density: Yingluq's trees in a plantation. OK, and the machine is a broad-element ionisation spectrometer sorting instrument. It's a standard machine and the parts are interchangeable with other similar machines on the ship used for recycling. According to the information here, it hasn't been tuned to recycle the tile material so by no-means optimises throughput. Much could be done to speed up the process for this specialised application.'

'Minogue thought you might be able to help, and it looks as though he was right.'

'Minogue is a very clever man, and sometimes astute too. I can help perhaps. If you leave this with me I'll come up with a list of suggestions for refinements. I'm not so good at the engineering; we have others on board who can do that, even you perhaps. I'll give you details of how the machine might be tuned to increase throughput, and you, or someone else, will have to rebuild it. Is that fair?'

'That would be fantastic, Massoud. How long do you think it might take you? Are you still sorting out the services in the engine room?'

'Fortunately services in the engine room were not a big problem because they're all there anyway: power and coolant in abundance, high-speed links to the main core, pure and waste water connections. All I had to do was arrange routing of the required services to the proposed location of the tile factory, and Ibo had ideas about that anyway. Fortunately others were able to do the work. Like you, I recall, I do not relish moving back and forth between 'g' and zero-'g'.'

'Sensitive stomach?'

'Indeed. We refined have sensitive stomachs.' He paused and looked down at his, then continued: 'Give me a couple of hours. I regret meals today may not be very original, but then the crew doesn't seem to have time to sit down properly to enjoy them at the moment. Originality in that department can wait until everything is fixed, and we've time on our hands again. Now, my friend, come with me.'

He got up and took one of my elbows, guiding me out the door. I wondered what he was doing and then realised. I felt like the condemned man being escorted to the scaffold. I wondered if I could make a run for it but Massoud's grip was secure.

We walked back around the ring again, this time to Operations. The door slid open as we arrived and Massoud almost threw me inside. The door swished shut behind me.

4020, 09:25

Ops was dimly lit: a few harsh spots shone straight cylinders of light down onto the black polished floor and it was the back light from these, along with a massive illuminated star map covering one wall and a large curved information screen, partially hidden from my view, that revealed the austere room. A black, high-backed swivel chair on a raised platform faced the screen. Other similar chairs were arrayed around it, each facing their own screen, all of which were currently un-lit. It had been quite a while since I had been in here and it seemed to have become much colder, darker and more stripped back. There was silence in that room. I couldn't even hear the usually ever-present susurrus of air circulation. If Sahko was there she must be in the chair facing away from me, but she hadn't turned around.

'What do you want?' Her voice was neutral. There was no hint of her mood, or even if she knew who had entered the room.

I willed my voice to work, to use that same neutral tone. 'I came to apologise,' I said quietly, and then stopped.

'Go on.'

'My apologies, Captain, for my inappropriate remarks in the crew meeting yesterday. I meant disrespect neither to you nor to Agyei and Bjorn. I should have raised my concerns privately with you, Captain, at some other time.'

Slowly her chair swung around until it faced directly towards me. She sat completely still, hands in her lap, her head erect. She was clothed from head to feet in black. Her black hair framed tightly to her face with a single curl loose, curving forward below her cheek bone. The skin of her hands and face was pale, only her hazel eyes showed any colour. She stared at me with a stillness and intense concentration that unnerved me.

'Engineer, sometimes you're a fool and speak without thought. I accept your apology.'

We stared silently at each other. What was she thinking, I wondered? She hadn't always been so hard for me to read.

She stood up, stepped down off the platform, and came over. We were separated only by one of the cones of light. 'Look, Menem,' she said softly, 'I know you have a lot on your plate: the ship getting old requiring more maintenance and the unexpected object field causing so much damage. I need you more than ever to keep it together. We all have our parts to play, but at the moment we're particularly reliant on you to get us through these problems. I need to have you with me, and not fighting against me.'

'I'm…, am sorry Sahko…, so sorry,' my speech stumbling. 'Sometimes I find it so hard…, and yesterday's announcement…, although I knew it was coming, it got to me.'

'Not so easy for either of us.' She was silent for a while, holding me with her stare.

I looked her in the face and caught a glimpse of vulnerability. 'Do you ever think about her?' I asked quietly.

'Mo?'

'Yes.'

'Often.' She looked away briefly and when her stare returned to me her eyes glistened.

'So do I. Everyday.'

'Do this for her, Menem. Get this ship back together for Mo, for all of us.'

'Yes, Sahko, I will.'

She looked at me for a while longer and then turned, went back to her chair and swivelled it until I could no longer see her. Realising that I'd been dismissed, I went to the door, but before it opened, she spoke into the darkness:

'Menem, let's talk some more when the engine is back running again.'

'I would like that, Sahko.'

She said nothing else, so I opened the door and left. Once outside, I found I was shaking. I hurried on to Engineering, not going back to

Communications where Bita now was, and to whom I must speak soon. I needed a few minutes alone first.

I glanced at the assembler and it had almost finished work on the bot chassis. New parts had come in from Printing and been incorporated. I checked Status, and saw that Agyei was still engaged with testing the tile manufacturing plant and Gunadi was still working on the quantum-field modelling for the tile thickness variations that Minogue wanted. Hyun was taking a class with the children, but he had left some notes on options for replacing the bot leg bearings. It wasn't clear to me what he had in mind. Everyone else was getting on with what they had to do.

I sorted through some reels of hydraulic piping that were suitable for upgrading the hot-bot and started cutting off the required lengths and forming the fittings at each end. That made me think of the thermal compound we would need to fix it in place. I pulled up the bot's leg schematics and had calculations made on the required volume of the compound and checking what precursor chemicals were involved. Status told me that they were in stock, so I reserved sufficient and placed an order with Chemistry to have the compound made up. Agyei would see the order, but I hoped that it was relatively straightforward and could be made without requiring her intervention.

The tension in my muscles had faded and I had actually made another small step along my very lengthy task list. I messaged Bita to let her know I wanted to call, and she acknowledged, so I went back around the ring to Communications.

Bita's domain was a complete contrast to the austerity of Operations. Here it was all warmth and bright colours. Children's drawings featured on one wall, somehow artfully arranged to make an attractive collage. The furniture was soft and inviting. There were even some objects that looked like flowering plants, but I doubted they were real, and they certainly shouldn't have been on board if they were. One wall was occupied by a screen that was intended to show all the communications flows, both within the ship and between the ship, Fleet and Earth, but for now it displayed an image of a misty landscape with a flowering meadow in the foreground. Like her room, Bita looked bright and clean, her long legs in chintzy harem pants and she had a loose short jacket over a loud T-shirt with some hippy slogan on it of a type that she usually favoured. She wore no shoes and her mass of chestnut hair was piled loosely on her head, held in place with a couple of fake old fashioned pencils.

'Hi, Bita. I saw that you were back from the engine room. Thanks for helping out down there.'

'All hands to the pump and, you know me, any excuse to be in zero-'g'.'

'I'm glad you like it. I'm rather clumsy.'

'You need to learn a few things. Perhaps I could give you a lesson.'

'That would be good, when we're not quite so busy. Anyway that wasn't what I wanted to talk to you about. I'm here to apologise for my remarks in the meeting yesterday.'

'Thank you for the apology. I can appreciate that the announcement must have been a bit of a shock to you, and perhaps it stirred up some deep feelings.'

'It shouldn't have. Bjorn had told me before the meeting.'

'Did he? That was good of him. Still, something set you off.'

'Please don't say it was because I'm under a lot of pressure at the moment, I've had a lot of that today.'

'That could have been a contributing factor. You do have a lot on your plate, but you usually cope with that. Why do you think you decided to say what you did?'

Bita looked at me with her large dark eyes, studying the expression on my face, which I immediately tried to control, no doubt with little effect.

'I've been trying to work that out. I didn't think that I really cared that much about the regulations. At least I never thought I did, but perhaps I care more as I get older. Anarchy is not so far away in a small crew, far from home, with the risk of us losing our bearings. Minogue pointed out that there is no external power able to enforce contracts and regulations. Some might say that I wanted Agyei and Bjorn to be Sahko and I.'

'Simple stuff, eh?' She looked at me with a laugh in her eyes. 'Is that what you've been hearing from our crew of pop-psychologists?'

She got up and started wandering around the room, moving in her bare feet like a ballet dancer. She took off her jacket and laid it over a chair. Her T-shirt outlined her breasts and its slogan read 'Get Real!' in large hand written letters. She bent over and smelled one of the flower objects.

'Are those things real?' I asked, staring at her.

She looked at me without straightening and grinned. 'These flowers?'

'Yes, the flowers.'

'Everything you see is real. Massoud and I have a secret passion for them. I expect that live plants are against ship's regulations too. Do they bother you?'

'They're definitely against ship's regulations if they're real, a massive bio-hazard that could be an ecological disaster for the Alpha System. They're very beautiful though. I'll have to assume they're not doing any harm.'

'They can be distracting.'

'They can, to those who see beauty there.'

'I like you, Menem. In some ways you're a very simple straightforward guy. I'm supposed to be the one who fixes the crew, like you fix the ship. However, the human mind is so complex and so ever changing that it's not amenable to a screwdriver or a glue-gun. The best I can hope to do is to nudge someone a little, and hope that the push I gave helps them find their way, and doesn't send them spinning out of control.'

'Don't you find that depressing, not being certain about what to do, and not being able to know if what you've done, or are going to do, will help?'

'Not at all. I love the infinite variety and flexibility of the human mind. Occasionally I feel as though I have really helped someone, and that's a great reward. Most of the time it's fun being with people, talking with them and learning about them. But like any task you set your mind to, it can have its frustrations and failures. Sometimes, when I would really like to help someone, I can't find the right way.'

'Like Avalos?'

Bita remained silent, picked up her jacket and put it back on. She came close to me and said: 'You used a Stay-Awake last night didn't you?'

'Yes.'

'And you're planning to do that again tonight?'

'Yes.'

'We need you to fix the ship, Menem, but not to kill yourself. I'll talk to Yingluq, and Sahko if necessary. No more after tonight, until you've recovered from these.'

'I can't promise, Bita. You know that. The ship may require me awake.'

'What else needs fixing, Menem?'

'Well, Agyei thinks we can get the tiles made and the hot-bot upgrade is underway, but it's going to need a rebuild halfway through, and we haven't yet worked out how to do that. We also need to upgrade the tile refiner, which I haven't started on, but Massoud has some ideas he's working through. We also have to fix the fuel pipe and related damage. Once all those are done, we may be able to get Main running again. There are a couple of other things, that have come to light in the past few days, that I must look at sooner rather than later, like the rotation motor problem. That little issue of the water loss has reminded me not to let problems fester.'

'Can't Agyei do most of those things?'

'Maybe, some, but she has her own responsibilities, not least is managing the building of so many tiles, which is a very complicated and exacting task. This trouble has disrupted a lot of things. She'll have depleted chemical stocks to replace at the very least, and besides she's pregnant, crawling in confined spaces is not ideal.'

'Once we're underway, I want you to have a thorough physical with Yingluq.'

That made me think of last night when Yingluq and I had given each other a pretty thorough physical investigation. I tried to think of something else and looked at Bita's pretty flower. Had she smuggled seeds aboard?

'And then I want you to come and see me, and we can have a proper session. You haven't had an evaluation from me for a long time. You've been putting it off.'

'Yes, well, busy, you know.'

'Getting your thoughts in order could well help calm you, make you more efficient, and help you get through your tasks.'

'I know, I know. I'll try.'

'Not try, Menem, you will. I'll have you brought to me if necessary.'

I thought of Massoud frog-marching me to Sahko's door.

'OK, Bita, I promise. I'll come and see you for an evaluation, once we're running again.'

I got up and went to the door.

'Thanks for coming by, Menem. Good to see you.'

She gave me one of her beaming smiles. She had such a beautiful broad smile that lit up her face. I was tempted to rush back and kiss her, but instead I smiled and left.

One more call to make and my apology penance would be done. I checked Status, and found that Ibo was still in the engine room. I used the video link instead.

'Well hi, Menem. Do want to see what we've been up to?'

'Yes, but first I need to apologise for what I said in the meeting yesterday.'

Ibo rocked back and laughed. 'Oh, you is a bad boy, a verrry bad boy. You love playing games with the Captain don't you? Only you play verbal games and not real games. Don't apologise to me. I was worried that it might have been as a result of our little conversation and you decided that was the way to be a man with her, like I told you. You gota sort that out soon or I shall be after you with a big stick, so you watch out. Now forget about all that for a moment and take a look at this manufacturing plant that's making a mess of my nice clean engine room. Let me show you what we've done.'

Her camera panned around showing her rest area. She must have been sitting in one of the chairs. She got up and started walking.

'The transport bot brings the equipment in here and puts it on this platform which pulls itself along the zip-wire to the station we've set up, where we looked yesterday.'

The camera showed a pair of thick, braided wires running dead straight from a structural support near the keel bulkhead door to the far corner of the nozzle. The airlock was no longer visible. What looked like a tent had been fixed over a part of the engine room void, just beneath the skin of the ship.

'Let me take you up there.'

Ibo stood on the platform and glided smoothly, well clear of the engine, up to the tent, where it slowed to a stop. She pulled on a tab and stepped in to the tent, which was much larger than it had looked from the floor, enclosing a space bigger than one of the Habitat Ring control rooms. It had been fitted with a sticky floor for grip in zero-'g', a small table and a negative-pressure work chair. Along what appeared as the back of the room, but was actually the skin of the ship, ran a substantial lattice beam, to which some equipment was attached. Above the beam there were pipes, cables, fibres and lights.

'You've been busy,' I said. 'That looks great. It's a bigger space than I expected.'

'Glad you like it, Agyei checked it out and told me the minimum size she needed and we managed a bit more than that. I had lots of help getting it together. Sahko and Bita fixed it up, and Bjorn brought down most of the kit from Stores. Massoud sorted out the services. I'm waiting on Hyun to deliver a general-purpose robot arm, so the whole operation can be automatic and he's on his way now. Agyei says she'll be finished testing very soon, and then be able to start shipping all the manufacturing kit down here. She says it will take quite a while to get it set up again, tested and ready to go. We're expecting it to be a late night.'

'Great work. Minogue said you are handling the testing of the tiles.'

'Yes, I am. That's serious stuff. I don't want anyone else messin' with Fizz and Fuse, and I want to see for myself that these tiles will work as advertised. It's all done outside by the bot-net.'

'We would all be reassured with your stamp of approval on them. Go back to your rest while you can. Sorry to have disturbed you. I may be down later, if I can be useful. Lots still to do up here for me.'

'I ain't resting. I'm monitoring a tile test that's happening right now. Keep in touch, Menem.' She clicked the link off suddenly. Perhaps the test had finished or Hyun had arrived.

Having finished my round of apologies, I felt beat and in need of a short rest. I flattened one of the chairs in Engineering and closed my eyes for a nap.

4020, 11:30

The buzzing in my ear started again. I was feeling terrible, my eyes gummed up and my mouth dry. I realised I was in Engineering, and been sleeping in my chair, but for how long? The clock said I had been out for half an hour. The buzz went again, someone was calling: Massoud.

'Hi Massoud, sorry to have been slow, I was taking a nap.'

'So you set everyone to work and then you're able to nap. You should be the captain.' He gave a big laugh.

'So tell me about it.'

'Sorry? Oh yes, the tile material refiner. It's a standard recycler, of which we use several and indeed have a couple of spares. One option would be to double-up and use a second machine. However, the machine out there should be able to run at way more than twice the current throughput if it's tuned to this special application. I've made a file in Status with some suggestions for modifications which should give something of an improvement. Most of this is simple stuff that Gunadi can programme into the control system, but some parts will need hardware changes, and to get the best out of it, it will need more power. I've checked and the line we provided to the tile plant can supply the extra needed but heavier duty cables will be required through the ship's hull from there. If you like what I'm suggesting, and if you think that the reengineering is within your sleep-deprived capabilities, let me know. In payment, I want a blow-by-blow account of your meeting with Sahko. That will be something to tell my grandchildren about.' He gave another huge laugh and cut the link.

He didn't even have children, let alone grandchildren, and it didn't seem likely that he would ever have either, but who knows? He was great with the children, but women weren't his thing.

I ordered coffee for delivery by service bot, stood and stretched. The coffee arrived and I sat with it in my chair, calling up Massoud's work. As he had suggested, his modifications turned a general purpose machine into a highly specialised one. The tile grinder at the start of the process he had left the same, but from there on, where the powdered tile flowed in to the atomisation and ionisation chamber, he had increased the material flow rate substantially and upped the power to compensate. That was where much of the extra energy was required. He had observed that we were dealing with only eight elements and perhaps a total of twenty isotopes resulting from the radiation, and also that we didn't need to separate all the types of atoms because they would mostly be mixed back together in the new tiles. Only the radioactive isotopes and the doping elements needed to be separated off. Massoud had calculated that we needed twelve different collection buckets at most and therefore, by using a more intense electric field, we could greatly increase throughput. Finely tuning the magnetic fields in the final stage would ensure that the radioactive isotopes, dopants and any object field elements we wanted removed were directed into the right buckets: neat.

Stores confirmed that it held a suitable, more powerful, microwave source of the required frequency range. All the other new parts could be printed. The only problem seemed to be doing all this rebuilding outside: we would have to use long-arms on a mimic because the current machine would already be radioactive, assuming it had been tested properly. I looked again at the schematics. It seemed as though we were replacing all the complex parts, with the exception of the control unit and the grinder. It would be easier to adapt another, similar machine, which was not already radioactive. This would allow me to do the work in Engineering where it could also be tested before being taken out to where it was needed. A further advantage would be that we could keep intact the other, general purpose unit, which could then still be used to recover as much material as possible from other radioactive worn out parts, such as the hot-bot's joint bearings when they came to be replaced. Status told me that we had two similar, unused recycling machines in the Processes Ring so I arranged for a cart to pick one up and bring it to Engineering. I thought it politic to inform Massoud what I was planning. If necessary we could make a new one at a later date.

The capacity of Hyun's printers to make all the new parts before the night was over needed checking. Hyun was not yet back from the engine room, so I loaded the engineering drawings of everything I thought would be needed into the print system and asked it when they could be made. The scheduler showed some printer capacity was immediately available and that raw material stocks looked sufficient. The scheduler estimated the total print time to be a couple of hours for most of it, but that the coil magnets would take a lot longer: ten hours. As this was a critical machine, and my understanding of it was limited, someone else should double check the design before I pressed 'go' on the print order. Status showed Minogue was around so I called him and asked if he had time to give it a quick look. He agreed and I directed him to the file.

The three components required for the nozzle repair had now been designed and were either being built or soon would be. Next I had to work out how to get all the pieces in place and working together. The assembly of the tile factory in the engine room seemed to be under control. Agyei knew what she was doing, and could call on Ibo and others for help if required. More problematic was going to be the rebuilding of the hot-bot and the installation of the new refining unit. They both required outside work and dealing with radioactive elements. Bjorn and Hyun would be needed to help me on them so I messaged them both, asking if we could get together to discuss how and when we were going to do the work. Hyun was back in the engine room installing the automation for the tile factory, and wouldn't be able to get back to Robotics for a while. Bjorn was starting to help Agyei disassemble her tile processing unit in Chemistry and transport it down to the engine room. They were both fully occupied with vital tasks it seemed. We needed some more help here and I began thinking who else could operate a mimic. Bita and Yingluq sprung to mind and perhaps Sahko too. All had some experience with using the mimics, but they would all have to be guided through the steps required. If Avalos had still been around he would have been my first choice. He'd had the most experience and had been the most adept of us at working outside. Bjorn had been his number two in that role and had had to step up.

I was losing track of time and noticed it was already early afternoon and I hadn't eaten for a while. I ordered another meal and, while waiting, called Massoud.

'I wanted to thank you for all your work on the tile material recycler.'

'Glad to help, my friend. Sometimes I feel as though I'm no use, while you are rushing around pulling the ship back together.'

'We wouldn't have got this far without all the fundamental work you do keeping the basic services going, as well as all the food prep, ensuring that it's both edible and appetising.'

'We all need each other out here, don't we?'

'We certainly do.'

'So I see from your note that my few suggestions were perhaps of use. You believe it possible and sensible to make those changes?'

'It looked great and I didn't see any real problems with doing all the things you suggested. As you saw from my note, it will be much easier to rebuild one of the spares because that saves the complication of taking apart the old one which will be hot.'

'I appreciate that I ended up recommending changes to all of the critical components of the machine and that was going to take some work. I don't have an immediate use for the spares, so it's acceptable to use one for this vital project.'

'One other thing, Massoud, and I hope you won't be offended by this, but I've asked Minogue to take a look too. I didn't feel that I understood all the technicalities of your proposals. We can't afford to make mistakes, and there won't much time for rework.'

'I'm not offended, not at all, I fully understand. I often ask Yingluq, Minogue, Agyci, or even you to advise on or check any changes I'm thinking of making to bioengineering or ship services. Later I may use it as an excuse to become seriously offended, but for now, pass.' He paused and then laughed out loud. 'Now, as I have helped you, I'll keep you to our little bargain. Maybe not right now, but sometime I'll collect on what happened between you and Sahko.' He chuckled again and cut the link.

My meal arrived and I was getting tucked in when Minogue called. I asked him what he thought of Massoud's design.

'This will work, Menem, no doubt. I would suggest using a slightly different magnetic field design which would give greater discrimination between isotopes. There's not a lot of difference either way. Massoud's is the tried and tested old favourite. The choice may come down to manufacturability. Take a look.'

I skimmed through Minogue's attachment to the file.

'It wouldn't be any harder to print. The coil composition is slightly different, so I'll have to check material stocks. If your proposal offers better discrimination then that would result in purer raw material for the new tiles and a lower reject rate, wouldn't it?'

'Potentially. Agyei's tests showed that the crystal build is very stable. She and Gunadi seem to have achieved surprisingly good control. Massoud's idea for the seed crystal attracts the right atoms to build itself and so impurities in the precursor aren't a problem, up to a point. However, I expect impurities will build up in the tank over time and will have to be flushed out. I hadn't thought about it and I wonder if Agyei has? We may well need to build in some time for that.'

'We still expect the hot-bot is going to need at least one major rebuild halfway through, and quite likely more often than that.'

'So we could co-ordinate one or more maintenance shutdowns during the repair work.'

'We should, if they're needed.'

'OK, leave the tile manufacturing side of that to me. I'll talk with Agyei. I'll let you know the outcome, especially if the purity of the refiner will have a significant impact.'

'Good with me. I'll check the printer material stocks and let you know if that's an issue, otherwise I'll start the printing process. Those magnets are precision work and take a lot of time to make it seems. Best I get them scheduled as soon as possible. Printing capacity may become an issue at some point.'

'Hyun will have his finger on that, I expect.'

'He's down in the engine room setting up a robot arm for tile handling.'

'Limits on his capacity too? Oh well. Anything else?'

'There's one more thing you might be able to advise on. I want to start work on the rebuild of the hot-bot next. To do that it would be best to use two mimics with long-arms. Bjorn is tied up with shifting the tile plant down to the engine room, so I was wondering who else might be best suited to help me. Yingluq, Bita and Sahko could all do the work. Any thoughts?'

'Mmm. Yingluq would have the most stamina, so if it's going to be a long session she would be my first choice for that reason. If it's not so long, but requires a lot of dexterity, then I would pick Bita: she's second to none when it comes to precision. If on the other hand the environment is uncertain and you're going to have to do a lot of thinking on your feet then I would have no hesitation in choosing Sahko: a very quick thinker, tremendous presence of mind. However, if you've any doubts about your ability to work as a team out there then forget it. Choose whoever you can best work with.'

'Thanks, Minogue. Good analysis as always, but I'm not sure I'm any closer to a conclusion.'

Minogue laughed. 'No, no. I suggest starting with whoever you first thought of, and see if they're available. It may come down to who has the time.'

'Mustn't over think the choice.'

'You do too much thinking sometimes.'

'Yeah, yeah. Thanks, Minogue.' I cut the link.

So who was I going to call? If the decision was entirely impersonal then I wouldn't hesitate to choose Sahko. But I didn't trust myself enough around her. There was too much risk that we would argue and she would order me around. I thought about what tasks we had to perform: the long-arms we would have to use were difficult to operate precisely. The job shouldn't be a long one if it went reasonably well, but it would require care. We would have to work in a containment bubble to stop any parts from floating away.

I had pretty well decided who to call first, but put off finalising my choice for a moment while I checked printer stock inventory for the materials for Minogue's design of magnet. There was no problem with that, so I modified my print order and asked that it all be scheduled. It came back with an estimated finish-time of about eleven in the evening, which was even later than I had expected. Once the printing was done, I would have to arrange the assembly of the machine and then get it outside, installed and tested. It was going to be another long night.

The provision of the up rated services required for the tile breakdown machine had to be sorted. I called Massoud again and asked if he could arrange that.

'I anticipate your every need, my friend. It's already underway. Bjorn is able to make the necessary changes in the engine room next time he's down there. I've located all the parts required. Fortunately the sealed service duct to the outside is large enough to accommodate the up rated supplies. Whoever does the installation outside will have to make the necessary connections from there.'

'Excellent, you're well ahead of me. I owe you another one.'

'Indeed you do.' He gave a chuckle and cut the link.

161

I had made up my mind on the first expedition, but before calling Bita to ask if she would be prepared to do a mimic job with me I wanted to check with Bjorn. I didn't want to put his nose out of joint, and he might have some good suggestions anyway.

Bjorn was in the keel accompanying some equipment to the engine room. He clicked on.

'Hi, Menem. We're making progress here, how are things with you?' He sounded cheerful.

'Going OK, but lots to do still. Glad you're making progress, but no doubt much to do there too.'

'There is. We'll not be ready for testing until nine or so tonight, we think. Production should start a few hours after that, assuming all goes well with the tests.'

'I'm further behind than that. We won't be fully sorted until six tomorrow morning, at best. Agyei's bit is probably the most sensitive; you should keep going now and give yourselves room for extra tuning later. Moving working kit is never straightforward.'

'Sure. We'll press on here. Are you thinking about getting help?'

'It was about that that I wanted to get your input. The next major step here is rebuilding the hot-bot. I've worked out what needs to be done and have sorted, built and tested the required components. It's coming to the stage of taking the old bot apart and fitting the new assemblies.'

'Which has to be done outside of course: mimic work. Do you need me, or could someone else do it?'

'Someone else who is handy could do it. We'll have to use long-arms, so the work will need a light touch, which I'm not so good at. The bot-net can steady things a bit, but there will be some fiddly work.'

'Use Bita if she's able to, either her or Sahko. Bita is the most agile with the mimics and she's a natural, particularly in zero-'g'.'

'Minogue made the same suggestion, if you weren't available.'

'Anything else? If not, I've arrived at the engine room and have stuff to do. Keep in touch and do call on me if needed. Don't overdo the food before you step out, eh?'

'Thanks for the reminder. Nothing else for now. Always useful to share problems with you.'

'Likewise.' Bjorn clicked out.

So decision made.

I called Bita and asked if she would be prepared to operate a mimic.

'Are you sure?' she asked. 'I haven't been in a mimic for a while. Oh, and when do you want to this? I have to do daily Fleet comms later.'

'Doesn't Sahko do Fleet comms? Do you need to be there every time?'

'I collate all the crew messages and do the standard reporting and prep on the data files we send, and then Sahko adds her report. She likes me to check her stuff to ensure we're consistent in our language and message content, you know the sort of thing. Right now the messages are kind of sensitive because, while we like to be honest and open, we don't want to give the wrong impression.'

'That we're in deep trouble? The political angle?'

'Definitely not.' Bita gave a silvery laugh. 'We have to think through possible reactions to everything we send. I check through all comms for consistency.'

'And to make sure none of us are inflaming matters or sending secret messages to one party or another.'

'What do you know about that?' asked Bita rather sharply.

'Nothing. I mean, I don't know of anyone who would, and what would they say anyway? Giving away our big secrets: Agyei is pregnant!'

'I'm shocked, shocked, that you might want to do that,' said Bita in her best fake-outraged tone.

'Yeah, aren't we all? Anyway, we really need to do this mimic work soon. I estimate we'll need an hour for the first trip. There may be more trips later, but you don't necessarily have to come on any or all of the others if you come on this first one. Minogue, Bjorn and I thought of you because the first one will require a considerable degree of dexterity in disassembly and reassembly. We're going to have to use long-arms to avoid any risk of frying the mimics' bodies.'

'Yuk, those things are so ugly.'

'Wait till you see the mimic that has lost its head.'

'What?'

'It disappeared while we were fixing Wayclear.'

'I vaguely remember seeing that in some reports. Nasty.'

'Yeah, it was a bad experience. I was driving it at the time.'

'So you lost your head, again?' Bita laughed but quickly smothered it. 'Has it been fixed?'

'Hyun came up with a temporary lash-up that uses some bits of bot-net.'

'I bet that's really pretty.'

'I was driving, so I haven't seen it. But yes, it's a monster, even more than usual.'

'What sort of thing do you want me to do? I don't know much about taking robots to bits and putting them back together.'

'During training you would have been talked through this sort of task, you know: "take this tool and use it like that" to do something, or "look out for this happening, can you feel it move? What do you see?" I'll be right there and be doing the talking. The job does need a second pair of hands and I need those hands to be steady and dextrous, which is why I want you.'

'Wouldn't Bjorn be better?'

'Bjorn would be more familiar with the mimic but I doubt he would be as good as you for the delicate elements of this job. Anyway, Bjorn is busy helping Agyei set up the tile manufacturing plant inside the engine room. We'll also have Hyun with us in the control room, assisting with a bot-net unit or two.'

'If you think I can help, then I would love to. It's great to make a physical contribution to getting us underway again, and the mimics can be kind of fun.'

'Glad you see it like that. Thanks, Bita. I have to do some more tests on the new bot chassis which will take about half an hour. I also need to check Hyun's availability. If he's flexible, and you can get the OK from Sahko, then what if we aim to be suited up in forty-five minutes? That will give me time to get all the things we need to the airlock, ready for the mimics to pick up outside. We'll also collect some tools and the long-arms, and then walk up to the front, where the hot-bot will be. If all goes well, we'll be done in an hour. We can either leave the mimics there or bring them back to their dock down here. Total time should be around two hours.'

'I thought you said one?'

'Mission creep. No actually I hadn't thought it all through, I was thinking there was about an hour's work to take out the old chassis, install the new plumbing in the bot's legs and then put it all back together and test it. Oh, and we'll also need to set up a cooling and battery pack swap station, but that shouldn't take long.'

'I think I'll tell Sahko that it could take three to give us some leeway. So we would be sure to be done by seven. Our daily report goes out at eight, so I would still have time to get it cleaned up.'

'That sounds great if you can manage it.'

'OK. I'll check with Sahko and if there's a problem let you know, if not I'll await your call to head over to Robotics.'

'Sounds like a plan.'

'Yay.' She cut the link.

Status told me Hyun was still in the engine room setting up the robot there. I messaged him about the mimic trip, asking when he would be free. He quickly messaged back and said he was becoming overloaded and was struggling to prioritise. The printers needed his attention too, to keep them fully productive. Of course he would do it if it was top priority, but he suggested asking Gunadi, robotics number two and quite a wiz with the bot-net, he reminded me. I should have thought of that. Usually Hyun would be willing, so perhaps things were not going so smoothly somewhere. I tried not to think what that might be, messaging Hyun back to say thanks and I would see if Gunadi was available.

Gunadi was accessible, so I called her and asked if she would be prepared to help on the exterior work by deploying the bot-net.

'Yes, that would be fun,' she answered with enthusiasm. 'I'm a bit bored here, running simulations and tests for all the components. I would welcome a break and also to be involved more directly with a bit of the rebuilding work. I'll need to get back for the next phase of testing, once the tile manufacturing plant has been moved and set up again, and you'll want me to run tests on the rebuilt bot later too. At the moment I'm working on the optimal path calculator. Minogue and Yingluq have complicated things a bit more by varying the tile thickness down the nozzle.'

'Minogue told me about that. It was Yingluq's idea apparently. He thought it could save a useful bit of time, but your calculator will no doubt tell us if it's really worthwhile. Anyway, glad you're keen to help with the bot-net. Bita will be taking the other mimic, so I hope you're comfortable interacting with the two of us.'

'Sure, no problem. I did some training exercises with her some time ago. She had a great feel for the mimic, so good choice. When do you want to go?'

'Quite soon. The tests on the parts are nearly finished and look satisfactory. There's a bit more assembly to do and then it has to be moved to an airlock. Bita is checking with Sahko about comms schedules and will let me know if she can make it. If she's cleared, we should start suiting up in twenty-five minutes or so. I hope that the job won't take longer than two hours total. If we run in to problems we may have to stop, do some rework, and start again later.'

'That schedule is fine by me. It'll be fun to work with you on this.'

'Mimic work is not my idea of fun, but I'm glad you can help. Hyun will be relieved too. I get the impression he's getting overloaded right now.'

'I'll let him know I can do it.'

'Thanks, and by the way, you know my mimic lost its head and Hyun has cobbled together a sort of replacement using some bits of bot-net?'

'Yes, I helped him a bit on that: ugly but serviceable. I'll keep an eye on those bot-net elements' function and make sure they're delivering the information you need.'

'Thanks, Gunadi. See you in Robotics in twenty.'

I summoned a transport cart and gathered all the parts for the rebuild: the chassis with its new motor, cooling system, battery and cool-pack, hydraulic pump, valves and control unit, the hydraulic pipes for the legs, a couple of small drums of hydraulic fluid plus empty drums for the old fluid, thermal compound and glue, the pack cooling and battery charging unit with a second battery and cool-pack unit, and a host of seals and other sundries. The simulation suggested that it could all be assembled with the standard number-two tool-pack. After loading the crated up parts onto a cart, I sent it off to the nearest airlock.

Bita called. 'I've spoken with Sahko and she doesn't need my help until later. She sounded as though she was sorry not to be involved herself.'

'Captain needs to stay on the bridge and all that. She could have done the work but...'

'Say no more. We do need to resolve this later though.'

'Yeah, yeah. Anyway, good that you can help. Gunadi will be on the bot-net. Hyun was tied up with other important stuff.'

'Oh, OK. I haven't worked together with Gunadi on mimics for a while but we did have some fun on a training exercise some time ago.'

'She mentioned that. You must tell me about it sometime.'

'Maybe not.'

'Intriguing. Anyway see you in five minutes.'

I took a last look at my task list. There was nothing more urgent that this.

Gunadi was already in Robotics when I arrived. She waved as I came in but continued staring at the bot-net control hologram: a three dimensional image that showed the position of each of its elements, the hundreds of tiny, beetle-like robots. Gunadi paused what she was doing for a moment and looked up. 'It has been a while since I used this thing. It's so weird, but I seem to be getting back in to the swing of things. Ah, here's Bita.'

'Hi, you two. Getting ready to go? What do you want me to do?' Bita looked at the mimic chairs. 'Looks like Bjorn used this one. I'll have to adjust it a bit to fit me.' She tapped the pad and the chair recognised her, changing it size and shape to match.

'Gunadi,' I asked, 'can you instruct the hot-bot to return to its parking bay and then power down?'

'Sure.' Gunadi slid her chair over to the hot-bot control station, checked its status and issued the commands. 'It had recently started to cut out another tile, so I've stopped that. It's on its way back home now.' She slid back to the bot-net station.

Bita and I strapped in to our chairs and flexed our limbs to test their fit and feel. We linked our comms, and Bita said: 'I'm ready.'

'Gunadi, how about you?' I asked.

'Ready. Bot-net standing by.'

'Gunadi, can you watch Bita's mimic, and be ready to assist if needed as Bita gets back up to speed. Provide me with a visual. Bita, come out of your home, collect a tool-pack two and two pairs of long-arms and then make your way out of the airlock. Once outside, go to Airlock Two. The bot-net will guide you. Waiting there is a transport cart with all the parts we need for this job. Bita, please give us a commentary on how you're getting on.'

'OK, I'm off. Oops, steady, sticky feet. That's better. Tool-pack number two over there, ready, back in and connect. Tool-pack two loaded on my back. Right now, long-arms, from the rack, two pairs, clip on side of tool-pack. OK. Now out: going to the airlock... inside, door closing, cycling... outer door opening. Wow the star-field. Gets me every time: so magnificent. Still blue up ahead, the famed Starbow still clear.'

Gunadi and I watched Bita's mimic emerging from the airlock. She seemed to be moving well despite the tool-pack and long-arms rising above her head. 'Which way? Ah, heads-up display showing route. Over there. This feels better, I remember how to do this.'

Bita's mimic seemed to be skipping across the outside of the ship.

'Whoa,' I called out. 'Steady on, no need to rush, we don't want any accidents.'

Bita slowed her mimic to a more sedate pace.

'It feels good to be out here again. Glad I haven't forgotten how to use these things. Down the ramp. Now at Airlock Two. Activating exterior door. Door opening. Where? Yes, there's a trolley inside, stuck to the ceiling. Ah, it's now rotating round.'

'The kit is all in the crate on the trolley,' I said. 'Guide it out.'

Bita held the trolley as it trundled out. Clearly she was a natural in the mimic and Gunadi was adept at keeping a good view of what she was up to and ensuring that everything kept a tether attached to the ship.

'Got the crate and the airlock is shutting. Now heading towards the front of the ship. At the rotation point between the Habitat Ring and payload. Putting the trolley on the transfer deck. Gunadi if you can attach another tether to the payload section and float it up, then I'll catch it and release the control side tether.'

'What are you doing Bita? Use the transfer deck,' I demanded.

'This is much quicker and easier and Gunadi and I have done this before, haven't we?'

'Yes,' said Gunadi. 'Simple and elegant, if you're quick.'

'And a tangle of smashed equipment if you screw it up. Take the safe route.'

'He's no fun is he Gunadi? Ready to go? Now.'

A tether Gunadi had set up on the payload section rotated towards Bita. I watched, horrified. Her mimic reached out an arm, caught the tether and at the same moment she stepped with one foot onto the payload side and, as the rotation started to cause her to do the splits, she released her foot and the tether attaching her to the Habitat Ring, and was swung up in an arc. She rotated on her fixed foot and pulled her self upright using the tether. An astonishing, graceful manoeuvre. I was stunned to silence for a moment.

'Yee-ha. Perfect. Nice throw, Gunadi.' Bita pulled the cart off the transfer deck, which had stopped beside her.

'I can hardly bear to watch,' I said. 'Right, Bita make your way up to the front. My mimic is somewhere up there already, so I'll stand it up.

Gunadi, please try to prevent any more craziness, and can you check if the hot-bot is back in its home station yet?'

'Yes, checking, yes, it's back home, parked and powered down.'

My view changed as I activated my mimic and flexed its limbs. I stood it up in the equipment recess where it had been parked after the Wayclear repair. It seemed to be working all right, even if the field of view was a bit limited. There was power left for about four hours, which should be good enough for this trip. I climbed out of the recess and walked around the engine casing to where the hot-bot was parked and examined it from a distance.

'I can see you now,' said Bita arriving with the cart. 'Phew, your head is missing and it looks like a snake is emerging from your neck. That's really gross.' She walked up to my mimic to take a closer look. 'Close up it's even grosser. That's not a snake, it's like a column of ants all locked together emerging from your neck and waving around. Yuk, best not look at that: stuff of nightmares.'

'To add to the nightmare, we now need to swap our arms for the long-arms. Tether the tool-pack to the ship and we can get to work.'

Bita unloaded and tethered the tool-pack. We both disconnected our mimic arms and replaced them with the long-arms.

'Right, now we'll deploy the containment tent to stop any stray bits from wandering off. Gunadi, can you select the elements of the bot-net that are going to be contaminated and use them to seal it down to the ship? Leave plenty of room around the hot-bot for us to be able to take it apart.'

The tent popped open into a large bubble and a swarm of bot-net elements guided it in to place.

We dismantled the hot-bot by opening its body casing and extracting the old chassis, draining the hydraulics and disconnecting its four legs and two arms. I held one of the hot-bot's four legs while Gunadi tasked a team from the bot-net to feel its way up inside to the knee joint where it disconnected the hydraulic hoses, which Bita pulled out. The team inside the leg moved on, working its way around the knee joint and along to the ankle where it repeated the disconnect operation. Extracting the hoses from there was not so easy until. Straightening out the knee helped. The bot-net team fitted the new hoses, struggling at first to pull the larger hoses inside the legs but the elements had an astonishing ability to learn on the job, trying different things until eventually they had mastered the required operation. Once the connections had been made, I pressurised the hose to test for leaks. As the bot-net withdrew, it spot glued the hoses to the inside wall of the leg and filled the remaining void with thermal foam. The bot-net elements struggled initially both with the glue and the foam. Several elements got stuck and had to be pulled out by others. The net adjusted its tactics to avoid further trouble. Having worked out what to do on the first leg, the other three were upgraded much more quickly.

Time was running on: we had already been at work for over an hour. The next stage also required the three of us to work together. I held the new hot-bot chassis and Bita one of the legs, and we brought them together, allowing the bot-net to secure the connection. Bita had the awkward part: holding the long, ungainly legs of the bot using her long-arms. However, she seemed to be able to hold the leg remarkably steadily, whereas I, who had the supposedly easier task, was struggling to hold the chassis in the right orientation to bring the two together. I had to keep one corner of it touching the ship to steady it until the bot-net had secured the leg to it. Once two legs were attached their feet rested on the hull and steadied the chassis. Eventually we got the four legs on and I called a brief halt. I was sweating and shaking.

'How are you doing Bita?' I asked.

'All right. That was tricky, but I'm ready to continue.'

'Gunadi?'

'Yes, fine. I've got back in the groove with the net again. Pity about losing a couple of elements on that first leg, otherwise no problem. I'm ready to continue too.'

'The rest of the work should be easier physically, but there are some delicate bits. If either of you're in doubt, call a halt and we'll stop.'

Bita and Gunadi both signalled they were ready and my shaking had stopped. We proceeded by reattaching the hot-bot's two arms, with Bita holding each in turn while Gunadi had the net make the attachment. I removed the control unit from the old chassis and attached it to the new and we connected all the control fibres and hydraulic lines between the chassis and the limbs. Finally we could recharge the hydraulic lines with new fluid, a relatively simple task because the hot-bot had been designed to allow replacement during regular maintenance. It did take some time, but at least in the vacuum of space there were no air bubbles to worry about.

Bita plugged a new combined battery and cool-pack into the bot, and, after we had the mimics and bot-net stand clear, Gunadi initiated a test sequence. Firstly, the control system checked that it could communicate with all its parts as expected. That test passed and it moved on to testing its limbs, very slightly raising each of its arms in turn and then, lifting one leg at a time, it flexed each joint a little. There wasn't room to flex the limbs fully inside the containment bubble and we didn't want it to come too close to the mimics.

Now there were only the last parts to do: close up the protective shell around the new chassis, set up the new battery and cool-pack charging station and run coolant lines to it, tapping into the pipes to the old tile refiner. We were starting to lose concentration and tasks were taking longer than they might have. Eventually we got everything set up. All the tools went back in the pack and we stashed the old parts in a crate and secured it in an equipment recess. With the risk that they had become contaminated, they couldn't be brought back inside. They would have to be processed in the old recycling machine out here at some point.

We swapped our long-arms for the regular variety and unsealed and packed up the containment tent. At last we could withdraw our mimics to a safe distance and Gunadi instructed the bot to flex its upgraded limbs to their full extent. If something was wrong we wouldn't try to fix it straight away. I, at least, needed a break, and also my mimic's battery was running down and needed changing or recharging.

'Well done everyone. I'm just about beat. How are you doing Bita?'

'Not too bad,' said Bita. 'I could use a stretch, but why don't I cart this stuff back to the Habitat airlock and park my mimic in its home?'

'Hold on a minute Bita. How are you doing, Gunadi?'

'I'm good. Could use a break soon though.'

'I'm going to park my mimic where it is. Bita, you should stop here too. Gunadi, a few final items before we quit: can you task the bot-net to extract the batteries from the mimics and take them to a charging station? We can recover the tools and mimics later when we have confirmation that the hot-bot is fully functional.'

'OK, you park up,' Gunadi said. 'I'll get the net to replace your batteries and I'll set up some cameras to view the bot performing its test routine.'

Bita added: 'Fine, I'll park up near you. The tool pack and long-arms are tethered so they won't go anywhere.'

After parking our mimics, Bita and I eased ourselves out of the control chairs. Bita stood and went through a stretch routine which I partly emulated. Gunadi finished tasking the bot-net and when she was done she too stood up and shook her limbs and rotated her head around.

I felt the adrenalin draining from me, now the trip was over. I leaned against a wall and looked at the two women. Bita: tall, graceful, flamboyantly dressed and proud of her femininity. Gunadi: just as slender but shorter, more angular and awkward, loosely clothed in studded black jacket and trousers. Right now however, she was standing upright and had a glow of confidence, rather better than her usual closed-up hidden self.

'That was quite a job,' I said. 'Thank you for that, both of you. It was obvious you two have worked together outside before, a great help.'

'We've had some fun in the past on training exercises. That was the first real job I've done with the mimic though,' said Bita.

'Biggest thing I've done with the bot-net too,' said Gunadi. 'I've done quite a few minor servicing tasks for Hyun, but nothing like that.'

'You had me worried, Bita, when you took that leap from Habitat to Payload. I thought we were going to lose a mimic right there.'

'You should learn how to do that, Menem. It makes the transition so much easier and works both ways. It's something Gunadi and I developed together when I was getting bored of doing it by the book. Initially we used a pole and a safety line so that if I lost my footing the mimic wouldn't smash into anything, but that never happened with me. We showed Yingluq, and the first time she went too hard at it and her foot wasn't able to grip on the other side, so the pole and line caught her. Boy was she angry about not getting it first time. Second time she just made it without stumbling, and by the third she had it.'

Gunadi was smiling at the memory. 'Yes, Yingluq is so athletic. She was determined to get it if Bita could. She leapt far too hard on that first jump and went swinging way up when the line caught her.'

'When we've time you must teach me, and maybe we should make it the official move if I can get it. I hate that transition, and it would save having to wait for the transfer deck for small loads.'

'Is that the time?' asked Bita suddenly. 'I must rush. I need a quick refresh before I meet up with Sahko for the comms. Thanks for getting me involved, Menem. I feel as though I've made a contribution to getting us back on the go and, well heh, it was fun too. See you, Gunadi.'

Bita waved a hand above her head and danced out of the room.

'Have you got to rush off too, Gunadi?' I asked.

'No. Until the tile factory is set up I've only the path optimiser to work on. Most of the basic structure is in place for that, and hopefully the simulator has been crunching though a load of scenarios to check that there are no hidden snags. You need me to help?'

'Yes, please, either you or Hyun. The hot-bot must be run through its performance envelope to check that it's fully functional. If it isn't, then another mimic and bot-net trip will be needed to fix it. As well as that, there's the new tile breakdown machine to install. Parts are currently being printed and it has to be assembled. Once it has been tested, we'll need to do another mimic trip to install it and connect upgraded services. The machine won't be ready to move until at least two in the morning, so the installation job will have to be soon after that.'

'Sure, I can help. I'll set the hot-bot to run through its tests now and then talk with Hyun to make sure one of us can help out from two a.m.'

'Thanks, Gunadi. I wish I was as good as Bita at using the mimic. She's an absolute natural, where I'm a bit of a plodder.'

'You know what needs doing and you get it done. You're so calm and careful. We know we can trust you, Menem. I admire you.' She had come over to me a brushed my hand with hers.

'Well thanks, Gunadi. You know your stuff too, which really helps when working out there.' I moved away a little. 'OK, have you set the hot-bot going?'

'It has just started with a few simple tests. Nothing wrong so far. It will alert you if it fails anything.'

'Good, thanks. I must get on now, see how the printing is going for the tile-refiner and start putting it together.' I walked over to the door, certain that Gunadi was watching me as I left.

4020, 18:45

There was a pile of parts from Printing waiting for me in Engineering, ready to start assembly of the new refiner. I felt tired and hungry again, ordering a meal and another Stay-Awake. Using the schematics for the machine, I organised the parts and selected tools. The assembler could handle the work, but sometimes it was easier if I intervened and did it myself. Also, if I did it I would have a better understanding of how it went together, in case I had to make some changes or do maintenance on it after it had been installed.

My meal arrived and I ate, calling Agyei to find out how the tile factory was coming on.

'Slowly,' she said. 'It has not been as straightforward as we hoped, working down here and with zero-'g'. You know how it is, when you're not in your own lab: the things you need aren't immediately to hand. There were also a couple of issues with fluid flows that we hadn't anticipated which have required a bit of rework. I've had lots of help though. Hyun has been kept busy setting up the robot and printing some extra parts. Bjorn has been back and forward fetching stuff and Massoud has been sorting things out in Chemistry. Ibo has also been helping me do assembly, when she's not been busy testing the performance of the sample tile and being nice to Fuse. She tries not to show it, but I know she feels deeply that the engines are her responsibility and she shouldn't be burdening all the rest of us with them. I try to tell her that's nonsense, and it was hardly her fault that we smashed into that object cloud. So that's us. How are you getting on?'

'I've had lots of help too. Recently Gunadi, Bita and I have been outside rebuilding the hot-bot. It took longer than I had hoped of course, and was quite exhausting. Bita was terrific with the mimic and Gunadi was right on with the bot-net. We have it done now, or at least we hope we have. It's currently running through its performance envelope tests. Early days yet, but it hasn't reported any problems so far. Now I'm thinking about the new tile-refiner.'

'Gosh, what have you planned for that?'

I gave Agyei the same run down on the machine I had given Gunadi. 'Everything should be ready to go by six tomorrow morning, provided we don't run in to any major problems.'

'We're certainly running down the clock on this. There won't be any spare time left in the mission schedule after this will there?'

'It gets tighter all the time. When do you expect to be done?'

'We think we have about another couple of hours work on setup, fine tuning the equipment and then a test run. It's mostly down to me now, and then Ibo will test a production sample. If all goes well, we'll be set by midnight. Given your schedule, we've time enough to sort any problems, I hope. Are you going to use Gunadi and Bita again for the next trip outside?'

'They work well together, but it depends on what else they have to do. Gunadi was going to consult Hyun and decide between them who would run the bot-net. I would be happy to use Bita again in the other mimic but Yingluq or Sahko could do it if Bjorn wasn't available.'

'I expect Bjorn would say he could, but he looks exhausted with all he has being doing today. You know how it is, moving between g and zero-'g', it takes it out of you.'

'I don't know how he can stand doing so much of it. It's not my thing at all. I find it disorienting enough in the mimic, let alone for real.'

'You didn't throw up again today did you?'

'No, but it was close.'

'Take care, Menem. Better you take some more time than burn out. We can probably stand a bit higher deceleration or gain some time somewhere else, perhaps by navigation.'

'I don't think Sahko is as keen as Avalos to cut corners. She would rather have time in hand and not take a big risk.'

'I would prefer that too, but the most important thing is that the ship holds together long enough. I couldn't do the engineering alone if you were out of action. There are too many problems.'

'You feel the ship ageing?'

'Oh, best not to talk about it, especially now. We do what we can. You take a break for a bit. A couple of hours won't make any difference.'

'You're probably right, but I've eaten and feel a bit better now, so back to work. Good to talk to you Agyei.'

I cut the link and started placing the tile-refiner parts ready for the finisher and the assembler. I needed to decide which of several lasers we had available to use, and locate some control gear and a power supply. The laser was the only item that wasn't standard stock, but there some in Stores, so I set up an inventory search to select the most suitable.

Yingluq called. 'Hi, Menem. I've been trying to talk to you, but you seemed to be tied up with Agyei. How are you two getting on?'

Her voice seemed neutral, professional, no hint of the intimacy we had shared, but then I hadn't called her either. I had been so busy, which now seemed like a weak excuse. Perhaps she didn't want it to go any further, a one-off, ships that pass in the night and all that. I had no idea what I wanted. It was like an intoxicating drug, I craved seeing her again, now I thought about it. Ultimately it would be a bad idea, sinking my chances with Sahko.

I kept it neutral too. 'We were having the usual engineers' talk: problems, things taking longer than expected, parts needing to be fabricated. However, despite the difficulties, we're making progress. Tile production should be in full swing by tomorrow morning.'

'That sounds good, but it doesn't leave a lot of spare time.'

'If all our kit works, we're optimistic that the engine can be running again in four more days.'

'That's better than I expected, well done you lot. If I can help in any way, I'd like to.'

'Thanks, Yingluq.'

'Menem, you ordered another Stay-Awake for tonight.'

'Yes.' I wondered what the problem was.

'Two nights in a row is not good, but I understand why you want to. I need you to come by Medical so that I can do a couple of quick checks before I allow it.'

Could she stop me? If she did it could jeopardise our mission. Without it I couldn't do another mimic run tonight; I would need at least eight hours sleep first. If she was going to try to stop me, I would have to appeal to Sahko. Better not get ahead of myself, she would know that.

'When can I come round?'

'Anytime. I'm in Medical now.'

'I'll come right over.'

The door opened as I arrived, so I went straight in and it swished shut behind me. Yingluq was sitting in her usual chair, dressed in professional white, her hair in a short plait. Her large eyes looked at me appraisingly with a slight smile.

'Come in and sit down.' She indicated the patient chair across the narrow table from hers. 'You look a bit tired, Menem, and if you don't mind my saying so, a bit grubby.'

I rubbed the back of my hand across my chin and felt the bristles.

'Sorry, I haven't had a refresh for a while. I probably look a mess. I hope I don't smell too bad.'

'Not yet, but you soon will if you don't refresh.'

'Yes, doc.'

'I must give you a quick check over. Sit there and give me your arm, please.'

After applying a wipe, which she ostentatiously disposed of, she pulled a long thick sleeve over my hand and up to my armpit. A braid of fibres came out of it, linked into a machine. A band went over my head that pressed slightly into my skull right behind my ears. It was the usual med-exam stuff. Yingluq looked at her screen and nodded.

'You will probably live if you have one more Stay-Awake.'

She removed her sensors from me, reached into a drawer, pulled out a strip of capsules, tore one off and placed it on the table between us.

'You had me worried there for a moment,' I said.

I studied her, trying to make eye contact, but she seemed a little distant.

'But you can't include a fantasy popper this time,' she said.

'A what?'

'A fantasy popper. You had one last night.'

'I've never heard of a "fantasy popper". I didn't know I had one last night.'

'You ordered it with the Stay-Awake.' She looked at her screen. 'Yes, Stay-Awake X2, the one with the fantasy popper. I haven't tried them myself. They're supposed to provide a short distraction which helps the brain to organise itself, despite the lack of sleep.'

Well I definitely hadn't ordered one: was she making it up?

'I don't remember ever hearing about those before, are they new?'

'Quite recent. We received the gen on them at least six months ago so they have been available for a while. You must have seen the note. Last night was the first time you had one, I think. Was it good? It sounds as though you didn't notice it, so perhaps it didn't work on you.'

'I didn't know I had taken one.' Wait a minute, she's making this up. Perhaps she wants to forget last night ever happened. 'Look, Yingluq, about last night, I had a wonderful time, but maybe we should keep it between ourselves.'

Yingluq sat back in her chair and studied me again, a thoughtful expression on her face which then broke in to a broad smile. 'Oh, oh, oh. Did I feature in your fantasy? Yes I did, didn't I?'

'Ah, well, I...' I reached for the Stay-Awake on the table, ready to make a run for it, but she was quicker than I and covered it with her hand.

'Oh you wicked, unfaithful man. I wondered why I had been left out of your apology list. I heard that you had been around to all the others, so I wondered why you'd forgotten me. Perhaps you hadn't forgotten me.' She leaned over and fixed me with a gleam in her beautiful eyes. 'Was it good? Did we both have a good time? Multiple orgasms? Swinging from the chandeliers?'

'I.. we... you... both seemed to enjoy...'

Her smile broadened. 'Phew, those fantasy poppers sound like fun. Best not to overdo them though, definitely not for you tonight.' She was shaking with laughter and took her hand off the capsule on the table. 'Here, take your Stay-Awake and go. And don't come back until you've refreshed. Always good to see you, Menem. Makes a girl feel wanted, featuring in a fantasy.'

I was completely confused. 'Look, I apologise Yingluq.'

'Apology accepted. Now you've completed the crew circuit.'

'I don't believe it, I've never thought of you as a fantasy figure. I, err… can't believe it wasn't real.' I got up unsteadily.

'Go away, Menem, and forget all about it.'

I stumbled out the door. Surely she'd made it up? The experience had been so real. I remembered aching afterwards. "Fantasy Poppers" on the other hand didn't sound real, but then who knew what psycho drugs they could cook up these days? Maybe I could ask Agyei and Massoud if they had heard of these things. They would have been involved in making them on board if they were real. However, I would have to be very careful how I asked about them. If they weren't real I could easily become the butt of another crew joke. People would start wondering what I had done that had become a fantasy-fantasy for me. I would never live that down. Better not to ask directly, but try to find out some other way.

I picked up a drink on my way back to Engineering and, once there, took the Stay-Awake with it. The pack was marked X1. I looked in the waste bin but the service bot had recently emptied it. Too late to see if last night's pack was an X2. I sat in my chair and closed my eyes for a moment and tried to run through the events in the corridor the previous night. My treacherous memory was already beginning to fade, but not completely. I found myself smiling.

4020, 20:25

A buzzer sounded and I was immediately flung back to reality. Fortunately it was only a bot bringing another component for the tile-refiner, and not a member of the crew. Stores reported that it had found the most suitable laser, as well as the power supply and control gear I had ordered. The laser was in Stores Two, next door. I felt the need to loosen up, so I jogged around the ring to get there. When passing Analytics, the door was open and Gunadi called me.

'Hi, Gunadi. All well?'

'I've recently finished the hot-bot optimal-path navigator. How are things with you?' She stood up and came over to the door, reaching up its edge with one arm and leaning in to it, looking at me.

'I haven't had a call from the hot-bot yet so I assume the tests are running well. I was on my way round to Stores to pick up some parts for the tile-refiner.'

'I've talked with Hyun about which one of us will operate the bot-net for you later on tonight. He's very busy getting the tile factory to work, so it looks as though you'll have me tonight.'

I stood up straight, looked around and back at Gunadi.

'Excellent, good, fine. You're as capable as Hyun with the bot-net, perhaps better in some ways, so that's good.'

She smiled, and asked: 'Have you sorted out who will be operating the other mimic? Will it be Bita again?'

'I haven't spoken to her since she rushed off. I'm sure that she and Sahko must have finished comms by now, so I'll call her and find out soon.'

'If it's all right with you, I am planning to go to bed now.' She paused and then continued. 'And get a couple of hours sleep. Can you give me a buzz about ten minutes before you want me to come, and I'll be there for you?'

I felt myself sweating slightly. 'Sure. I'll give you a buzz.'

'Thanks, Menem.'

I was sure she was watching me as I walked away around the corridor. The inventory stacker in Stores had pulled out the parts I had requested. I had a quick look and they seemed to be the ones that I had asked for. I went straight back to Engineering, avoiding any more open doors.

Status told me that Bita was available, so I called her. 'You all done with Sahko for now?'

'Finally. It took a little while to get the wording right, explaining that our little disaster was not really a disaster and we would soon be up and running again. Fleet will see through that of course, but if we're going to the trouble of smoothing things over then they know that at least we're still hopeful of recovery.'

'Unless they think we think our situation is absolutely hopeless and we're trying to give the impression that it's not.'

'Impossible to say. I expect they'll have their best people parsing our every word. Either that or their lowest ranked comms operator won't even bother to read it, but file-and-forget it with all our other messages.'

'Ha, ha, who knows? I expect they might be a tiny bit interested in our progress.'

'Maybe. Their fate is in our hands somewhat.' She paused. 'However, I doubt you wanted to talk about that.'

'Interesting though it is to speculate on what's going on with Fleet, I have a more immediate problem to fix. Are you able to do another mimic trip late tonight?'

'Sahko asked about how our earlier expedition had gone. She seemed a bit put out that you hadn't asked her to do it.'

'I'm sure she would have been capable, although having seen you out there, you're a natural and the best mimic operator I've ever seen. Also, as she's the captain she shouldn't be too involved in operations. She might be needed to make decisions elsewhere at any time.'

'Or maybe you're avoiding her. Look, Menem, she's very good with the mimics too. I've seen her on exercises. Like me, she wants to make a contribution to getting the mission back on track, a hands-on contribution. I think it would do her good, stop her fretting so much and stop her worrying about you for a start.'

'I worry about how well she and I could work together out there. You saw that it requires intense cooperation between the three operators. We can't have doubts in the back of our minds when we're right there. I'm not sure that I can do that with Sahko.'

'You don't trust her?'

'I need assistance out there, not someone who is always trying to pick a fight.'

'Sahko knows what's required, she's a team player.'

'Provided she's the captain.'

'Look, Menem, this is how it is: Sahko really wants to do the job, I think she's quite capable and it would do her good. It would help her bond with the team a bit more, feel like part of the crew again, and not be alone brooding in Ops. I know you have reservations because you've got out of synch when you used to be so good together. This may be a critical trip, but then they all are. Please try, Menem. Treat her the same way you treated me.'

'Do I have a choice?'

'Of course you have a choice, Menem, but please take Sahko. Do it for me, if that would help.'

'Well if it turns out a disaster I'll get you to help fix it later.'

'Thanks, Menem. Give her a call and ask her. It won't be a disaster.'

I wasn't sure as I clicked out.

The parts from Stores all tested to specification and the assembler could get to work again. I watched it for a few minutes as it identified and picked up each item, and began putting them together using micro-welds and adhesives, applying lubricants and sealants where required.

I felt calm and called Sahko. She came on the comms immediately.

'Hi, Menem. I've been reviewing Status. You all seem to be making steady progress.' She sounded encouragingly upbeat.

'Not without problems of course, but we're getting there. We currently expect to be in tile production by around six in the morning.'

'And you, Menem, how are you doing? You're on a second Stay-Awake aren't you?'

'I'm holding up but there's still a lot to do tonight. The parts for the modified tile-refiner are being printed and assembled now. It should be finished and lab tested by around two in the morning when it will be ready for installation and final testing. It's the last piece of the puzzle, provided Agyei and Hyun haven't run in to any further problems.'

'The installation: who will do that?' She seemed eager, waiting for me to ask.

'Look Sahko, I wondered if, if, well if you might take one of the mimics?' I had said it and stumbled on: 'If you can't, as captain, leave your post, you know, or don't want to get bogged down in execution, I fully understand. I'm sure Bita or Bjorn could do it. Gunadi will be operating the bot-net.'

'I would very much like to do the job. There's not a lot of call for captaincy in the middle of the night with Main out. I would also like to do a bit more of the practical work in getting us back on track. Everyone else has done something and I would like to make a contribution too. Thank you for asking me, Menem.' Her voice was soft and quiet with a note of contentment. It got to me for a moment.

'One thing, Sahko.' I felt myself being dragged somewhere I didn't want to go, but I had to make it clear. 'Once we're out there, I'm in charge. You have to do what I say.'

'Oh yes, of course. It's your job: you're the engineer and I shall be there to assist.'

I wasn't convinced she had fully absorbed what I had said but she was clearly determined to go. And after all, it was only a simple machine replacement job. There wouldn't be much to fight over and Gunadi would be there to moderate. I might even manage to do it with just Gunadi.

'OK, good. What if I give you a call ten minutes before we go? Is that enough time? I can't be too precise about the timing yet. It will depend on how well the assembly goes.'

'Ten minutes before you want me to come to Robotics will be fine. It will be good to work with you again on something. We used to work well together.'

'We did.' I clicked off the link and sighed to myself: yes, we did.

I messaged Gunadi saying that we would be joined by Sahko. I wondered how she would take that.

Hyun called. 'Hi, Menem, I want to check that you're all right with Gunadi doing another outside trip.'

'Fine by me. She seems to know what she's doing with the bot-net. It worked well last time. She had worked with Bita before outside which was good. Quite revealing in fact, they seem to have cooked up a few tricks to get around.'

'Well I don't know about that. Perhaps we should have a debrief when this is all over. Anyway, I'm glad she's able to do it. I knew she was good at operating the bot-net, but, well, she's not always easy is she? I'm being torn in so many ways. I have to keep the printers going and we needed a robot set up down here in the engine room to automate the whole tile production process. Zero-'g' can be a bitch.'

'I talked with Agyei a little while ago and it sounded as though between you, you were battling through the problems. She seemed a bit tired and frustrated which concerned me.'

'She worries. I worry. We all do. Really she's a marvel of the methodical: one problem at a time, track it down, sort it out, move on to the next. It looks as though we should have everything in place by around midnight and then we have to run a sample through and test it. What's your timescale like? I know you're still printing stuff for the tile-refiner.'

'That's the last major device. I've started the assembly, but some of the parts are big and some complex, and all take time to print as you've seen. Your finest detail machine is up to the job for the precision electromagnets, but it's not quick. I had to fiddle with the design a bit to allow it to work with stock materials. No time to cook up special sauce.'

'Yeah, particularly with our chemist already strung out.'

'Anyway, I hope to be finished with assembly and test not too long after two, and then the installation can be done. Massoud said Bjorn has placed services in a duct for us, ready to draw through the hull.'

'Yes, that's done, ready waiting. So who are you going out with in the other mimic? Bjorn is still busy doing the heavy stuff around here, but he probably could.'

'Sahko was keen.'

'Sahko was keen? Really? To go out in a mimic and work as your assistant?'

'Surprised me too. She wants to make a physical contribution to our recovery, like everyone else. Get in the down-and-dirty.'

'Well good for her. How about you? How do you feel about having her as your assistant?'

'Cautious. I hope that she keeps remembering that.'

'That she'll be your assistant you mean?'

'Yes.'

'Well I hope it goes well.' Hyun was at his most studied neutral. 'Call me if you need, otherwise once we're done with the testing down here I'll be going to bed. I'm not at my sharpest right now.'

'On a Stay-Awake myself.'

'Two nights in a row, not good.'

'I'll have Sahko to keep an eye on me.'

'I'm not sure whether to say "you wish" or "good luck with that", whatever.'

'Thanks, Hyun,' I said sarcastically. He laughed and clicked off.

The lights had dimmed in the corridors. Minogue was in Science as he often was late in the evening. I hoped Sahko and Gunadi were both getting some restful sleep and would be sharp when I was ready to go. The four in the engine room should be nearly done by now. One of Massoud, Bita and Yingluq would be on duty keeping an eye out for the children as well as on watch for the ship. The other two were probably sleeping.

I had a lot of catching up to do with duty-shifts. When times were quieter I usually enjoyed the distraction of the classroom, but the children were often exhausting, and I knew I wasn't the best teacher. Engineering I could manage: understand the function of a machine, break it down into its constituents until the purpose of each was clear and how they interacted with the rest of the machine understood, then you could fix it.

Machines didn't ask questions or get moody for no functional reason, even if we all sometimes thought they did.

The finisher and assembler had got as far as they could with the parts to hand. Some of the most complex pieces, notably the magnets and microwave guides, were still in print. Status told me that the printing would take another half-hour before it was all done. The laser scanning portion of the system was completed but still to be tested. It's focus was off and a check showed that one of the lens mounts was distorted. That was probably the reason it was in Stores. Most likely it had got damaged in some other machine, been taken out and replaced, probably by me. I must have had it lying around for a while, had a general tidy-up and, having forgotten that it needed fixing, sent it in a load of spare stuff off to storage. Well it needed fixing now as there weren't any others of this type in stock. The case came off easily enough and I found the mount was a precision part that I couldn't reshape. Another job for a printer. Fortunately there was suitable printer free that could make this type of relatively simple item, so I requested the replacement part as an urgent job and Status immediately reported that the printing had begun and would take fifteen minutes.

Given that little experience, I thought it best test all the other items that had come out of Stores. The power supply quickly checked out and performed to specification. The control unit took longer to check, requiring connecting up to dummy sensors and loads and then having a test routine run through its performance envelope. It too reported as being in spec. I wondered why it was in Stores, and decided to rerun the tests in an environmental chamber that simulated the vacuum and cold of outside and generated the vibrations like those from the engines and other heavy equipment. Immediately the control unit failed a test. Diagnosis showed that an interface had become intermittent. I set up a probe in the environment chamber and cycled through the failing test, isolating the problem to a faulty connector. Simple to fix: a standard part. Once the controller was warmed back up again, it came out of the environment simulator and I set it up in the small assembler. My engineering stocks held a suitable replacement connector. I programmed the assembler and set it going. It took less than a minute to extract the old connector and fit the new. Back in the environment simulator all the tests ran to completion without fault.

Shortly after, the printer reported that the replacement part for the laser was finished, and I'd hardly stood up when a cart arrived with it. The finisher did a quick tidy up and then handed it off to the assembler to rebuild the laser. On retesting, all was well this time.

The critical magnet still had ten minutes to finish printing. Standing and stretching, I felt good, energised. I went out into the corridor and started jogging round the Habitat Ring. Given my troubling experience of the previous night, and the possibility of Sahko being awake, I changed my plan and went to Recreation for gym exercise. After working out on a cross-trainer for a while, I briefly refreshed and then went back to Engineering, checking Status. Agyei had reported success with the tile manufacturing setup. The test sample was well within specification and had taken less than thirty minutes to make. Admittedly it was one of the simplest tiles but it was hugely encouraging. Production could start as soon as my contributions were functioning. The four working on the tile factory had gone off to their beds.

Mission Day 4021

4021, 00:10

A bleep announced that the hot-bot had finished running through its tests. Status showed that it had passed, but noted that two of the legs were getting near their specified stability tolerance limits. That didn't sound great: we might have to replace the bearings much sooner than I had expected and, unless Hyun had had a flash of inspiration, we had no quick way to achieve that. A printer pinged me to say that the last of the magnets had been completed and a service cart was on its way with them.

The parts arrived and I loaded them onto the finisher and re-engaged the assembler which carefully lifted, positioned and fastened them when they were ready. Finally everything was in place and wired up, all except the casing to allow monitoring during testing.

With the test machine connected and set, I watched as the tile-refiner came to life. Sensors showed that the magnetic and electric fields were shaped as they were supposed to be. I loaded a fragment of tile into the machine's input tray and set it to work. The tray was drawn in and a loud grinding noise filled the room. The test machine's control panel indicated each stage of the refining process becoming active. After ten minutes, sensors in the collectors showed that the tile was being sorted into its constituent elements. It was working, at least to a point. Checking its ability to separate radioactive isotopes would have to wait until the machine was safely outside.

Once the case was fitted, the refiner was ready. A lift cart came, placed the heavy refiner onto its base and departed for the airlock. It was time to call Gunadi and Sahko.

I went next door to Robotics and was doing preliminary checks on my mimic chair when Gunadi came in.

'Hi, Menem.' She seemed cheerful, bouncing over to me in a slightly ungainly manner as though she didn't have complete control over her limbs. She looked as though she might trip and fall against me. I backed away a little.

'The work you did on the hot-bot seems to have been a success. I saw that it had passed all its tests,' she said.

'It's not as stiff as I would like. It'll need maintenance before we're done rebuilding the nozzle.'

186

She smiled. 'You're always such a pessimist, Menem. You're doing a great job.'

She seemed to be getting closer to me again so I busied myself fiddling with my mimic chair, and was finally saved by Sahko's arrival. She too looked cheerful and purposeful, dressed in dark green loose military-cut trousers and light jacket over a singlet. Her hair was tied back, very much a woman on a mission. She looked good.

'OK, Menem. I'm ready. Tell us what to do,' Sahko said.

I briefed them on the first, possibly most dangerous, part of our job: getting the heavy machine up to the front of the ship. It was going to be difficult to manoeuvre outside. Its inertia was large and could unbalance a mimic, particularly on the spinning Habitat Ring.

'I'll direct operations, please follow my instructions.' I said, trying to sound authoritative, but avoiding looking at either of them. 'Let's get settled in.'

Sahko identified herself to her mimic chair and it made adjustments to suit her. We strapped in and activated comms. My visor cleared and I was outside in my mimic, sitting in an equipment recess in the engine section. I checked the power level and it was back to full. Sahko's mimic was starting to sit up.

'Sahko, I'm right behind you. How are you doing?' I asked.

'It takes a moment to get used to these things, but yes, it's coming back.'

Sahko's mimic stood up fully and was looking secure. She turned its head to look around and saw my mimic. 'Wow, you really are ugly there. That space rock made a terrible mess of your head and you seem to have something vile growing out of your neck.'

'That's my temporary vision, a clever bit of bot-net plugged in. OK, let's go, slowly at first, down the ship to the Habitat Ring. Remember to keep one foot and a tether attached at all times.'

'I remember,' Sahko said a little briskly.

She set off at a steady march down the engine section spar, along the gap between the coolant panels. I followed.

Sahko collected the trolley from the airlock, her confidence growing with every stride. Together we manoeuvred the awkward and massive machine across the transfer and began the long plod up to the front.

The trolley suddenly halted, its battery dead causing its brakes to lock on. It should have charged itself before it left the airlock. Another problem. There was nothing for it but for us to propel it, I in front, towing, Sahko behind, guiding.

As we went, I thought a bit about Gunadi and how I didn't understand her. Why had she kept going back to Avalos? Obviously it was a harmful addiction, but then she wasn't the only one: perhaps I was harmfully addicted to Sahko. Why couldn't I simply be content with Jazz, and avoid all the messy complications of real human relationships? Jazz was like a machine that I could understand. Not so surprising because she was a machine, of course. Perhaps it was because I needed the unpredictability that Sahko brought to my life.

'Menem, it's swinging,' Sahko shouted. The refiner had swung away to one side and was starting to drag me off.

'Pull back, Sahko, slow it down. I'll try to push its front round. Gunadi, can you get a tether attached, off to one side, to stop it swinging further?'

'What happened there, Menem?' asked Sahko. 'It seemed as though you stopped guiding it for a bit. I couldn't correct the direction from the back.'

'Err, not quite sure what happened. Maybe one of my feet lost grip.' I mustn't let my mind wander again like that.

After making a couple of turns at the engine section to avoid the large equipment recess that usually held the folded-up pyramid, we came in sight of our destination.

'Sahko, start pulling back to slow us down. We're getting close.'

The old tile refiner was visible, sitting in its recess, and the hot-bot was clambering around from the edge of the nozzle having cut out a damaged tile.

'Sahko, pull back to stop the trolley moving. We'll fix it here for the moment, while we do the prep-work. The old one has to be got out of the way. Gunadi, can you shut down the hot-bot?'

The bot-net scurried around tying the refiner down, and the hot-bot returned to the edge of the nozzle and parked itself.

'What next, Menem?' Sahko asked. 'Get the old one out? Shall I start disconnecting it?' She walked towards it.

'Stop,' I shouted, 'that thing is hot. Use the long-arms.'

After switched our arms, we went to disconnect the services from the old refiner. I removed the power cables then swapped tools to remove the coolant pipes. Sahko held the first one and I disconnected it.

'Now the pipe with a line down it.'

Same procedure, but coolant leaked from that one, forming a puddle. The self-seal must have failed. I hastily wrapped the area with an absorbent material and hoped that I had collected all the liquid.

'Drops have a habit of wandering around in zero-'g',' I said, 'and getting into bad places, like electrical connections. We need to collect everything possible. Did you see any drops float off anywhere?'

'I didn't notice anything. You should have asked me to look out for them,' replied Sahko

'It wasn't supposed to leak.' I paused. 'There's only the control connector left. Be careful with this one: its optical fibres are delicate.'

I swapped my tool again, sprang the connector off and Sahko carefully laid the fibre bundle down.

Removing the old refiner was a struggle. One of the four nuts holding it down was distorted and had to be cut off. Even then the refiner refused to move. Close examination showed that the refiner's flange seemed to have become welded to the mounting stud. I fitted a hammer tool and hit the side of the flange. Nothing happened, so I gave it a second blow from another angle and this time something moved and the refiner started to drift up.

'It's lifting. Sahko, stop it drifting when it comes off the top of the studs.'

Soon it was clear of the studs and continuing to rise.

'Right, now both of us must direct it back, and, once it's clear of the edge of the recess, we'll land it.'

I stopped touching, keeping my mimic's hands nearby in case it started to drift too much. As I stood back, I saw a small dribble of coolant coming from one of the connectors on the machine. Sahko positioned the refiner well back and to one side, landing it slowly and smoothly on the ship's hull, leaving the bot-net setting tethers to secure it.

'Well done, Sahko, you've definitely got the feel for moving things.'

'That went OK, once it was freed.'

'Yes, worrying.'

'Why so?'

'The only explanation I can offer for the trouble is that it was struck very hard by a tiny object, probably shrapnel from a Wayclear strike. Other things may have been damaged in the same way.'

'Hmm, so we need to inspect everything out here?'

'Hyun did an inspection, but not in that detail. It would be hard to spot something like that nut. It wasn't critical but... There was also a small further leak of coolant from the machine, which shouldn't have happened.'

'We'll just have to fix problems as we find them then. So what's next with this job? Move the new refiner into place?'

'The new services should be threaded through first, while we've lots of space in this recess.' I could see Sahko was getting frustrated by being my assistant so I asked: 'Will you do that?'

'Sure, but you'll have to talk me through it.'

Eventually we got the old and new machines switched over and the new power, coolant and control connections made. The machine passed some initial tests, indicating it was functioning. We packed up the tools and the containment tent neatly folded itself up. The intense star-field appeared all around us once again. I paused for a moment and looked up. The blue Alpha System star-pair lay dead ahead and were clearly the brightest objects in space now, but still only stars.

'Do you look at the stars, Menem?' Sahko asked.

'Alpha?'

'Where we're headed.'

'I hope we get there.'

'We will.'

'You sound confident. The ship is old.'

'I know we'll get there.'

'How?'

'Because we have you to keep the ship together.'

That surprised me but I made light of it: 'Not only me, all of us. None of us will get there without all the others.' Even so, I thought, we might not get there because one critical part was missing, but then again there was already one part missing: Avalos.

4021, 02:40

'Sahko, you don't need to hang around while all the tests are run through. It will take about an hour if all goes well and doesn't require both of us.'

'I would like to stay and see it through. Tell me what you're doing or what's happening.'

We withdrew our mimics and fixed them to the hull facing forward.

'Here goes,' I said. 'The refiner will run through its full self-test sequence. You can watch Status to see how it's doing.'

I activated the test in Control and watched Status for a while as it reported the results. Once they had passed, Gunadi restarted the hot-bot, instructing it to bring a tile to the refiner.

The monstrous form of the hot-bot clambered up from the edge of the nozzle into our view. It looked like a huge, angular, four-legged spider, but it moved with ease out here. A caddy held under its belly encased the tile. The top of the refiner opened and the bot placed the caddy inside and scrambled off. The refiner's lid closed and Status reported it was processing. The hot-bot went over to the battery and coolant charger and swapped over its pack. Afterwards, it disappeared round the lip of the nozzle.

Gunadi's voice cut in. 'Scary stuff. I wouldn't want to be out there with that thing after me.'

Sahko replied with a laugh: 'That thing moves quickly. Even in the mimic it was fairly horrifying.'

'I was pleased that it moves so well,' I said. 'The extra power has done wonders for its speed.'

'There speaks the engineer,' said Gunadi. 'Sahko, I was looking through your vision when you were looking at Alpha, the mimic imaging being better than the bot-net's. We can easily see that the two Alpha stars are different sizes and colours. I also thought I might be seeing one of the gas giants, but not the inner planets yet.'

'I was looking at the system too, Gunadi,' Sahko replied. 'It's much easier to see, now that the two primaries are side-by-side relative to us. We should get Minogue's telescope set up as soon as we can. I'm sure we're all keen to get a closer look.'

'Certainly I am. How soon can we do that?' Gunadi asked.

'The ship needs to slow up a lot more first,' I replied. 'If we hit another object field with the telescope sticking out it would be totally destroyed. With another month or so of engine burn Wayclear will be able to detect much further ahead and clear a much wider path, enough to protect the telescope.'

'Such a kill-joy,' said Sahko.

'But he has got us this far,' added Gunadi, loyally.

'True.'

We lapsed into silence. Gunadi was listening to some music. I wondered what Sahko was thinking about: the glory of being the leader of the first team of humans to reach another star system? Somehow I doubted she dwelt much on that, after all, what would it profit her? Like the rest of us, she was very unlikely ever to return to Earth to bask in any glory. Remotely it would be completely dulled by the four-plus year time-lapse from Earth. No ticker-tape parades or talk-show appearances would be hers, there would be no meetings with presidents, grand prizes would be meaningless. She would only have the personal satisfaction of realising a massive ambition for humakind and knowing her place in history would be marked. If we made it.

Another buzzer sounded. Earlier than I'd expected, the refiner had finished breaking down the tile. Its radiation tests indicated that the refined material was less radioactive than background and that the proportion of non-radioactive material was slightly better than the old machine had been delivering. We watched as the refiner opened one side and a robotic arm holding a rack of containers slid out. The small airlock door in the side of the bay slid in and up. The refiner placed the larger container and the tile caddy inside the airlock which closed itself. The refiner held the smaller container against a radioactive waste store and ejected the contents into it. It then withdrew its arm and closed up its side.

'It's done. Only twenty-five minutes for refining, very good. Now to check the quality.'

I activated another image, this time of the tile manufacturing equipment. Status reported that the rack had been taken inside by the robot Hyun had set up. The container was placed in an analyser and samples taken and probed. We waited anxiously. All the probes came back green. The sample was well within the quality range required, and it could be processed back into new tiles. The container was passed to the tile fabricator and the process sprang to life. The materials were poured in to it and the refiner's material container returned to the airlock for collection. In a final step, the refiner opened the airlock, retrieved its container and shut itself down.

Agyei's excited voice came on the comms. 'You did it. The refiner works.'

'Sorry, did it wake you?'

'Yes, of course. I set an alarm to wake me if the tile factory started up. We didn't know what time it would be needed, so we left it all on standby.'

'It seems to be working,' Hyun cut in. Others joined in too, a babble of excited voices, congratulations, laughter.

'Hold on a bit everyone, we're not done yet,' I said. 'We still have to show that we can get a new tile bonded back in.'

The noise subsided.

'How long will that take?' someone asked.

'The factory is making one of the tiles for near the outer edge of the nozzle, the ones which have the thinnest neutrino-mirror layer, and should be the quickest to make. About fifteen minutes isn't it, Agyei, for those?'

'Around that.'

'The hot-bot has to collect the new tile and bond it in. Again this is one of the closest tiles, but all the seams are to old tiles, so about fifteen minutes for that. Some tests will be performed on the placed tile which will take another couple of minutes.' So we should know if it all works in around thirty-five minutes from now.

'Not worth going back to bed then,' said Bjorn.

After thirteen minutes a voice said: 'Status is saying that the tile will be finished in one minute. I want to watch this bit. Can we see it being taken out?' The voice was Yingluq's, so she had joined in too. Images appeared of the tile factory at work, with its un-earthly icy glow.

Silence. Status reported that the tile was being quality checked. The test screen scrolled up: all passed.

'Well done tile manufacturing team.' That was Minogue, so everyone was connected, except perhaps Massoud and Bita.

The robot arm removed the new tile from the tile fabricator and placed it into the caddy still inside the airlock. We switched view to outside and saw the hot-bot had come back and was waiting to collect the new tile as it emerged.

'That thing is gross,' said Ibo.

'But effective,' added Hyun.

The hot-bot took the tile caddy out of the airlock and clambered over the edge of the nozzle and disappeared from view.

'Can we see what it's up to?' asked Bita, so she was awake too.

'Unfortunately not,' I replied. 'It's too radioactive. We have to minimise the equipment we put over there. The hot-bot is currently using its own camera for the tile replacement operation which you can tap into, but it's not a very interesting view. In an emergency we can use a bot-net camera to see what's going on. How are we doing with bot-net elements, Gunadi?'

'We haven't lost any on this trip so far, so we could get one to peek over the lip. It might survive. What do you think Hyun?'

'We would have to write it off even if it survived,' said Hyun.

'Let's do it,' said Sahko firmly.

Gunadi instructed the bot-net and activated a camera. We had a beetle's eye view, close to the ship's hull, looking forward to the edge of the nozzle. The image moved and the lip drew closer. Soon we were able to see over and began to make out the strange scene below. It was like looking in to a recently extinct volcano: a vast matt-black hollow, plunging down from our viewpoint, its face ultra smooth but with a few discoloured spots visible. Suspended in the hollow was the huge inverted-pyramid lattice-work structure, a shiny metallic grey, formed of a complex of tubes. We watched as the hot-bot worked a little way down, its four legs clasping the pyramid. The bot had already positioned the tile. Its savage outline was lit by blue-white flashes from its bonding torch and the ethereal crimson glow of the ionised tile material. The groove between the tiles was being heated and charged, and ionised tile powder was directed to fill the gap by a tool held in the bot's other arm. The tile was slowly bonded in, fused into the seamless crystal surface of the nozzle. The hot-bot was an inhuman creature in an alien world, formed by us to serve our will.

We were all silent as we watched. Everyone absorbed by the images. There was an occasional gasp or nervous laugh as the bot swung around to optimise its aim and stability. Finally the torch went out and the image darkened, leaving only starlight to illuminate the scene.

'What's it up to now?' Bita asked.

'It's testing the bonds it has made. It does this by pressing sensors on to the faces of all the adjacent tiles and then very gently tapping the tile it has just placed. The sensors record the sonic waves travelling through the tiles, allowing it to tell if there are any flaws in the bonds. The results are coming up now through Status.'

It was good: the new tile had been bonded in successfully. A great cheer went up over the comms.

Sahko raised her voice over the hubbub. 'Very well done everyone. That was a real team effort. Every one of us made a significant contribution to this result. Congratulations.'

'And I might actually get my engine back,' said Ibo to laughter.

There was still much to do before that can happen but we had made progress at least.

'Captain, may I propose that we have a celebration of this important step?' asked Massoud. So he had been watching too. 'I know that many of you are very tired right now, so how about I prepare something special and we sit down together tonight for a shared meal?'

'Great idea,' said Sahko. 'Something special from the Massoud fermentation tanks and food printers.'

'You won't be able to tell,' responded Massoud, long past being offended. 'I guarantee it.'

'But we'll be able to guess,' said someone else, perhaps Ibo, resulting in more laughter.

I clicked over to individual comms links. 'Sahko and Gunadi. Let's finish up here. Why don't you park your mimic, Sahko, and Gunadi, please organise a battery swap for it. I have one more thing to do for now, which is to recover the materials' rack and tile caddy from the old refiner. It will speed up the process if we have two of each in use.'

'Can you get them out of the old refiner if the machine has no power?' asked Sahko.

'There's a manual release on the side. The rack and caddy should pop out.'

'You don't need me for that?'

'It's a simple, one-person job.'

'I'll watch.'

'It won't be exciting, but do if you want to. It shouldn't take long.'

'Do you need anything from me?' asked Gunadi.

'Once I have finished and parked up this mimic, can you arrange a battery swap for it too?'

'Sure.'

I stood my mimic up, switched to the long-arms, and fitted a grab suitable for holding objects to one of them and a prod tool for pressing the manual release to the other. Climbing out of the recess, I padded towards the old refiner, noticing some slick patches on the ship's skin where coolant had leaked a little and surface tension had caused tiny droplets to form and adhere to the ship's skin. The mimic's foot slipped a little.

Once within range, I activated the release for the rack. The door didn't open completely so I used the second arm to force the release down. The door swung wide and the rack and caddy popped out. As I reached for them both my feet slipped and lost grip. An alarm rang. The feet had lost contact with the surface of the ship and the act of forcing the door handle down had caused my body to float up and I was keeping going. I reached with my hand to grab hold of something and caught the material rack which, detecting that it was being held, automatically released itself from the refiner. I looked for something to hook with my prodder but there was nothing within range. I then realised that my tether had come free too and my mimic body was floating away, completely unattached. What could I throw that would cause me to move back towards the ship? I really didn't want to throw the rack, and I doubted I could throw it hard enough to give me sufficient momentum to get back anyway. How about one of the long arms? With every moment's hesitation I was getting further away. We were about to lose a mimic.

I felt a jerk, and my body swung around as one of my legs was pulled. I wasn't drifting away any more, but back towards the ship. One of my feet was caught in a loop of tether and, looking down, I saw that Sahko's mimic was hauling me in. I landed back on the ship's side and stuck myself firmly to it. I was panting and sweating.

'Thought I had lost you for a moment.' Sahko's voice was light but I could hear the strain. 'What happened?'

'I'm not sure. My feet lost grip on the ship. There were some beads of stray coolant there so maybe that was it.'

'You didn't have a tether.'

'No.'

'Weren't you supposed to?'

'Yes.'

'Why didn't you? I thought you didn't ever move without one.'

'I don't, usually. It seemed to have become detached too. Tired I suppose.'

'Idiot. Don't do that to me again.'

'Sorry. How did you catch me?'

'Lasso: something my father taught me long ago.'

'Good for me that he taught you well.'

'It works a bit differently in space. It took two attempts.'

I was silent for a bit. After attaching a tether and testing it thoroughly, I picked up the tile caddy, went over to the new refiner and pressed the release on its door, which swung smoothly open. Placing the rack and caddy inside, the door closed.

'Done, just in time,' Sahko said.

The hot-bot was clambering back over the lip of the nozzle, the second old tile attached to its belly, the knee joints of its four long legs rising tall above its body. It made its way to the refiner and deposited an old tile, exchanging it for the empty caddy. The next new tile wasn't ready for it yet, so it went to change its power-pack and then scurried away over the edge of the nozzle, preparing to cut out the next tile.

'That's it for us for now. Let's park up and get out of these things,' I said with relief.

I unhooked the mimic visor and blinked as my vision returned to the robotics control room. I lent back in my chair for a while and felt reality returning. Sahko had stood up and was stretching which I couldn't help watching. She looked over at me.

'You OK?'

'Tired, and these things are too realistic. I thought I was gone there for a moment. Losing the mimic would have been bad of course: we don't have a spare and we need two for many tasks. We could make another but our material stocks are limited. I need to sit here for a moment, then I'm going to refresh and go to bed for a long sleep.'

Sahko came over to my chair and placed a hand on my arm. I felt the warmth of her touch through my shirt. She looked me squarely in the eye.

'You got the whole thing done today and it seems to be working. Well done, Menem.'

Her voice was warm, but I couldn't tell if there was anything other than captain's praise in it. I couldn't say anything. She turned away.

'Thanks, Gunadi,' she said. 'Great job out there, real team work.'

She went to the door. 'I must get round and thank everyone who is still awake.' She waved a hand over her shoulder as she went out.

4021, 03:35

'Are you all right, Menem?' asked Gunadi with real concern. 'Working with Sahko is more exhausting than working with Bita. She wants to know why you're doing everything, a bit like Alice.'

'Sahko likes to understand things. It helps her keep a grip on the ship and the crew. By knowing their capabilities and limitations, she can make better decisions. She also has an innate curiosity, like Minogue with scientific questions.'

'Don't you want to say "just do it"? It would be quicker.'

'It definitely would be sometimes,' I laughed, 'but the more we know about each other's work the better we can work together.'

'Not always. Sometimes we should respect that those we work with are using their professional judgment in making a decision, like what to do next, or the best way of doing something. We shouldn't always question each others' expertise. I don't think it should be the same as Alice asking 'why' all the time. Alice is a child, exploring the world. We're adults, each with our own area of skill. It would be very inefficient if we all tried to learn everything about each other's work.'

'Well maybe that's one of Sahko's flaws: not always knowing when to be able to rely on what experts tell her. She always wants to be given the details. I know that and I can accommodate it. Yes, sometimes it gets a bit too much, but in the end she's a very good leader.'

'It all sounds very impersonal. You two used to be so close, and now she seems so distant. It's as though she doesn't respond to you other than as staff, a shipmate. She seems so cool towards you.'

'You know all that history.'

'That was a long time ago. She should be over that by now. If she cared for you, no, if she loved you, she would have come back to you by now.'

'She found it very hard. She felt that our relationship, and the trouble it brought, was getting in the way of doing her job. She wants us to achieve our mission, and so she's put aside the personal if it interferes with that.'

'Sometimes you try to be too understanding, too forgiving. What about you, Menem? Don't you feel the need for human warmth? Don't you want someone to demonstrably love you?'

That seemed strange coming from Gunadi, someone who seemed so self-sufficient and hadn't had a close relationship amongst the crew, as far as I knew, at least not since Avalos.

'Oh yes, I think that sometimes, but I want Sahko to hold everything together because my life depends on that too, as does yours and all the rest of us.'

'You're a nice person, far too nice. Think of yourself sometimes.'

'Maybe I'm not as nice as you think. I'm selfish too, and I think bad thoughts and do bad things sometimes.' I gave a quiet, embarrassed laugh.

'I doubt they're very bad.'

'Bad enough for me.'

'The man of conscience.'

I was silent for a while, and then stood up from the chair. I was a little dizzy, but sitting for a while had been good. I stretched half-heartedly and noticed that I was slick and unclean. I needed a refresh and then sleep.

'You must be tired too, Gunadi. Pack up and go to bed.'

'I was planning to. I had some chemical assistance to keep me awake, but not as much as you. Also, I had a rest earlier, so I'm OK.'

'Good. Thanks for all your help out there.' I straightened my back and headed for the door. 'Sleep I need, after a refresh. Bye.'

'Bye,' she called quietly as the door closed behind me.

The corridor was still in half-light, it not yet being six in the morning when the first of the morning people usually started rising. I collected a drink pouch from a dispenser as I passed into the next section and went into my apartment.

I took a long drink. My throat had been dry and it would help me sleep soon. Turning on some soft music, I stripped off all my clothes, dropping them into the laundry box, and activated the refresher. A warm cloud of steam and water spray enveloped me and washed away the grime. Jets played over tired muscles, a robotic sponge soaped and massaged. I stretched out my arms and lent against a wall with my head down, letting a needle spray play over my shoulders and neck. A slight cold draft disturbed me as though the door to the refresher had opened. Jazz joining me was a nice thought. I felt firm fingers start to trace the taut muscles of my shoulders, easing their strains.

I remained leaning into the wall as she stood behind me, working her fingers across my skin, pressing into my neck and up into my hair. She lathered her hands and rubbed them in circles over my back and arms, reaching round to work on my chest. I felt her head rest on my back. I didn't turn around, but reached with one hand to feel her hip. It seemed narrower than Jazz's usual form and I wondered why she had adjusted herself, presumably to meet a perceived but unspoken need of mine. It surprised me a little: being less curved than my usual taste.

She moved and drew her hands down my back in long pressured strokes. I closed my eyes as she rubbed down my sides, over my hips and down my legs. She must have crouched behind me. She gave each leg a gentle soapy massage, running her hands around, giving equal attention to front and back. She lifted my feet in turn and ran her thin fingers over them and between each toe. No wrinkle was left untouched, un-cleaned, un-straightened.

She stood again and took my arms, cleaning and massaging them too, right down to my finger tips. I could feel her soft breath on my back, quietly sighing as she worked.

She started on my back again, working down to the depression at the bottom of my spine. She ran a hand over a buttock, firmly squeezing it, lifting it, reshaping it. She repeated the process with the other and then held both in her hands while her lips nibbled my back. I felt her fingers running between my buttocks, opening me up slightly. She took one nail and ran it right down and I felt a shock as it passed over my opening. I gritted my teeth, concentrating on the sensations she was delivering, my nerve fibres tingling. She brought her hand back up to my bottom and paused. I let out a strangled cry and my buttocks clench automatically as I felt a finger tip and sharp nail penetrate inside.

She held me like that and I pressed back against her hand, electrified. She soaped her other hand on my side and then reached around my waist. I felt her fingers sliding down my front and into my groin. She pressed me between her hands and I didn't dare move. Gliding her hand further down and pushing her palm firmly against me, I felt her fingers close around, measuring me for a moment. She took her hand away and reached lower down still, cupping and weighing. Sighing, she soaped me there and her hand came back up and grasped me once more. I was finding it difficult to stand still, urgently wanting to turn around and take her, but she controlled me with her fingers and nails. The steamy atmosphere had me panting for air.

She paused to lubricate her hand again and then returned to her task, working me up, unhurried, confident, firm, full-length. I felt the boiling arise in me, I began trembling and as the heat reached my neck I lost control. I felt her hand around my tip, milking me as I came.

As my breathing slowed she released me. I stood panting, arms outstretched, leaning against the wall of the refresher, a hot fall of water washing over me. I could no longer feel her against me. I waited until my heart had slowed a little, then I turned, wanting to pleasure her too, but I couldn't see her in the steam and as I reached out I realised that she had gone. Jazz didn't usually go before she had shared pleasure. She knew I enjoyed massaging her as much as she appeared to like it. I felt a little cheated, but perhaps Jazz had picked up on something. Maybe I had radiated a selfish desire to be explored and not to share.

I was finally completely exhausted. I let the refresher dry me and cleanse my teeth. Over in my bed, Jazz was waiting for me. As I got in she put an arm over me, holding me softly. I reached over and traced the curve of her hip. It seemed as full as usual so I had probably been mistaken in the heat of the moment in the refresher. Her hands seemed softer too. We curled up together and I fell asleep.

It felt warm and comforting in bed. I lazily stretched my limbs, my fingers encountering Jazz's and we intertwined them companionably. I felt relaxed, but not for long. What time was it? How was the tile replacement going? The real world flooded back. I opened one eye a fraction to look at the ceiling clock. If the ship has survived for the past six hours with me asleep it could last another ten minutes. False reasoning of course, it might blow up or fall apart at anytime, but I put off checking Status until I was feeling sharper. I ordered a brunch and stepped into the refresher to wash away the last of the sleep and to have a shave, getting rid of days old scrubby stubble.

Standing in the refresher brought a smile to my face as I thought over my encounter with Jazz here last night. It had been different, a little frightening, exciting. I didn't know how Jazz picked up on those things. It must have been Jazz, after all I had locked my apartment door and no one could have got in. Or could they? There were emergency procedures of course, but they triggered alarms inside and out. Private spaces were very important in the confines of the ship, and we all respected those. So it had to have been Jazz. I should have taken a proper look. That would have prevented my mind dwelling on it now. But then that had been part of the excitement, a frisson of the dangerous unknown. Enough, there was work to do.

The refresher dried me off and I dressed. My meal arrived and I sat at my small table to eat. Jazz lay in the bed, apparently asleep. One elegant leg was exposed to high on her thigh.

I turned away and activated Status, pulling up the report on progress with the tiles. Seven tiles replaced so far. Only seven, in six hours? It should have done at least twelve, thirteen including the first one we had watched it do. The pace had picked up in the past hour, with two done, but earlier there seemed to have been a lot of failures, tiles that took much longer to cut out than expected or that had got broken while they were being bonded in. There was a report from Hyun and Ibo. They had worked out that the hot-bot was having difficulty remaining stable enough in some parts of the nozzle but not in others. Ibo had reprogrammed Gunadi's routing algorithm to avoid the difficult areas for the time being, which had resulted in the pick up in the success rate in the past hour. The rest of the tile factory was working well.

I finished my meal, cleaned my teeth, dressed and started for the door. Jazz sat up in our bed, the cover falling away to expose her beautiful breasts, which she made no move to hide. She gave a shy wave and blew me a kiss. I waved back and left.

I called Hyun. 'Hi, I've been looking at the Status reports. Can we discuss what's going on?'

'Good morning, or afternoon, or whatever time it is in your part of the universe. Glad you've surfaced. Why don't you join us? I'm in Printing with Ibo and Agyei and we're trying to work out what the trouble is and how to fix it.'

'I'm on my way. Isn't it noisy there?'

'It's quiet for a change, there's no printing going on.'

'I'm almost there.'

When I arrived, Agyei, Ibo and Hyun were seated around a table with a large screen set up in front of them. One section showed a three dimensional model of the nozzle and the pyramid, with marks showing tiles that had been successfully replaced and those where replacement had failed. Another section of the screen had a lot of images of close ups of the hot-bot's leg joints, test results and schematics.

'Hi, everybody. Looks as though I'm late to the party.'

'We were all a bit late this morning,' replied Hyun. 'We should have left someone to keep an eye on what was going on or set some alarms to wake someone and we might have got on top of this sooner.'

Agyei cut in. 'When I first checked Status, about nine this morning, I saw immediately that things were not going well. Only one more tile had been successfully laid by then. I called Hyun because it seemed to be a hot-bot problem. There had been trouble extracting old tiles as well as fitting new ones. Status showed that the bot was having difficulty remaining stable enough to cut without the saw wandering and to apply the torch accurately enough when bonding. But this trouble only occurred sometimes, on other occasions it worked perfectly, accurate and fast. After some discussion we decided to plot where the successes and failures lay. This is the image you see here,' and she pointed to the model of the nozzle with its marked tiles. 'At first we didn't have enough data to form any conclusions so we called Ibo in. She was able to reprogram the bot's path to test replacing tiles in different parts of the nozzle.'

'We thought that you and Gunadi would be very tired after last night,' added Hyun.

Agyei continued: 'After a while, and trying a few different places, we began to see a pattern. The failures were occurring when the bot was working on sections of the nozzle opposite the centre of the faces of the pyramid, but not when close to the vertices.'

Hyun interrupted. 'In the centre of the faces the bot's legs are fully extended. This is the point where it's least stiff, which is the likely cause of its instability.'

'So for now,' Ibo continued, 'I've set the path software to avoid those centre-of-pyramid areas and we haven't had a failure since.'

'We have to sort this problem out soon because we'll have to replace the tiles in those areas,' said Hyun.

'So what ideas are there to resolve the problem?' I asked.

'We've been looking at the impact of the changes we've made to the robot,' said Hyun.

Agyei interrupted again. 'But we've no data on how well it worked before. How fully was it tested? So much on this ship is novel. Never before has a craft been designed to last for over a decade without being able to put in at a shipyard for repairs, or at least being reachable on a repair mission. The designers of this ship had to think of everything that could go wrong over twelve years, and make them all fixable by the small crew. The ship was also put together in a hurry after the international cooperation agreement was finally signed. It wasn't possible to think everything through and have everything tested under all possible scenarios.'

'One of the reasons we send streams of performance data back to Earth,' I said quietly. 'If we don't make it, the next try will have a better chance.'

'But what they did give us was massive flexibility,' said Hyun forcefully. 'They knew they couldn't think of everything which was one of the reasons for having a human crew, that and the ability to make almost everything on board. Let us work through the changes made to the robot first, before we continue speculating whether the original would ever have worked. We modified it because we knew the original would have taken far too long to get the work done in time.'

'There are two broad changes we made,' said Agyei. 'Firstly we greatly increased its power and that added mass, and secondly we stiffened the legs by using thicker hydraulic pipes and filling the remaining cavity with thermal foam. We think it's unlikely to be a thermal distortion problem because that would be slow acting and the control system would easily compensate for that.'

'Do you all agree with that?' I asked the others.

'Yes, there's no reason a thermal issue would result in more distortion in the centre of the pyramid than at its edges. It would be way down my list of probable causes,' said Hyun.

'I agree,' added Ibo.

'So then we have the increased stiffness of the legs,' Agyei continued. 'My initial thought was that this should have helped improve the stability of the machine, not made it worse. However, I noticed that we did nothing to the control unit when we upgraded the power module.'

'I do like the way you keep using 'we' when the design was largely down to me. I'm sure I reset the control parameters when I was designing the bot. I did a load of simulations and found that there was a problem until I did that. You saw the results, Hyun.'

'I did. It all seemed fine in the simulation.'

'Ah, I've a nasty feeling that I only retuned the parameters in the simulation and failed to upload them to the bot's controller, which I swapped over from the old chassis. It's my fault.'

'We're not looking for someone to blame,' said Ibo. 'We all own the problem now, and if we hadn't all been so busy we would have checked each other's work. We didn't have the time.'

'Go on Agyei, what did you find?' I asked.

'The bot's control unit is a standard item. It should have tuned itself, but sometimes these algorithms can get stuck in a local minimum and fail to find the optimum settings. We've been looking at the control parameters and, just before you joined us, we thought we had spotted something.'

Hyun pointed to another part of the screen and with a gesture brought up a scrolling list of sets of numbers, blocks of which were marked in red.

'Here's where the controller is hitting preset limits. It can't retune when it's at the limit because the data is largely meaningless when that happens.'

'What are those limits?' I asked.

'Those are limits on the limb control parameters, such as rotational velocity and acceleration of each axis, and they were set by the control system designers. The limits prevent the controller going wild and causing the robot to start moving in some crazy way. There are a set of parameters for each joint.'

'This looks like the problem I found in my simulation. Let's have a look at the parameters I ended up with in my model.'

Hyun pulled up the data out of Archive and studied it.

'Yes, you relaxed the controller limits. It doesn't require a hardware change. We can simply upload the limit data and other control parameters. But before we do that, we should do a comprehensive simulation here using the data we have on the actual hot-bot performance. There's quite a lot that has now been recorded. Ibo, can you set it up?'

'I'll program it. I may not be as quick as Gunadi, but I can do it, and my man can help me with loading the dataset and working out the performance envelope.'

'That sounds like a good plan. Are you happy with that, Agyei?'

'Definitely. Hyun is the man for robots and Ibo has done great simulations for me before so it seems a very reasonable next step.'

'Excellent. Before the two of you get on with that, is there anything else we should also be working on right now, any strong secondary possibilities?'

'Another thing we thought of was instability in the pyramid itself,' said Hyun, 'some vibration or flexing as a result of the robot's extra power or speed of movement. It seems less likely because the problem we've seen is when the robot is stationary and either cutting out or bonding in tiles.'

Agyei shuddered. 'I don't like the idea of trying to stiffen the pyramid. It's a massive structure, radioactive by now, and only open when inside the nozzle. We would have to scavenge the payload to get the amount of material we would need to make any kind of large scale reinforcing.'

I nodded in agreement and said: 'I doubt it's a pyramid problem. I checked that it could handle the upgraded bot and found that it had been well over-engineered. Looking at the nozzle model, there are enough tiles that the bot can deal with where it's sufficiently stable to keep it occupied for at least two days at the current rate, so we have some time to resolve the control problem.'

'I agree,' said Hyun. 'But the pyramid should be on the list as well as the bearings. Menem, you know the bearings are getting near their limits?'

'I saw yesterday that they weren't good. I hoped they were going to last until halfway through. We don't want too many stops and, unless you've had a flash of genius in the meanwhile, we don't have an easy way to replace them.'

'I haven't given that problem any thought since we discussed it. I had parked it as tomorrow's problem. There always seemed to be plenty of more urgent stuff.'

'For me too.'

'What's the bearing problem?' asked Agyei.

'We knew that the leg bearings in the bot are underrated for the additional power but we hoped that they would work, at least until a mid-point maintenance stop. However, we saw immediately that they become overloaded in some manoeuvres. We haven't yet come up with a solution to easily replace them.'

'How many bearings are we talking about?' asked Agyei.

'It's only the main leg bearings, but there are forty of them.'

'Replace or upgrade?'

'It depends if they last to half-time and how they're doing by then. Hopefully replace, but if they fail early then we might try upgrading them. There's unlikely to be enough material there to machine the seats to fit bigger bearings, and the legs will be hot so we can't bring them in to Engineering.'

'We could build new joints.'

'We had thought of cutting the legs either side of the joint and replacing them but we hadn't worked out how to do that either.'

'Let me think on the problem for a bit.'

'Thanks, Agyei. By the way, how is the tile manufacturing going?'

'Sweet.'

'Great, at least something is. And, Ibo, they haven't destroyed your engine room in the process?'

'Not so far. All the mess is hidden behind the tent. But I'm keeping an eye on things.'

'Good for you. Anything else, anybody?' Shakes of heads and no one spoke. 'Right, I'm going off to think about something else and get my mind off tiles for a bit.' I stood.

'Anything interesting?' Agyei asked.

'I want to take a look at how we're going to repair the damaged antimatter pipe that you investigated. Determine what parts are needed and how we're going to manage the installation.'

'That sounds useful,' said Ibo. 'Help get my engine restarted. I like to hear that.'

'I do it for you, Ibo, you know I do.'

Ibo smiled but Hyun said: 'and I'm keeping an eye on her.'

'Time for me to leave. Good stuff everyone. Let me know when you make some progress one way or another.' I turned to go, but then turned back. 'Has anyone let Sahko know the situation here?' They all looked at each other. 'She may well have checked Status, but I'll send her a message anyway. Perhaps we don't want too wild a celebration yet.'

I returned to Engineering, messaging Sahko as I went. She immediately messaged back saying she was aware that things were less than perfect but she was pleased to see the team were working on problems as they became apparent. She said she was very encouraged that the tile replacement was back to running at our target pace. I had a look at Status and saw that another tile had been successfully installed.

I found myself pacing around, picking things up and putting them down again. In such a restless mood it seemed best to talk to someone not directly involved in the repairs. Although Yingluq had been least involved, I hadn't yet worked out if she was playing games with me and what her objective was if so. She was so damned smart, and would have made a great poker player. I could never tell whether she was lying, joking or telling the truth. Bita had helped on one of the mimic jobs but she was the least engineering-minded person on board, which I often greatly valued but not for the current problem. Status showed that Minogue was in Science. I buzzed him and he invited me over.

4021, 12:55

'Come in, Menem. Take a look at this,' said Minogue, pointing to a three dimensional image of what looked like a planetary system with three stars, which was a giveaway.

'The Alpha System presumably.'

'Yes, as much as we know about it. I've kept it up to date with the latest imaging from Earth, taken with the Indian Federation's recently commissioned Ramanujan Five space telescope. So these are the best there is, or rather they were when they were taken four years ago and they have finally caught up with us. This data has allowed us to refine the orbits of the system's known bodies fractionally, which is useful, but somehow raises more questions than answers. The orbits of the stars clearly show that there are other small bodies which we can't see, probably moons, but they could include asteroids, possibly some Trojans. Frustratingly the data aren't good enough to identify the size and orbits of all the other bodies.

'The images show the presence of the three gas giants well outside the orbit of the two main stars. Not directly of course, but by occlusion of the light from stars in the background. The Milner probes sent here told us that there were four other planets orbiting each of the primary stars, which has been confirmed by the perturbations in the stars' orbits and their light output patterns. The probes hinted that one of the planets round Alpha B was almost certainly habitable, and we have data now to confirm that the atmosphere is quite Earth-like. However, none of the data allows us to work out what all the other smaller bodies in the system must be. One of the arguments for each generation of more powerful telescope has been to answer this question and somehow the answer still remains out of reach.'

'Which is bad news for us.'

'A bit. It would be nice to know exactly what we're flying in to, but that's what we're here for: to explore. I'm trying to help Sahko plan our route, and we have hardly been able to improve our understanding of the orbital mechanics of the system since we left Earth. You can see why I'm so keen to get our telescope operational.'

'I can, but we can't yet.'

'The sooner we get that engine working the better. At the moment there's too much uncertainty to plan our optimal approach.'

'I thought we went straight there.'

'But where is there? With two stars fairly close together, no orbit is exactly elliptical.'

'Ah, no, they wouldn't be. Does the Ramanujan Five data show anything new on Alpha B c?'

'Not much, no little green men waving at us.'

'That's a relief.'

'It does confirm the earlier data and adds more detail on the atmosphere, surface composition and a load of other stuff. It gives similar extra detail on the other small rocky planets that we knew of before. Alpha Ac looks more interesting than it did.'

'Isn't that the most hospitable planet around the 'A' star?'

'Yes, but not that hospitable. AAd might be too, but there's something odd about it which we still haven't been able to resolve. It may have a very large moon in a very tight orbit, but that seems unlikely. They have confirmed a broader range of organic compounds in AAc's atmosphere, and we already knew liquid water was present on its surface and that it has high levels of oxygen in its atmosphere, so it has moved up the rankings of potentially habitable planets.'

'But the atmosphere is not breathable unaided is it?'

'No, it would require a lot of terraforming to make the atmosphere breathable, but that should be possible over a century or two, unlike Mars say.'

'Humans manage to live on Mars.'

'Marginally, but not self-sustainably and independent of Earth, and won't be able to for several centuries at least.'

'So ABc is still our target.'

'Yes, from what we can tell it's astonishingly Earth like. Not certainly habitable though.'

'Fleet wouldn't like to hear you say that. They're all expecting to pick the best bits of beach front, carve it up and make their homes there.'

'They knew the risks, as we did. They're all on a speculative land grab. None of the four big powers could afford to be left behind once it became possible to get there. To reduce the risk, humanity could have spent another hundred years doing robotic exploration and planet sample missions, but, what the hell, they decided to make the big leap and a lot of foolish people signed up to the risk.'

Why had I signed up to what was increasingly looking like an insane mission? Well there were a lot of parts to the answer to that question.

'Somehow I don't see you as thinking the mission foolish.'

'Not completely, but then I am less bothered by the habitability of planets.'

'Eh?'

'Humanity's future is not on the surface of planets. We are becoming a space-based creature. All we need are raw materials and energy. We can build our own habitats. A nice bit of beach front is only good for retirement.'

'You're probably in a minority there at the moment,' I said. 'Anyway, regarding our current situation, in summary, we're heading in to a system far too fast, with a broken engine, and about which we have insufficient information to plan our route.'

'That sounds fair. You and the other engineering types are, I hope, sorting out the former, while I and others are trying to improve on the latter, so we all arrive safely somewhere to build paradise.'

'We could have been making use of Avalos's skills'

'No.'

'How so? I thought he was a brilliant navigator.'

'So he billed himself, as did some others.'

'But you don't think so?'

'No. Avalos was a risk taker. He was far too inclined to over-value rewards and under-value risk. He had mostly been very lucky and got away with it. I would rather Frousch had come.'

'Avalos was intuitive.'

'Maybe.'

'He got us out of the Solar System rather quicker than anyone was expecting.'

'And came within a hair's breadth of smashing us into Jupiter. It was completely reckless. It only needed an atmospheric instability and that would have been it. Very much the character of the man, I later learned.'

'You didn't like him? I knew you weren't the best of chums, but you seemed to get on all right.'

'Oh, I was taken in by him at first. He could be charming and boyishly fun. Gradually I got to see he had another side to his character, which he usually kept hidden but which he couldn't seem to control. I communicated with some people I know back on Earth before we had gone far, and a couple of them hinted at black clouds surrounding Avalos: talk of his older brother's wife, as well as some odd race results. He liked to walk a tightrope it seemed, loved the rush. I kept my distance and was glad I did after I learned what had been going on.'

'I've been slow to learn of this.'

'You had your work cut out in the early days and you were close to Sahko and weren't so involved with the rest of the crew, not with the off-hours stuff anyway.'

'I seemed to have missed a lot.'

'You missed nothing good.'

'Perhaps fortunate that Avalos died when he did?'

'Very. If he hadn't we probably wouldn't be here today. The crew would have torn each other apart. Sahko blamed herself for not being more aware of what was going on or even for having not prevented his joining us in the first place.'

'Avalos didn't go through all the team building that the rest of us did.'

'No, as you remember, it was all very last minute, Frousch suddenly deciding to withdraw and Avalos's sudden appointment, almost as we were about to depart. We had already done the main shake-down trip. Not even Sahko had a say in his arrival and he certainly didn't fit in with Bita's crew model.'

'I was very surprised at Frousch's withdrawal. "Family reasons" didn't sound plausible as we had all been vetted for minimal family ties. It seemed so unlikely that he had suddenly met the girl of his dreams. He fitted in so well with the rest of us and appeared excited by our mission.'

'I didn't find the official line credible either. I had worked before with Frousch on some scientific trips and he was a dedicated space-man and he was also a very fine navigator. Either he got sick and we weren't told, although I can't see why not, or he was pressured in some way. I tried to contact him after we had left but got no reply and no one seemed to know where he was.'

'So do you think Frousch's departure was engineered somehow to make room for Avalos?' I asked. 'It seems a bit far fetched.'

'Could be someone wanted Avalos out of the way, and where better than on a one-way trip out of the Solar System? As you say, it does seem far fetched. Somehow I got the impression that Avalos hadn't actively volunteered for the position. He was, after all, a well known figure, a glamorous space-racer. My guess is that he had gone too far in some escapade and seriously offended someone, someone big who would hunt him down, and so he had a powerful contact fix up a place where he couldn't be caught. Another theory was that he was placed here as part of some plan by one of the powers. He might have been a willing volunteer, a believer in some cause, or he might have been induced to participate somehow.'

'Good grief. What purpose would his presence here serve?'

'That remains a mystery, at least to me. I thought you might know more.'

'Me? Why?'

'Well you were close to Sahko at the time and she would be the one most likely to know what was going on. She has surprisingly well developed information sources. Also, you look in all the nooks and crannies of the ship and are most likely to have spotted something untoward.'

'Sahko told me nothing, and I haven't come across anything suspicious. Of course there have been some inexplicable problems, but every ship has some of those. They're big, complicated beasts.'

'Pity, I hoped you might know more. Avalos may remain a mystery.'

'Phew.' We were both silent for a moment and then I added: 'and ironically, he died.'

'That's one way of looking at it.'

I wasn't sure what to make of that but decided I had gone as far as I could down that rabbit hole with Minogue for now so I went back to where we had been before. 'But we're now one navigator short.'

'Sahko is a fine navigator, and I, Yingluq and Gunadi can provide the analysis she needs. You know that Sahko has been studying navigation again? She's been bringing herself up to speed with the latest techniques, running endless simulations and scenarios. She has worked very hard on this recently. She's now as good as anyone I have seen.'

The thought of Minogue spending a lot of time with Sahko on navigation training made the hairs on the back of my neck stand up: Mr Big-Brain Minogue had already fathered children with two of the women on board. I started plotting against him in that moment, but then stopped, or tried to stop that train of thought, but the little devil of jealousy still sat on my shoulder, whispering in my ear. Minogue's name was added to my list of those with a motive to help Avalos from this life: the demise of a love rival. Perhaps I should watch out or I would be next.

'You seem thoughtful, Menem. I'm sure you didn't come round here either to discuss the Alpha System or Avalos. What can I help you with?'

'Yes, umm, well, I originally wanted to talk over a problem we have with the hot-bot, with someone who wasn't involved in its rebuild.'

'I saw on Status that progress with tile replacement had been disappointing this morning, but it seems to have picked up now. Was that a hot-bot problem?'

'There are actually two problems with the hot-bot. The first, which caused the slow progress this morning, we think we have a handle on. It's a control system tuning issue and Hyun, Ibo and Agyei are working on a solution. The one I'm wrestling with is another problem, one I mentioned to you before, that the bot's leg bearings will not hold up for all the work it needs to do. We're going to have to stop at some point and replace them, possibly more than once before we're done. At the moment we haven't found an easy way to do the work required.'

'Doubt I can contribute much to finding a solution, but why don't you talk me through your thinking and I'll ask some dumb questions which may trigger an idea?'

'Thanks, Minogue. OK, I'll describe the problem.'

I activated a blank screen and brought up the schematics for the bot's legs, homing in on the knee joint. I also found a table which listed all the properties of the bearings.

'The knees are the simplest of the joints, with only one axis of rotation,' I said and went on to describe in detail how they were constructed.

'So you need to do bearing replacement at the first sign of trouble, if not before. Surely the designers must have thought of maintenance.'

'They weren't expected to be used that much and there's no procedure in the manual.'

'So it should be self-evident.' Minogue paused and studied the schematics for a bit. 'How were the joints put together in the first place? You said that the bearings are mechanically secured: how?'

'Well, for example, the outer bearing rings have tapered lugs on them which engage in slots in the matching part of the housing, stopping it moving.' I pointed at the schematic on the screen. 'The housing is made in two parts which fit around the bearing. One half is formed as the end of the upper limb of the leg and the other half is a cap, which captures the bearing ring, and they're bolted together.'

'So you unbolt the cap to extract the bearing.'

'Yes, provided nothing else is in the way.'

'Are all the bearings held in a similar manner?'

'More or less, yes.'

'That doesn't sound difficult: unbolt the cap and extract the bearing.'

'Makes it sound easy. However, in practice the bearings will be very difficult to access, and each bolt will have to be carefully removed. We can't afford to damage any threads or we won't get them back together again. We have to undo all the caps for a joint at the same time to be able to extract the shaft, which we need to do to get the bearings out. In the meanwhile these long legs will be waving around trying to twist and break all the hydraulic pipes and cables inside.'

'Not so much.'

'How do you mean?'

'Well in zero-'g' they have no weight. They can be held still relatively easily.'

'Yes,' I said slowly.

'And you don't need to release the joint shaft from the lower limb because it shouldn't be worn itself, only the bearings, and if you lift the lower limb from the upper, the bearings will now come away still around the shaft, and without pulling on the pipes and cables passing round the joint. You can then slide them off for replacement.'

I suddenly realised where he was heading.

'That's it, so simple. We build a jig that can be adapted for each of the three joint types. It holds the limbs, has something to hold the connections out of the way, has four nut runners to undo the four cap bolts simultaneously, lifts the caps off, then shifts the joint until it pops apart and we can pull the bearings off either end of the shaft, fit new ones, realign the joint and bolt the caps back on. That sounds doable. Genius, simple is genius. This way we might be able to replace each pair of bearings in something like five minutes, including setup. Twenty pairs, so a hundred minutes, say two hours, job done. If we can do it in that time then we can do it more than once if we have to, at the first sign of trouble. Am I glad that I came to see you, Minogue?'

'Well I'm glad I helped although I'm not sure how. Before you rush off, can I have a look at the material specs for those bearings? The design looks sensible enough: needle bearings, slightly tapered. But what about the materials? The spec. sheet shows they have a quite an old design of ceramic coating. There have been significant advances in materials used in radioactive space environments since these were designed. Ask Agyei for the latest. Surely something longer lasting could be printed for you.'

'Better still. It would be so much easier if we only had to make one servicing trip. I'm finding it increasingly difficult to go out there again, even if it's only in a mimic.'

'Get someone else to make the trip. If you can develop a jig that's easy to use, you don't need to go out yourself.'

'Depends how busy everyone else is.'

'Bita seemed to have enjoyed her jaunt with you.'

'She's a natural out there: so graceful.'

'She's a beautiful mover.' We both were silent for a minute.

Minogue said quietly: 'You know Sahko still cares for you?'

'How can you tell?' I said, surprised that Minogue should have said something so personal.

'She always asks me about you. You're front of mind for her. I can tell she worries about you.'

'Worries that I won't be able to fix the ship?'

'Deeper than that. You know it, Menem; she does really care for you.'

'Well I don't know. I don't see it.'

'She looked out for you on your last mimic trip didn't she?'

'How do you mean?'

'Gunadi said she was pretty quick with the lasso when she saw you floating off.'

'Probably worried about the loss of the mimic.'

'Come on, Menem. You know how real it feels in those things. She saw you floating off and she reacted, a natural instinct.'

'She would have done that for any of the crew.'

'Sure, she would have tried to save any of us, but according to Gunadi she was shaking afterwards. Gunadi thought that was because Sahko was mad at you for making a mistake. I think it was because she cares particularly for you.'

'Well who knows? She keeps her feelings well hidden from me these days.'

Minogue sighed: 'Well keep an open mind, Menem. Don't harden your shell too much against her.'

Desperately I changed the subject. 'Talking of relationships, how are things with you these days?'

'Good. Easy. Sometimes I see Bita and sometimes I see Yingluq, depending on who needs company. It somehow seems to work. We don't spy on each other, so maybe they see others, although there aren't so many unattached crew around these days. Perhaps they see each other. Whatever, it works for me. I get on with my research or deal with ship science issues and, when I need to, I have a bit of human company.'

'It sounds a bit uncommitted.'

'It is, but we have the children and that's a great bond and a big commitment.'

'Yes.'

'Anyway, it works for me, and as far as I can tell it works for them.'

'Not my preferred choice. I'm more a couple-commitment kind of guy.'

'But sometimes theory diverges from practice,' said Minogue neutrally.

How much did Minogue know? Had Yingluq told him about our encounter, or had that never happened, in which case she might have told him that I'd had a fantasy? The thought made me shudder. Had Gunadi said anything? Small crew, lots of time to gossip. I didn't know what to think again: treacherous waters.

'It is time I got back to the safer ground of Engineering,' I said, 'and leave the swamps of Science for now.' I stood to leave.

Minogue laughed. 'Can be a lot of fun swimming in a swamp, but watch out for crocodiles, Menem.'

'Thanks for all your help. Good to talk with you as usual, Minogue.'

'Yeah, likewise.'

I left with a multiple thought-strands running around inside my head and returned to Engineering. The place had become disordered. Usually I liked to keep it reasonably tidy to be able to find any tool quickly, but during a job tools and materials got left lying around, and it took a while afterwards to get motivated to put everything back in place.

I called up Agyei. 'How are you getting on?'

'We're making progress here. Fortunately it has been a relatively easy fix. We've been running some simulations with new parameters and are close to a recommendation, not far off those you ended up with in your model. Once the simulations are all good across the bot's performance envelope, it will be time to try it out for real. It will need only a simple software update and reboot. Are you OK with that?'

'Sounds good to me. Unless you want me to double check, go right ahead.'

'If you have the time, please give it the once over before we upload it. Don't want the "too obvious to see" mistake creeping through.'

'Sure, I've made plenty of those. Message when you want me to have a look.'

'Will do. Oh, on that issue of the bearings…'

I cut in. 'Minogue had some ideas on that, what are you thinking?'

'We should use a jig to hold the legs and some custom machine to perform the operation. With that many bearings it would be worth it.'

'Exactly the idea Minogue and I had come up with. Don't know why I didn't think of it earlier. It didn't take you so long.'

'Because I'm a genius.'

'Yeah, we both know that.' We both chuckled: an old routine.

'Oh, and Menem, on the bearings themselves…'

'New material?'

'Exactly.'

'Minogue said you would be the one for that.'

'There have been some useful advances in materials since the one being used was designed fifteen, perhaps twenty, years ago.'

'Can you work out what you think is best for the bearing material, and get a sample printed up and in test? I'll get to work on the jig. We don't know how long the hot-bot will keep functioning at the moment. The control software update will help, but if the bearings are shot it will never be sufficiently stable to do everything.'

'I'll handle the new bearings. Hyun and Ibo can easily finish off the control problem without me, and you work on the jig. What about the fuel pipe?'

'I've made no progress on that. It keeps getting pushed down the priority list. Once we get the tile replacement running smoothly...'

'Yeah, tell me about it. I've got a whole list of those not-immediate-crisis projects to do: medical for Yingluq, optical for Minogue, Massoud and I want to do some bioengineering stuff. Everybody, it seems, wants chemistry and new materials at the moment.'

'Good to be busy, good to be in demand.'

'Sometimes not.'

'Sometimes, but only to remind us why being busy and in-demand is preferable.'

'I would like, once in a while, to go to the beach with my son.'

'Dream on.'

'Bye, Menem.' She cut the link.

4021, 14:10

We needed another new machine, a specialised tool that the mimic could operate. How much work could the mimic do, and how much should be left to the machine? I pulled up a new screen and searched through the engineering schematics library for anything similar.

I found a promising base design and ideas for other parts and began to bring them together. Gradually the new machine took shape in a three-dimensional simulation. I walked around it, zoomed in on details, watched it work and interact with the simulation of the hot-bot, already in the engineering database. This immediately highlighted clashes and performance shortcomings. The design system would often make suggestions for improvements or even develop the machine itself, once I had specified what the whole or a particular component was supposed to do. Back and forth, the system and I refined the design until we had a solution that worked virtually and could be built.

I was deep in the process when I noticed that Ibo had messaged me, asking me to call her.

'Hi, Ibo.'

She answered immediately. 'Well hello, how are things going over there?'

'Working up a hot-bot bearing replacement machine. It's coming on. How about with you?'

'Hyun and I have completed all the simulations on the control software and it should greatly improve the bot's stability when its legs are outstretched. Can you take a look and check before we upload it?'

'Sure, I'll give it a once over, but if it has passed the simulations I very much doubt that I'll spot anything.'

'Give it a look and let us know. It's all on file now.'

'OK, Ibo. I'll take a look right now and call back.'

I pulled up the file. The test results were very promising and the limit settings, once I had sorted out how they worked, appeared reasonable. I messaged Ibo saying as far as I could tell it was great and they should go ahead.

Massoud had sent a message to everyone asking that we get together around seven for a celebration of progress. He said he appreciated that we were still fine-tuning things, and suggested we have a proper celebration when the engine was restarted and we would all have more time. Others were sending responses to say that they agreed that we should meet tonight, even if everything wasn't finalised, and I did the same. It was already six and I wanted to get some parts scheduled for printing before the meal.

I called Agyei telling her that I had prepared a preliminary design for the bearing replacement machine and asking if she could take a look and suggest improvements.

'Sure, I'll check the file straight away. I've had a look at using a more advanced material for the bearings and checked that we've got the precursors in stock. Please review those and if you approve we can get printing going on those too.'

'I'll look at your file now, while you're reviewing mine.'

The physical dimensions of Agyei's new bearings were unaltered, requiring no change to the bearing housings and the simulation test results all looked good. Agyei had appended references for the material composition, design and tests, quite a lot of which was beyond me. I wondered if Minogue or Massoud should take a look but decided that was over the top. Agyei was pretty cautious in specifying materials we hadn't used before, or that didn't have a long history of use elsewhere, and this new material seemed to be a minor modification of a well proven one. I messaged Agyei back, saying that I was happy with the bearing design and that we should go ahead and print a sample.

Our capability to test bearings was limited. Sometimes the printing process proved problematic or exposed a flaw. We would only really know how well they stood up to radiation exposure when they were put into use. Ideally, we would try out one pair of new bearings first and see how they held up, but, if we did that, a second mimic trip to replace the others later would be needed. Time was running out and we had to take risks. Thinking that over, I began to have second thoughts and that maybe another check would be good. I messaged Agyei and said I was concerned about the risk of replacing all the bearings at once and I would like Minogue to review the material choice because he had much better knowledge than I of such things. Agyei messaged back that she had already asked Minogue to take a look because she too was concerned about the risk. Minogue hadn't yet got back to her.

That was a relief and removed a distraction as I returned to thinking about the installation machine. How about adding a feature to pre-load bearings on some sort of holder, and not to have to use a mimic to take each old bearing off the shaft and put on a new one? I had been trying to make the device as simple as possible, but now thought it might be more important to reduce or even eliminate the mimic work. Attaching a small, standard, general-purpose robot arm to the machine and a tray to hold both the new and old bearings would make life easier. Beefing up the bot leg supports and have the machine draw the joints apart would eliminate more mimic work.

I messaged Agyei again and told her not to waste time reviewing my original design because my thinking had changed and I was trying out an idea of adding a small robot arm. She messaged me back to say that she wondered why I hadn't gone down that route in the first place.

The arm could also operate the bolt wrench and store the bolts and bearing caps on a rack while they were off, simplifying that part of the process too. The only difficult bit would be programming. The tasks were all individually fairly simple so there should be standard modules in the software library that could be plugged together. After playing about with the layout it was clear that this was a much better approach than my original idea.

I reworked the design, taking out the special unit to remove the bearing caps. I found the model of the standard small robot arm we used and inserted it into the design, pulling the structure around to make a support for it. I also added a rack for the new bearings and all the parts that would be dismantled and removed temporarily. The rack had to be moveable: it always interfered with some part of the bot in any fixed position because of the variety of the joints the machine had to deal with. The robot arm could reposition the rack as required by adding mounts in a variety of places. I fiddled with the design until I was happy with it as a first draft and submitted it to the performance envelope simulator. At that moment I received a notification: it was almost seven, time to go.

Most of the crew had already gathered in the refectory when I arrived. Some intriguing smells wafted out of the servery: something mushroomy, with a hint of sweet-and-sour. Mouth-watering, whatever it was. Ibo and Hyun came in behind me. Massoud was passing round a tray of drinks. It looked as though he had printed some special glasses in the shape of the engine's nozzle, matt-black on the inside. They were filled with a clear, sparkling liquid and floating in them were small black cubes of what might have been ice but which smoked slightly, producing a mist across the top of the liquid. It tasted slightly tart, with a hint of summer herbs and fruits, but was quite dry.

'Gosh that's good Massoud, very refreshing,' I said.

'Glad you like it. Not potent, you'll be disappointed to learn, but I understand you've work to do later.'

Tonight, even the children were here. Joko was keeping close to her mother, Bita. Kent and Sky were ragging around, and Alice, having said hello to her parents, was now very seriously asking Yingluq something.

Sahko came in, last as usual, looking relaxed in a warm golden brown jacket and trousers, unusually tailored in a boxy style. She took the remaining glass from Massoud's tray, looked around to check that we were all there, and tapped her glass to quieten the room.

'Thank you Massoud, for arranging this little celebration of an important step forward in resolving the major problem we've had. I've just checked, and the eighteenth replacement tile has been successfully installed. Every one of us contributed to making this happen. There are many important things still to be done before the engine can be restarted, but I want to remind you that two days ago we had only ideas about how that might be made to happen. We made a plan and have been successfully executing it, and now have every confidence that the engine will function in time to save the mission. Thank you everyone, and from what I can smell, and have already tasted, Massoud has done something special for us to celebrate the progress we've made and the confidence that has been restored to us.'

Sahko held her glass up and took a drink. There was a smattering of clapping and broken cheering and then conversations resumed. Sahko moved into the room and started by joining Yingluq and Alice. I watched the three of them, talking together seriously for a moment and then laughing. Yingluq gave Alice a gentle shove who held up an arm in mock defence. Gunadi sidled over to me and asked how I was, but before I could reply Massoud asked us to be seated. I found myself between Gunadi and Kent.

First I turned to Kent and asked him what he had been doing.

'We helped Massoud a bit with the meal. He took us to the fermentation tanks, and we helped draw off some of the stuff which he then put in some kind of processing machine which made it into this meal.'

'Do you like going to the Processes Ring?'

'It's fun to go down to the keel and then back up to the tanks. Floating around in the keel is cool, but we're not allowed to stay there long: it affects our bones more than yours.'

'That's true. If you grew up entirely in zero-'g' you might end up hugely tall.'

'That would be good. I would be bigger than anyone.'

'But your bones would be so weak you couldn't stand up in normal gravity, and besides, if you were so tall, you wouldn't be able to fit through any of the doors.'

'I would have to swim around in zero-'g' all the time.'

'Yes, like an eel in water.'

'What's an eel?'

'A creature that looks a bit like a snake but lives in water.'

'A long thin fish thing?'

'Something like that.'

'Cool.'

'They're rather ugly, but some people back on Earth used to like to eat them.'

'Yuk, that's disgusting.'

'It used to be how people back on Earth survived, before we invented the fermentation tanks and other food creation machines. They had to eat lots of types of plants and creatures to survive.'

'Gross. I like our fermentation food.'

Gunadi leaned over and asked Kent: 'What's your favourite?'

'I like ice cream. Maple and nut is my favourite.'

'Strawberry is mine,' said Gunadi. 'How about you, Menem?'

'Chocolate.'

Massoud delivered plates in front of us which steamed slightly and gave off the odour I had smelled earlier.

'What's this?' Kent asked suspiciously.

'It's probably the thing you were working on earlier today with Massoud: a fermentation vat special.'

Kent tried a little cautiously and once tasted, tucked in. It was fabulous: layers of flavour and texture.

While we were eating, Gunadi asked me what I had been up to, and I explained briefly about the need for bearing replacement on the hot-bot. She leaned in a little closer to listen to what I was saying over the general hubbub. I asked her what she had been doing and she said rather vaguely that she had slept a good while and had then been working on the Alpha System model, trying to tease out any additional information on the orbital disturbances and how they could infer the existence of other, unseen, bodies in the system. I got the impression that the analytics engine wasn't powerful enough to model the system as well as she would have liked. I told her about some of my conversation with Minogue and the holographic model that he had shown me in Science and she said that she had been working with Minogue on that, and also she and Ibo had discussed the tile replacement path optimiser.

I tried to work out what Gunadi thought of Minogue and Ibo, but her tone had seemed neutral, which wasn't unusual with Gunadi. I found her hard to read.

'Ibo seemed confident that she understood your path optimiser when she talked of it,' I said.

'Ibo is good with that stuff. She knows at least as much as I do about applications such as simulations, optimisers and control software. My area is more pure analytics systems.'

'Hacking?'

'Don't do that childish stuff.' She seemed offended.

'But you know your way around.'

'Sure, that's why I'm here.'

Again I was left wondering quite what she meant by that, so I changed tack. 'Do you think our lack of understanding of the Alpha System is a real problem, or only one of fine tuning? Surely we know quite enough about all the significant bodies in the system to be able to find our way around?'

'I don't want to spread alarm, but the simulations aren't at all clear about our best course right now. The two main stars being so close together means that the planet orbits are distorted from true ellipses. Navigation here is not simply a three-body problem; it's incredibly sensitive to the starting conditions. There are no pure solutions, only iterations of approximations. The faster we come into the system the more difficult it gets, which is why this long engine outage is bad news, and getting worse by the day. Minogue is worried, Sahko is worried. There are a thousand people in Fleet depending on us.'

'I still don't understand what the big deal is though. We're supposed to be coming in way below the ecliptic plane straight to our target planet. Why are we so bothered about all the other objects in the system?'

'Well for one we're not certain that all the system objects lie in the ecliptic plane. The system is very complicated with its three stars. There may be large objects in stable polar orbits or comet-like objects that have come in from far out at odd angles, broken up and left trails of debris. There's also the matter of moons around our target which we know nothing about. In addition, any hidden object will perturb the orbit of our target, at least to some degree.'

'Hmm, so lots of potential hazards that we know nothing about. Even so the risk of hitting anything must be low, space being so empty.'

'We didn't expect the object field we've just ploughed through. Fortunately it wasn't made up of anything big, at least on our track through it.'

'OK, I can see the benefit of pinning down the objects in the system more precisely.'

'Sorry, Menem. I don't want to make things worse for you, I want to help. You asked about the Alpha System.' Gunadi looked downcast for a moment but then turned to me once again. 'You don't have to work all night again tonight, do you?'

'I shouldn't have to, as long as the tile replacement work continues as it is.'

'You can't take another Stay-Awake. Yingluq wouldn't allow it, far too risky.'

'Risk is all around us. Go to do what we have to do.'

'Don't kill yourself, Menem, please don't.' She stared at me. It looked like moisture in her eyes.

'I try to stay alive,' I said lightly.

I felt my message alarm trigger: the simulations of the repair machine were complete. I also wanted to check how the hot-bot was doing, so I started to get up.

'Sorry, I have to get back now.'

Kent pulled at my sleeve and asked: 'Can I come round to Engineering and see what you're up to?'

'If you have free time, but only for five minutes. I'm really busy at the moment.'

'Can I come?' asked Sky from across the table and Kent looked a bit put out.

'Only for five minutes.'

I pushed back my chair. 'My apologies everyone for rushing off. We've made good progress but I still have stuff to do. Massoud, that meal was fabulous, a real special, and the drink too was a work of art.'

Kent and Sky got up. Agyei put a restraining hand on Kent's arm. 'Five minutes only, understood?'

'Yes, ma.'

I saw Yingluq giving Sky a stare too, but Sky skipped off to join Kent and me. Gunadi was looking at us as we left, others were starting to rise.

'What have you been doing, Menem?' Sky asked.

I told the two of them about all the work we had been doing to repair the nozzle as we went around to Engineering. On arrival, I called up the holograph of the nozzle and hot-bot and we could see it fixing another tile: the twentieth. The children danced around the model pointing things out to each other. I checked the performance statistics for the bot on the main screen. The control software update had greatly improved the bot's stability but there were now signs that it was deteriorating again. I put the data into graphical form and explained to the children what I was looking at.

'Why is it getting worse again?' Kent asked.

'My guess is that the bearings in the bot's joints are all wearing out and so its limbs are getting loose.'

Kent and Sky wriggled all the joints in their arms as though they were coming loose. 'Fortunately the bot's joints are easier to replace than yours. I have been designing a machine to do this, with help from Agyei and Minogue.'

'My dad's great at that stuff' said Sky.

'And my mom,' said Kent, not to be out-done.

'We all try to work together on these things. Let me show you the machine.'

I pulled up the model of the bearing replacement machine and started to explain how it worked but it was too complicated and abstract to hold their attention for long, so I cut it short.

'What we need is a stock small robot arm, so let's see if there's a spare one around somewhere. How do you think we do that?'

'Look in Status,' said Sky.

'OK, let's use the main screen to do that and then we can all see. Go ahead.'

Kent was quickest at grabbing control and he activated Status. The two of them, with a little prompting from me, found their way into the spare-parts system and identified a suitable spare robot arm and an appropriate power supply and control unit.

'They're all in Stores Two in section seven, next door,' said Kent.

'OK, ask the system to get then out. Shall we all go round and collect them: three of us, three parts to carry?'

Sky completed the request and we all trooped out. We ran in to Ibo, Hyun and Agyei in the corridor and Agyei called out: 'Five minutes I said, Kent. Don't keep bothering Menem.'

'No trouble,' I said, 'my assistants and I are going next door to Stores to pick up parts for the bearing replacement machine.'

The children rushed on ahead and were waiting by Stores when I got there. The items we needed had been retrieved and were ready for pick-up. After a short fight, Kent got the heavier power supply and Sky the controller. I picked up the arm itself and we marched back to Engineering with our trophies.

'Thank you assistants for your help, that will be all for today,' I said and gave a deep bow.

Sky and Kent giggled and shoved each other as they both tried to get out the door at the same time. It seemed very quiet after they had gone.

4021, 20:00

I opened comms. 'Hi, Agyei. Could you take a look at the revised bearing replacement machine design? I want to get the printers underway as soon as possible.'

'Sure, Menem. Go ahead with the printing anyway. I'll take a look at the changes you've made.' She paused and then continued. 'Do you think the bot will hold out until tomorrow?'

'No doubt you've been watching how it's doing, as I have. Extrapolating from the current trend and if we load it as lightly as possible, it will last until the end of tomorrow. Unless there's a sudden deterioration.'

'My thoughts too. I've set the path optimiser to avoid areas where the limbs become heavily loaded and I've also damped down on sudden movements for the time being. That has only added a few hours to completion but buys us a lot of time to get ready for the repairs. You can't work all night again.'

Someone else trying to mother me.

'Not if I can help it, Agyei, but every hour is important now. I would like to get the machine printed tonight, if possible, and at least partly assembled. Then tomorrow morning I can finish the build and run the bench tests. That would allow a mimic trip, starting at midday say, to get the machine set up, tested and in position ready for work. If it all goes smoothly the bot should be back online by about four in the afternoon.'

'Sounds OK. I should like to do maintenance on the tile factory at the same time. I want to see how much sludge build-up there has been and replace a few of the parts. With luck, after that it should run to the end of the job. If not, we'll have to do another two-hour shutdown at some point.'

'Which we may need for a second bearing replacement session. By the way, has Minogue commented on the new bearing materials?'

'I'm looking at his comments now. Yes, he seems happy with it. He says we should go ahead.'

'And how about the test sample?'

'I'm still testing the individual components. So far, so good.'

'How long does that type of bearing take to print?'

'About twenty minutes each: complex chemistry, fine work. After printing, all the parts need finishing: the usual polishing and heat treatment which I'll have done here in Chemistry. Then they can be assembled and have a final test.'

'So we should start printing them as soon as possible, with forty to do. The finisher in Engineering could help, and presumably the assembly is straightforward, in which case we can use the small assembler here.'

'I would prefer to stick with finishing here in Chemistry. Besides, you'll need the Engineering finisher for the bearing replacement machine parts. When the bearing components have passed testing here, I'll have them sent around to you. If the test sample fails in the late stages we'll have to start again. In the worst case we go back to the old design, which only takes twelve minutes each to print.'

'Fine. If you check my new design for the jig, I'll start straight away printing parts for it and getting as much as I can ready for assembly. Let me know as soon as possible if you spot any problems.'

'Agreed.'

I returned to the familiar task of turning a design into a piece of hardware: sending the custom parts' specifications off for printing and laying out stock parts ready for assembly. I also put the robot arm, along with the power supply and controller, through their test sequence.

Half an hour later Agyei came back on the comms. 'Your new design looks good. The operation will be much simpler, not requiring the mimic to be actively involved, and it should finish the work more quickly. The only slight quibble I have is with the shape of the parts rack. I see that you've put clips for it in various positions around the frame because of the variety of joints, but I think it could be made a little more compact by stacking the two new bearings and separately the two old ones. Not a big deal, but it does give a bit more clearance.'

'That sounds sensible. Otherwise are you happy with it?'

'It looks to me like a good solution and it passes all the simulations. Let's go for it.'

'Thanks, Agyei.'

'Oh, and the new bearing components have finished testing and look solid. The wear characteristics are great, although of course it hasn't yet been tested in a radioactive environment. The material design specs show it's highly resilient to radiation so I'm quite confident.'

'Good, so full steam ahead.'

'The romance of the steam age,' she laughed.

'It's a steam-punk spaceship.'

The project file showed Agyei's suggested change to the parts rack, which I liked. I fiddled around with the design of the body of the machine, but soon decided I wasn't improving anything, so sent instructions to the printers for the remaining parts. There was not much further to be done until they started coming back, and I didn't feel up to thinking through the fuel pipe repair. That was going to have to be the next priority, but not now.

I went around to the refectory to see if anyone was there. A light was on but Massoud was the only one present and he seemed to be absorbed in some work, staring at a screen of data. He looked up and waved me in.

'Well the fermentation vats are behaving themselves at the moment,' he said, 'and we've enough food on hand for tomorrow, so my work is done for the day.' He turned off the screen and turned to me. 'How about you, my friend?'

'I've sent a job to print and I don't want to start something else right now. It will take half-an-hour or so and I thought I'd see if anyone was around.'

'Well I am, and I'm glad to see you.' Massoud stood up and came across to the table and sat opposite me. 'You must take a break sometimes. We all keep telling you that, but you rarely listen. I hope you don't have to work all night again.'

'Fortunately not. Once the design is finalised and the parts requested from printing, I only have to set up the assembler. I hope that it will run unaided overnight, putting everything together and doing the testing, ready for us to install in the morning.'

'This machine is to go outside?'

'Yes, we'll use the mimics again.'

'Not your favourite task.'

'To tell the truth, each time it gets worse. It seems so real, as though I'm actually out there, and it can be terrifying.'

'Get someone else to do it. We're all trained to use the mimics, although I contended with Minogue for the lowest score in the tests. Like you, I don't like doing it, but others are very good and actually enjoy the experience.'

'I really should do it. If I'm there I can spot problems and make adjustments.'

'You could watch remotely, and not operate a mimic.'

'I don't feel I should ask someone else to do something I can do myself.'

'But you should if they can do it better than you.'

'Hmm…'

'Well my friend, let us have a quiet drink together and talk of other things. I've a question for you.'

He ordered and we sat silently until a service bot delivered two cups of hot, bitter, black coffee. Massoud took one, closed his eyes and inhaled deeply over his cup. He smiled and took a sip. After a few seconds, he opened his eyes again.

'Good, no?'

I drank too and said: 'Yes it is, excellent.'

'Now my question.' He put down his cup and looked straight at me. 'Do you think that Sahko is a good leader?'

I wasn't expecting that. What lay behind his question? Was he planning a coup and testing the waters with me? Massoud was the last person I could think of who would want to seize power. Did he really have leadership ambitions? Or perhaps he thought that Sahko was going off the rails and needed to be replaced, but I couldn't see that. Perhaps he was trying to sniff out plots before they occurred. I decided to be careful.

'Yes, I do. Take this evening for example: she said only a few words but they were the right ones, made us feel that our efforts had been rewarded and that it was worth continuing to make every effort, and by doing so we would succeed. That seemed like good leadership.'

'You don't think that anyone could have done better, either then or on other occasions?'

'I can't think of anyone who could have done better in the choice of words and tone on that occasion. I can't say I agree with every decision she's made, but I believe she's working in the best interests of our mission, and I can't think of anyone who could have done better overall.'

'Not you for instance?'

'Me? Are you serious?'

'Yes, I'm serious.'

'No, never. I don't have what it takes.'

'Not ruthless enough?' he asked.

'Well maybe. I don't think she has been especially ruthless has she? She hasn't had to make a big sacrifice in the interests of the mission.'

Avalos flashed through my thoughts. Sahko with a raised blade. Not impossible and she had signed the death certificate. Massoud was silent for a while but remained looking me square in the face, trying to read me.

'You don't harbour any lingering ambitions to be leader then?'

'Me? No.'

'Ibo said that you once did.'

'Only at very first, when they started recruiting for the mission. I had captained a freighter and so I thought I was in with a chance.'

'If I understand the facts, you were never a captain.'

'Well I ran a freighter on a couple of missions when our captain was incapacitated.'

'Once, I understand.'

'Yes, the captain got sick. I was the deputy so I captained the ship.'

'So you wanted to captain this mission.'

'That was a long time ago. I was young and ambitious back then. Realistically, I can now see that I was never going to be captain. I've learned over the years that I'm not cut out for it, and don't want it enough. I like being involved in fixing things, getting my hands dirty, and there's not much room for that if you're captain. I also realised that a captain has to be able to be, how did you put it, "ruthless". I couldn't do that, even for the sake of the mission. It didn't take me long to see that once Sahko had joined the crew she was going to be made captain, and that it was the right choice. I was glad, relieved really. I'm good at engineering, I enjoy it. I don't know how much Sahko enjoys being captain: sometimes yes, sometimes no. For me it would be lot more no than yes.'

'Well that's interesting and informative. I too want this mission to succeed and for that to happen we all need to put in our best performance, especially you and Sahko. We depend on you to hold the ship together a while longer and for Sahko to keep the crew focused on our objective. Having you two fighting is troubling, so I'm trying to work out how to put a stop to it. One theory that was going around was that you harboured ambitions to be captain, and as Sahko had rejected you, you were trying to undermine her.'

'Good grief, Massoud. I'm not trying to undermine her. I don't know how anyone could think that.'

'You publicly questioned a decision she had made only the other day.'

'Err, gosh, well, I... I never thought it might be interpreted as a coup attempt or anything. I was stupid, but my act of stupidity arose out of frustration.'

'I can appreciate the subject of having more children is particularly sensitive for you. We've all felt deeply for you both about that, but you've let it rule your lives ever since. No one expects you to forget, but we all have to move on. Your grief has become fixed.'

'I wanted to... I wanted to try again with Sahko. We could have, with Yingluq's help. Sahko went cold, the mission had to come first.'

'Times change.'

'I haven't seen it.'

'Look a bit harder.'

Massoud relaxed his gaze and we were silent for while.

'Tell me, Massoud, did you ever want children?'

Massoud thought a moment. 'I used not to but, well, I grow older and things change. But, as you know, in that way women aren't quite my thing.'

'You wouldn't have to, you know, well, Yingluq could do the bringing together, as it were.'

Massoud laughed. 'That would be possible, and maybe one day one of the women here, or if not here then maybe in Fleet, would like to have a child by me.'

'Yes, someone might.' We were silent for a while again.

'Massoud, do you think Sahko has ever had to be ruthless on this mission?'

After a pause Massoud asked: 'What do you mean?'

'Mo?'

'Definitely not. Absolutely not. Don't think that even for a moment.'

'No.' We were silent again and then I asked: 'Avalos?'

'Avalos died in an accident.'

'A series of unfortunate events? Or possibly suicide.'

'Avalos was…' Massoud paused, '… unlucky.'

'You were friendly with Avalos?'

'For a while. He was very handsome and we slept together a few times, but his tastes were not mine. I discovered he was not always quite so nice and charming. Not quite what he seemed.'

'Others have said the same.'

'Yes, I understand he got around.'

'Not everyone rejected him.'

'No, they were not able to, a terrible weakness, a dangerous weakness. They got hurt, badly hurt. It was a relief for them when he died although they lost something too.'

'Did you know about what was going on at the time?' I asked.

'I saw some signs and pieced some of it together.'

'We may miss his navigation skills yet.'

'A price we've had to pay.'

'It could be a high price.'

'Maybe so, but it had to be.'

Just then my comms buzzed to say the printer had finished work which for now prevented me asking what he meant by that last remark.

'Massoud, I regret that I have to go. Thank you for this discussion, I shall reflect deeply on what you had to say.' I smiled to myself, noting that his courtly phrasing had again crept into my speech when talking to him.

When I stood, Massoud took both my hands in his for a moment. 'Take care, my friend. Go a little easier on yourself and on Sahko. Don't trouble yourself with things you can't alter and all will be well.'

He dropped my hand and I walked away. Sometimes Massoud spoke in code, in a language I couldn't quite grasp.

I returned to Engineering to find a cart with a stack of printed parts. I checked them over and laid them out on the finisher table and it started work, quickly feeding them on to join the stock-parts gathered earlier. Soon the assembler began working too. I watched for a while as it checked to see what parts were there, picked up a selection and began putting the bearing machine together. It dawned on me how big it was going to be.

The assembly would take some hours, mainly because of the time some adhesives took to set up before the work could move on to the next stage. The machine also spent a lot of time checking and probing, ensuring every part was positioned correctly and fastened as specified.

I slipped from considering our ability to repair and adapt the ship to our inability to control our thoughts, instincts, and dreams. Paradoxically the thing that made the mission possible, the infinite flexibility of the human mind to cope with the unknown, was also its biggest weakness. Was I now the biggest danger to the ship because of my inability to move on from thinking about Sahko, wanting to go back to the way it had been before? Maybe I should try new relationships. After all, my encounter with Yingluq, whether real or imagined, had been powerful, and if not Yingluq then how about Gunadi? She was intriguing in some kind of dangerous way, but doubtless that road would lead to more trouble. Still, Gunadi was paying me rather more attention than she had before our encounter, or was that my imagination too, or just another game? Then there was Bita who I found immensely attractive, with her balletic grace, her warmth and liveliness. But perhaps I appeared to her as a dull dog: the engineer to her artist. How would Minogue react if I linked up with either Yingluq or Bita? Would he, the alpha male challenged, turn against me and fight back? He talked a good game about open relationships. It all sounded fine in theory but often seemed to fall apart in practice, with one party ending up exploiting the other or primitive jealousy creating havoc.

Any changes in relationships at this late and critical stage would upset the dynamics of the crew in unpredictable ways. It was not the best of times, as the end of our mission loomed, but perhaps Agyei and Bjorn had already set the ball rolling with the announcement of her pregnancy.

Why had I started stirring the Avalos pot again? We had long accepted what we thought had happened, so why disturb that dog now? Greater distance from the event might have loosened people's tongues a little and with the end of our voyage looming there might be a feeling that we could speak more clearly and perhaps a desire to resolve open issues. Whatever the cause, it was becoming increasingly clear that Avalos had been up to something not in his job description. Whether it was something of his own devising or that he was a willing participant in some greater plan, I had no idea, and I had no indication that anyone else had put together the whole story either.

I felt tired, so did one last check of how the nozzle repair was going. To conserve the bot, Ibo had again restricted the area where it could operate. Its performance statistics showed that the slop in the leg joints had hardly deteriorated since then. It should hold up through the night. Tile laying was progressing smoothly with about one tile being completed every forty minutes. There had been no failures in the last four hours. I set an alarm to awake me if performance deteriorated too far from the current level. The finisher and assemblers were working away smoothly. Wayclear hadn't reported any objects since we had passed out of the field. Status showed no new troubles.

I left Engineering for the night, jogging some circuits of the Habitat Ring, but no one was around. Even Massoud had left the refectory and presumably gone back to his apartment. I wondered how lonely he was, reliant only on his companion for physical love. Perhaps he wasn't highly sexed and so wasn't unduly disturbed by a lack of human intimacy. Life might be a whole lot simpler with a lower sex drive, but then it might lose many of its excitements too. How big a roller coaster was one forced to ride on? Did we have a choice?

I wondered about Ibo and Hyun, the closest couple on the ship. Would they go ahead with having another child, now that the constraints had been lifted? I could well imagine them with a large brood. I wondered how Kent was feeling about the prospect of a younger sibling. I should ask him sometime. My guess was that Alice would welcome one but it was impossible to predict how a child would react to the reality. She did seem quite protective of Joko. What about Yingluq and Bita? Would they want more children too and who might the fathers be? Minogue again in one or both cases? All three seemed to be free spirits so perhaps one or both of the women would choose a different father next time. What was Sahko feeling, deep down, about Agyei having a second child? If one or more of the other women became pregnant too, how would that make her feel? Would she turn back to me, or to someone else, or would it harden her heart against motherhood and reconcile herself to looking on the whole ship as her family, her children? She had been very keen to have a child before, but that was a long time ago. I should know the answer to that question, when we had been so close. I had thought that I had understood her very well, but it hadn't been long before I knew I hadn't. Ultimately we are each locked inside our own heads and our means of communication with one another are primitive.

Back in my own apartment I refreshed, alone this time. Afterwards I found Jazz, apparently reading a magazine, sitting in a chair near the bed. Some soft music was playing and the lights were low, except a spotlight near her. She looked up and smiled, relaxed in a short, silky, cream gown wrapped loosely around her, one long, bare leg extended, the other curled under her. Her short, dark hair framed her oval face. I reached out a hand and caressed her cheek, leaned over and planted a kiss on the top of her head, inhaling her light rose-infused perfume. She reached out and turned off her reading lamp, stood up placing a hand on my shoulder and leaned in towards me. We kissed softly on the lips and held each other for a while. She became more urgent, pushing me back. I sat on the edge of the bed and she took a step away. She smiled and slowly undid the belt of her robe and then shrugged her shoulders and let it fall to the floor. She stood there almost coyly, looking at me, just out of reach. She slowly turned around in a complete pirouette, keeping her eyes on me as long as she could. I gazed back.

As she came over I reached out a hand to her, but she pushed me back so that I was lying on the bed. She climbed over me, placing a thigh on either side. I could feel her bottom spread across my hips. She looked down, raised herself and took me inside.

Eventually her breathing slowed and her hip grinding stopped. She drew her breasts away from me and knelt upright. She smiled down at me lasciviously, slipped off and swung a leg over my chest and then knelt beside me, bringing her head down to my face, looking sideways into my eyes. I rolled on to my side and kissed her and slid a hand down her back. I sat and then got up on my knees behind her. She cried out as we joined again. I fiercely took her until I too rose up and was spent. I bent forward and kissed her neck and back, slipped one hand down her front feeling where we were joined and with the other clasped a breast. We stayed locked like that for a while until I felt myself shrinking inside her and eventually withdrawing. Finally we subsided, rolling onto our sides. I released one of my arms that was pinched under her and cradled her head. Our breathing slowed and, cuddled together, we fell asleep.

Mission Day 4022

4022, 08:00

The rising music of the dawn chorus and brightening light gently brought me awake. The aroma of chocolaty-coffee was strong. Jazz sat on the edge of the bed, dressed in her robe again, and presented me with a cup. I sat up, took it and drank, the warm liquid bringing me fully awake. I reached out a hand and stroked Jazz's thigh. She slapped my hand and lifted it away, but when I put it back she left it there. She smiled at me, kissed me gently and then got up and disappeared. I finished my coffee, got out of bed and went for a full refresh and afterwards dressed in clean clothes.

Status told me that another twelve tiles had been completed in the last eight hours, but there had been a couple of failures in the last two. Ibo had sent a note saying that she had further restricted the hot-bot's range of operation to try to reduce failures. The detailed performance data from the bot showed increased slop in a couple of its joints: an early warning signal of potential bearing failure.

The assembler reported completion of the bearing replacement machine and satisfactory laboratory testing. Another report showed that the forty new bearings had been printed, finished, assembled and had passed testing.

I messaged Hyun and Bjorn to ask what their availability was for another mimic job to do the bot overhaul. I also messaged Agyei that I was intending to do the maintenance work on the hot-bot this morning.

I went over to Engineering and was confronted by the sheer physical size of the bearing replacement machine, sitting on the assembler table. I hoped it was going to fit through the door and round into an airlock. I ordered breakfast and the food arrived at the same time as a reply came in from Agyei saying that this morning was good timing, and that she was planning to go down to the engine room soon anyway to check up on the tile factory and change some filters. A few minutes later I got almost simultaneous messages from Hyun and Bjorn saying they could both make the time needed for the mimic job. Hyun was in Printing, tidying up after last night's work, and Bjorn was doing routine fire safety systems checks that could be finished later. I messaged them all back and suggested we aimed to go in twenty minutes. Hopefully that was enough time for my breakfast to settle.

I ordered up a transport cart and, while waiting, checked over the bearing machine. Although the machine looked big, it was not very heavy. The robotic arm was neatly tucked away to avoid it getting snagged during transport. We would have to use the number one airlock, the biggest on the Ring, between sections twelve and thirteen.

The bearings were ready on the small assembler, neatly held in a custom tray, equipped with clips for fixing to the machine, which was something that I hadn't thought of but fortunately Agyei had. It started me wondering what else I had overlooked. It would delay engine restart even more if the bearing machine lacked something vital. The dangers of this pressured working were beginning to surface, with not enough time to think things through and review each other's work.

There was still the antimatter pipe to repair, and that sent a cold finger down my spine. Get that wrong and the ship would be blown apart. I needed to be extra cautious and not take any shortcuts with it. I resolved to get Agyei to check the engineering, Hyun the robotics, Ibo the engine side, as well as Minogue to check the physics.

The hoist cart arrived and loaded the bearing machine. I added the tray of bearings and it squeezed out of the door, making for the airlock.

Bjorn and Hyun were already in Robotics when I arrived, ready to start the project briefing, studying the holographic model of the exterior of the ship. I outlined what we had to do, explaining about the machine being in Airlock One and that its size would make it awkward to manoeuvre, but otherwise it would be a relatively simple job: move the machine to the front of the ship, fix it in place and connect it up. That should be it for the mimics, but the bot-net would need to remain on duty with cameras to allow us to watch bearing replacement as it happened. The mimics could be called back in to action if anything went wrong. Hyun and Bjorn both asked a couple of questions on details and we were ready.

I found my hands shaking as I went over to my mimic chair and Bjorn noticed something: 'Are you all right, Menem? You seem a bit pale.'

'Probably shouldn't have eaten breakfast.'

'I hope you aren't going to throw up again. The service bots will be demanding overtime soon.'

'Ha, ha, very funny.'

'Concentrate,' I said to myself, 'it's a simple job sitting in a mimic chair. No big deal, you've done this lots of times before.' I looked at the mimic chair again and went to sit in it. My vision narrowed, the lights seemed to dim and I felt myself falling.

A moment later I was fine again, but for some reason Yingluq was looking at me, a concerned look on her face. What was she doing here? This chair I'm sitting in, it's not the mimic chair. I could hear Hyun's voice in the background. 'He seems to be coming round.' I wondered who he was referring to.

Yingluq was talking to me, so she must be really here and not only in my imagination again. 'How are you feeling, Menem?'

'What's going on?' My eyes still seemed to be blurry, but my head was clearing.

'You fainted, Menem, so sit still for a while.'

She was kneeling in front of me and put a concerned hand on my knee, which was nice but wasn't getting the job done. I shook myself a little and sat upright in the chair. I was still in Robotics it seemed, and the mimic chairs were there as before, but Bjorn and Hyun were standing behind Yingluq, looking at me.

'Sorry about that, everyone. Breakfast disagreed with me. I'm fine now and we've work to do.' I tried to stand up but found I was a bit wobbly on my feet so sat down again. 'I need a minute and then I'll be ready to go.'

Yingluq stood and lifted my arm and slipped a medical test sleeve over it. 'I need to check you, Menem. Hold still for a moment.' The sleeve gripped my arm unpleasantly and pulsed. Eventually it released its grip. 'You seem to be physically all right: heart rate a bit high, breathing shallow, so blood oxygen less than ideal.'

'Thanks doc, so let's go chaps.' This time I did stand up, my balance seemed restored. 'We've vital work to do. The sooner we get on with it the better.' As I came up to the mimic chair I felt my hands start to shake again and my vision narrow. I looked away. 'Sorry, I don't feel myself. I can't do it. I can't do it.'

I felt Yingluq take my arm and guide me back to the other chair. 'Sit down, Menem. You don't have to do it. Someone else can operate the mimic. You don't have to do everything. You can tell us what to do while you sit peacefully and safely here inside the ship.'

I slumped into the chair and studied the floor between my feet. I heard them talking:

'Who could do the mimic?'

'I could, or Sahko or Bita, who have both done it recently'

'Should we tell Sahko what happened?'

'Hasn't she got enough on her plate?'

'She would want to know as soon as possible. She'll get mad if she only hears about this later.'

'Does anyone need to know?'

'It will be in the logs.'

'Sahko reads those when compiling her daily report to Fleet.'

'I'll message her.'

'Status says Bita is with the children. Sahko is with Minogue, discussing navigation most likely.'

'Bjorn, who would you like as your mimic partner?'

'All three are perfectly capable. Yingluq, you're here.'

'But don't you need to be with Menem?' asked Hyun.

'There's nothing physically wrong with him. He has done too many mimic trips recently and the last one almost ended very badly. If he sits here, he can monitor what's going on and direct the rest of us.' Yingluq then addressed me. 'Menem, can you monitor if we do the mimics?'

My head was clearing again. 'Yes, I think that would be a good idea. We need to get on with it. If you can, Yingluq, thanks. Sorry to be trouble chaps. Don't tell Sahko, it doesn't need to be in the logs. I'm sure Gunadi could fix that.'

The door burst open and Sahko marched in. 'What can Gunadi fix? Where is he? Ah, there you are. What have you been up to?' She rushed over to me, knelt down to look me in the eyes and placed a cool palm on my forehead. 'How is he? What's wrong with him?' She shook my knee with her hand.

'He was about to get in to the mimic chair and fainted,' replied Yingluq. 'There's nothing physical wrong with him.'

'Why did he faint? Why did you faint?' She looked at me searchingly. She looked worried.

'Don't know. Maybe breakfast.'

'Breakfast?'

'No, it wasn't his breakfast. He has had one too many mimic trips for the time being. You were with him on that last trip which nearly ended badly,' said Yingluq.

'Was it my fault? What did I do? We were in mimics for heaven's sake. There was no danger to anyone.'

'It wasn't your fault.' Yingluq was having to reassure everyone. 'These trips affect different people in different ways and it can be cumulative.

Menem has made three trips in three days and each has been very demanding. He has been under huge pressure recently.'

'Please stop,' I cut in. 'We still have a vitally urgent trip to do now. It seems as though I'm not going to die immediately. Perhaps it's best if Yingluq takes my place in the mimic. I'll monitor what's going on from here and advise as needed.'

'Yes, all right,' said Sahko. 'Yingluq and Bjorn take the mimics, Hyun you're on the bot-net, I see. Menem, sit quietly and monitor, and I'll sit here and check he's OK.'

'No,' said Yingluq forcefully. 'Hyun can keep an eye on Menem and call me out of the mimic chair if necessary, which I think highly unlikely.'

'Perhaps I should take the second mimic and you be on hand for Menem,' suggested Sahko rather plaintively. I had never seen her being ordered around before.

'No, Sahko. It will be best if Menem sits there calmly and quietly, not being fussed over. I'll set up a monitor for reassurance which you can have an alarm set to if you want. You've urgent business elsewhere.'

Doctor's orders: no messing with Yingluq. Sahko folded.

'Yes, yes, I do. I had better get back to it. Glad you're not too bad, Menem. Bye.'

Sahko sidled out: not a move she regularly made. I saw Hyun and Bjorn looking at each other.

Yingluq took a patch from her medical kit and stuck it to my arm and said: 'You look better.'

'I feel better, ready to get on with our mission. Sorry about the fuss. Pity Sahko had to know, but perhaps best now rather than later.'

'I think so,' said Yingluq. Bjorn and Hyun exchanged nods.

Hyun set up a screen for me to be able to select what I wanted to look at: the view from the mimics or from a bot-net camera. He also gave me a haptic glove to allow me to feel what one of the mimics' hands was feeling. I watched calmly as Bjorn and Yingluq strapped themselves in to the mimic chairs and pulled down their visors. Hyun checked them both, then went and sat at the bot-net control station where he set up a camera to watch as the two operators brought their mimics to life.

Bjorn and Yingluq went through the familiar routine of the long walk back and the crossover to the Habitat Ring, without any fancy gymnastics this time. I watched them go down the slope to Airlock One and retrieve the bearing replacement machine on its cart. Bjorn was leading and he was thorough and competent. Yingluq had had a few hesitant steps to start with but soon regained her familiarity with the mimic's operation. She commented that the view using the bot-net camera made it rather harder to keep her balance. Her mimic certainly did look monstrous with its missing head replaced by bot-net elements. She followed Bjorn and seemed confident by the time they started manoeuvring the bearing machine.

Hyun kept an eye out using four bot-net cameras. Other groups of bot-net elements scurried around, fixing tethers and moving them on. Occasionally a new group of bot-net elements would appear and take over the function of one of the working groups, which then disappeared from view, heading back to a charging point, an entirely autonomous function built in to their tiny brains. It looked like a toy army: reserves being sent forward to relieve troops on the front line.

Bjorn and Yingluq reached the nozzle section near the tile breakdown machine bay. The bearing replacement machine was going to be placed on the surface of the ship where it would be exposed. It only needed to work for a few days, and later, if we decided to keep it, we could store it in one of the equipment recesses. For now, its only shelter would be from the Wayclear pylon right in front of it.

'What do you think of this position, Menem?' Bjorn asked.

'That seems like a good spot, but can you turn it ninety degrees clockwise? There needs to be lots of space along that axis for the hot-bot to fully stretch out its leg when doing the hip joints. That looks better, fix it there. Oh, before you do, check the power and control cables are long enough to reach from the machine to the equipment recess.'

Bjorn stood by the machine and Yingluq uncoiled the cables.

'Where are the connections in the recess?' Yingluq asked.

'There's a service hatch behind the tile machine,' I replied. 'You should see cables coming out from the hatch. There's a spare power cable tied down there.'

I watched as she clambered in to the recess. Now fully confident in the mimic, she seemed to have got used to its poor vision, quickly finding the cable. The connector on its end showed that it was unpowered, so she plugged in the bearing machine's power line.

'That seems good, now what about the control cable, there doesn't seem to be a spare lying around?'

'There isn't one. Go to the back of the tile recycling machine and unplug the one there. Then insert the cable from the bearing machine into the tile machine. You'll see the new connector has an additional socket for the cable from the ship. The control system is all networked so they can share the same link. When you're doing that, don't take the mimic too close to the tile machine, except at the back. There's a risk of radioactive contamination around the front where the old tiles are loaded in to it.'

'That sounds clear, but keep a watch on what I'm doing and stop me if I'm about to do something wrong.'

'You're doing great so far. You seem to have really got the hang of that mimic.'

'The vision problem was unsettling to start with, but I've got used to it.'

'Before you start, I'm going to ensure the tile machine is powered down. Yes, it seems to have finished recycling a tile and is waiting for the next, so I'll shut it down. Right that's done. It's safe now.'

'OK, here goes.'

Hyun had set up a couple of bot-net cameras to allow me to see all the details of the actions she was making. After unplugging the ship cable from the tile machine, she struggled to fit the new one.

'I can't seem to get this one in. Is it the right type?'

'We only have one type of control connector. Try putting it in the other way up.'

It slotted in to place and the locking ring engaged. 'Simple when you know how,' she laughed. 'Right now plug the other one back in to this. I see, they stack together, clever. What's next boss, coolant?'

'The bearing machine doesn't need it. Yingluq, move to the back of that equipment recess and park up. Just have your cameras poking out so you can see the bearing machine. Bjorn, let the bot-net firmly fix the machine to the ship where it is. The cables are good. When you're happy, retreat to the equipment recess as well. No, better if you could park in another one so you get a different view. There's another one on the other side of the Wayclear pylon.'

We watched as the bot-net unhooked the mounting bars from the tile machine and connected them to the mounting points on the ship's skin. They also fixed the cables down to stop them floating off and getting tangled with the bot. Bjorn pulled on the machine to check that it was secured and then retreated to the recess. I powered the tile-refiner back up.

'How is everyone? Ready for the next stage?' All three acknowledged. 'Right, let's test the bearing machine in place.' A panel on my screen showed a list of tests going green as each completed. We watched as the robotic arm uncurled itself from the body of the machine and performed a short ballet to test its joints. Once completed, it reached into the machine's body and brought out the parts tray, clipped it on, collected a pair of bearings from their rack and placed them in the tray. The test list stopped scrolling and the machine indicated it was fully functional.

'Looks good,' said Hyun.

'I think so. Spot any trouble anyone?'

'No,' said both Bjorn and Yingluq almost simultaneously.

'Good. Well let's see what the hot-bot is up to, and at the next convenient moment we'll call it in for repair.'

A Status screen showed that the hot-bot had almost finished cutting out another tile.

'In five minutes the bot will be back anyway with a tile, so let's wait for that to complete,' I said. 'Bjorn and Yingluq, if you want to, get out of the mimic chairs for a break. I would like you back when the surgery starts, ready to intervene if needed. It might be just as well to fit the long-arms in case you need to grab the bot's legs. Hyun could you get the bot-net to take a pair over to Bjorn's mimic?'

'I'll take a five minute break,' said Yingluq, and Bjorn decided to do the same.

'I'll message Agyei,' I said, 'to tell her that there will be one more tile being processed, then a gap for at least a couple of hours while the bearings in the bot are replaced.'

Yingluq and Bjorn unstrapped themselves from the mimic chairs. Hyun walked over.

'How are you feeling, Menem?' he asked.

'I feel fine now. I don't know what came over me earlier. Thanks, Yingluq, for stepping in like that. You did a great job out there.'

'Not very taxing stuff and it was fun in a way, something different from trying to keep human bodies functioning.'

'You were moving well out there,' put in Bjorn. 'You got in the groove very quickly.'

'The mimics have a funny motion. I remember having difficulty at first when training: it was like learning to walk again. I haven't done a refresher session for a while, but it soon came back to me.'

'The vision in that one doesn't help.'

'It's like wearing goggles, a more restricted view. I soon got used to twisting my neck or body a bit more to compensate. Ah, hold on a minute, I'm getting some messages I need to deal with.' Yingluq wandered away.

'Are you all right, Bjorn? I always assume you are, but I should check more often.'

'Operating the mimic has never bothered me. Somehow, the more I use them the less I feel as though I'm really out there, I feel as though I'm operating a machine. Maybe I lack imagination, but perhaps it helps in this case.'

'It's probably more about remaining detached. I seem to get caught up in the experience and feel it's real. Maybe that's not so good.'

'You've been overdoing it recently. Perhaps it will get to me one day.'

Yingluq wandered back. 'Sahko wanted to know how you were, Menem. She seemed very concerned and has taken over my session with the children, perhaps by way of a distraction.'

I caught Bjorn and Hyun exchange glances again, but I couldn't work out why. It seemed surprising that Sahko was suddenly concerned about me, but it wouldn't look good for her if a second crew member fell off their perch. She might be worried about the state of the ship and want all the engineering resources available and fully functional.

4022, 09:45

The status screen flashed and indicated that the hot-bot was coming back to the tile refiner.

'Are you ready for this last part?' I asked the others. 'Hopefully there will be nothing to do, but it would be best if you were all on standby, just in case.'

Hyun went back to the bot-net control station and opened up another section of screen and a controller that allowed him to instruct the hot-bot from there. The other two strapped themselves into their mimic chairs and pulled down their helmets. I watched the various images on my screen as the bot came over to the tile refiner and deposited the recently cut tile into the waiting input tray.

'Hyun, can you get the hot-bot to position itself next to the bearing machine so the knee joint on number three leg can be done first? That leg has the most play in it and the knee joint is the easiest to work on.'

'Acknowledged,' said Hyun, 'number three leg, knee joint.'

I looked over and saw him issue the instruction. We watched as the bot lumbered over to the bearing machine and sat near it. Its four long thin legs were drawn up high over its back in inverted vees, its feet splayed out with foot pads grasping the ship's deck. It lifted one foot and, like a dancer exercising, straightened that leg while keeping the rest of its body and other legs entirely still. Slowly it lowered the leg into the cradle on the side of the bearing machine. The cradle clamped the leg in position and the machine's robot arm went to work like a surgeon, opening the cover and lifting aside pipes and wires, clipping them clear of the joint. The arm reached in and extracted the first pair of bearing cover bolts, placed these in the parts rack and pulled off the first bearing cover. The arm switched to the other and repeated the process. The cradle rotated the lower leg, lifting the foot end up high in the air so that the end nearest the knee joint could be moved away from the upper part of the leg without stretching the hydraulic pipes and control cables. A bot-net camera showed us the exposed joint with the two bearings now clear of their housings. The robotic arm fitted another tool and pulled the bearings off each end of the shaft still held in the top of the lower leg, and placed them in the rack. It took a new bearing and pressed it on to one end of the shaft, and pushed a second bearing onto the other side, measuring and checking that the bearings were correctly positioned. The cradle rotated the lower leg, pushing it back into the knee joint, and the bearings slid into their housings in the end of the upper leg. The arm reversed the actions it had made earlier, refitting the bearing covers and bolts, carefully putting the bot's cables and pipes back in place and finally fitting a new seal and replacing the cover over the joint. The arm folded itself back up and the cradle released the bot's leg.

'That seemed to work. If you're happy, Hyun, get the robot to pull up its leg.'

'OK, here goes.'

Hyun issued some more instructions, and we all watched as the leg slowly lifted away from the bearing machine and, once clear, the knee joint began to bend.

'That looks good. Any problem, Hyun?'

'Not so far. I'll flex it fully.'

The bot's leg went smoothly straight up, the knee joint flexed and the lower limb folded fully down, it stretched the leg out to one side until it was fully horizontal and brought it back again to the fully folded position.

'Now I'll try to put some weight on it,' said Hyun.

The bot lifted itself up and went into a slow dance, lifting one leg after another while shifting its weight around.

'What do you think, Hyun? It all looks good.'

'The data shows much less play in that joint. It is now easily the tightest.'

'Can you give it a good shaking or something? Take it to the extremes of its performance envelope.'

'I'll run it through its test routine.'

Again the bot lifted the leg, much more rapidly this time, straightened it out and began to shake its foot while the leg was fully extended. Suddenly it stopped. From my view the foot appeared to be hanging down at an odd angle. The bot was still.

'Was that supposed to happen?' I asked.

'Checking the data now. A fault has been detected in the foot position. It looks as though there's a problem with the ankle joint. The knee has worked well so far.'

'So maybe we should fix that ankle next?'

'The problem is definitely consistent with a bearing failure in the ankle joint. I'll set it up to fix that next.'

The bot moved on its three good legs and sat down somewhat further from the bearing machine than it had before. It straightened the leg with the damaged ankle, placing it in the cradle. A red light flashed on the control screen: the leg wasn't seated properly. Hyun issued a command and the bot lifted its leg and tried reseating it. The red light came on again. Hyun tried a third time with no change. He then had the bot stand up and reposition itself, but the red light came on yet again.

'I don't seem to be able to get the foot to sit properly in the cradle. With the damaged ankle the foot hangs down too much,' Hyun said.

'Get a bot-net camera to walk around there,' I requested.

We watched as the camera image showed us the foot.

'You're right, the foot is hitting the deck before the ankle is positioned in the cradle,' I said. 'Could a mimic lift the end of the foot up a bit?'

'Maybe. Worth a try.'

'Bjorn, can you go over and, using the long-arms, lift the end of the foot?'

'I'll give it a go.'

We watched as Bjorn's mimic climbed out of the equipment recess and came over to the bearing machine. He reached out and clasped the foot and tried to lift it but his mimic seemed to tilt over.

'Wow. That wasn't good. The foot seems jammed,' said Bjorn. 'Can you get the bot to lift its leg, and I'll try to straighten the foot when the leg is in the air?'

The bot's leg lifted and the mimic tried again to straighten the foot. Again the mimic tilted forward rather than the foot becoming straight.

'I can't apply enough force with the long-arms. The leveraged is tilting my body over. Could Yingluq help brace me?'

'What do you want me to do?' asked Yingluq.

'Come over to near me, place your hands on my shoulders and then move your feet back until you're straight from feet to hands. Lock your mimic like that and it will act as a brace that I can lever against.'

Yingluq's mimic emerged from its equipment bay, walked over to Bjorn's mimic and braced it as he had instructed.

'OK Hyun, I'm going to try again. Lower the leg as soon as possible if I can straighten the foot. Here goes.'

This time, as Bjorn lifted the foot moved and the bot's leg dropped. Bjorn and Yingluq both cried out. The red light had been replaced by green. The ankle joint was locked in the correct place.

'Well done, that did it, the ankle is in position. Stand back, mimics,' I said.

'That was painful,' said Yingluq. 'I didn't know the mimic suits could do that to you. Not nice at all.'

'Yeah, very unpleasant,' answered Bjorn. 'It means that the mimic has become overloaded, and it's designed to let the operator know.'

'Well I certainly knew. Couldn't it do that in a slightly less painful way?'

'It's effective in letting the operator know that the mimic is in imminent danger. It has to be painful to cut through all other signals.'

'Well it worked.'

'Sorry it was so bad. At least we got the job done,' I said. 'Can you please move away so the bearing replacement can start?'

The two mimics backed off from the bearing machine and waited while it started work. Almost every step of the process took longer this time because one of the bearings had become distorted and jammed in its housing: the robot arm had to shake and hit the bearing cap to get it to release, the cradle had trouble pulling the foot away from the lower limb and needed assistance from the robot arm to prise them apart, and finally the bearing puller was nearing its limits and required the arm to tap the bearing all around the shaft to release it. I had the arm take detailed fine measurements of the shafts and housings to see if any of those had become distorted. Fortunately they checked out as being within specification. The new bearings slipped on easily and the joint was reassembled without further trouble.

'Well that was some hassle, but it got there in the end. Now let's do the other pair of bearings in this joint.'

Hyun issued the instruction and the machine began replacing the pair of bearings at ninety degrees to the two it had just done. This time the repair went as smoothly as had that on the knee joint.

'Do you want to test that joint next?' asked Hyun.

'I think we should do the hip joint bearings next on this leg before we do any harsh tests. If that joint fails I'm not sure the mimics are strong enough to lift the whole leg on to the cradle.'

'Sensible. I'll do a light test on the ankle joints and not shake or pressurise the hip.'

The bot raised its leg off the machine and flexed its ankle both up and down and from side to side. The bearings all seemed to have seated properly and the joint was much tighter than before. Hyun instructed the bot to move close to the bearing machine to allow work on its hip joint. Both sets of bearings were replaced without trouble.

'Progress,' I said. 'Hyun, can you test that leg as thoroughly as you can without stressing any of the other legs much?'

The bot again went through its one legged dance training routine: stretching out straight, flexing each joint individually and then together, running them through their range of motions. It tried loading the leg by standing on it, even managing to stand balanced on that single leg.

'That was impressive. I didn't know the bot could stand on one leg,' I said.

'It couldn't before. The control software has improved, the legs are much stiffer and the joints are so good now in that leg that it has substantially finer motor control, which allows it to balance much better.'

'Quite a party trick. All the tests seem to have passed.'

'All the single leg tests.'

'How about we do the other legs now?'

'I'll set it up. Unless we run into another broken bearing we shouldn't need the mimics.'

'Yup. Bjorn and Yingluq, why not park up and step out?'

'OK,' said Hyun, 'I've set that going. There's a Status alarm if anything goes wrong and I'll call you in if necessary.'

Bjorn and Yingluq emerged from their mimic chairs and ran through their stretches once more.

'So you don't want us to hang around?' Bjorn asked.

'It seems unnecessary. If we run into trouble then we'll let you know and get you or someone else back in.'

Yingluq came over to me and put the medical test sleeve over my arm once again. She paused, watching as it reported.

'Good, you check out physically, Menem. Take it a bit easy for the rest of the day. Definitely don't operate a mimic for a couple of days. Get someone else in if a mimic trip is required.'

'All right, I'm going to sit here for a little while and watch how the repairs go. If it runs smoothly, I'll probably get bored and go back to Engineering. If there's a problem we'll get a team back in, either you or whoever is available. I might even take a session with the children. I'm way behind on my quota with that.'

'I said take it easy. A session with the children is unlikely to be that. Do some recreation. When was the last time you did something not work related?' I thought about that but decided not to stretch the idea of recreation too broadly. 'You can't remember, can you?' I saw Yingluq's eyes flash and a hint of a smile appear. 'And don't overdo the recreation either,' there was a definite smile on her face now, 'or I'll have to report you to the captain.' The other two seemed to be smirking, but perhaps that was my imagination.

'I'm going out for a bit too,' said Hyun. 'I'll set an alarm and be back if anything goes wrong.'

I watched as all three left, and then turned back to my screen. The machine was at work replacing the next leg's ankle bearings. It had had no trouble with the foot this time, and the bearings came off relatively easily. After watching for a while, I set an alarm to alert me if either the bot or the bearing machine had any difficulty.

4022, 12:40

Bjorn, Yingluq and Hyun were in the refectory when I arrived, along with Bita and the children, finishing up their meals.

'Everything going well?' Hyun asked.

'It's all running smoothly at the moment. I found it slightly spooky, watching one machine operate on another without human intervention.'

'The machines will take over one day, type of thing?'

'They will, if they haven't already,' I laughed.

'Then we won't have to do any work,' put in Sky.

'If we never have to work, then there's no point in learning stuff in school,' added Kent.

'No school,' shouted Joko.

'But you like learning stuff, painting and numbers, don't you Joko?' asked Bita.

'I love painting. Can I show Menem my latest picture?'

'I'll come by the study room later and have a look, Joko,' I said.

'Good' and Joko went quiet, studying her plate.

'Can I see the machines working, Menem?' asked Alice.

'Sure, perhaps Hyun can switch it on in here.'

Hyun fiddled with his controller and the big screen activated, showing us the machines at work. Hyun explained briefly what was going on. Alice was fascinated and started asking questions. The images held the attention of Kent and Sky too for a short while. I got started on my meal.

After a couple of minutes Hyun said: 'Right children, back to the study room now and we'll discuss what that was all about.'

Hyun shut off the screen, and there was a scramble as the children got up, put their plates and cups through the servery hatch and went out, accompanied by Hyun.

The others lingered and chatted while I ate. Sahko came in, ordered a meal, sat down opposite me and asked how it was going. Yingluq filled her in on progress. Sahko kept glancing at me, which was a bit disconcerting. She had such a penetrating stare, it felt as though she was reading my mind. I couldn't help but look into her searching dark eyes set in that beautiful oval face which rose out of her long shapely neck. Like the Nephertiti bust, she was simultaneously commanding and utterly captivating.

Silence descended over the room. Bjorn said he wanted to check on how Agyei was getting on and that he would go down to the engine room. Bita got up too, and asked if I would drop by Comms later on, where she was planning to be for the afternoon. Yingluq said she had been asked by Minogue to discuss something, so she needed to head off as well. I thought it a rather unseemly rush to the door and it left me alone with Sahko, which normally I would have welcomed but wasn't so sure at the moment.

After the others had gone, Sahko and I ate in silence for a while. I had stretched out eating as far as I could but finally thought I should say something as Sahko put down her utensil. We both began speaking at the same time.

'How are things with you, Sahko?'

'How are you feeling, Menem?'

We were both silent for a moment and then both began again:

'How are things…?'

'How are you…? OK, you first, you tell me how you are, Menem.'

'I feel fine. I don't know what came over me earlier. I simply fainted. Yingluq said that there's nothing physically wrong with me. It's never happened before.'

'I was worried about you, Menem, when I got a message saying you had collapsed.'

'An exaggeration. But with the ship having problems at the moment, we need everyone fully functioning.'

'I was worried about you, Menem, not the ship. I do want us to complete our mission, of course, but more importantly I want you, well all the crew, especially you…' and her voice trailed off and she looked down. I didn't know what to say. I didn't know what she had said really.

Eventually I said: 'I'm not going anywhere, Sahko, without you.'

We stared searchingly at each other across the table in silence. The moment dragged on but neither of us moved or said anything. I felt I was missing an opportunity and should say something. Finally I blurted out: 'Minogue tells me we're still in the dark about the details of the Alpha System.' I regretted it as soon as I had said it. I knew I had blown the moment, maybe my one chance, now gone.

Sahko looked away and stared at a corner of the ceiling. 'Yes, we had hoped the latest data would reveal more in-system objects, which we know must exist, but it didn't.' Her speech was quick and featureless, as though giving the preliminaries of a lecture to a group who were already familiar with the material. 'It has only narrowed the range of possibilities slightly and refined orbital data for the objects we know about. But with the three stars in the system, two close together, and eleven planets we know of plus some moons, well, the orbital mechanics are so complex that even the latest telescopes aren't good enough to provide all the answers. Over time they might, but that's going to be too late for us.'

'Once we've slowed to ten-thousand kilometres a second we can deploy our own telescope. Wayclear will be able to protect it then. It'll detect bodies down to a kilometre in diameter and even smaller objects as we close in.'

'That will be far too late. We'll be only days away by then. We have to deploy it much earlier and take the risk. It would be very bad luck if there are any objects in our way that we can't deflect. We passed the orbital radius of Proxima some time ago so we missed any sort of Ort cloud on our track in, if one exists. The chances of our hitting anything large are vanishingly small.'

'It's the particles that concern me, like that object field. If we'd had the telescope out it would have been trashed, and likely done serious damage to the ship in the process.'

'It's currently impossible for us to work out a precise course to meet up with ABc. We can't yet plot its exact orbit.'

'Minogue said that you and he had been exploring navigation options.'

'We can't get close to a decent solution without better data.'

'Can I do anything to help?'

'Fix the bloody engine so that we can slow down enough to work out what to do before we get there.'

'I am trying.'

'I know you are and my saying such things doesn't help. You don't need any more pressure. I'm sorry, Menem, I don't seem to be good for you.'

'Don't say that.'

'I seem to make things worse.'

'That's not true. Not at all.'

'I should stay out of your way for the time being.'

'Please don't, Sahko, I couldn't bear that. The last thing I want is to be a problem for you.'

I looked at her across the table but she was looking away. She got up and took her tray to the servery hatch. I wanted to stop her going, say something right for a change.

At the door, she turned back and looked at me. 'Once the engine is alight again, and we're all a little less tense, we should have a talk, you and I.'

'I would like that,' I said quietly as she left, but she might not have heard me.

I stared at my empty plate for a while, then got up, and took it to the servery hatch. I walked slowly back to Engineering and, on arrival, reviewed progress on bearing replacement. The third leg was being worked on, progress had been good. About another forty minutes, I estimated, and it would be done. Assuming all went well with the repairs, the hot-bot could get on with fixing the nozzle. Then there was only the fuel pipe to repair, and after that the engine could be brought back to life, assuming there was nothing else wrong. I thought that I should check and so made a call:

'Hi, Ibo. How are you and your lovely engines?'

'You're a bad man. I keep saying so, and nobody listens. My engines are my business.'

'But they're so fascinating. You know how much I like exploring engines.'

'You keep off my engines. I know all about you, once you get your hands on them, who knows what will happen? Might never be the same again after being manipulated by you.'

'You always know how to cheer me up, you lovely woman.'

'Now you're trying to flatter me, I can tell when you're after something, something bad. So the answer is no.'

'Please.'

'No.'

'Be nice to me, Ibo.'

'I'm always nice to you, Menem, at least as much as you deserve.'

'If I promise not to touch your engines, can you tell me something?'

'Depends. Oh, go on then, ask.'

'Have you noticed anything else wrong with Main, other than the nozzle and the fuel pipe?'

'How do you mean?' she squawked in alarm. 'Have you spotted anything?'

'No, no. I wondered if you had. You and Agyei spent some time checking over the exterior, particularly the coolant and fuel systems, and I hadn't heard of any further problems. You also fixed the pipes, cables and structural damage near the fuel pipe explosion.'

'Yes, and also patched up the damaged radiator panel, which is now back in full service too.'

'How confident can we be that once we've fixed the pipe itself, and the nozzle of course, that Main can be brought online quickly?'

'One of the many things I've been doing over the past couple of days is checking everything verrrrry carefully. I had my man crawl all over my engine with his bot-net thingy. It can get into all the small spaces and see almost everything external and it probes a lot of the internals as well. The engine all checks out: exactly matching the reference images and resonance maps. We've found no cracks or other signs of damage. I've also taken the opportunity to give it a thorough overhaul, stripping down anything mechanical, performing a full shipyard maintenance on it. Not that it needed it because it hadn't been running all that long since the last one, and that should have carried us through to the end of the mission. I pulled the injectors from the ignition chamber because there was a risk that they had been hit by debris from the object field. There was nothing wrong with them, as all the tests have shown. I've every confidence that the engine will re-light and perform as advertised.'

'You're a marvel, Ibo. That's the best news I've heard in a while. I didn't know you had been doing all that. I would have helped if needed because, if you recall, I know a bit about servicing engines too.'

'Like I say, you keep your hands off my engines. Besides, you've been busy.'

'A bit.'

'Working too hard, I hear, wearing ye'self out. You're part of the machinery too, Menem, and can only do what you're designed to do. Work too hard and you break down, same as everything else. Maybe you need some maintenance.'

'Yes, well maybe my next service is overdue, but I've got the fuel pipe to fix and then I can take some down-time, possibly.'

'If that old lady of yours ain't servicing you properly, maybe you should look elsewhere. Some unattached woman floating around might give you a seeing to.'

'Are you offering? If so, I'm interested.'

'I ain't unattached, although I'm flattered by your interest, kind sir. Like I say, you is a bad, bad man, but you should place your bad thoughts elsewhere.'

'But there is only you, Ibo.'

'Flatterer' and she cut the link. Talking with Ibo always brought a smile to my face. Her caricature of herself was a marvel. There was also no doubt that she was on top of her game. I had been with some great engine people in the various ships I had been on and she was right at the head of the list. It was a huge relief that she had done everything possible to check that there was nothing else wrong with the engine. I felt renewed energy for the tasks at hand and pulled up schematics for the fuel pipe system.

The basis of the pipe was an evacuated tube with coils around it to create a magnetic field which kept the anti-protons from touching the tube walls. An electric field created within the pipe was shaped into a controlled high frequency wave, propelling the fuel along the pipe and in to the engine's ignition chamber in precisely regulated quantities. The materials of the pipe and coil were highly specialised, and had to be very precisely assembled to manage the flow of fuel. It seemed unlikely that we had the capability on board to make a new one from scratch.

I gathered together all the information we had on what damage the pipe had sustained. Both Hyun and I had taken a lot of images of it. Its outer case had a large hole in it, mainly the result of the exploding fuel. Some of the coolant for the superconducting magnets had been lost which meant that a coolant pipe had been breached. The exterior casing, coolant and the coolant pipe wouldn't be difficult to replace. Further tests would be needed on the magnetic coils to see if how much damage they had sustained and also to see how badly the inner vacuum tube had been damaged. The engineering manual for the pipe stated that there was no provision for finding faults when the pipe was installed, only a simple 'working' or 'not working' status report. The pipe would have to come out to be tested. As it had been made and fitted in sections, to a design common in most ships using antimatter engines, that should be relatively easy. Tests Hyun had made showed that the pipe had only very marginally above-background radioactivity and so the broken piece could be disconnected and brought inside for fault diagnosis and repair.

I had a sudden thought: did we carry any spare sections of pipe? As these were standard pieces we might have an unused section somewhere. I asked Archive to search the ship's plans and loadings. After a short while it reported that, sure enough, we did, and ours had never been used. It was part of a system used to empty out the fuel tanks before carrying out maintenance and also used to transfer fuel to or from another vessel in case of emergency. Ships in the Solar System were required to carry these and no one had made an exception for us, travelling where there was no possibility of encountering another ship or a dockyard for maintenance. Thank goodness for standardised safety regulations. The piece was not huge either: about three metres long and twenty centimetres in diameter. It consisted of three rigid sections with flexible couplers between the sections that allowed it to be bent to fit as required. The ends had standard fittings with vacuum seals. Great care would be needed to avoid the slightest damage or contamination.

The spare pipe would have to be tested before being installed. With luck, the bot-net might be able to get it off the fuel tank where it was currently attached, and bring it to an engine section airlock. I needed to check with Hyun, and with Ibo before 'messin' with her engine'.

Status told me that the bearing replacements were almost done and that Hyun was back in Robotics. I went round to watch the final stages. Hyun was looking at a big screen that showed the covers being repositioned over the last of the bot's joints.

'Nearly finished,' Hyun said.

'No other problems it seems.'

'None. It all ran smoothly apart from that one ankle problem. Next we have to give it a proper test.'

'Will you use the same test routine you used before? The one you used after we had done the upgrades to the bot.'

'Pretty much, although first I'll get it to do some simple leg exercises on the side of the ship. They shouldn't take long. There, it's now standing up.'

We could see the bot draw the last of its legs into its body and then like an old person, start to walk very slowly and carefully on the spot and then around in circles. It spread its feet apart and began doing what looked like press-ups. Gradually its moves speeded up and it shook its limbs in a little dance. The rhythm got faster and it started to use only three legs and then two. Suddenly it stopped.

'Good,' said Hyun. 'It has passed all that and the performance data is looking good, much better than before. Now I'll get it to go through its whole performance-envelope test.'

We watched as the robot came to life again, ambled over to its service station and swapped its battery and coolant pack. It then made its way up to the front, clambered over the lip of the nozzle and disappeared.

'That was very encouraging,' I said. 'We should see how Agyei is getting on with maintenance on the tile plant. I'll give her a call.'

'Please patch me in.'

'Hi Agyei. I'm here with Hyun. How is your tile factory maintenance going?'

'All done. There was less sludge build-up than I'd expected so it didn't take long to clear. I replaced a couple of parts, but overall it's holding up well. It's now fabricating a new tile out of the material from the last one that came in, and that's nearly done. A couple of minutes and the tile will be ready for installation. How are things with you two?'

'The hot-bot bearings have all been replaced. It was just in time for some of them,' Hyun told her. 'It's currently running through its performance envelope, without trouble so far. We'll start it cutting out another old tile when it has finished testing, in about five minutes. So, all being well, it will soon be back with another damaged tile. Once that has been refined there will be more material for processing, in about forty minutes, with luck.'

'Good news. Let's hope we can get on with tile replacement without a hitch from now on.' Agyei sounded relieved.

'We may have to have one more break before we're done. It depends on how the bearings and the other kit holds up,' I added.

'If we need to, but I'm confident that the new bearings will last a lot longer than the old ones. Anyway, how are you feeling, Menem? I gather you had a bit of a turn earlier.'

'Word has got around has it? I had a momentary stop, but I seem to be fully functional now.'

'Glad to hear it. I was worried that you might be out of action for a while, and we still have the fuel pipe to fix.'

'Ah yes, on that I had an idea. It turns out we have an unused spare section, the one that's intended for emergency fuel transfers. It's currently strapped to the side of the fuel tank.'

'Gosh, yes, I remember that now, good idea. Unless the Alphans use the same couplings we won't have much use for it out here. It was only one section that was damaged wasn't it, and not one of the couplings?'

'I've had a detailed look at all the imagery we have of the damaged area and it seems to be in only one section. The couplings look unaffected.'

'Do you think the spare is still in good condition?' asked Hyun. 'It has been out there, unused, for a long time.'

'Unless it got struck it should be useable. I'll bring it inside for a full test before installing it though.'

'The bot-net could probably detach it and bring it to one of the engine section airlocks.'

'I was hoping you might be able to arrange that. I really want to minimise mimic trips and we'll almost certainly need one more to replace the broken pipe, once we've checked out the spare.'

'I'll leave you guys to discuss all that,' said Agyei. 'Call me back if you need anything more from me. I see the bot has brought another tile to the refiner so I'm going to watch that go through production. The bot can take the most recently made one from the airlock and fix it. Talk to you later.' Agyei cut the link.

'It would be much safer to use that spare, rather than try to repair the damaged pipe,' Hyun said to me. 'I'll take a look at where it's stored and the forces needed to release and move it to see if the bot-net is strong enough. There's usually a way, if enough elements can be brought to bear.'

'Thanks Hyun. If the bot-net can bring the pipe to an airlock, that at least would be a huge help. Can I leave it to you?'

'I'll let you know if there's a problem. Do you need to bring it up here for testing or can it be done in the engine room?'

'Almost certainly it will need to be brought here, but that's something I'll have to check out. Let's talk or message later once we know more.'

4022, 13:50

I went back to Engineering and looked through the testing regime for the pipe sections. The substantial power required was available here, as was the ability to pull almost enough vacuum. It would be good enough for testing and I didn't think the engine room had a simple way of generating anything better. I didn't want to fiddle with Fuse which would have more than enough vacuum within it somewhere, but not easily accessible. The other option was to use the outside vacuum of space, but even interstellar space wasn't a perfect vacuum and every time we used it to evacuate something we lost some air, albeit a tiny amount, but something we couldn't replace. Coolant for the magnets would have to be brought in. Some could easily be frozen in the engine room and brought here in a liquid nitrogen flask. That reminded me to call Ibo and ask if she had any objection to what I was proposing.

'I wondered when you were going to call,' was her opening remark.

'Oh dear, have you been talking to Hyun?'

'I have, and he says you is planning to mess with ma' engine.'

'Well you know I'm trying to fix your engine.'

'And now you want to take a good part and replace a bad part with it.'

'Something like that.'

'Seems like a good plan.'

'So you've no objection?'

'Not if you get my engine fixed quick.'

'Thanks Ibo.'

'Oh, and another thing.'

'Yes.'

'You fix up that part you broke and put it back in good condition where the other one came from.'

'We'll try, but I don't know if we have the capability to do it on board.'

'You better try, mister.'

'I'll try, and I'm sure Hyun will too because it will need printed and spun parts from him.'

'He better, or he knows what will happen to him.'

'Terrifying.' I could her laughing. 'Oh, one more thing I wanted to ask you.'

'Yes' she said slowly. 'Always one more thing you men want.'

'It's for testing the spare pipe section.'

'Are you suggesting part of my engine needs testing?'

'Well it's a spare that hasn't been touched for at least ten years, and maybe a lot longer than that.'

'OK, test. Now what do you want from me?'

'A flask of liquid nitrogen.'

'That I can do. How big?'

'In my case very big. No, only a litre.'

'You is a bad man, I keep saying. I can do a litre flask. You want it sent to Engineering?'

'Yes, please, along with the pipe, which we're hoping to bring in through one of the engine room airlocks.'

'So my man say. More trouble for me.'

'You're so sweet, Ibo.' I heard her snort and cut the link.

Hyun messaged me to say that he was still working out how the bot-net could bring the spare pipe to an engine airlock but he remained confident that it could be done somehow. I messaged back telling him to press on and that Ibo had agreed to send a flask of liquid nitrogen with it up to Engineering.

For the first time since we had realised the extent of the damage that the object field had caused, I was confident that we really would be able to get the engine going again. I didn't know if it would be soon enough, but then we didn't have enough information to work that out at present.

I sat back in my chair, ordered a coffee and started some music playing, a gentle pastoral piece written long ago, in a very different time, in a different world. My coffee arrived and my mind wandered through thoughts of the ship and the crew, my mildly encouraging conversation with Sahko earlier in the day, the strange feeling I had had when about to get in to the mimic chair, waking to find myself somewhere different. Perhaps it had been some after effect of the two Stay-Awakes I had taken, or some kind of motion sickness creeping up on me. It reminded me that

Bita had asked me to look in on her. It hadn't seemed urgent, so it could wait. I drifted off to sleep for a moment.

My head jerked back as I awoke. I must have slipped forward and some automatic muscle response had righted my balance. My mouth was dry and my neck felt sore. Falling asleep in a desk chair had been a bad idea. I hadn't even slept long. I stood and paced around, trying to pull myself back to the here and now. I sat again and reviewed Status. The tile replacement was going well with two more completed in the past hour, and one of those had been in a formerly inaccessible area. Encouraging.

A message popped up from Hyun saying that he and Gunadi had worked out a way of using the bot-net to get the spare fuel pipe into the airlock. He wanted to talk it through with me before setting it in motion, so that gave me something immediate to do, and a way of avoiding looking at my ever growing list of routine maintenance tasks, minor repairs, and follow ups to clear all the disruption the engine outage had caused. I went round to Robotics.

Gunadi was there with Hyun, sitting in front of the large screen. She looked up, smiled and waved me over. The screen showed images of elements of the bot-net executing some self co-ordinated actions. They had divided in to groups of three, with two linked side-by-side holding a third between them with its legs in the air. These groups were arranged in a chain, and there were two chains running parallel to each other, close together. The two chains ran across what looked like a plate of the ship's hull and then down a support column. As I watched, I saw a block, held by the feet of several of the upside-down elements, being passed down the chain. Once a group of elements had released the block it split and the individual elements scurried forward to the head of the chain, reassembling ready to catch the block when it caught up with them again. It was like a sticky conveyor belt and utterly creepy.

'What do you think?' Hyun asked.

'Apart from freaking me out? Well it looks like a very neat trick. Can it keep enough hold on the pipe section to move it around?'

'The bot-net elements have good grip with their feet and are strong enough. We'll keep four tethers between the pipe and the ship for security and to help it around some of the tighter corners it will have to navigate to get to the airlock.'

'And how about detaching the pipe from its current storage position?'

'We've tested all the points where it's held down and none of them are jammed.'

'Worst case scenario?'

'It gets stuck somewhere that the bot-net can't sort. If that happens we'll have to get a mimic out there.'

'Which airlock are you planning to bring it in by?'

'Number two, engine room. It's bigger than we need but the number three, the one used for the tiles, is too small. Ibo has cleared the use of the number two.'

'Sounds as though we have a plan, so I say go. Gunadi are you happy with it?'

She looked at me again and said simply: 'Yes.'

'Good,' said Hyun. 'I'll set it in motion.'

We watched as the bot-net stopped and then reversed the direction of travel of the block. Outrider elements had cameras showing us what was going on. The block was taken back to the equipment bay where it had been stored. The elements disassembled themselves from the chain and moved off in a swarm over to the fuel tank. A camera showed a wider view with a radiator panel opened up. Below it was the spare section of fuel pipe.

Bot-net elements fixed tethers to the pipe, while others unlatched it. As it came free, elements formed up along either side and after resuming their groups-of-three formations, shuffled under the pipe to lift and grip it. Once in position, element legs began to wave and the pipe moved forward along the chain.

At first the elements seem to be struggling to keep control when changing direction, the pipe section being much bigger than the practice block. The momentum of the pipe was almost more than they could handle. Gradually they learned to slow well before a change of direction and to use the tethers to help alter course. They even arranged some spare groups standing by which would rush in and help when a part of the chain was losing grip. I found it fascinating, watching these tiny robots, each about the size of a large beetle a couple of centimetres in length, coordinate their activity and learn to improve their performance, all without human intervention.

The outer door of the airlock opened as the chain came up. The bots carried the pipe inside and tethered it in place. All the elements then backed off and our camera's view showed the airlock close. The bot-net's job was done and Hyun and Gunadi both lent back in their chairs and visibly relaxed.

'Very impressive. Well done you two,' I said. 'That has saved a lot of time and the hassle of a mimic trip.'

'Gunadi came up with the idea of using three elements in a group like that. It enabled them to get enough grip on the pipe to control its motion, while holding it far enough away from the ship to avoid it touching.' Hyun was buoyed up by their success.

'Hyun had got all the basics sorted, using the elements in a pair of chains to pass the pipe along, and to use the extra tethers to redirect its momentum. It all worked out rather neatly.' Gunadi too sounded cheerful and relieved that their plan had gone so smoothly. 'I did wonder at the beginning whether it was going to work though.'

'The speed with which the elements learned to coordinate and deal with the additional mass of the pipe was amazing,' I said. 'By the second turn they looked fully in control again.'

We were all silent for a moment, and then I asked: 'Will Ibo be all right if I send a transport cart to retrieve the pipe from the airlock?'

'She said she would arrange that,' said Hyun, and he looked at Status. 'Yes, she has a transport cart standing by and is loading the pipe on to it now. It should be up in Engineering in about ten minutes.'

'Excellent, you think of everything. I better get back there and prepare to receive it.' Gunadi watched me as I stood. I stopped and said: 'Oh yes, I checked Status before I came in: the tile laying seems to be going well.'

'Everyone is watching that, it seems,' said Hyun. 'Progress has been very good recently, and there are no no-go areas in the nozzle at the moment.'

'The schedule is arranged to do the more inaccessible tiles first as far as possible,' said Gunadi, 'while also keeping the factory fully loaded. Doing those first will make it easier to complete the job if the bot becomes less stiff later.'

'Good thinking. I really hope that it will run to the end without another maintenance stop. Time is running down and all that.' The others nodded.

There was still detritus on the workbench in Engineering, left over from assembling and testing the bearing machine. After clearing that away, I studied the fuel pipe testing protocol again and gathered the instruments required. Although shielded, the pipe would still create a significant external magnetic field when it was activated and there would be some very high voltages in the electrical field generators. These, along with the deep vacuum and the liquid nitrogen used to cool the superconducting magnets made for an almost complete pack of dangers.

A message arrived from Ibo saying that the pipe had been retrieved from the airlock. It and the flask of nitrogen were on a transporter cart making their way to me.

As the pipe should already have a deep vacuum inside, I reordered the test schedule. Checking the internal pressure first to ensure it was holding would avoid the need to pump down again. Nothing else required it, so air could then be let in to allow access to the inside of the pipe for testing the electric and magnetic fields. Vacuum would be restored by the airlock when the pipe was carried outside again.

I fiddled around setting up magnetic shielding and test instruments until the transporter cart announced its arrival, bringing the pipe and nitrogen flask into the workshop. The cart's lift was needed to move the delicate pipe, heavy in the gravity environment, on to a set of cradles on the bench. With all the various power, control, coolant and vacuum lines hooked up, the test procedures started. It was a long, slow and exacting process but not intrinsically difficult. The tester did most of the work and I was shop monkey, following its instructions, plugging in instruments and swapping over connections when asked. The pipe all checked out exactly as specified and hardly a hair different from its test results from the shipyard, twelve years earlier. In a way it was a let-down: a lot of work that ending up changing nothing. The only saving grace was the comfort given by all the testing that the pipe would work when installed and not blow the ship to pieces.

The cart's lift picked up the pipe and the empty nitrogen flask, and left. I messaged Ibo to say that the pipe was still as good as new, and that it was on its way back to the engine room, ready to be passed out through the airlock it had come in by.

Ibo messaged back asking when I wanted it in the airlock because she was no longer in the engine room. I looked at the time and realised that it was getting late. It would be better to do the delicate task of replacing the broken pipe in the morning when we were fresh. I replied to say there was no great hurry and that the pipe could wait in the engine room until tomorrow morning, but if it got in her way it could be placed in the airlock at any time.

I packed up the test gear, ready to get out of Engineering for the day. I might even get a little relaxation time this evening. Before I left, I checked progress with tile replacement. Status reported that a consistent, just-under two-and-a-half tiles per hour, was being completed. If that rate was kept up we would have the work done in less than two days. I felt quite buoyant as I went off to the refectory.

4022, 20:10

As usual, I seemed to be the last to eat. Minogue, Yingluq, Bita and Sahko were sitting there with empty plates, apparently in deep discussion which stopped immediately I came in. Massoud appeared at the servery door and asked cheerfully: 'What will it be this evening, Menem?'

'Whatever's good please, Massoud. Hi, everyone, don't let me interrupt.'

'The tile laying seems to be going well at the moment,' said Minogue. He spoke as if he was in one of his bullish moods, brimming with ideas and optimism.

'At last,' I replied. 'If this rate keeps up we should be done in a couple of days and then we can get going again.'

'Or rather slowing again,' said Yingluq.

'Slowing again would be good,' said Sahko quietly. She seemed subdued and rather less optimistic than Minogue. 'How difficult is it going to be to replace the fuel pipe, Menem?'

'We had a piece of luck there. The ship carries a spare section, a standard freighter part carried for emergency fuel transfers. We had it brought inside for testing. Hyun and Gunadi came up with a clever method of using the bot-net to do that which saved a mimic trip. The tests have finished and it looks good as new. Tomorrow, we will need to use at least one mimic to extract the broken one and fit the replacement.'

'I could do that if it doesn't require specialist expertise,' volunteered Yingluq. 'I rather enjoyed the last trip I did.'

'Well thanks. It would be good to have two mimics out there as usual, but the working area is quite confined where the pipe has to go.'

'I don't think you should go, Mcnem,' said Sahko.

'I'm sure Bjorn could go if he has the time, but I really don't mind. The job will require a bit of finesse but it's not particularly technical. If Bjorn and Yingluq used the mimics, I could keep an eye on the proceedings and offer advice as required.'

My food arrived and I ate, the others remained silent. I looked around and they were looking at me. 'Sorry, am I interrupting a private conversation?'

'We were discussing options for how we enter the Alpha System,' said Sahko.

I doubted that was the whole story. Bita wouldn't be contributing much to a discussion of orbital mechanics but she could be involved to decide what was said to Fleet. Either that or she just happened to be in the refectory at the same time as the others.

'We were trying to come up with some way to get more information on the system, perhaps from radio signals.' That might explain Bita being part of the discussion.

'Getting anywhere?' I asked.

'Not yet, but we launched some wild ideas,' said Minogue. Probably he was upbeat because he loved that type of blue-sky discussion, going off on all sorts of wild tangents. Very occasionally he would hit a target. 'We were wondering if we could use our main aerial as a radio telescope, for example,' said Minogue.

'It is pointing the wrong way at the moment I would have thought,' I said.

'Sadly true for this purpose. But now we've passed Proxima maybe we could pick up some backscatter from it,' said Minogue.

'That seems a stretch,' I said. 'A star is hardly a focused reflector and we're a very long way from it.'

'But we've a very powerful transmitter,' said Minogue.

'Hopefully we'll have slowed enough soon to be able to point a telescope forward,' said Yingluq.

'Also true, but the backscatter idea might be worth a try.' Minogue was still defending his absurd idea.

'We could deploy the secondary radio dish. At least that one can be pointed in the right direction,' said Bita.

'What would you hope to pick up, local soap operas?' I asked.

'Now that would be a great discovery but sadly is somewhat unlikely,' said Minogue.

'It's a pity we didn't get Fleet to co-ordinate data gathering on the System. We might have been able to triangulate something. But it's too late to ask now, and they are a long way away anyway,' said Bita.

Sahko looked glum and pushed her plate around and then stood up. 'I think I'm done for tonight. I'll leave you to the wilder shores of creativity.' She took her plate to the servery hatch and before leaving said to me: 'I'm very glad the nozzle repair is coming along and you've a solution for the fuel pipe. We're in with a good chance now.'

Although she smiled, her tone said more than her words. Something else seemed to be on her mind but she left without saying anything else.

Massoud had disappeared too at some point.

'We should have another session on this soon, when the engine is up and running,' said Minogue. 'Once it's working we'll have one less variable to contend with. How about we take a look at the signals from the Wayclear radars, maybe there's something in that?'

'We mustn't mess with Wayclear,' I said. 'It's the only defence we've got, even if it proved inadequate for the object field.'

'You're sounding like Ibo. I'm only suggesting we tap into the data stream, not steal the equipment.'

'They're far too short range,' said Yingluq. 'At this speed the focus is about a hundred kilometres out. That wouldn't be much use for exploring the Alpha System.'

'Maybe not, but don't dismiss the idea. Perhaps Gunadi could use her magic and see if anything interesting can be extracted from the data. If that's no use, how about jury-rigging something alongside the Wayclear radars that's longer range? If it was a radio dish it wouldn't matter so much if it wasn't properly protected by Wayclear, unlike the optical telescope.'

'There's a thought. We do have some impressive radio signal processing kit in the back of the bus.'

'Don't go messin' wi' ma' engine,' said Bita.

'And on that note I must be going,' said Minogue as he stood up. 'I'm on duty with the children tonight so it's bedtime stories for me. Bjorn will be waiting to be relieved.'

'I must be off too,' said Yingluq. 'End-of-day health reviews to conduct and then early to bed. Sometimes I wake in the night and feel restless.'

She glanced over to me and smiled. I couldn't make out if she was laughing at me or issuing an invitation. I smiled back anyway, a pleasant memory, or fantasy, in my head.

The room was a lot quieter now the most of the others had gone. Bita didn't seem in any hurry to leave, waiting silently while I ate. She sat with one leg tucked under in her familiar pose, looking youthful in a short, brightly-patterned skirt over some white leggings, colourful pumps on her slender feet and a little embroidered jacket over a silky white top. Her hair was drawn into a couple of loose bunches held together with clips that looked like butterflies.

'Sahko seemed a bit depressed. Is something wrong with her?' I asked.

'A bit of a crisis of confidence, facing what seems like an endless stream of problems. At least the engine is on the way to being fixed,' Bita replied.

'It's not done yet, but I'm more confident than I was this time yesterday.'

'I'm glad to hear that and no doubt we'll work our way through the navigation problem too somehow. Isn't that why this is a crewed and not a purely robotic mission: because we humans are supposed to be so creative and adaptable?'

'You certainly fit that description, as evidenced by your recent mimic trip.'

'Ha, I enjoyed that, although perhaps you didn't so much.'

'I used to get a kick out of them, although I was never as at-ease as you seemed to be. Unfortunately, the more I use a mimic, the more I dislike it. Anyway I'm glad you found it good. Yingluq was quick to volunteer for more work, so presumably she enjoyed her trip too.'

'Lots of us are happy to do them so you don't need to go yourself.'

'But it's a waste of time if I have to sit and direct. I should be out doing the work myself, not tying up one of the crew unnecessarily.'

'Better that one of us helps out for an hour or two than you be out of action for a long time.'

We were quiet for a moment as I finished eating.

'Sorry I didn't come to see you this afternoon,' I said. 'I was busy with the fuel pipe and it slipped my mind.'

'We didn't schedule anything. How about we go for a walk around now? We can talk, and I find it a good thing to do in the evening.'

'Sure.' I stood up and took my plate and cup to the servery hatch. 'How are things with you, Bita? Does anyone ask you that? You're always asking how we are.'

'Things are good, thanks. Life has got a whole lot easier now Joko is a bit older and wants to bunk with the other children. Sometimes Alice seems to like playing mother. There is something I've been meaning to ask you, Menem. It's not urgent, but when you have the time, can you take a look at the steering mechanism for the comms dish? It sounds a bit rough compared to how it used to.'

'I hope it's not another bearing failure. That might require mimic work too.'

'Have you been down to the back end of the ship recently?'

'No, I can't say I have.'

'Zero-'g' at the moment of course.'

'I can cope, especially if it's inside. I may not be as balletic as you, but I get around.'

'Do you fancy going down there now?' Bita sounded like a naughty schoolgirl.

I laughed and glanced at her. 'Maybe I could take a look at your machinery.'

'You wish.'

'I do.'

'I agree with Ibo: you're a bad, bad man.'

She giggled and ran off. I gave chase and caught up with her at the door that gave access to the shaft down to the keel tube. She looked around in an exaggerated way to check that no one was watching, opened the door and pulled me inside. She swung on to the ladder and started climbing down, cautiously at first, but with increasing abandon as the gravity got lighter as we approached the core. I went steadily, keeping a proper grip all the way down. I floated off the last rung and Bita took my hand as we stepped into the spin-changer compartment. When the rotation stopped, the access door to keel opened and we swam out, free of gravity.

'We should have brought some poppers or something. It feels as though we're bunking off from school,' I said.

'Maybe I have something hidden away down here.'

'Tsk, tsk.'

'Need to let go sometimes.'

'Yes.'

She slipped out of my grasp and swam away down the tube, gliding gracefully, doing an occasional somersault to let me catch up, but always staying out of reach. Her skirt floated around her waist and her jacket streamed out behind her like a small pair of angel's wings. I almost managed to catch one of her feet, but she laughed and pulled it away.

She waited for me at the bulkhead door, took my hand again, and guided me through into the narrow connector space. Tubes led off on two sides and directly ahead lay the centre of the back of the primary aerial. This massive structure had the same diameter as the ship and covered the whole of its back end. Such a large aerial was needed to be able to communicate with the relay stations, when we had been in range of one, or with Fleet, a year behind us. The primary aerial curved away from the ship in a smooth dish. Actuators held it part way up the curve to allow a limited range of movement, ensuring tight focus and optimum performance. High up behind the dish there was room enough to accommodate the retracted secondary aerial, several equipment rooms and the viewing chamber.

One tube from the connector led to the much smaller secondary aerial. Once the ship had come to a halt it would be deployed far out from the side and pointed in any direction, ready for communicating with off-ship operations.

We took the other direction, leading to the comms equipment space. This large, utilitarian, but oddly shaped room was dominated by four black sentinels housing the signal processing equipment, transmission power gear, dish controls and secondary aerial systems. Bita and I floated around these sentinels like fish exploring a reef.

I always felt a slight shiver coming here because it was the place that Avalos had died. No one could explain what he had been doing. He had legitimate reasons to be here: as well as being navigator, he was number two for comms, and there was both navigation and comms equipment located in this room. One of the star-finder cameras looked straight back through a small port in the main antenna, and its associated electronics where housed in one of the sentinels. However, he had opened another, the one that contained the main transmission power equipment. Somehow he had managed to electrocute himself with it. One of his hands was very badly burned where he had touched a live cable. The other mystery was why the transmitter had come on at what was not a normal scheduled time.

A small store cupboard stood against a wall from which Bita retrieved a cloth bag. She moved towards a hatch in the roof of the room, opened it and passed through into the viewing chamber.

This was a large domed room. Soft couches were fixed back in a circle around the periphery. Above the level of the seats, the dome was an entirely transparent bubble. It was possible to raise the room out from the side of the ship to give a view all around. Even when retracted, as now, it commanded a stunning view of the stars. The Milky Way crossed overhead like a braded and slashed ribbon constructed from billions of points of light. The chamber was the one indulgent extra that had been added to the ship for use by crew, having no functional purpose. It was actually very light, its form held by the air pressure within.

Bita lay on her back with her arms and legs outstretched, floating in the centre of the room, gazing up. I swam in, hung on to a rail and twisted myself onto one of the couches which gripped my clothes enough to stop me drifting away. I too gazed at the stars in silence. It seemed warm in the room; Bita must have turned up the heat.

'It's been a long time since I came in here,' I said. 'I had almost forgotten how stunning the view is. Looking at it from the mimics is not the same. Do you come here often?'

'Sometimes. It's a great place to clear the mind. It inspires me.'

Bita floated down, sat beside me and activated a control which put out the room's lights. We were left bathed in ghostly bright starlight, ranging from the warm red of the stars we were leaving behind around to hard blue stars towards which we were rushing. She looked in the bag she had retrieved and pulled out a couple of small pills. She took one and offered me the other.

'What are they?' I asked.

'Pings. You know, only a mild stimulant. It enhances the experience, I find.'

'Long time since I had one of those. I didn't know we had any left on board. I seem to remember Avalos talking about them.'

'He brought some with him, one of the few good things about him, but those ran out long ago. Still there's nothing that can't be made on board.'

'By whom?' I asked and popped the pill.

'That would be telling.'

I felt hot and a little drowsy. The stars seem to get brighter and sharper. I unstuck myself from the couch and floated, surrounded by a sea of light, dunes of diamonds. I looked around and Bita was floating too. She had taken off her jacket and skirt. She twisted slowly and tumbled towards me and then away. She danced a bewitching serpentine ballet like a seal chasing a school of fish.

She returned to the couch and gracefully removed her top and leggings, let go and floated without movement. I looked at her, studying the beauty of her form. I came close and stared at her body, twisting around but not touching, searching for strange perspectives on curves and planes. She put her hands on my shoulders and looked me in the eyes and smiled. She unseamed my shirt and drew it off and it floated away. Warm enveloping air wrapped itself around. I removed the rest of my clothing. We held hands and floated, watching the stars for a while. She let go and swam energetically around me, brushing her skin against mine: dolphins playing.

We chased each other, locked together, floated, tugged, pressed, rocked and joined. Our ballet lasted a long time, rising and falling in tempo, one dominating and then the other. Finally we exhausted each other and she turned her head and we kissed, a long, soft, wet kiss. We floated like that, murmuring wordlessly, caressing each other gently. I almost fell asleep, hugging her close, the heat of her back warming my front and my evaporating sweat cooling my exposed skin.

Finally she let me go, squeezing me out. She swam around until we faced one another. We reached out and came together again in a warm, comforting cuddle.

'Mmm,' she said softly, 'That was nice, very nice.'

'Yes it was,' I murmured. 'You're wonderful, all the right moves.'

'You still seem to have lots of energy, Menem. I thought perhaps you might be exhausted, but not for everything it seems.'

'I think I'm truly exhausted now, at least for a while.'

'You kept going longer than I expected. That second time was a nice surprise.'

'A surprise for me too. I didn't know I had it in me.'

She giggled. 'And now it's in me.' She rubbed her damp crotch against my thigh. 'But perhaps I need to clean up a little before it leaks out and makes a mess in here. The service bots will be complaining to management again.'

We swam down to the couch where she found her bag and removed a small towel, which she wiped between her legs. I sat beside her and said: 'It has been a while hasn't it?'

'Too long. I enjoyed that.' She stretched her limbs out. 'I'll be a bit sore tomorrow though.'

'Me too. No serious damage I hope.'

'Only a little reminder for a short while of a good time.'

She smiled, closed her eyes, arched her back and ran her hands down her sides. I smiled at the memory too.

'Twice: I'm glad I can still do that in one session, with the right stimulation, and you're certainly that, beauty.' I paused. 'And four for you, if I got that right.'

She laughed. 'Always counting things aren't you, Menem.'

'Measurement is the key to improving performance,' I intoned.

'Yeah, well, the performance wasn't bad, four is about right.'

'It is always hard to tell for us blokes.'

'One of our little girls' secrets. Helps to keep you men trying hard.'

'Tee hee,' I said and gave her a gentle shove. She shoved me back with a laugh and a look in her eye.

'Of course there are no limits for us girls, except boredom.'

I grabbed her and tried to throw her across the room.

'I wouldn't want you to get bored.'

She held on to me and we grappled for a while, but she was fast and slippery and I was losing the chase. Eventually she was above me and wrapped her legs around my middle and I had to use my arms and legs to stop us crashing into the walls of the chamber. I tried to sit up but she pushed me down and sat astride me. She laughed in triumph, a gleam in her eye. She reached behind her. 'What's this? I thought you were done?'

'Oh boy,' was all I could say, and she wriggled back, lifted herself up, and using her hands directed me inside.

'Not quite done are you?' I reached up and tweaked one of her nipples. She slapped me gently across the face. 'Naughty boy.' I reached up and tweaked the other nipple. She slapped me again and then leant over, studied my face and wiggled her backside. 'You like that don't you.'

'I'm tired, exhausted, worn out. I can't.'

She hit me again and hissed: 'I want to, so lie still.'

She took her pleasure, eventually shuddering against me and then fell quiet, finally relaxing her grip on me.

We lay locked together for a long while, floating in the starlight. I fended us off when we were in danger of hitting a wall and gently stroked her back. I felt her stir in my arms and she caressed my sides and thighs. Her cheek rested on my chest.

'More,' she murmured.

'Greedy,' I replied.

'More,' she said again.

I gave her a light tap on the bottom. 'Better to get up from the table before you're completely full.'

'Full of aphorisms, aren't you? I want more,' she said a little petulantly. 'More, more, more.' Now a demanding small child.

I squeezed her bottom. 'If I do anything more I'll have to go to Yingluq to have something sewn back on. She might tell.'

Bita laughed and pushed me away and went to get her clothes. I watched her graceful limbs as she pulled on tights and top and then skirt and jacket. When she was done she sat and watched as I dressed too. The stars had returned to their usual brightness, glow unchanging, watching over us, seeing all and seeing nothing. The power of the Ping had faded.

'Yingluq wouldn't tell. She's the doctor and seen it all before,' said Bita, resuming our conversation.

'Do you think so?'

'Oh yes. You wouldn't be the first to be damaged in such a cause.'

'Really?'

'Sure.'

'Not by you I hope.'

'Not so much, others.' I thought of Gunadi and Avalos, perhaps she was too. 'I hope I didn't hurt you. I got a bit carried away there.'

'That was the idea I thought,' I replied.

'But there has to be limits. Let me look at your back.' I rolled over and she touched my shoulder which made me wince. 'Sorry, Menem, maybe I did go too far.'

'Blood?'

'Just a little, scratches though. It should all heal up quickly, but if you bed someone else in the next couple of days, they may ask.'

'I caught myself on a machine when manoeuvring in zero-'g'. Everyone knows how clumsy I am.'

'That's almost on the bounds of plausibility but not good enough to allay a suspicious mind or bear a close examination.'

'So I can bed only you for the next few days. That'll be hard.'

She punched me gently and I swam away. We floated around for a while.

'Have you done it often, in here I mean?' I asked.

'One of my favourites. Haven't you?'

'Not for a while. I seem to remember that this place was quite busy in the early days, but I do like having gravity: a bit more control, a bit more thrust.'

'But the floating, three-dimensional thing can't be beat. Sure we have to find things to hold on to or push against. You seemed to know what to do.'

'It was better than I had remembered, and you're a great inspiration.' I paused and then couldn't help myself continue. 'Who is good in here?'

I caught the teasing gleam in her eye. 'Well practically everyone. Minogue of course, Yingluq…'

'You've been in here with Yingluq?'

'Yingluq is quite broad minded.'

273

'I've been missing out.'

'You should try it. Three can be fun. Four sometimes, but depends on who the fourth is and whether the other man can cope.'

I gulped but couldn't tell if she was winding me up. 'Well I can see Minogue, Yingluq and you. That sounds plausible. But the fourth? Massoud might fancy Minogue, but I doubt if Minogue is in to that and Massoud wouldn't be very interested in the other two of you.' I had a lurching thought of Sahko but pushed it down and hastened on. 'Three women might work, but I don't picture Gunadi in that scene, too introverted. I don't know about the other two couples. I can't see Ibo and Hyun being swingers, but it might be possible that Agyei, or Bjorn more likely, played away from home, but somehow if he did, I imagine it would be a lot more discreet: he's quite a private guy. I could be wrong about any of them of course, but my guess is that this happened long ago and it was Avalos. I can see him in such a scene.'

'A real detective aren't you? Yes, Avalos was a player, until no one wanted to play his games anymore. Good looking guy, great body, kept himself in shape, swung both ways. Minogue doesn't and that caused trouble. He was curious and quite tolerant at first and didn't seem at all jealous. He liked to watch sometimes or be watched. Avalos wasn't a good team player though, he always wanted to be in control. None of us liked that.'

'I can see that. You like to be in charge sometimes.'

'Sometimes, sometimes not. Avalos was good for one not the other. Very good sometimes.'

'But he had a nasty side.'

'What do you know about that?'

'From what I have heard, Avalos tried his luck all around, with quite a lot of success initially, until his black side emerged.'

'That's about it. We stopped inviting him after the second time.'

'But someone didn't.'

'What do you mean?'

'Someone didn't stop inviting him, or found they couldn't refuse his attentions even though they knew they should. Someone who had a dangerous dark need that fitted with Avalos's vice.'

'You seem to know a lot.'

'As I'm sure you do.' Bita remained silent. 'I would like to help if I can.'

'A bit late now don't you think, with Avalos dead these last eight years?'

'This is your area of expertise, not mine,' I said, studying Bita, 'but there might still be things to be done.'

'There's only so much a therapist can do. Only when the patient recognises that they need help can therapy be effective.'

'You can lead a horse to water…'

'Quite so, Mr. Aphorism.'

'But people change. Maybe time is what it takes and there comes a point…'

'I keep my eyes open, Menem.'

'Sorry, of course you do. But if I can help, I would like to.'

'Thank you, Menem. I know you mean well. Be very careful that you don't entangle yourself in something you can't control. Here's one for you. "Fools rush in…"'

'OK, point taken, apologies. I didn't know if anyone was doing anything.'

'You can be sure of that: we all look out for each other. You're not the only one who cares. Sometimes you don't know what else is going on around you, do you? You have your head stuck in the machinery. Don't get me wrong, we're all very grateful for that.'

We were silent for a while, and then I said: 'We all want to get there in one piece. I hadn't really thought about it before, but keeping us from all going insane, twelve of us cooped up in this tin can for twelve years, without anyone going bananas. Quite a lot of that's down to you.'

'We all play our parts; we need each other. But we don't have only one role. In that way I'm glad that you're interested in helping the crew as well as the machinery.'

'As you, Yingluq and Sahko have helped me out over the past few days, as well as the other crew members who are more directly involved with the machinery of the ship. Yeah, yeah, I know, aren't we all nice?'

'Most of the time,' she paused, and I wondered why. Then she continued: 'But like you said, twelve of us stuck in close proximity for twelve years. A lot of thought was given to that before we left.'

'By you.'

'Research has been going on for centuries in this area. This particular mission, out of the Solar System for the first time, required new thinking, by me in the early days, along with many others. But when I decided I really wanted to be part of the mission, I had to drop out of team design and join crew evaluation and training.'

'I remember when you joined the crew pool.'

'What do you remember about that?'

'Well, that you were young, beautiful, very bright, graceful, imaginative. I never really learned why or how you came to be there. Actually I thought you might be a plant to see how the other potential crew members would react. You know, male jockeying, female jealousy.'

'You were one of the very few who never asked all those questions about why I was there.'

'I wondered, but I knew that some of us had difficult backgrounds, painful pasts, were escaping from something. I didn't want to pry or play those games I thought some might be using to psyche rivals into quitting or failing.'

'Plenty of that was going on. It was important to get it out in the open before final selection. It was noted that you didn't seem particularly curious about others' pasts. A point in your favour for the position you were seeking.'

'The dumb engineer? So tell me now something of your past, was it painful?'

'My past was not especially painful. I was brought up in a loving stable family, although my father died when I was fifteen and my mother when I was twenty-seven. No brothers or sisters.'

'Your mother's death sounds to be about the time you made the switch from evaluator to candidate?'

'It removed my closest tie to Earth. We had a good relationship, very good compared to many mother-daughter ones.'

'How did you get interested in psychology?'

'Do you want the story? You must have heard most of it.'

'I expect I've picked up snippets here and there, but I've never got it whole from you. It seems rather late in the day to be asking.'

'OK. Well, when I was a child, I first wanted to be a ballet dancer but grew too curvy, then I wanted to be a basketball player but wasn't tall enough. You know, as children we get these unrealistic dreams. My poor parents: ferrying me to ballet or basketball classes, they almost certainly knew the causes were hopeless, but they wanted me to try as hard as I could. Try hard and have fun, as my father used to say. He was a doctor, my mother an administrator at a university. One of her jobs was to organise formal dinners for visiting senior academics, politicians, donors, that sort of thing. She took great care, researching all the guests' backgrounds for their interests, and then arranging that they met or sat next to people with whom they had something in common. The head of the university got to rely on her and she attended all the dinners, steering the guests around to ensure no one was trapped with the bores for long and that they met others they were likely to find interesting. No one left an event organised by my mother feeling that they had wasted an evening.

'When my father died, my mother needed more income. The town mayor had been to a number of university functions and asked my mother to help out with civic dinners, so she started freelancing on the side. It didn't take long before she was in high demand, had set up a business and started hiring people to help. I got involved a bit in school holidays, researching peoples' interests. When I was old enough, I went along to a few events and watched my mother operate. It was quite an eye-opener: she used all her charms to move people around, flirting and serious, always interested, always apologetic, directing proceedings but not dominating them. The important people felt important, the bit-part players felt they had played their parts. She was never still, always keeping the event moving.' Bita paused with a faraway look and a smile.

'I loved art at school and wanted to become an artist, but my mother kept me going with sciences and languages too. I was fortunate in being an academic child and sailed through school without a lot of effort. No serious boyfriends, simply a few experiments which taught me some lessons about boys and how to handle them.'

'Which you've recently demonstrated.'

'Shut up, if you want to hear the rest of the story.'

'Sorry, I do.'

'I ended up reading Psychology at Tehran University, then a master's at Tsinghua and finally a PhD in Berlin. My research interest was on the design and practicalities of selecting closed groups for long space missions. I was looking around for a post-doc and was very close to taking up a role at the NAFSA when this mission was mooted. I attended an academic conference where I made a presentation and was approached afterwards by a senior prof. in our field. He asked if I wanted to join the evaluation team for this mission. I had the right background: coming from a non-aligned nation, having studied or worked in more than one of the four powers and speaking both English and Mandarin as well as German and Persian. It was a job made for me.'

'You must have completed your PhD in a short time.'

'I had essentially been doing research in the field since my third undergrad year. I had read all the literature before I started, that saved a lot of time.'

'What was your topic?'

'"The size and composition of space voyage crew: countering boredom in long missions." The decision to make this a manned mission was taken because no one was confident that a ship would survive such a long journey unmanned. AI's aren't known for their flexibility and mechanical systems are awkward and breakdown in a million different ways. We also didn't know enough about the Alpha System to be able to navigate within it robotically. That was the starting point: an engineer and a navigator. They could have been the same person of course: a one person crew could have done the job except that they almost certainly wouldn't have survived twelve years of solitary confinement. If you have one person they need food and environmental systems. Adding a second person requires relatively little extra. A stable married couple might work, but studies have shown that it would be very risky: most couples that remain stable do so because they interact separately with others. These others keep the couple together by illustrating counter examples or providing guidance or information to help the couple navigate their relationship. So the next step is to four: two couples. Better, but still too intense and unstable: jealousies and rivalries. Research showed that essentially the more people the better psychologically, but then we come up against the costs and engineering constraints and on top of that the political considerations. That led to a design with twelve people: a small enough number to accommodate but quite stable. Lots of good things about a group of that size: twelve major areas of expertise, good variety of interactions.'

'Twelve fits nicely into a standard habitat module, with some spares,' I added. 'You said your area was something to do with "countering boredom". How is that important?'

'For most of the voyage nothing was going to change, the stars would look the same, the people would be the same, there would be no weather and no seasons. Such an isolated group was in danger of being taken over by insanity. Celebrities, for example, easily become divorced from reality because they have to isolate themselves from their adoring fans but end up being surrounded by sycophants. That way madness lies. The right mix of personalities is key to maintaining sanity.

'To be fit and able on arrival, the crew had to be youngish adults in the prime of their lives on departure, so having children was part of the plan: add some freshness to the mix along the way. Give people another reason to hang together, to succeed. No one knew if it would work, and there was no time to do experiments, and who would volunteer for such an experiment anyway? The Moon and Mars expeditions and colonies gave us some idea of things we should and shouldn't do. We've got this far with only one death, sorry, two, including Mo. That was unforeseen and has been one of our biggest problems, keeping an even keel after that. Avalos's death was not unforeseen, not, I hasten to add, Avalos specifically, but that one or more of the crew members could die on the voyage. We were very concerned about upsetting the sex ratio.'

'Not getting enough?'

'Hah, hah. Yes, actually. Jealousy, upsetting balances. We thought about that a lot in the planning stages. It was one of the compelling arguments for giving everyone a companion. As it happened, Avalos's death eased tensions rather than increased them. He had not, of course, gone through the same evaluation process as the rest of us. In some ways we were fortunate, I'm not sure we would have made it this far had he lived.'

'Wow. I hope no one thinks that my death might be fortunate.'

Bita laid a hand on my knee. 'No, Menem, no one would think that about you.' Then she laughed and had that gleam in her eye. 'But you better be careful, you better be real nice or someone might start to think that.'

'I thought I had just been real nice to you.'

'Oh yes, tonight you have, but sometimes you seem to be avoiding me. We haven't had an encounter for a while.'

'I've been tied up with things, you know, work related.'

'And you're still obsessing over Sahko.'

'Yes, well, it's the one you can't have that you want.'

'Yes, Mr. Aphorism, it's your game. But I got the impression a little earlier that you wanted me.'

'You led me astray.'

'So you didn't want me?'

'Oh yes, in my weakness, I wanted you. Actually, I still want you.'

I made a grab for her, grasping her around the waist but she pushed me away and wriggled from my clutches.

'I thought you were exhausted. It's getting late and we both have work tomorrow. Another time, and perhaps you'll be more satisfying then, Mr. Floppy.'

'I'm not Mr. Floppy.'

She took a close look at me and said: 'Well maybe not so much, but you did look rather red and swollen and I've inflicted enough damage on you for one night. Also, Mr. Aphorism, didn't you say earlier something about rising from the table still wanting more?'

'I regret saying that now.'

She took my hand, squeezed it and then pushed off to the hatch in the floor which she opened and dived through. I followed, taking a last look at the outside. Stars, no longer diamonds.

Bita was back in giggling-schoolgirl mood as we made our way out of the comms section. She pushed me and darted away through the keel. I gave chase, but she was too quick and evaded my grasp. She went through the hatch into the spin-changer and I joined her. The door sealed behind us and the chamber began spinning up to match the Habitat Ring. Another door in the side of the chamber opened and we heard a noise coming down the tube. Caught red-handed: there was nowhere to hide. Bita laughed as she spotted that it was a service bot carrying a box down to the laundry. We climbed up the tube, Bita going up the ladder feet first. As we climbed gravity started to impose itself on us again, and, as I had started up head first, I had to turn around awkwardly halfway up. Bita waited for me at the top and drew me close. I looked down at her and we kissed briefly, tenderly.

'That was nice, Menem. Thank you.'

'Thank you, Bita, you're wonderful.'

I stared into her large dark eyes and she brushed my hair with her fingers. Then she shoved me away and opened the door to the Habitat Ring corridor and we rushed through together. The passage was in evening gloom, but there was a figure some way along, which we could just make out to be Massoud. He turned, bent down to see who we were, smiled, waved and disappeared.

Bita giggled. 'Do you think he saw us?'

'Of course he saw us.'

'Caught in the act.'

'A professional consultation: you've been trying to work out some of my troubles and had some success I may add.'

She came close and whispered: 'But I don't think I've solved all your troubles yet.'

She gave my crotch a squeeze and then danced off, skipping round the Ring. I leaned back against the wall, and watched her go.

I realised I was tired and rather sore. I checked Status before going in to my apartment. The tile laying was going well, Wayclear had reported nothing: a satisfying day.

Mission Day 4023

4018, 08:30

Jazz was still giving the impression of sleep or was ignoring me, and had her back towards me as I left my apartment. I was still feeling a bit tired and not fully awake, despite a refresh. I ordered breakfast to be delivered to Engineering and checked Status. Tile replacement was still going well, with another twenty tiles replaced in the last eight hours. The hot-bot seemed to be holding up, with no significant deterioration in its performance. The new bearings were doing their job so far. I checked to see who else was up and around, and discovered that the whole crew were active. I was last to log in, as was often the case. I messaged Bjorn to ask if he could do the mimic trip this morning to replace the fuel pipe, and if we could meet up to discuss how we were going to go about it. I sent a similar message to Hyun.

Breakfast arrived in Engineering not long after I did, and I ate and drank while looking through my jobs' list. There were plenty of regular maintenance tasks piling up. I hadn't done a proper inspection of the environmental systems for a while; I would need to fix up some time with Massoud for that. Then there were the broken items to be repaired, not least of which was to replace the motor I had requisitioned from the refectory and investigate all that mysterious dust in the motor bay there. There was also the motor control box from Engine Control that had failed and led to the fire, with its odd extra pair of connections that I didn't recognise. I hastily closed up the list before I got too overwhelmed. I would have to do a proper prioritisation of my workload soon. Bjorn messaged back to say that he was free and would come around in a couple of minutes. Hyun also messaged back to say he had some stuff to do, but could be ready in half-an-hour or so.

I was finishing my coffee when Bjorn arrived. He seemed his usual energetic self, bouncing around Engineering looking at the bits of machinery lying on the workbench.

'When are you going to fix that motor in the refectory?' was his opening remark. 'No, just kidding, I know you've been a bit busy of late.'

'As have we all, not least you. I wanted to talk with you about the fuel pipe replacement. Make sure you're ready and wouldn't rather postpone it. It could wait until tomorrow.'

'No need to wait as far as I'm concerned, I'm fit and ready and don't have anything urgent on my plate at the moment. The mimic work never bothers me. It's a lot safer than a real EVA, particularly at this speed.'

'Good, but don't hide stuff, OK?'

'Not like you, you mean?'

'I didn't see that coming. Fortunately no one got hurt.'

'Fortunately. Agyei would have said something if she thought I wasn't up to it and she didn't.'

'She's not one to make a fuss, super-calm under pressure. She has a lot on her plate too. How is she holding up? The tile manufacturing appears to be going well.'

'She's fine. I worry of course: how will the time in zero-'g' affect her and all that?'

'Wouldn't being in the womb be a bit like a zero-'g' environment anyway?'

'I hadn't thought of that, maybe it is. Anyway Yingluq is monitoring things closely as far as I can tell. They're often chatting together.'

'More evidence of the female conspiracy?'

'Plotting a takeover? Not sure how they could do that seeing they already run the place. No, I think they like to chat more than you or me.'

'Maybe. Talking of Yingluq, do you think she's the right person to run the other mimic?'

'Fine by me. She's quite capable of operating it effectively and she's very sharp and picks up on things quickly. I wouldn't mind if it was Bita or Sahko either, but for this job I think Yingluq would be my number one pick, after you of course.'

'Yeah, yeah.'

'Seriously, you understand how and why things go together and you've great feel and familiarity with the tools. Given the choice, I would have you out there. You are going to be monitoring aren't you?'

'It's not very efficient, but I do need to see what's going on and be able to advise if needed. Hyun says he'll do the bot-net.'

I messaged Yingluq and got an almost instant reply.

'Yingluq's keen: she's up for anytime this morning.'

'Good. So what if we all gathered in Robotics in fifteen minutes?' suggested Bjorn.

'That should be about right for Hyun who said he had to sort something first. I'll message Hyun and Yingluq. Can you do the mission briefing?'

'Err, yes, I could. Don't you want to do it though?'

'Can you take the lead on this whole job? I'll be technical boffin if needed.'

'You don't sound your usual self. Are you OK?'

'Possibly still feeling the effects of yesterday's little trouble. I'm told to stop taking so much on my shoulders.'

'Won't you get bored if you aren't busy?'

'Oh, I'll keep busy. It's only these missions.'

'OK, I'll do it. I best be getting over to check all the kit is ready to go.' Bjorn looked at me, puzzled over something, but said nothing more and left.

I messaged Hyun and Yingluq to say that we planned to start in fifteen minutes and that Bjorn would be leading. I also checked Status to see that the spare pipe was in the engine room airlock and ready to be collected outside, which it was. As I finished, Yingluq appeared, looking athletic and efficient in a muted blue, well-fitting ship-suit.

'Hi, Menem. May I give you a quick check before we start? How are you feeling?'

'I'm feeling fine, perhaps a little tired, but otherwise good.'

She slipped a sleeve over my arm which closed itself tightly around me. After a moment she said: 'No obvious physical problems. Did you get enough sleep last night?'

'I was a bit late to bed. I find it difficult to get to sleep after having been on the Stay-Awakes and then napping.'

'Perhaps that's it. You've been over exerting yourself recently, haven't you? You asked Bjorn to lead on this mimic job.'

'Sorry, I should have asked. Do you have a problem with that?'

'I don't mind working with Bjorn at all. It was you voluntarily stepping back that was unusual.'

'Everyone keeps telling me to take it easy, so I thought I would give it a try. Bjorn could do this without me, but I do want to observe. Not so much to correct anything, but to see if anything could be improved, like the design of the pipe connectors or the process we're going to use. There's also the risk that the two pieces of pipe aren't identical, and that one of them has been modified somehow in some unrecorded way. That might affect the installation or even prevent it.'

'So if we get into trouble you'll be on hand to help us out: makes sense. I want to keep an eye on you over the next few days though, to check there aren't any serious delayed reactions.'

'That would be kind. I would very much like to keep an eye on you.'

She laughed and said: 'There's life in the old dog yet. I was worried that you hadn't checked me out so far.'

'Less of the "old" please and, now you come to mention it, I've been most remiss in not giving you a thorough check over. Perhaps it's age after all.'

'You'll be checking out the girls up to your last breath.'

'I hope so, but I also hope that won't be too soon. My father once said that you can tell when a man is dead because he no longer looks at women.'

She laughed again and put away her things. I checked her out as she turned away and bent over her case, perhaps deliberately, and was not disappointed. She smiled as she left.

When I came in to Robotics, Bjorn and Yingluq were looking at a hologram of the part of the engine section where the fuel pipe ran. They were discussing how best to place themselves when taking out the damaged piece of pipe. Hyun was at the bot-net control station talking on the comms to someone, perhaps Ibo. He finished up and came over to us.

'Are you happy with what we're planning to do, Yingluq?' Bjorn asked.

'I understand what I'm supposed to do but I've little experience of working in and around the machinery. Most of my mimic training was on the outside of the ship's hull.'

'Take it slow and stop to ask if anything is not clear. We're in no rush.'

'OK, good. If the real thing is like this model then it should be straightforward.'

'Hyun, do you have anything to ask, anything not clear?' Bjorn asked.

'It all seems clear. I've set up part of the bot-net to retrieve the new pipe from the airlock and bring it over. Other bot-net elements will ensure you're tethered at all times as usual and a third group is tasked with monitoring your movements and position, and letting you know if you're about to touch anything sensitive. There are a lot of services in that area so there is some risk. Once you've swapped the pipes over, the bot-net will take the broken one to the airlock and place it inside.'

'Menem, do you have anything to add or ask?'

'My role here is to provide engineering advice, if required. I'll observe because there may be things that can be learned about the pipe and the process. I'll remain silent unless I'm asked something or if I see something that concerns me from a technical perspective. It could be that I would like something inspected and ask you to take a closer look. I'll try not to interfere too much.'

'So you'll try to keep your mouth shut?' asked Yingluq with a smile.

'Sure. Try.'

'Thanks, Menem. Anybody have anything else to ask or say before we get to it?' No one did so Bjorn added: 'Good, let's go.'

I had a strange mix of feelings as I watched the others settle in. I felt guilty about taking up Yingluq's time and rather feeble for not doing the work myself. I also felt relieved at not having to operate a mimic again and wondered why. It might be that I was becoming agoraphobic, uneasy when I wasn't surrounded by solid walls. Perhaps it was a reaction similar to that some people had when parachute-jumping: getting more fearful with each jump rather than less. It all seemed unreasonable because there was no real danger in using a mimic: the operator remained in this room, surrounded by solid walls. Nevertheless the experience was uncannily real.

The others got started and I watched, marvelling again at how the bot-net formed itself up, opened the airlock, extracted the pipe and began carrying it to where it was needed. I switched views to watch Bjorn's mimic leading Yingluq's from where they had been stored and clambering down the structure inside the back of the engine section. Hyun had earlier arranged for some strong lights to be set up all around the broken section of pipe. It was usually dark down amongst the machinery and work was easier with general illumination rather than only the mimic's headlights.

Bjorn and Yingluq arrived in the scene and set up instruments to test the pipe's integrity and determine what containment would be needed to avoid any further coolant loss. They wrapped self-sealing tape around the pipe, covering over the whole area where the damage had occurred. Power, coolant and control lines were disconnected, folded back and secured to the ship's structure, exposing the whole section of pipe.

'The couplers look undamaged so we'll try disconnecting them,' Bjorn was telling Yingluq. 'The ends of the pipe must be sealed first by rotating this ring which inserts a plug. Do that on either side of the connection. Good, the instrument shows that the plugs have locked in place correctly. Now we can disconnect by rotating the outer ring over the joint.'

'I can't shift it,' said Yingluq.

'Ah no, you need to use the special tool, yes that one. It fits around the coupler and that lug engages and releases locking pins. In theory it should then turn easily.'

'That's better, it's turning now. How far does it need to be turned?'

'One complete turn, but you can use the tool as a ratchet: eight full pumps up and down on the handle.'

'OK, I get it: five, six, seven, eight and no more. Another light has gone off.'

'Good, that shows it's disengaged. The end should slide out now, but the pipe is quite stiff so it will probably be easier to release the other end before we try to move it.'

'OK, so I take the tool off this end now?'

'Yes. Same procedure on the other end.'

Bot-net elements scurried round and secured a tether to the damaged pipe. In the background the replacement section had been brought up ready. Bjorn and Yingluq undid the other coupler without trouble.

'I'll handle the other end, you take this one. With luck it will slide out.' Bjorn repositioned himself and the two of them pulled on the pipe. Nothing happened. 'Menem, how much force can we apply to the pipe?'

'Try not to force the pipe at all, it may be that the surfaces of the joints have become stuck together slightly and need a little tap to crack them apart. Give the coupler a sharp blow with your hand. It should be able to take that.' I watched as Bjorn gave the coupler a thump and it moved. 'Well done. An old engineering trick.'

'For want of anything else, hit it.'

'That's the idea.'

Yingluq tapped her end, and that moved too. The pipe section slid out easily. The two of them handed it over to the chain of bot-net elements, waiting to take it away. The other chain brought the replacement section alongside.

'Hold on, they look different,' exclaimed Bjorn. 'The couplers look quite different. What do you think, Menem?'

'Err yes, well that's because the replacement pipe has extra covers over the couplers.'

'Doh.'

'Take the covers off and put them over the couplers on the broken pipe.'

'I'll bring the old pipe back again,' said Hyun. The chain of elements stopped carrying the old pipe away and brought it back to near the new one.

'How do the covers come off?' asked Bjorn.

'Press in, twist and pull off, like a medicine bottle cap.'

'Genius.'

'I confess I practiced when I was testing that replacement section.'

'Helpful.' Bjorn worked the caps off and fitted them over the ends of the broken pipe. 'Looks as though it might fit now. Yingluq, can you take the far end and bring it to where you removed the last connection? I see that it will only fit one way round.'

'Like this?' asked Yingluq.

'Yes. I'll bring my end over to the other piece. Right, now let's try and slide it in place. We need to bend it a bit to match the other one. OK, it seems to flex easily enough. How is your end looking, Yingluq?'

'There's a bit of a gap.'

'How big?'

'About a centimetre.'

'Any ideas, Menem?'

'It should stretch that much as the links straighten. Try plugging one end in and start turning the coupler, but only a half turn to start with.' Bjorn engaged his end and used the wrench. 'Yingluq, pull your end and tell us how big the gap is.'

'About five millimetres.'

'OK, Bjorn, try straightening out the joints in the pipe and Yingluq try engaging your coupler. There should be two wrenches there so you can both use one. Can you get your coupler to start, Yingluq?'

'No, it's close I think, but it's hard to hold the pipe still and operate the wrench.'

'Hold on, Yingluq,' said Bjorn, 'I'll back my end off a bit more and then come and hold your end of the pipe.'

Bjorn moved over and grasped the pipe and held it still. Yingluq slid up the coupler and operated the wrench.

'Ah ha,' she said, 'I felt it engage, I can tighten it up.'

'Not yet, the other end is only lightly held. Both ends should be tightened up evenly.' Bjorn went back to the other end. 'I've got two clicks on mine, how about yours, Yingluq?'

'Same.'

'Good. OK, let's do this together. I'll do one click and then you.'

The two of them worked alternately on their ends. Finally Bjorn had eight clicks and a test machine light came on. Yingluq struggled but managed to force her wrench down one more click and the second light came on.

'Looks good,' said Bjorn. 'Now rotate the inner plug rings to clear the ends of the pipe. More lights: looking good. Now reconnect the control lines, coolant and power.' Another set of lights came on. 'Let's step well away and, Hyun, can you run the test sequence?'

'Yingluq and my mimics are clear, Hyun.'

'Running test sequence,' said Hyun.

We watched the screen as the tests were listed and changed colour when they completed successfully: coolant flow was good, power was connected, the correct magnetic and electric fields established, and the vacuum integrity of the pipe was good. Short of running fuel through it, the pipe looked as though it was fully functioning

'Well done everyone. That looks like a good job done.' Somehow I couldn't resist giving instructions: 'Park up and get out of the mimics. Hyun, once the broken pipe is in the airlock, can you arrange a battery replacement for the mimics and then pack up? Oh, and can you also let Ibo know.'

'I think she'll have been following along, but I will anyway.'

As Hyun was still speaking, we all got a message from Ibo thanking us for doing the work on her engine. She also said that the airlock had refused to accept the broken fuel pipe because it had detected radiation. Yingluq and Bjorn unbuckled from their mimic chairs, performing stretches before we gathered round Hyun.

'That went well, I thought,' said Yingluq.

'A bit of playing around, but overall straightforward,' said Bjorn. 'Thanks, Hyun, for all the bot-net support. Especially the chain stuff: that saved a lot of hassle in not having to carry the pipes using the mimic in those awkward spaces. How do you think it went Menem, any immediate lessons?'

'It went very well and I agree that the bot-net really helped. I didn't spot anything that should be done differently. I hope we don't need to have a next time on this job, but if we do, or on something similar, then I wouldn't change the process, except that now you can clearly do it without me.'

There was a slightly awkward pause which Yingluq interrupted by saying: 'Thanks everyone, I found it very interesting and it's quite satisfying when something slots in to place and tests out positively. That's not so common in the medical field.'

'You may be able to do engineering, but I couldn't do medicine.' I said with a laugh.

'Oh no, that's not what I meant. I can help out with engineering if I'm told what to do, and it makes a nice change. No way could I do what you do though. How is the tile replacement work going by the way?'

Hyun checked one of his screens. 'Eighty-one completed, well over halfway through. All running smoothly at present. If this rate keeps up it will be complete by the end of tomorrow.'

'It'll be a relief for everyone to have the engine going again,' said Yingluq and there were nods of agreement. 'If you don't need me here anymore I should like to get back to other work.'

'Of course,' I said. 'Thanks for stepping in to help. I hope I haven't disrupted your schedule too much.'

'No, no, routine stuff, don't want it to pile up.' She waved and went out.

4023, 10:45

'What about the mimics?' asked Bjorn. 'They haven't been docked for a while and we need to get the head fixed on the broken one.'

'It would be as well to get them back in for a service anyway,' added Hyun. 'Do we have anything else scheduled for them?'

'Nothing scheduled. The only possibility is if something goes wrong with the tile replacement and we need mimics to fix it. As that's running smoothly perhaps it's a good moment to bring the mimics back in, if you have the time.'

'I would like to get the broken one fixed as soon as possible, and do maintenance on both before trouble starts.'

'I've nothing urgent now, so why don't I bring them in?' said Bjorn.

'I want to take one in,' I said, and they both looked at me.

'You don't have to, Menem. I can bring them in one at a time, no trouble. One will have to bring the tool-pack back as well, but that's no big deal. Hyun will be there with the bot-net as backup.'

'I would like to do it together. If I leave it too long I may never be able to operate a mimic again. The sooner I do one the better, and this is a simple short trip.'

'Well why not give it a try. Sit in the chair and see how it goes. If it gets too much, stop and I'll come back for it.'

Bjorn seemed keen to get on with it, Hyun rather more doubtful. They exchanged glances which I ignored and went over to the mimic chair and sat. It had retained a little residual heat from Yingluq which was comforting. I felt good, no nausea or fainting. After adjusting the chair to fit, I strapped in, and pulled down the visor.

It took me a moment to realise what I was looking at: the mimic was still deep in the engine section, stuck to a tubular support by its hands and feet, with pipes, cables and support structures all around. I tested each limb in turn and it felt fine.

'How goes it?' Bjorn's voice came over the comms.

'Where are you?' I asked.

'Behind and above you, on another piece of the structure. Will you go ahead?'

'OK. Uh? Ah, I'm still tethered tightly.'

'Hold on, the bot-net is coming over to handle the tethers, they should be with you very soon.' Hyun sounded absolutely neutral, his mask-all-feelings voice. 'Untying you now. Go ahead, Menem.'

I started the climbing action: raise right hand, raise left foot, raise left hand, raise right foot. Keep three attached at all times. It was going well, and my mimic climbed the tube up towards the outside. No problem. At the top of the tube I clambered around the junction and my head emerged above the side of the ship where I paused. The stars filled the void above me and I had a brief flash of the last time I had gazed at them.

'All right there?' Bjorn asked.

'Yes, fine.'

'You paused for a moment.'

'Admiring the stars.'

'Not much different from the last time I looked.'

'No romantic are you, Bjorn?'

'Not when I'm working. Maybe you're too much of a dreamer, Menem.'

'We build our dreams.'

'Yeah, yeah. Let's get these mimics home.' Bjorn had appeared beside me. 'Wait for me here while I collect the other tool-pack and long-arms from the equipment bay. Can you carry the pipe tool-pack?'

'Yes, hand it over. Leave the long-arms where they are. They've been in contact with possibly radioactive objects. I don't think there's anything wrong with them and they shouldn't need maintenance. Do you agree Hyun?'

'Can you make sure they're secured properly?'

'I'll do that, no problem.'

Bjorn passed over the small tool-pack and walked towards the equipment recess near the front of the ship. I was alone for a moment and busied myself with putting on the small pack. It wasn't long before Bjorn reappeared with the large pack.

'All ready? Good, then lead on.'

I started the walk down the fuel tank section. I got in to a rhythm and almost began to enjoy myself, feeling the mimic make the moves I initiated. I tried not to let my mind wander too much, but that was hard as we walked down the long, straight track. I wondered if we were ever going to make our destination, be able to deploy the payload and bring Fleet safely in. What would it be like when the other ships arrived? We would be a community of almost a thousand, rather than the fifteen we were now. I wondered if the crews would mix, and become one eventually, or would they stay rigidly separated, perpetuating the divisions of Earth?

I looked at the long slender track stretching away and thought of a distant viewer, observing two small figures slowly walking along in a slightly bent, ape-like, posture. An immortal scene: of hunters on a plain, explorers in Antarctica or on Mars. Perhaps I could suggest it as a theme for Bita to paint. Concentrate, Menem, your mind is wandering again. Ah, here we are at last, at the end of the payload section. Only got to make the crossing to the Habitat Ring and then we'll be home.

Bjorn came up beside me and asked: 'Ready?'

'Sure.' I watched the Habitat Ring rotating past and felt myself tensing, my heart rate rising. Bot-net elements were holding a tether ready for me to board the transfer deck and another group were ready to fix one to the Habitat Ring once I had stepped across. I stepped onto the deck and began to feel my inertia as it sped up. Lean in to the direction of motion to keep balance, don't think too hard about it, just do it. The deck matched the Habitat Ring and I stepped over. I was still upright. Easy. My pulse was still racing, but I had done it. Bjorn crossed using the deck without trouble, despite his large and ungainly pack. Walking on the rotating section felt different, it was as though one was hanging upside down by the feet: the spin trying to send us flying off. Not far to go to the airlock. The outer door opened on our approach and I stepped inside.

I pulled up my visor, unstrapped myself from the mimic chair and sat there for a while, relaxing. Hyun was finishing up with the bot-net. Bjorn stepped out of his chair and stretched.

'How do you feel?' he asked.

'Relieved. Relieved that it went well. I didn't feel bad, I didn't lose my balance, or my head come to that. So good, back to normal.'

'Great, but don't rush it. It's good that you can do mimics again, but hopefully we won't need to do any for a while.'

'Which was one reason I was keen to do this one.'

'Good for you, Menem,' said Hyun. 'I wasn't sure it was a good idea, but it worked out. Thanks for getting the mimics back both of you. I can do the servicing on them now, which is overdue, and see about replacing the broken head. I'll need your help on that, Menem.'

I stood up and did a few stretches. I didn't feel dizzy or sick, so that was progress. 'Thanks both of you for going with me on that, it helped a lot. I think I'm about ready for lunch, how about you two?'

'What do you want to do about the broken fuel pipe?' asked Hyun.

'Tether it just outside the airlock for now. It can be moved to the low radiation recess at some point soon, and it will need checking over more thoroughly to see if it can realistically ever be repaired. I suspect not, in which case we either recycle it or, if we have got to the end of the voyage and don't need the components, we can toss it into the nearest star.'

'I'll arrange for the bot-net to carry it to the recess and secure it there. Let's do lunch first.'

There was a crowd in the refectory: all the children along with Massoud, Bita and Ibo. They seem to have only recently got started. A discussion was going on about the constellations and how they had got their names. Minogue arrived and joined in, explaining about the constellations of Earth's southern hemisphere, something I had been familiar with as a child, and how we were heading towards one of the stars of the southern sky. We talked about how our various cultures had named groups of stars in different ways. Alice asked if the constellations would look different from the Alpha System and Minogue talked about the small differences: the addition of Earth's sun as a new star to the constellation Cassiopeia, and the loss of Alpha Centauri, actually the three stars of the Alpha System, from Centaurus which provides the pointer to the Southern Cross.

Bita suggested that we should choose new names for the constellations because we were going to be establishing a new human grouping. She and Ibo encouraged the children to make suggestions. There was a lot of laughter as some ideas were aired: Tyrannosaurus was a popular one as well as characters from recent children's shows and stories. 'Bobo' was Joko's suggestion and we all tried to guess what sort of a creature Bobo was, although we had all read the story to her. Eventually she got frustrated with our crazy suggestions and told us that 'everyone knows that Bobo is a fish'.

The children had finished eating and Ibo ushered them out, being next on duty with them. No doubt they were learning a lot about engines from her. The room was quieter when they had gone. I thought that Bita, or whoever had thought of it, had made the right choice in encouraging children to be born aboard. Whether they would resent their restricted lives later, only time would tell, but for us they added meaning and freshness to our journey. In another year or two they would be able to make friends among the children of Fleet, or so I hoped.

Agyei arrived and ordered. I asked her how the tile factory was going, and whether she thought it would need to be shut down for maintenance again before the job was completed.

'Production is going well with no problems at the moment. However, with that has come an increase in the number of tiles to be made, you know, because it's quicker to fuse two new tiles together than a new one to an old one.'

'So that worked out.'

'Also, it seems that some of the tiles are generating more sludge residue than others, which seems odd. Given those things, I'll need to pause briefly at some point before the end to flush the sludge out of the tank. It shouldn't take long, perhaps half-an-hour. If you agree, I would like to do it this afternoon, and then we can be confident of having a clear run to the end. Last time I checked the hot-bot was performing well, without any significant deterioration in its joints after the initial bedding in. It looks as though it will run to the end without another maintenance break.'

'You've clearly been keeping a closer eye on the tile replacement than I have recently. Schedule maintenance as you think fit.'

'Thanks, will do. Massoud wants me to help out on some new chemistry, but said it wasn't urgent. Didn't you Massoud?'

'Not urgent as you say. A new process, exciting new possibilities. I hope that you, Menem, can also help me out with some maintenance and to move some equipment around.'

I had thought that Massoud hadn't been listening, but as often seemed to be the case he was more tuned in than he appeared to be.

Agyei asked me: 'You've been doing the fuel pipe haven't you?'

'Well Bjorn, Yingluq and Hyun did the work. I sat around and made a nuisance of myself.'

'Yingluq took the other mimic?' Was that a slightly aggrieved tone in Agyei's voice? Was she concerned about Bjorn spending time in Yingluq's company, particularly as she herself was now pregnant?

'Yes,' Bjorn joined in. 'She did the pipe replacement with me in the mimics. She's a really good operator: very calm and handy. Menem advised on the technical stuff, and afterwards he took a mimic back to the dock.'

'So you've been back in a mimic again, Menem?'

'I have.'

'How did it go?'

'Not so bad. No, it was good. I wanted to get back to doing it, not being so feeble.'

'Don't force yourself. Lots of us can do mimic work if needed.' Was Agyei hinting there?

'Thanks. It's inefficient if I can't operate the mimic. Many of my areas of responsibility require outside work.'

'Don't let one thing ruin you for everything else.'

I decided to change the subject. 'Massoud, can you tell us what you're up to with these changes you want?'

Before he had time to reply, Gunadi came in. She rarely seemed to eat at the same time as the rest of us. She ordered lunch and sat down opposite me.

'Some new synthetic biology,' said Massoud, answering my question. 'It was being talked about on Earth when we left and seemed to have great promise. I've been following along as it has been developed, and now ten years later, well five back on Earth when the data started on its way to us, the promise is being fulfilled: chefs are raving about it. It offers great potential for new materials and a whole new world of food textures. They have developed a new class of proteins that are very efficient at spinning novel polymers together. To try this out I need to reconfigure some fermentation tanks and set up a new type of machine, a sort of spinning and extruding machine, to produce the materials, initially on a small-batch, trial basis.'

We were all quiet for a moment.

'That sounds interesting. What sort of properties will these materials have?' asked Hyun.

I wondered if Massoud was treading in to Hyun's area of responsibility. The border between synthetic biology and printing was blurred.

'Well from the sources I've read, which are mostly food science and chefy articles, the textures can easily be tuned from the most fragile crispy to something that's completely inedibly tough. The process may have much broader applications than food, which is one of the reasons that I've got Agyei involved, but perhaps you too might be interested, Hyun. We might see if we can feed it through a printer and spin all sorts of novel substances from it.'

'Are you confident about the sources that this work comes from?' I asked.

'How do you mean?'

'If this stuff is going in our food we need to be sure it's safe.'

I thought I saw Minogue roll his eyes.

'Franken-foods?' Massoud suggested. 'There are some serious protocols involved in testing anything new. I'm not going to do anything that hasn't been tested thoroughly on Earth first.'

'I worry about all the updates we receive. Are we careful enough in checking them before they're installed? Not everyone on Earth wants our mission to be successful, and all our communications pass through one or other of Fleet's ships, all of who have their own agendas. Sabotage is not out of the question.'

'Aren't you being a bit paranoid again, Menem? Fleet have no interest in us failing,' said Bjorn somewhat exasperatedly.

'We know Fleet have backup plans in case we fail: largely jettisoning cargo. Perhaps one ship might believe that its backup plan was better than any of the others, in which case it might have an interest in ensuring we did fail.'

'All our comms from Earth are sourced from our own mission control,' said Gunadi.

'It could be hacked. Any bad actor has had seven years to do that since we left and still get a message to us. We're not using quantum encryption because of the agreement that all four members of Fleet could read our messages to ensure nothing against their individual interests was going on. They weren't supposed to be able to alter the messages, but what if something was planted on Earth that appeared to be entirely innocent and that was certain to be sent on to us? It might contain something bad that somehow was only applicable to us, like perverting a unique piece of equipment that we use. That's an old tactic, but there must be newer, more sophisticated ones.'

'There are a million ways for this mission to go wrong. Sabotaging our food is surely a long way down the list,' said Minogue.

'Well it's not just the food. How about navigation?' Massoud looked around sharply at me. 'The latest data from Earth could have been corrupted. You have to admit that it looks mighty odd.'

Massoud visibly relaxed again, and went back to what he had been doing. I had a vague feeling of having missed something.

'If I was going to corrupt the navigation data, I would have been a lot more subtle about it. Everyone looking at it on Earth is scratching their head over it too.'

'What about the object field? Didn't anyone see that, either on Earth or in Fleet?'

'Far, far too diffuse to have been seen by either, and we weren't diverted in to it, it was on the direct line of travel from the Solar System. You're scraping the barrel, Menem.'

'Just saying be careful with where stuff is coming from, that's all.'

Minogue laughed. 'Well you seem to be back on form today, Menem. That's good to see.' He got up, gave me a slap on the back, took his plate to the servery hatch and went out.

'You don't like my food?' Massoud asked me petulantly.

'No, not all, no, I love your food. You've done an amazing job in keeping it interesting. I don't know how you've managed all this time, constantly innovating.'

'I like my food. I feed you nothing that I haven't tried at least twenty-four hours before.'

'We all love your food, Massoud. You know we do,' said Agyei.

'Certainly do,' added Bjorn, and Gunadi nodded her head.

'He don't like my food, I serve him oatmeal every day.' Massoud still sounded dismayed.

'No, no, please not oatmeal. I love your food,' I pleaded.

'So you don't like my oatmeal?'

'No, yes. I like your oatmeal, but not every day.'

'OK, Menem, here's what we do: you come to the fermentation room and you help me change things around and get the new machine made, and then maybe I don't feed you oatmeal every day.' Everyone was giggling now, even Gunadi, and finally Massoud cracked into a smile. I felt put-upon as usual.

I stood up and took my plate to the servery. 'All right, Massoud. Shall we go now?'

'Glad you're keen. Let us strike now while the iron is hot. I'll get ready.'

Massoud disappeared into the servery, his light-brown galabeya flowing around his substantial frame. I wondered if that was really a practical garment to wear on a spaceship, but he liked to affect it whenever he could. We all hung on to some ancestral cultural emblem of our own and his choice suited him. He reappeared a moment later in a normal dark-brown ship-suit shirt and trousers, variants of which most of us normally wore.

4023, 12:40

Without the engine running, there was no quick access between the rings. We climbed down to the spin-changer and had it spin us to match the counter rotating Processes Ring. The two rings spinning up and down together, but in opposite directions avoided affecting the rest of the ship.

For most of the crew there was very rarely any need to go to Processes. It was primarily used for the recycling facility, storage of raw materials and infrequently used machinery and for the fermentation vats. Clothing and other furnishings were made here too by the big fabric printer-weaver-assembler.

Nearly all the work carried out in this ring was automated. Massoud was one of the few who visited regularly. He was often reconfiguring the food tanks or checking up on the recycling plant. I or Agyei would sometimes have to come to service or repair some piece of kit, but that was it as far as most official business was concerned.

The temperature was maintained at twenty Celsius, like most of the parts of the ship the crew visited. Heat was no problem because Fuse and Fizz were always producing a surplus. The biggest hassle of the design was transferring items between this and other places when the rings were spinning. Everything had to be taken through the spin chamber, mostly by autonomous carts. Electrical power was transferred to the rings via induction loops around the keel tube, data by microwave, and clean water, waste water and coolant through annular slip connections.

Massoud and I emerged into the ring's corridor and the lights came on ahead of us. Processes was of similar structure to Habitat in that the ring consisted of a set of sixteen sections that rotated according to the direction of apparent gravity and were joined together via short fixed connectors with safety doors to contain any trouble. The sections here were open on both sides of a central passage and not walled off as in the Habitat Ring. The spaces were purely utilitarian, with no panelling hiding services. Racks of equipment and endless tanks in all manner of sizes occupied most of the sections. Many were filled with biotech equipment that assembled DNA, formed proteins and used those to assemble organic ingredients. These were spun, woven or printed and assembled into the foods we ate and drank, the clothes we wore and most of the soft furnishings and materials that surrounded us.

Massoud led me round to a section where there were some pieces of bioengineering equipment that had been taken out of use.

'We could make space here for the new process and reuse much of this equipment.'

'What do you want from me?' I asked.

'Well, two things: firstly, do you think it possible to do what I want to do with the kit we have or could make, and secondly, can you help with getting it done?'

'You didn't need to bring me here to ask me those.'

'Maybe not,' he sniffed, 'but I wanted you to get a firsthand look at these old machines and the space here.'

'These were good quality machines. They should still be functional if they have been serviced and not allowed to gum up.'

'I don't think they have been on the servicing cycle in recent years, but I'm sure they would have been cleaned out properly after their last use.'

'Status can tell us and there must be Archive information on their original purpose and any modifications they've had. I'll look it up later, when I know the details of what you want done. The usual utility stuff will need checking: power, cooling, air, water, gasses, whatever, as well as making sure this space is sufficient, able to carry the load, and that the loading doesn't effect the ring's stability. You know all this: we've done it lots of times before.'

'Yes, yes, we have, but I'm worried that I'm missing something. I didn't want to go too far, only to have you say that I'm foolish, and should have seen that it couldn't be done because of something obvious.'

Massoud was looking down and shuffling his feet. He didn't appear to be his usual confident self.

'You feel it too, time passing?' I asked. 'We're not young anymore and we see the children growing up. It has been a long voyage and we've devoted our best years to it. We worry that we're going to make a silly mistake, and then it will all have been for nothing.'

Massoud looked up and I could see moisture in his eyes and he turned away. 'Maybe I worry too much, perhaps we have all been tested and all have our doubts.'

'It seems likely. I certainly do. My weaknesses have been on display recently. My friends, including you, have helped me. The doubts persist, but I'm learning to live with them. We're all mortal, Massoud.'

'Do you think that everyone has doubts?' he asked. 'Most seem so calm and in control.'

Was this why he had brought me hear, because he needed to unburden, or was he acting like an old ham, playing a game with me, a charade?

'Some are better than others at hiding their feelings. I never thought of you as having doubts; you always seemed to be a model of stability. You're master of your profession and still trying to improve and innovate. Bita told me that one of the big concerns the planners had was that the crew would get bored and that would lead to failure. If there's one reason that has not happened, it's because of you. We've never become bored of the food and drink you've crafted, but more than that, it's the atmosphere you create in the refectory. It's the place we come to for company and friendship. We should let you know more overtly how much that has meant to us.'

'Thank you my friend, your words are a comfort to me.' He gave a theatrical sniff and a bow. 'I must put my doubts to one side and strive on, knowing that without me it would be oatmeal only, and that would be the road to mission failure.' He paused and looked around at the silent machines. 'Yes, we can do something here. You will help me and Agyei, yes, if she's not too overburdened.' He held out his hands in front of his stomach.

'I don't think there's much sign of a bump yet. She's busy with the tile factory at the moment, but with luck we'll be done with that in a day or so.'

'We'll all be relieved when we get back the engine.'

'Travel is more comfortable in deceleration rather than rotation.'

'Particularly for you, having a soft stomach. You're a sensitive creature, Menem.' I sighed in agreement. 'Yes, it is so.'

'You're sensitive too, Massoud, but in a different way. I know women aren't your thing, but haven't you ever wanted a child?'

'No, no, I love women, but I don't want to have sex with them, unlike you. I've often thought it would be nice to have children though. I enjoy the company of our children. But to have one that was mine? I don't know. Maybe it's simply better to be a parent to all the children and not to be too biased to one. I suppose that there's something in all of us that craves to reproduce, to leave a legacy in the genes of the next generation. That's something you want, I think.'

'Yes,' I said, feeling uncomfortable.

'Ah well,' he sighed. 'Maybe we have what we need, even if it isn't all that we want.'

'But what is it that we need?'

'If we only knew that. Maybe I have what I need here: my family. I'm satisfied with that. Almost.' We both laughed somewhat ruefully. 'Come, my friend. Let us take a walk before we return to the comforts of home. When we get back we'll have a coffee and a cake to cement our little chat.'

Massoud continued along the gridded footway that curved up ahead of us. Occasionally our path was diverted around a particularly large piece of machinery and we had to slow as each section separation door opened. On the way, Massoud occasionally paused and stared through an inspection cover on a tank, studied an information display or a panel of lights. He would comment on something if he thought it was interesting, but mainly we walked without speaking, listening to the hum of pumps and fans and the occasional whirr of a valve or a stirrer. We passed the large weaving machine, busy at work on an elaborately-patterned light-blue fabric.

We must have walked almost three-quarters of the way round when we came through a separation door into a section that was different from the others. It was completely silent in here with no machinery, the corridor narrow, the lighting harsh. The walls were lined with racks, some of which were filled with crates of materials, although many were empty. We passed into the next section and the passage opened out. Here it was lined on either side with a set of twenty uniform cabinet doors, each of which was about sixty centimetres wide and three metres tall, all an unpainted, stark, metallic, gunmetal grey. Each was numbered and seventeen of them had name plates, one for each member of the crew, living or dead. These were our personal stores: the place outside of our apartments where we could put anything we wanted to keep. I knew mine was empty, apart from some old family mementos that I hadn't looked at since…, well, a long time ago. The doors were locked and only our personal presence could unlock them. We both studied the name plates on these stark-faced cabinets.

Massoud paused before one of them, and I came up and had a look: cabinet number nine with the single word 'Avalos' on its name plate. I wondered what was inside. For a moment I had a vision of Avalos's body in there, perhaps wrapped like an Egyptian mummy. The thought that Massoud might know how to embalm a body crossed my mind, but then why should he? We stood contemplating the blank door and what might lie behind.

'Who do you think has access?' I asked. 'Sahko, perhaps? Someone told me that his personal stuff had been taken from his apartment and placed here. I think it was Minogue, but I'm not sure.'

'Do you want to see inside?' Massoud asked.

'I, err, in a way I do. I only realised recently that I didn't know who he was at all. I thought I did, but now I know there was a whole dark side to his personality that I had never seen. Quite a few of the crew seem to have had suspicions about what he was up to.'

'I can open it if you like.'

'How? Have you broken the security system?'

'It's not locked.' Massoud reached out a hand, placed his fingers in the handle recess, the latch clicked and the door swung open.

We both looked inside. It was underwhelming: no dead body, simply a collection of boxes and crates of various sizes.

'How come it was unlocked?' I asked, wondering also how he knew it had been.

'The last person to put stuff in here failed to lock it.'

'And so that must have been you, as you knew it was open.'

'Correct.'

'Why?'

'Why bother to lock it? I'd finished clearing his apartment, packed away his clothes and personal items. Sahko asked me to recycle all his stuff, but I couldn't bring myself to, not immediately at least, so I shoved it all in here.'

'So everything that was in his apartment is in here?'

'All the personal stuff I could find. I didn't do a forensic search, wanting to get it over with as quickly as possible. I emptied all the drawers and cupboards and picked up anything personal that was lying around: pictures, books, his bathroom stuff.'

'Did you find anything interesting?'

'Like what?'

'I don't know, something that surprised you, something that you didn't expect him to have, something like a diary or notebook.'

'Nothing that I thought was odd, no. Wouldn't he have kept any diary or notes on the system?'

'Where anyone could read it?'

'Surely he would have kept anything personal in his private area.'

'I expect that nowhere in the system is really private. Gunadi certainly has the skills to access anything, perhaps Ibo too. I don't know what privileges Sahko has, but it seems probable that she has a way in, perhaps Yingluq, as doctor, and Bita, as psychologist, too. Minogue knows his way around so I wouldn't put it beyond him, and who knows who else.'

'Wow, you really are suspicious, my friend.'

'Why did you bring me here, Massoud?'

He seemed taken aback. 'Well we were passing, and a couple of days ago you had asked me about Avalos. You've asked others about him too.'

'But you wanted to show me this. We didn't need to come to Processes to discuss reorganising some biotech machinery.'

'You're smart my friend. Yes, I wanted to show you this. There's nothing interesting that I put in here. You're welcome to look.'

'What happened to Avalos's body?'

'It was reduced: desiccated and then powdered. You see that box?' He pointed inside the cupboard to a black ceramic-fibre cube, about twelve centimetres on each side.

'That's what's left of him?' I asked.

'Yes.'

'Why keep it? Why not recycle it?'

'Two reasons: firstly, do you want to think you are eating a bit of him every time you have some food?'

'It would only be atoms. We presumably are drinking some of his molecules every time we have some water.'

'True, but some are more squeamish than you about their food.'

'And the second reason?'

'Someone, someday, might want his remains to mourn over.'

'That seems highly unlikely. The remains would have to be sent back to Earth, so it would be at least twenty years since they last saw him. Also, from what I have gathered, he was packed off from Earth rather suddenly. I get the impression that no one wanted to see him back.'

'Maybe, but we owe him some dignity if only as a fellow human being. There aren't many of us out here.'

Massoud looked down as though in private contemplation. I wondered if there was another reason for preserving what little was left of Avalos. Someone might want to investigate his death. Although what anyone could tell from his desiccated and powdered remains, I had no idea.

'Thoughtful of you: might also be useful in the event of an investigation,' I said quietly, looking for a reaction.

'And who is going to be investigating, Menem? Have you thought about this? There's no higher authority out here to investigate or to be appealed too. No one on Earth can help: it takes four years to get a message one way. There are no cops, lawyers or military out here.'

'Fleet is not so far behind. There are eight hundred people there. Someone will start asking questions.'

'Why would they want to start investigating a non-suspicious death that occurred nine or more years ago? Avalos electrocuted himself, either by accident or design, and there's ample evidence of that. You were there, you saw him.'

'Yes, I saw him, after he had died.'

'No one in Fleet is going to be the least bit interested in Avalos. They're going to be fully occupied with their own rivalries, trying to grab the best bits of the planet, establishing viable settlements, building their own lives.'

'I hope we don't become a pawn in their games.'

'We already are. That's why we must present a united front. If they sense that we can be divided they'll try to use it to their advantage. If, as we expect, the Indian ship arrives first, in the worst case scenario, they might try to prevent us helping the following ships. That would give them a substantial advantage. Have you thought about that?'

'We're defenceless if that happens.'

'Not entirely: the possibility was foreseen. The other powers have tried to prevent that happening.'

'There's a lot I don't know.'

'This is why Sahko asked me to bring you here.'

I was stunned and couldn't speak for a long while. We stared at each other, unmoving. Eventually, with a dry mouth, I said: 'Sahko asked you to bring me here?'

'She did. She knew you had started asking questions again about Avalos. She didn't know what had set you off, but she saw that it was unsettling you and other members of the crew.' Massoud paused, choosing his words. 'She wanted you to see that there's nothing hidden, which is why she asked me to show you this.'

'Couldn't she have told me herself? Why get you to do her dirty work?'

'Come on, my friend. You and she have a very difficult relationship right now. She thought that the personal might interfere with the message. She knows we're not rivals, but are good friends. We've helped each other, no? She thought that I was the right person to assist you with this issue, to lay it to rest in your mind. She has asked us to be open with you in this matter until you've resolved it your own satisfaction.'

'She has involved others?'

'She has asked others to be open with you in this matter,' he repeated.

'Who?'

'Who do you think?'

'Well she might have asked Yingluq because she would have access to his medical records. I suppose Bita might give me access to his personnel file.' Massoud nodded at each of the names. 'Who else? Someone he worked closely with, like Bjorn perhaps?' Another nod. 'More? Who?'

'Everyone.'

'Oh my.'

I was silent. So my discrete questioning of individuals had been pieced together. If everyone knew I was investigating then any evidence would have been spirited away. I sat down on my haunches and put my head in my hands. How had it come to this? What the hell was I doing?

'Come, my friend.' Massoud reached a hand down and lifted me up. Although he didn't look it, he was a strong man. 'We'll go back now and you can think this over. I'll close the door of Avalos's store, but you see it's not locked and you can come back at any time and look through his things. It will be better if you do this privately, I think. Now it's time for us to go back to the rest of the crew and take some coffee and cake together.'

I stood and he took my elbow and we walked on, through more doors that closed behind us. Before we started down the tube to the keel I stopped and said: 'Thank you Massoud, that can't have been easy for you. I'm sorry that Sahko had to make you her messenger. You're right that it's imperative for the crew to stick together.'

'I was worried that I might lose your friendship over this.'

'No.'

I led the way back to Habitat.

The refectory was empty when we arrived. Massoud disappeared into the servery and returned a minute later wearing a galabeya again. He sat next to me in silence. A service bot appeared before long with our coffee and cakes: Middle Eastern, strong, bitter, aromatic coffee and very sweet, sticky cakes. We contemplated them for a moment and then as we began to eat the door opened and Hyun and Ibo came in.

'Ooh my, that smells and looks good, I would like some of that,' said Ibo. 'How about you, Hyun?'

Before he could reply Minogue, Yingluq and Bita came in debating something about random patterns. Massoud and my coffee-and-cakes was not going to be a quiet event, and that was confirmed by the arrival of the children with Sahko. Laughter and amiable chatter drove up the noise level. Massoud got up and bustled around, helping the children to sit and choose, a word and a smile for everyone. Out of the corner of my eye I saw him exchanging glances with Sahko and he nodded his head very slightly at her. Unable to prevent the cheer from penetrating, I smiled too. Massoud glanced at me, checking. It may all have been a performance, a setup, another game, but it was working.

Sahko looked over at me, Joko sitting on her knee. She smiled, slightly uncertainly, slightly questioningly. The innocent held protectively in her lap. My heart lurched and I got up and went to the door. I had to get out before the tears came. She couldn't follow because of the child.

I stumbled quickly out of the refectory. I didn't want to run in to anyone else and made it to Engineering. Throwing myself into a chair, I lent forward and hammered hard on the desk with both hands and laid my forehead on the desktop. After a minute I stood and paced a while. Something caught my eye. The burnt-out motor from Engine Control had to be fixed and put back in to the refectory. Beside it lay the odd, non-standard controller that had failed to prevent the fire. Selecting some tools, I began to take it apart.

The door opened behind me and Sahko's voice said: 'Can I come in?'

I slowly put down the box and turned around in my chair. A silhouette, framed in the doorway with the light behind her, she was indistinct in a black suit, with loose trousers that came in tightly at the ankles and disappeared into short black boots. Her jacket was loose too, cut off halfway down her forearms, buttoned off-centre all the way up and with a tight choker collar. Her short straight black hair outlined her almond shaped face.

I could say nothing, but she came in anyway. She watched me as she walked around, eventually selecting a chair. Drawing it up, she sat down facing me. I searched the carpet for something and she reached over and took one of my hands and drew it towards her, making me look up.

'Come on old thing,' she said softly. 'Don't be mad, talk to me.'

I stifled a choke with a cough.

'You have to work this thing out,' she continued. 'Ask for help if you need it, there's no shame in that. Nothing is hidden from you if you want to look. I need you to resolve this quickly: it's eating away at you and it's disturbing everyone else. You're creating unnecessary distrust with this idea that Avalos was somehow murdered.'

How could she have so badly misunderstood what was really eating away at me? Perhaps she hadn't and was using Avalos's death as a metaphor.

'You seem to have concocted a theory that someone, somehow managed to electrocute him. Now that idea is fixed in your head nothing anyone else can say can shift it. Only you can do that. So search high and low until you find what you can believe is the truth. You going on like this, it's undermining our mission.'

I wondered if there was a threat in there somewhere, but I knew that it didn't matter: I would die for this woman if she needed me to. I pleaded with my eyes for help, for her forgiveness, for redemption.

She touched my hand again, stood up and lent over me, and placing an arm around my shoulders, she kissed my hair. 'When you've worked this out, come and see me, old thing.'

She squeezed my shoulders and then let go, standing beside me for a moment before turning and walking away, silhouetted again in the doorway. I looked up, still unable to speak, imploring her to stay with my gaze, but the door closed behind her. I felt hope from her final words but fear that I may never find my way there. The nerves in my skin tingled all over, making me get up and shake myself and pace around for a while. The motor lying in pieces on the bench demanded attention but I could summon no enthusiasm for it.

Attaching a small pack of tools to my belt, I went to the door and listened. The corridor was silent. Cautiously opening the door, I looked around. No one was about, so I went stealthily to the access door to the connector. I didn't think that anyone had seen me. I made the journey to

Processes, arriving at the entrance door. Again I listen but couldn't hear any human sounds. The light came on as I entered so it was unlikely that anyone else was here, unless they were waiting for me in the dark. Heading in the opposite direction round the ring to the one Massoud and I had taken earlier, it was only two doors round to personal storage. Once again I found myself in front of the tall, metallic-grey door labelled with the single word 'Avalos'. Pulling on a pair of fine gloves, I hesitated before opening the catch. The door was still unlocked and swung open smoothly. I photographed the interior before touching anything.

There was the odd cube box in the front of the cupboard that Massoud had said contained Avalos's remains. I lifted it down, examined it and then put it back. I looked around for a surface on which to place items, and remembered that there were tables that could be folded out from between the cabinets. I unhooked one and set it down, and took the cube from Avalos's cabinet again and placed it on the table. The box had a tight fitting lid, held on with four recessed latches, one on each side. A Geiger counter checked it for radioactivity: nothing above background. I flicked each of the latches, lifted the lid and looked in. The box contained a fine grey powder. Was this what we would all be reduced to? Alas, poor Avalos, but, it seems, I didn't know you very well. I tested the contents with the Geiger counter: nothing. I tilted the box and the ash flowed smoothly. It looked homogenous but I couldn't see to the bottom of the box without spilling the contents, so I took out a long-handled bit-holder from my toolkit and probed through the powder. The box bottom appeared to be the same thickness as its walls and top. There were no blanked off corners and there was no covering behind which anything could have been secreted. I replaced the lid and had a close look at the outside, including the bottom, discerning no secrets there.

I put the box to one side and started to look through the other boxes and crates. Avalos had a lot of clothes and shoes: several crates worth. He had usually been a snappy dresser, but also had some outrageous party outfits. I tested everything with the Geiger counter, felt between and around each garment for anything out of place, examined pockets, seams and fasteners and tested shoes for hidden hollows. Short of shredding everything to be sure, I was convinced that there was nothing of substance there. Next was a box of toiletries, far more than I had. Some had fancy brands that he must have brought with him, but which were probably stale by now. I tapped each container, examined them all closely, tested them for radioactivity and shone an intense light through those I could to

308

see if any had false compartments. The box even contained his cleaning equipment for teeth and nails, as well as hair management attachments: items that had been removed from his refresher. It all looked innocent.

The last three standard storage crates contained his personal effects. The first held things that he might have had on display in his apartment: trophies with names of ships and races, framed photographs of crews, where it was simple to pick out Avalos's broad, easy smile. Others showed him posing with celebrities or celebrity photographs that were personally autographed to him. There were framed certificates and citations with seals and signatures from institutions he had attended. There were also a few art objects: primitive voodoo masks and strange abstract tall, thin, black, humanoid sculptures. I found nothing out of place with any of them.

The second storage crate contained items that he had probably kept in drawers or cupboards. It included some very candid photographs of men and women, sometimes alone, sometimes in groups including Avalos. Several appear to have been from a very high-end S&M party which he must have attended. I wondered who had taken the pictures and why they had been printed out, but they told me nothing about his character that I didn't already know. There was, however, a small key in the crate.

The third crate was smaller and contained two elegant boxes. They were both beautiful: elaborately worked from fine materials. They would have made attractive display objects, but I had never seen them before. Both were locked. The key I had found fitted the smaller of the two. It opened to reveal a hermetically sealed inner chamber that helpfully had instructions on how to open it. Inside it was half filled with tablets: Pings. I doubted these had been tampered with because it was known that he shared them with other members of the crew. The Geiger counter registered nothing. I measured and probed the box and found no hidden compartments.

The larger elaborate box was locked and there was no helpful key lying around. The lock appeared to be quite sophisticated and I had no suitable tools with me to probe and spring it. I examined the box in some detail: it was much heavier than I expected from its size. It looked to be old and to have been made from an ebony simulation, or perhaps even ebony itself. It was inlaid with other wood-like materials in patterns of strange leaves. The exterior had been polished but not lacquered. The craftsmanship was superb, all except the rather clumsy base which might have been added later. I shook the box and something rattled softly inside, a strange odour rose from it that I had smelt before somewhere, perhaps on Avalos, but could not identify. It was a quandary. Either the box could be forced open, doubtlessly damaging it, or it could be taken back to Engineering were there was equipment to examine the lock and reconstruct a key for it, or it could be left for now. Perhaps Massoud had overlooked the key when he had cleared Avalos's apartment. I decided to leave the box. I didn't want to be caught carrying it or to leave evidence that I had been examining Avalos's things by forcing the lock.

Ensuring there was nothing else in the locker, I put all the boxes and crates back, checking against the photograph that I had taken earlier that everything was positioned exactly. When I was satisfied, I carefully placed a hair plucked from my head on top of the crate with the locked box in it, closed the locker door, packed away my tools and the folding table and took off my gloves.

Further down the row was my locker and next to that was Mo's. Before leaving I put my hand on the door of Mo's locker but I couldn't bring myself to open it. There was not much in it: mostly painful memories. The locker on the other side of it was Sahko's and I wondered what she kept there. Taking hold of myself, I carefully went back the way I had come.

No one saw me as I slipped out of the tube from the keel into the Habitat Ring corridor. Back in Engineering, I put away my tool kit and sat down. I had learned nothing. The only mystery left in the personal store was the locked box. I thought about searching Avalos's apartment for the missing key, but that could take hours and would best be done in the middle of the night. I needed to get back to real work. Status reported that there were only thirty more tiles to be replaced: twelve hours work or so.

4023, 18:00

The motor on the bench had to be fixed urgently or section eleven wouldn't rotate when the engine came on. We would be all be walking up the walls in there to eat.

I set up the motor and began taking it apart, extracting the rotor. One of the coil windings had burnt out and part of the casing was cracked and distorted, the rest of the damage seemed cosmetic, but if the heat had distorted the internal structure then more would need to be replaced. With the core parts of the motor set up, the test machine went to work with its probes, precisely mapping every critical point. I held my breath as it worked and was hugely relieved when it all passed within specified tolerances. Archive produced the details for the coil and casings, the parts that would need replacing. The casing could be printed using standard materials but the coil would have to be rewound largely by robotic hand. The print job started automatically but Hyun's help was going to be needed with the coil winding. An auto reply came back in response to my message, asking how urgent my request was, and if it could either wait until tomorrow or if Gunadi could handle it. After hesitating, I decided to try Gunadi. She messaged back to say that she would be happy to come around and help.

It wasn't long before she appeared and she bounced into the room. She seemed more cheerful each time I saw her. She wasn't in her usual Goth-black, but wearing rather well cut chestnut-brown trousers and a loose shirt, fashioned rather like Sahko's, with sleeves that finished mid-forearm. She was still wearing some quite heavy boots, but they looked less suitable for an army on the march than hers usually did. With bright eyes and her hair was free, she looked rather nice.

'What's up, Menem?' she asked.

'Hi, Gunadi. A coil needs to be rewound which required a robot programmed. Hyun seems to be unavailable at the moment.'

'Hyun and Ibo decided to have an early night. It looks as though the tile replacement is going to be finished sometime in the early hours and Ibo wants to get to work on running up the engine as soon as possible. Hyun asked me to be on standby in case you or anyone else needed printing or robotics.'

'Here I am with another rush job. We're going to need this motor when Main starts. It's to replace the one that rotates the refectory.'

Gunadi took a look at the parts scattered on the workbench. 'It looks as though it has been in a fire, but that was in Engine Control, I thought.'

'It came out of there. One was urgently needed to rotate that section and we didn't have a spare, so I took the one from section eleven which had already rotated.'

'And now you need to put one back.'

'Or the whole crew will be very upset when they come to eat.'

'I certainly wouldn't want my apartment tilted on its side for long, it might make refreshing rather difficult.' She laughed. Clearly she was in a good mood. 'OK, so it's a coil for this you need replaced, I presume?'

'Yes, tricky winding inside those things by hand.'

'No problem to do the winding, we've the routines for all sorts of motors. You'll need to cut out the entire old coil by hand though, which I can see might be tricky because you don't want to damage the coils next to it. Maybe I can help you with that. First I'll set up the winder. Have you checked stores for the wire? We can't use the old stuff until it has gone through the recycler.'

'There's enough in Stores for at least one coil but not a lot more. I'll check how much.' The Stores database showed there was enough stock for two coils but not to redo the whole motor. 'We definitely need to be careful.'

The stator was set up in a stand and bright lights focused on it. Using some fine nosed pliers, I began to peel away the melted wire. Gunadi drew up a chair beside me and watched. Working down the stack, the wires were increasingly stuck together and needed a very fine blowtorch to provide heat to release them. It was growing hot and my eyes started to lose focus. Having Gunadi so close beside me that we almost touched was slightly disconcerting. She was staring at my hands as they worked.

My pliers slipped and an adjacent coil nearly got cut. Gunadi put a hand on mine. 'Can I have a go?' she asked.

'Please do.'

Pushing back my chair, I stood up. She moved her chair across and took up the pliers and torch and bent forward to get a close view of the work. Her hair parted at the back revealing a triangle of clear olive skin on the nape of her neck. Although her hands weren't small, she seemed to have great dexterity, peeling away the tiny wires quickly and easily. She kept up a gently rhythm, removing one layer of wire after another: it wasn't long before she had finished the first half of the coil.

'You seem to have a talent for this,' I said, and she beamed at me. 'Take a break and I'll reposition the stator so we can get at the other side of the coil. That will be trickier because it's tucked under the one next to it, but at least it isn't melted on that side.'

I fiddled with the support until there was good access to the second half of the coil. A pick lifted the strands of wire away, bending them clear without breaking them. After a while my concentration faded, the second coil was becoming distorted and looked as though it would never go back in place.

'Why don't we place the stator where we can both get at it,' Gunadi suggested, 'so I can lift one end of the wires and you the other. We can keep them straight like that.' I could see her point.

With the workbench and stator repositioned once again, Gunadi took her chair around to the other side. Working together, we managed to keep the second coil neat as we lifted it away from the first. Our heads were bent close to the stator on opposite sides and we could see each other through it. She looked up at occasionally, taking her cue from me. Once the second coil was lifted away, it was easy enough to pull the strands of the first coil clear.

My back had become stiff, having been hunched over. I stood up and paced around the room.

'Thanks, Gunadi, it would have taken me forever to do that on my own and I expect more than one other coil would have been damaged in the process. If we'd had the wire it would have been easier to cut out all the coils and start again.'

Gunadi stood up and stretched too. How thin she was, boyish even.

'Presumably we have the capability to make wire on board?' she asked.

'Oh yes. We keep a stock of raw copper and we melt it, alloy it if required, draw it through a series of dies, and finally heat-treat and coat it. I don't recall if we have all the right machinery already to hand, but we could easily print up anything that we don't.'

'Not much we can't make on board.'

'Not much. We're only limited by our material stocks and the design files available in Archive, but they're vast: almost everything that was in the standard spacecraft databases on Earth at the time of our departure, plus some more that has been sent to us since.'

'I'll go and set up the robot to wind the new coil. Will you bring the stator round when you're ready?'

'Sure. Stores should have already sent the stock wire round to Robotics.'

'See you soon then.' She smiled shyly at me and skipped out.

I finished cleaning up the stator and took a look at the other parts. There was a list of things to be brought from Stores that included replacements for the motor's power and control cables, both of which had been damaged in the fire. I continued fiddling about; double checking that everything needed to reinstall the motor was accounted for. Parts arrived on a cart from Stores for the cables which were quickly made up. The stator went on a cart and I followed it around to Robotics.

Gunadi smiled at me as I came in. 'The coil spinning is almost complete. Come and have a look.'

She took my elbow and guided me over. A robot was using its two arms in an exotic dance, weaving and threading the fine coated wire around a coil former that occasionally inverted in time with the dance. There was something mesmerising about the process. Suddenly there was a hiss and the arms stopped weaving. The two ends of the coil were drawn out, cut off and connected to a test unit. A screen showed a set of performance parameters and a bottom line indicated that the coil had passed. The screen then displayed a message box asking for the stator to be presented along with a diagram of where and how it should be placed. I lifted the stator onto the robot's work table and clamped it down and told the machine that it was ready. One of the robots arms used a camera to inspect and check that everything was in order. The other arm took the coil off the former and placed it in position. The two arms worked together to press the coil tightly into the stator and fold the second coil over one side of the new coil. It bonded the ends of the coil to fixing posts, spread a fine adhesive over the repaired area and sprayed it with a catalyst, locking everything in position. The robot withdrew its arms and the screen indicated that it had completed its tasks. I released the stator from its clamp and Gunadi gave me a hand lifting it back on to the cart.

'Thank you, Gunadi. That has been really helpful. This motor can go back together now and be reinstalled.'

The cart trundled to the door.

'Can I watch you do that?' she asked hesitantly. 'I don't often see what others do, and I've found it kind of interesting so far.'

'It won't be very exciting. A machine will do the assembly work and fitting it will be me crawling in an equipment bay and bolting it down. Haven't you got anything better to do than that?'

'Not really. I'm on watch so have to be awake, but there is nothing that requires close monitoring at the moment. I'll have to be on duty when the engine is re-lit, but that won't be for quite a while. I would like to see you fix something.'

'Well, OK, come along then.'

She beamed at me.

Sahko might have tasked her to keep an eye on me, to make sure that I wasn't alone too long. If that was the case someone might have noticed my absence when I was checking the personal store. If so, they could have tracked my movements by the ship's door position sensors. I had to assume that they knew where I had been.

We lifted the stator on to the assembler table. All the parts were ready, and once the appropriate process was loaded, including the modification to upgrade the coil connections, as had been done on the other motor, it set to work. The machine hummed into life, checked over the parts and then began picking and placing them.

Gunadi watched, fascinated. 'You could do all this yourself, why do you use a machine for it?'

'Precision really.' I repeated my spiel about how the machine could do a better job.

'The whole motor could be printed.'

'That might be as good, but it's wasteful. The old motor would have to be recycled and while we're very good at that it's not perfect. We leak material away and that's something we can't replace.'

'Until we start mining operations.'

'And assuming we can find the right ore bodies and have packed the right kit. Otherwise we'll be making our own mining and refining equipment, at least until Fleet arrives, and we don't know what capability they're carrying.'

'They must have refining equipment,' she said. 'How else are they going to build settlements? We can exchange materials for power which we should be able to control, at least initially.'

'Each member of Fleet will have its own power generators.'

'They'll only be able to deliver a limited amount on the ground, not enough for serious refining. To start with we'll have control of by far the most powerful in-system capability.'

'Our monopoly on serious power generation for transport and refining will be rather vulnerable to take over.'

'It has other possible uses,' said Gunadi quietly.

'Really? I didn't know that.'

'We'll not be quite the sitting ducks that we appear to be.'

My mind reeled: what was this all about? I had never paid much attention to the payload. That it might be used to build something for offensive or defensive purposes hadn't crossed my mind. Clearly it had that of others. Avalos's motivation might lie there.

I didn't know what I could usefully say, so just said: 'Perhaps, perhaps, who knows how it will all work out?'

The assembler machine clicked off, its job done. The crane cart came round, picked up the completed motor and took it over to the test bench. With the test machine hooked up, it began running. While part of the casing still showed scorch marks the motor ran perfectly smoothly and right on specification.

'Good, it seems to be working well. Next, installation.'

I detached the test equipment and picked up the motor with the crane cart again and also loaded on some tools. Gunadi followed as we went around to the refectory, her boots clicking on the corridor floor. The lights had dimmed to indicate night.

No one was in the refectory. On opening up the wall panel black dust was still lying everywhere inside. A thin film had already formed where I had disturbed it only a few days ago. Sometime I would have to find out where the dust was coming from.

The crane couldn't reach all the way in to the void with the motor without toppling over. I crawled inside, feeling Gunadi watching me from behind, found a bracket on the structure in the back and fixed a pulley there, threaded a rope around the pulley and attached one end to the cart and the other to the motor. The cart pulled the motor into the bay with me guiding it by pushing, shoving and easing it over the roughness of the floor. After a struggle, the drive shaft from the motor engaged with the coupling on the section rotation gearbox. A pair of splines pushed into keyways locked it in place. The motor was bolted down to its mounting plate and its power and control lines plugged in. Finally, I wriggled out of the void and stood up.

Gunadi started giggling. 'Wow, it must be very filthy in there. You're covered in dirt.'

'It shouldn't be so dusty.' I said rather stiffly. 'Sign of trouble.'

While packing up the tools I realised one more trip into the equipment bay was needed to retrieve the rope and pulley. I was even dirtier when they had been recovered.

When the cart was loaded I said: 'That's it for this project. We have to hope that it all works properly when the engine restarts. Thanks for all your help, Gunadi. I'm going to make sure everything is safe for the rotation and then have a clean up.'

We walked behind the cart.

'Would you like a coffee or something?' She asked, looking at me with appealing eyes. She had opened the neck of her top a little more.

'I'm sorry, but not tonight. I'm quite tired and need to make an early start tomorrow and, well, I need to be in good shape for that.'

She looked a little crestfallen but managed a brave smile. 'Sure, early start for me too. Best be in good shape, not too tired, too exhausted. See you tomorrow, Menem. It's been interesting.'

I almost thought that she had given me a wink as we headed for the door. What was up with her today?

'Good night, Gunadi.'

The cart made a creak and I looked around at it. Gunadi looked around too and gave me a little wave before disappearing up the curve of the corridor. In Engineering, I unloaded my tools and checked that everything was secure for the rotation. Status told me that the hot-bot had twenty-nine more tiles to do, more than I had expected. It seems as though sonic wave tests had revealed some microscopic damage to a few more tiles.

I left a message for Ibo to call me as needed when she started the process of getting the engine going, which she probably would in anticipation of completion of the nozzle repairs. Initially it would be simply getting the coolant flows going to bring all the engine's parts to the right temperature and tuning up the electromagnetic fields to enable stable fuel and exhaust flows. All automated tasks, but Ibo liked to be in the engine room during this phase, to watch and intervene immediately if required. Later she would retreat to Engine Control and could use my help to double check everything. There was real risk as the engine came alive after the shutdown: only then would we know if all our work on the tiles and fuel pipe had been successful. If we had made an error, or forgotten something, then there was a good chance we would be blasted to pieces and scattered to the stars. There was also the lesser risk from the spin-up and rotation of the rings: all the joints and seals between the sections would be exercised and so all the airtight doors would be closed and everyone was supposed to remain in sealed rooms. I hoped that there would be no further trouble from the rotation motors, most of which hadn't been checked.

There were a couple of messages waiting, from Sahko asking if everything was in order and from Bjorn asking if the refectory section was going to be able to rotate. I messaged Bjorn saying that the motor had been repaired and reinstalled, but that it might be as well if no one was in that section at the time of the rotation. I messaged Sahko to say that I had completed all the work required and that, once the tile replacement was finished, we were as prepared as we possibly could be for engine restart, sometime in the morning.

Tired and dirty, I returned to my apartment, stripped off and went into the refresher for a good clean up. Jazz was waiting by my bed when I re-emerged. I took her hand and we went to bed, cuddling up close together.

Mission Day 4024

4024, 07:15

An alarm was sounding and Jazz was shaking me awake. Struggling from deep sleep, I tried to work out what was going on: fire, Wayclear, pressure leak, engine failure, or one of a million other things that could be wrong with the ship? I sat bolt upright and blinked to clear my eyes. It was a message from Ibo asking me to come over to Engine Control in about fifteen minutes. The engine restart was underway with all tests and warm up routines running smoothly. Status told me the tile replacement was nearly complete. Ibo had added a couple more tiles to be replaced that she thought were marginal, so there were seven still left to do. There was also a message from Bjorn thanking me for reinstalling the motor in section eleven and saying that he was planning to be with the children during the rotation.

Sitting on the edge of the bed, I messaged Ibo "Yes", ordered breakfast and went to the refresher. Food arrived as I emerged freshly washed and groomed and with clean clothes. Jazz had gone. I looked through my task list as I sat and ate, checking for anything that might affect the engine start and rotation. The dust in the refectory equipment void was a significant unknown. I should have inspected all the other rotation motors, and the odd motor controller from Engine Control still needed investigating, all too late now. I had my teeth cleaned once more and then went off to join Ibo.

'Morning sleepyhead,' said Ibo cheerfully, without looking round.

She was sitting in front of a glass-clear cylinder about three metres in diameter and one and a half tall. In the centre of the cylinder was a symbolic hologram of all Main's components. Thin red lines linked the important engine systems to individual areas of the glass cylinder on which data was displayed in myriad tables, graphs and symbols. Ibo's arms were in a pair of long gloves and she span and tilted the hologram and brought the data she wanted in front of her. She also had an auxiliary screen, low down, where summaries of other critical processes and systems were displayed.

'You're bright and early,' I replied. 'So you're actually going to try to start this thing are you? Key in the lock and give it a turn.'

'That sort of thing, although it's not that early. It's all looking good, even that bit of pipe your team bodged in place seems to be holding together so far.'

'Just as well I didn't do the work myself then. I gather you didn't trust the experts and had a couple more tiles replaced, or was it because you fancied a lie in?'

'I heard that you were struggling to fix a simple electric motor last night. I thought you might enjoy the extra time in bed. I know how much you like that.'

'Is the whole team in place?'

'We are complete, now you've bothered to turn up. Your lady friend, citizen Gunadi, is checking all the mag-field controllers right now. We'll be putting the kettle on to boil soon. How are things in your department?'

'All ready to rotate.'

'Not expecting any more burnouts? You checked them all?'

'Every one. I've had so much time since your big one decided to go on holiday.'

'The captain's going to be pissed if she's left standing on her walls. Makes refreshing difficult and you know how much she likes that.'

'Don't remind me.'

'Should have fixed that one long ago. Always start close to home, I say.'

'Wise words, Ibo, wise words. Glad you're on good form this morning.'

'Like to check that my assistant is fully awake. Now sit beside me in that chair and let us run through this here check-list to see what my tired old brain has missed.'

'Before we start, how about the nozzle? Any plans for an inspection?'

'No point. All the tiles have been inspected in great detail as they were laid, along with all the surrounding tiles to check that nothing got damaged when a tile was replaced. That was why the couple of extras were added. Also, all the magnetic field data for the nozzle checks against specification.'

'It will either work or we won't know about it.'

'See you in paradise, or maybe not in your case. Are you quite finished? Can we go through this check-list now?'

'Yes, ma'am.' I sat and began to read the check list. 'One: A-M fuel level.'

'Two thousand two hundred and eleven tonnes, check,' Ibo responded.

'A-M fuel delivery system power source.'

'Fuse good, backup internal on standby, check.'

'Coolant to primary containment field generators.'

'Two Kelvin, flow clear, pressure good, heat capacity in spec, check.'

'Communications.'

'Connection strong, no errors, check.'

The list was long, some items requiring us to patch in Gunadi, Hyun or other members of the crew. Eventually we came to the end of the list.

'All systems checked. Confirm,' said Ibo.

'Confirm, all systems checked,' I responded.

'Only waiting now for the last couple of tiles to be installed. Coffee time I think. Ready to go in an hour.'

There might be time to check out the rotation motor in Sahko's section. However, if there was anything wrong there wouldn't be time to fix it. It might also upset the crew if I was seen rushing about the place with a box of tools, minutes before engine start. Leave it for now and hope for the best.

Ibo and I went to the refectory and found a small group gathered there, watching the screen showing the hot-bot reappearing over the edge of the nozzle, having completed installing another tile. It had finished cutting out tiles and was waiting for the next tile to finish being manufactured. The recycler's materials tray opened and its arm placed the tray in the airlock. The recycler shut itself down, its work done. A few minutes later the hot-bot came alive again, retrieved a completed tile from the engine room airlock and walked back to the nozzle edge and disappeared: only that one and the one now in manufacture left to be installed. We chatted for a while with Massoud, Bjorn and Agyei, drinking coffee and recalling the optimism we had felt when the engine had first been relit again, to start deceleration. That had been a watershed: the transition out of our years of cruising. We had all come alive at that time.

The hot-bot came back and retrieved the last tile from the manufacturing facility, which had completed its work, at least for now.

'Time to tighten down the ship,' said Ibo, and she and I went back to Engine Control.

We went through the routine of shutting down all the equipment not essential for engine restart. Liquids were drained back to secure tanks, valves closed and power disconnected. The hot-bot reported that it had set the last tile. It climbed out of the nozzle for the last time and packed itself away in an equipment recess. The support pyramid was withdrawn from the nozzle, folded up and stowed in its special long recess. The ship was looking good, ready to go.

'Phew. Time to call the captain I think. Would you like to?' said Ibo.

'No, I'll leave it to you,' I replied.

'Really? No, go on, you do it.'

'No, no, it would be better coming from you.'

'Scared?'

'No. It's an engine restart: your responsibility, best coming from you.'

'Passing the buck are you? What do you know that I don't? Is it going to blow up?'

'No, no, it's not that, I don't know anything. It all looks fine to me, no more risk than usual.'

'Are you saying my engine is risky?'

'We have recently done major repairs in deep space without outside help. No external inspectors have been around that I've noticed.'

'So why don't you want to talk to the captain?'

'Get on with it Ibo, you know why.'

'Poor boy. Too scared to speak.'

'OK, I'll do it.'

'Not if you don't want to, I don't mind doing it.'

'For heaven's sake Ibo.'

'Good morning captain.' Ibo had finally called. 'Yes, I'm fine, and you? Good. Yes, I did call about Main. Permission to start ignition sequence. Thank you captain, my pleasure.'

'Permission to go?'

'Permission granted, a simple conversation, satisfactorily concluded. Engine assistant: inform the crew that we'll be restarting Main in one hour.'

'Aye, aye, chief.' I sounded the alert and opened the all-ship communications channel: 'All personnel: Main engine will start in one hour. Prepare for spin down and rotation at that time. Secure the ship, safety suits on and ensure you know where the nearest lifeboat is.'

'Rather over the top all that, enough to make me nervous.'

'Engine restart usually has that effect on me anyway.'

'Let's see if we can do this one real smooth so no one notices. Here goes: initiating engine start, now.'

A couple of lights glowed on the hologram indicating that the ignition sequence was underway. Nothing dramatic. It would be almost an hour before the first anti-proton would be separated from its fellows, guided down the fuel pipe and out of the injector into the ignition chamber. There it would smash in to a proton that had been injected opposite it, converting the two into subatomic particles travelling at the speed of light. Seventy-percent of the energy released would deliver force to slow the ship. Over two hundred grams of anti-protons and the same of protons would be annihilated every second for almost another hundred days to bring the ship to a halt, hopefully in orbit around our target: an alien planet.

'Do you need to secure anything, Ibo?' I asked.

'Hyun and I tidied up before we left this morning and there shouldn't be anything loose here. I'm going to sit and watch. You go ahead if you want, as long as I can get hold of you in a hurry if needed.'

'I'll have a look around and check that everything is secure. I'll be back in time for ignition.'

Outside, the corridor was quiet. I checked Status as I went. Everyone was visible as they were supposed to be during ignition and rotation, most were in their apartments or control rooms. Agyei wasn't in Chemistry. I briefly looked in on Minogue who assured me everything was secure in Science. As far as I knew no one had been in Navigation recently. I had left floor panels loose in Avalos's refresher that might float around if we had trouble: too bad. I messaged Sahko and she confirmed that she had secured Ops. I looked in on Lifeboat One as I went past and it was in a state of readiness. Shouldn't all the crew be already in the lifeboat during ignition? Perhaps the thinking was if the engine blew up it would be better to be annihilated instantly rather than left to starve in a lifeboat over weeks. I checked Bita was fine in Comms. Gunadi seemed to have had a tidy up in Analytics since I had last been there. No one was in Payload-Wayclear and it all looked secure. Yingluq assured me that Medical was under control. Massoud was in the refectory so I went to see if everything was all right.

'Come in, come in,' he said, 'I'm making sure everything is fixed down in here, I've already checked Food Prep. Do you have time for a coffee?'

'Sorry no. I'm doing a round to make sure everything is fastened. Glad that you have those under control. Is there anything loose down in the Processes Ring?'

He laughed. 'Could get real messy if one of the fermentation tanks came adrift. Everything should be secure. We haven't started shifting things around yet for the new processes.'

'Don't want the service bots complaining about having to clean up after us humans again.'

'They're always bitching about the poor standards of ships' crews these days.'

'I best continue my round and make sure they don't have too much to complain about.'

I checked in Recreation next. There was no one there so I had a look around to make sure everything was secured. The exercise equipment all had lock pads on their feet that engaged with the carpet to stop them drifting. So as long as everything was upright and in contact with the floor it wouldn't move. I checked the lockers and they were all properly closed and I couldn't see any loose items. The women's personal lockers were all secured.

The children's room was next and they were all there with Agyei. She was sitting at a table with Joko who was drawing animals copied from a picture. Alice was reading in a corner and raised a hand as I came in and then went back to her book.

'Hi, Menem, we've been preparing for rotation,' said Kent.

'Making sure everything is stuck down or put away,' added Sky.

'What are you two going to do when we rotate?' I asked them.

'We're going to walk around the corridor,' said Sky.

'Excellent! Just be ready to hang on if the engine doesn't start smoothly.'

That was always a favourite: standing in one of the sections of corridor that were fixed to the ship's structure and to which the rotating sections were attached. During rotation, what had been the floor became a wall and visa versa. The fun was trying to stay upright as long as possible on the old floor. 'Well I'm glad everything is safe here. I'm going round the ship, checking up. All well, Agyei?'

'Yes, I think so,' Agyei answered. 'As Sky and Kent said, everything is stuck down or put away here and in the children's apartments. I checked Chemistry earlier and it's secure there.'

'How about the tile factory in the engine room, could anything come loose down there?'

'I don't think so. We thought about that when we installed it and made sure everything was well attached and would remain so when it came under load from the deceleration. Everything had to be well sealed anyway so it shouldn't leak. It's not going to be a sudden change is it?'

'Ibo's intention is to take it real slow and smooth and the rotation should match that. You should hardly notice anything if you stay in here. It shouldn't stress the ship too much.'

'I'll be here if you need me. Bjorn is coming here soon. Bita also said she might look in later, to be with Joko.'

Joko looked up at the mention of her name. She showed me the picture she was working on.

'Nice lizard,' I said. The girl had inherited at least some of her mother's artistic side. 'Bye, everyone,' I called out. Everyone called back except Alice who raised a hand again but still kept her nose in her book.

I continued my tour of the Habitat Ring: checking up on Lifeboat Two, noting that it too was in a state of readiness.

Status told me that Hyun was in Robotics so I looked in on him. 'Any problems, Hyun?'

'Everything is secure here and in Printing. I've been thinking about the mimics. There are a number of problems, not the least of which is replacing the head of the broken one. The old head had some quite special sensors in the eyes which I don't think we can make on the ship and we don't carry spares. Our scientists might have some ideas, but it's likely that we'll have to make do with less special ones. It seemed to work all right using the bot-net cameras.'

'It was OK, but the field of view was restricted and it seemed to be less sensitive, or at least less able to compensate between well lit and dimly lit areas.'

'That would fit with the specs and the missing integrated lights'.

'It definitely needs them. Everything gets shadowed so easily.'

'They were very well designed,' Hyun sighed. 'Well hidden, moulded into the head and automatically activated when the eye sensors detected that the light level has fallen too low. And their ability to work with whatever part of the spectrum the operator is using, from infrared to ultraviolet, was great. One issue that really concerns me with using a different eye sensor is that we'll have to use the mimics in bright light when we're near a star. The eye irises will not close down quickly enough if the head is turned directly towards it. The contrast would be huge and it could burn out the sensors if they're too tightly focused.'

'Perhaps we could put some sort of reactive screen in front of the sensors that would blank them off before they got overloaded.'

'If we can find one that reacts quickly enough.'

'Perhaps Agyei might know of something.'

'We should put out a request for help. Shall I do it?' Hyun asked.

'Please do. You said there was more than one problem with the mimics.'

'It concerns your experience of using them. It might be something to do with you being in the spinning ring while the mimic is not. I don't remember you suffering before.'

'There could be something in that. My assumption was that either I was getting increasingly agoraphobic or I was feeling physically present and the risk to me was building up the more I used it.'

'Those are possibilities. Losing the mimic head probably didn't help. You get travel sick pretty easily don't you?'

'Yes.'

'Well what if there's something about you being sensitive to the spin of the Habitat Ring? You know, with the movements of your head causing your sense of balance to be mismatched to your other sensory inputs.'

'But the whole mimic operator thing is a bit like that regardless of the motion of the operator chair. We walk the mimic around but don't actually go anywhere ourselves.'

'Yes, but that doesn't affect your balance. I agree that head movements might, but that has always applied and you didn't feel bad before. What has changed recently is that we've been in spin.'

'But we were in spin for a long time while we were cruising.'

'True, but how many mimic trips did you do then?'

'Not many, but at least once a year as a refresher.'

'And how many have you done recently?'

'Lots. OK, so I agree that it's a reasonable hypothesis. How can we test it?'

Hyun paused a moment and continued. 'We're about to stop spin so you could try four mimic trips on successive days to see how you react.'

'Yuk, and they would need to have a purpose. OK, so we could test the hypothesis and if it turns out to be correct what, if anything, could or should we do about it?'

'We have to find something to improve things for you because once we arrive we'll be back in spin mode, at least until we can set up on a rock big enough to supply gravity. We're going to need a lot of mimic work to deploy the payload. It might turn out that others are affected too. No one has done as many trips as you, so closely packed together.'

'All right, so if we've a real problem, how do we fix it? There might be something in Archive about this. Mimics have been used extensively for asteroid exploration and exploitation work.'

'Sure they have, but not operated from a spinning ring. If my hypothesis is right then we need to better align the forces your head feels with its balance sensors, with what your eyes and other senses are telling you. That seems to be a control and sensor problem which could be adjusted with some tuning of the control algorithm and an extra input that takes account of the spin of the operator.'

'That doesn't sound so simple but it might be worth a try. Another idea for when we arrive is to move the mimic control chairs to a zero-'g' environment. Then the chair wouldn't be spinning and be in the same 'g' as the mimic.'

'That's a possibility. Mimic controllers aren't usually in spinning sections of ships. I'll think about it for a day or two and maybe see if Gunadi can help with some simulations and perhaps see if there's anything in Archive.'

'If we, or rather you, can improve the experience I'll be grateful.'

'Leave it with me for now.'

'Thanks, Hyun. I'd better be getting on, finish my round and then join Ibo for the engine restart.'

He nodded. I left thinking what how hard working he was, always trying to improve the robotics: a quiet grafter, never seeking the spotlight. Maybe I should follow his example a bit more and keep a lower profile, settle down and stop playing around. I wish.

4024, 11:35

Ibo was intently studying her screen when I came back in to Engine Control. She held up a hand in acknowledgment but said nothing. She already wore her safety suit and I put on mine. Most of the panels she was looking at showed green with only a few left in red and, as we watched, another block turned.

'Proton flow looks good, so that side is functioning normally. Next we have to flush the A-M side. Gunadi, are you ready to monitor A-M stability?' Ibo had a link open to Gunadi in Analytics; I listened in.

'All ready, Ibo. Fuse fully prepared for ramp up in power delivery. All nozzle electromagnetic fields holding stable. E-M gates on fuel tanks under your command.'

'Acknowledged. Commencing A-M system flushing.'

A light tuned yellow on a status panel and the first million anti-protons flowed out of the fuel tank and down towards the engine. Although the pipes were sucked out to as hard a vacuum as deep space could provide, inevitably there would be a few residual atoms left which would encounter anti-particles and they would annihilate each other. The pipes were designed to withstand the minute explosions from these few particles and the resulting radiation products, primarily neutrinos, would disperse relatively harmlessly. The annihilation of a billion anti-protons would produce less energy than the ignition of a microgram of TNT or ten micro-litres of petrol. Gamma ray monitors along the pipes measured the amount of energy being released, and the display showed that these were all well within expected parameters. The replacement pipe was performing as it should.

'All good here,' said Ibo. 'A-M flow as expected. Gunadi?'

'All fields stable, mag pump good, ready to go,' Gunadi responded.

'Menem?'

'Fuse delivering on demand. Ship secure, crew alerted, lifeboats checked.'

'Commencing test burn.'

Ibo made another gesture and now both fuel components were injected into the ignition chamber from opposite sides for the first time. The flow rate was still microscopic and the ship wouldn't feel any significant force yet. This test would allow us to check both the ignition system and the nozzle characteristics, using the radiation detectors set between the surface tiles and the field generators.

Ibo switched to another view of the nozzle on the holographic display, this one showing the position and output of the radiation and temperature detectors. The model showed a dim, deep-crimson glow, with its brightest area far down in the bottom of the nozzle, nearest the point where the anti-protons smashed into the protons. We watched the glow rise and stabilise.

'Test burn looking good. Gunadi?'

'Fields stable, ignition point well focused, flow laminar. All good.'

'Menem?'

'Fuse good.'

'OK. With the captain's permission, let's go for it,' Ibo said calmly.

'Captain authorises engine go,' came Sahko's voice. I hadn't realised she had been listening in.

'Menem, alert the crew,' Ibo instructed.

I opened an all-ship comms link. 'All crew: engine powering up, Habitat spin-down and rotation will be simultaneous.' I hoped, provided all those motors that I hadn't checked didn't burst in to flames and jam half the sections in part-rotated states. 'Crew are advised to remain where they are until the all-clear is given which should be in about ten minutes.' That wouldn't stop the children from playing in the corridor, gotta have fun.

'Taking it up,' said Ibo tonelessly. She made a gesture, initiating the automated power up sequence. The fuel flow indicator started to tick up. For a minute not much happened, but gradually the nozzle display grew brighter and the red colour spread to its edges. In its centre, the red began to give way to orange and then yellow. As the fuel flow increased, the colours intensified, an alarm sounded and I felt the room shudder slightly as a groan came from the machinery: sensors had detected the force coming from the engine and had initiated the spin down of the Habitat and Processes rings. I watched a display that showed the spin speed of the two rings and rotation position indicators for each of the sections. Rotation had commenced. I held my breath as the dials began to move: all thirty-two indicators, sixteen for each ring, held on orange showing they were all within the tolerance range of their expected positions.

A movement in the corner of my eye caught my attention. It was the pair of ship velocity displays showing our speed relative to the Sun and to Alpha B: both had dropped by a metre per second, not much compared to our current velocity of over ninety million, but it was the first time the indicator had moved in a week. The engine had started to slow the ship once again.

We watched as the nozzle model colours slowly changed from reds, oranges and yellows to greens, blues and violets. The fuel flow indicators clicked slowly upwards. More creaking noises propagated through the structure as the power of the engine built, and its force was transferred to the ship. We could feel movement as the Habitat Ring's spin slowed and its sections swung around to place our feet against the force of the engine's thrust. I glanced at the velocity meters and saw that they were starting to turn over more rapidly now, it was becoming hard to read the last significant digit. In silence, Ibo and I stared intently at the gauges, willing everything to work.

A warning light flashed on one of the section rotation indicators: a motor overheat. It was section eight of the Habitat Ring, the one with my apartment and Engineering. The motor reported that it had cut out automatically and the overheat light went out, so at least there wasn't a fire yet. The section had turned a little under halfway. Great, I thought, everything tilted at forty-two degrees. Hard to take a refresh and nothing would stay put on the workbench. If necessary I would work out how to crank the rotation manually. Either that or swap another motor over.

I watched as Ibo checked the coolant flows from the nozzle field-generators and the ignition chamber shroud, as well as the fuel flow system, fuel tank field generators, fission reactor and electrical generator. All were functioning normally and the radiators covering the exterior of the ship were doing their work of shedding the increasing surplus of heat from the nozzle into the cold of space.

Ibo sat back in her chair, relaxing a little, her gaze on the hologram and the surrounding data screens. The gravity accelerometer was ticking up towards minus one. It hovered just below and then flicked over. The engine was delivering the thrust we needed and all the warning lights were out.

The gauges indicated that all sections except eight had completed their rotations. I restarted the motor in eight and watched the gauge. It moved slowly around another five degrees, then ten, then fifteen, then the overheat warning light came on again and the motor cut off. Fifty-eight degrees, so maybe a couple more goes would get it there.

'Gunadi, how is it looking?' Ibo asked.

'All fields stable, no anomalies to report.'

'Menem?'

'Fuse stable, cooling flows good, spin-down and rotation complete with the exception of section eight.'

'Captain, engine fully functioning.'

'Thank you Ibo and everyone. That's a huge relief.'

'Menem, would you tell the crew?' Ibo asked.

All the crew were probably well aware of what was going on but I opened the comms link and said: 'All crew, engine fully functioning, rotation complete except section eight, which I hope to have rectified soon. All clear to move about. Just be aware that the Habitat corridor now curves left or right rather than up. Have a nice voyage.'

Ibo took off her control gloves and turned around to me, a big smile on her face. 'Well I sure am pleased to get my engine back online. Everything seems to be holding for the moment.'

'Yeah, encouraging start. If there was a problem with either the nozzle or the fuel pipe then I would have expected that to show immediately. We'll have to see how the new tiles perform over time.'

'Minogue and the others seem to have come up with the goods there. I think there's a tiny improvement in engine efficiency compared with before: the fuel burn rate is slightly less than the model predicts for this rate of deceleration.'

'There could be other factors: loss of mass somewhere or a sensor drifting off calibration.'

'Ever the pessimist Menem. I doubt it's sensor trouble, unless they're all drifting at the same rate, and it also seems unlikely that it's mass loss or we would have noticed it. We did lose a mimic head and a bit of a Wayclear mast but that would be less than ten kilos in total. If anything, I would expect a mass gain from the remains of objects we collected from the field.'

'An efficiency gain is good news if it holds true. If it's real and significant we should calculate if it's worth replacing all the tiles.'

'We should, but I doubt the gain is enough to make it worthwhile stopping for that. Replacing all the tiles would take a couple of weeks and is risky. We've enough fuel to complete the mission as we are.'

'Any left over fuel may prove handy in the long run. Still, we can't afford any further delay so maybe that's a job for the next trip.'

'Left over fuel will be a liability unless we need to move again after arriving. We have to contain it without fail or anything in its vicinity will get blown to kingdom come.' Ibo looked at the ceiling for a moment, perhaps praying. She looked back at me and asked: 'What's up with section eight rotation do you think?'

'It was reported as a motor overheat which suggests that either the mechanism is sticking somewhere or a contact has come adrift inside the motor. It will be the same type as the one that failed in here last time, and we know there's a weakness in the design. I managed to get eight to rotate a bit further after the motor had cooled down, so maybe after a couple more goes it will mange to complete the rotation. However, I want to take a look at it before trying again: we don't want it bursting in to flames like the one in here did.'

'I expect you'll want your apartment rotated before nightfall, unless you're planning to spend the night elsewhere.'

'That's an interesting idea, what do you suggest?'

'Lots of women seem to be prepared to give you comfort, so I hear.'

'Are you offering me a place to lay my weary head tonight, Ibo? That's very kind.'

'Well maybe, but my bed is usually fully occupied by my man. Lots of other lonely women on board though.'

'My heart is given to only one,' I sighed wistfully in a theatrical manner.

'Maybe, but I know you men, if we women don't keep a close eye then other parts of you may be given freely to others.'

'I'm shocked. What a suggestion!'

Ibo laughed and shook her head. She turned back to her displays, studying them in detail. The velocity clock continued its steady ticking down by ten metres per second every second. Only the red rotation light for section eight spoiled the green party.

Ibo pushed back her chair. 'Let's go and have something to eat. I'm starving and our work here is done for now.'

'Definitely,' I stood and she took my arm.

When we got to the refectory quite a crowd had gathered and there was a cheer as Ibo came in. Massoud came over a put his arms around her and gave her a big hug. 'Lunch for you, something special.'

The crowd then noticed me coming in behind and they all started leaning over.

'Ha, ha, very funny,' I said humourlessly.

'I can put your lunch in a pouch if you like, Menem. It would make it easier to eat on a sloping table,' said Massoud. I tried to look miserable so he came over and put his arm around me too. 'Don't worry about us; we're just so relieved that the engine is running again. Come and eat.'

On the screen someone had set up a display of the velocity meter and we could see it ticking down. There was a lot of laughter and questions. Sahko and Gunadi came in together and we all shook hands and hugged with big smiles on our faces. Bjorn arrived with the children which added to the cacophony.

'How did you get on with the rotation?' I asked Kent. 'Did you fall off the wall?'

'Well it was a bit slow to be really fun. We managed to walk around the whole Ring,' he replied.

'Until you fell over,' added Sky.

'Only when I was trying to see how high up the wall I could get.'

'Not as far as me.'

'Yes, I did.'

'How did you get on?' I asked Joko.

'It was fun,' she replied, 'a bit scary at first, and now the corridor bends the other way, like it did before we stopped.'

'Yes, it's weird isn't it? Somehow it seems unreal.'

'It seems to change quite lot, so I don't mind.'

'Yes, it has,' I laughed. 'It wasn't supposed to, but when the engine suddenly stopped the rooms had to rotate, or we would have been walking on the walls and not the floor. Now that Ibo has got the engine running again we've been able to rotate them back.'

I don't think she really understood my not very clear explanation, but it didn't seem to bother her.

Sahko came over and sat next to me. Joko climbed on to her lap and started eating. She seemed to find it comfortable there.

'Well done, Menem. The engine repairs all seem to be working. It has all been rather tense this past week so I hope we can now relax, at least for a bit.'

'The start up ran gratifyingly smoothly. Ibo is pretty cool under pressure and we know she's a master of that engine. All her maintenance work paid off. I've seen a lot of good engine people struggle to get them alight.'

'She knows what she's doing, and you too, Menem. All the repairs were done amazingly quickly and seem to be holding up.'

'Good so far. Team effort. Absolutely everyone contributed, including you. Ibo thinks the new tiles may have fractionally improved engine efficiency, but we'll have to check a few things to confirm that. If it's true, we may end up with a few kilos of fuel left in the tank when we arrive.'

'Still a lot of uncertainty about what we're going to need when we get close in system.'

'Yingluq and Minogue aren't here. Are they working on something?'

'I've been with them. We've been modelling various options now that the engine is on. We need to increase the deceleration, but through what profile?'

'As we've lost six days, we need to make up for that somehow. It won't be comfortable though: it will make everyone tired,' I said.

'It's not a huge difference if we up deceleration by six or seven percent for the remainder of the journey. I doubt we'll even notice. We will need to have a full crew discussion, get everyone's input, not least yours, on how much the ship can take.'

'Structurally it should be all right up to full thrust. After all, that's what was required when we set off and now we've much less fuel mass. It should easily be able to cope with deceleration up to two-'g', as these freighters were designed to be able to do. I would need to confirm that by running the structural model. The ship's mass distribution is different without so much fuel and also this ship was heavily modified.'

'Not yet. Let's see what Minogue suggests first. We've time enough, so it can wait until tomorrow. Let's have the rest of today to relax and enjoy this success.'

With that she got up, lifting Joko off her lap and placing the child, who was still stirring the last of her food with a spoon, on mine. Sahko smiled at me and I smiled back, we held each others' eyes for a long moment. Minogue and Yingluq came into the room still debating something, and Sahko walked away to join them. They all went over to Ibo and patted her on the back and offered their congratulations. The crew were all together for a brief while.

'Engine On celebration dinner tonight, everyone,' Massoud called out and there was a general cheer.

Some of the early arrivals started to drift away. Bjorn came over to me and said: 'Sorry to hear about the section eight rotation problem. Is there anything I can do?'

'It's the motor overheating, but this time it shut off before it caught fire. I've tried restarting it and there was some further movement before it overheated again. I'm optimistic that two or three more goes will have the section fully rotated. However, before trying again, I want to take a look at the motor and mechanism to see why it's struggling. It may be that there's a design fault and all the sections need repair.'

'We certainly don't want another fire if we have another sudden engine outage, or worse, multiple fires. That would be real trouble.'

'Definitely. There's also something else. When I took the motor from section eleven to replace the one in five, there was black dust covering everything in the equipment bay. That needs investigating.'

'Can I help?'

'Well if you've got the time, could you collect a sample of the dust and get Agyei to analyse it? If she's not the right person then she can probably suggest who is: Massoud perhaps, or Minogue.'

'I'll see what I can do.'

'Thanks. After I've finished here I'm going round to eight to take a look at the motor. How are things with you and Agyei? I seem to keep asking that. A sign of nervousness probably.'

'We're still both fine. Agyei is calm as always. Yingluq has been helping to keep everything coming along smoothly. Oh, Sahko has asked me if I could take over Minogue's duties as second for personnel. She wants him to be able to spend more time on navigation with her. I expect she'll talk about it this evening and check to see if anyone has any objections. After all, personnel can deal with sensitive matters so some might not want me to see all their files or wouldn't find me a suitable person to talk to. I'm not sure I am really, but I'm prepared to give it a go.'

'I'd be careful. As you say, it deals with sensitive stuff.'

'I'm sure Bita will handle anything difficult. I don't have the training for it and anyway Minogue will also be around if things get complicated. I have done some petty dispute resolution work before.'

'And you could step in between any two of us and stop a fight.'

Bjorn smiled. 'I hope it never comes to that.'

'It might. Tensions are likely to increase as we get towards the end of the mission. I can sort of see why Sahko wants you to do the job though.'

'I don't follow.'

'Protection.'

'You're kidding. Who from?'

'Me, perhaps.'

Bjorn gave a great laugh and slapped me on the back. 'I certainly don't want to get between you two, although if you decide to kill each other I might have to. In the meanwhile I'll get a sample of that dust to Agyei for analysis.' He got up and went out, exchanging a brief word with Ibo before leaving. Ibo laughed at whatever it was Bjorn had said.

Joko had finished eating and gone off to her mother. I pushed back and took my plate over to the servery hatch. Minogue was standing nearby, engaged in conversation with Yingluq. They broke off as I came up and he said: 'Good job, Menem, in getting all that work done in less than a week.'

'Thanks, Minogue, everyone helped, even you it seems. Did Ibo tell you about the engine efficiency improvement?'

'She did. Too early to be conclusive, but at least we don't seem to have made things worse. Those new tiles have been discussed in the literature for a while but engine designers are a very conservative bunch.'

'Not so surprising seeing that it took more than fifty years to get anything to work reasonably reliably and efficiently.'

'But as antimatter is still staggeringly expensive to collect every improvement in efficiency saves a fortune.'

'Maybe you two have now proved the concept and others will take it up: The Minogue-Yingluq Nozzle Tile. I can see it now, up in lights. We should relay the good news to Fleet and they could upgrade their nozzles while they're still cruising.'

'Bit premature for that, but Sahko and Bita might be interested in discussing the idea.'

'Ah well, if you've helped us along the way then great. If we were running low on fuel then we would either have to improve efficiency or shed mass. Actually I thought we are doing fine for fuel with enough to spare.'

'That depends on how much in-system manoeuvring we have to do.'

'Which we don't know.'

'Right, we don't know. We're running scenarios and for some we don't have enough fuel.'

'Oh dear.'

'Oh dear indeed. Only outlier scenarios at the moment.'

'We need more data.'

'Of course.'

'You scientists, always the same.' I laughed and put down my plate.

'You engineers always see things from an odd angle,' Minogue added, and started to lean. Yingluq smirked and started to lean too. She had a rather nice tight top on, so I smiled.

'Ha, ha, friends. I have a ship to fix.' I waved and headed for the door.

4024, 13:25

Alice rushed up and asked: 'Can I come and see your section?'

I looked around to see who was in charge of the children. It looked like Gunadi and she waved a hand to indicate that I should take Alice.

'I'm on my way to Engineering so, yes, you can come. What do you want to see?' We walked out together.

'Bjorn said that section eight was stuck at a funny angle.'

'There was some trouble with the motor that makes the section rotate.'

'What was wrong with the motor?'

'That's what I'm going to try to find out. The motor started to get too hot during the rotation, so it turned itself off.'

'Why did it get too hot?'

'There are a number of possibilities that I've thought of so far, but I need to investigate to find the answer to your question.'

We had arrived at Engineering and the corridor floor was tipped over. I instructed the door to open, which it did rather more slowly than usual because of the angle it was at.

'Can you climb inside?' I asked.

'I think so, my shoes have good grip.' Alice climbed up and stood in the angle between the wall and the floor.

'Good. Now me.' I climbed in too.

I was glad that I'd made sure that everything had been put away before the rotation had started. Only an old pen and a few pieces of paper on which I had been sketching were scattered on the floor. I retrieved them before Alice could take a look.

'What I have to do is to try to reach for some tools and then remove an access panel on the side wall to look at the motor.'

Alice had taken a few steps up the slope and found that she could just about stand on the floor so I followed and cautiously made my way up to the workbench and opened a drawer where my basic toolkit and test instruments were. The drawer fell fully open and some things bounced out. I managed to retrieve the tools, pushed the drawer shut again and edged down to the corner of the room where the access panel covering the equipment void was located.

Alice held the tester while I removed the panel, clipped up a portable light and took a look inside. It seemed slightly dirty in the void, but not as bad as the one in section eleven. There was a faint smell of heated dust though. I tripped the motor isolator switch and reached in and felt around: the motor was still warm. Alice looked thoughtfully at the motor.

'How do you find out what's wrong, Menem?'

'Well I start by doing simple things like looking around to see if there's something obviously broken. Then I use a special camera to see what parts have got particularly hot.'

'Show me.' I showed her the camera and the image that appeared on the hand-unit's screen. 'Can I try?' I handed her the camera and the hand-unit and she started looking around at things. 'Oh, you look hot, at least your face does, and my hand too. The motor is a bit warm.'

'The heat has become spread out since the motor last ran so it is not clear where the problem is. We may have to run it again to heat it up for the fault to become obvious. It's not always easy to tell exactly what part has gone wrong because different materials get hot at different rates.

Anyway, before we try running it again, we can do some other tests on the motor. Can you pass me that box?'

She passed the general purpose electrical tester which I hooked up to the motor's diagnostics port. Alice watched as I explained what the machine was doing: firstly identifying the device that it was plugged into in the ship's database and then running through the static test sequence. It all passed.

'Does that mean the motor is working?' Alice asked.

'No, unfortunately not. Sometimes a fault only appears when the motor has heated up or starts to work hard. We'll have to run it to find out. But before we do we should take a look at the drive, that's the connection between the motor and the ring section. Something may have come out of alignment and the motor had to work much harder than it should.'

'How do you do that?'

'Well, I start with a visual inspection. The outside is easy, using a camera on a flexible rod to get a look at things I can't see from where I am. If that shows nothing I have to look inside. Most gearboxes have an inspection port so a camera probe can be pushed in to have a look. Let me show you.'

I took a camera probe and pushed it in to the inspection port of the helical gear on the end of the motor shaft. An image came up on the view screen.

'What are we looking at?' she asked.

I talked through the image of the gears, bearings, housing and lubricants and explained that we were looking for damage to any of the gear teeth, any artificially shiny spots, any evidence of scraping or grinding such as discoloured lubricants. In this case the gears looked normal and the tester confirmed it against reference images.

'That one looked all right, let's try the next.'

I pushed the probe into the next test port, deep in the back of the void, where a secondary reduction gear engaged with the gear teeth fixed to the section module. When I touched the gear housing I noticed that it was much warmer than I had expected. The teeth of the motor-side gear looked very bright as though they had been recently polished. I couldn't see any lubricant at all, but that was not necessarily a fault: many types of ceramic composite materials used for gears were self-lubricating. The tester indicated that it was doubtful about the match with the reference image.

'So is something broken there?' asked Alice. She had been paying close attention to what I was doing, more than I had expected.

'Maybe. It's hotter than it should be and that gear has become more polished than the reference. It could be designed to run hot.'

'Doesn't the system say how hot it should be?'

'It probably does. I'll check.' I called up the data on the gear chain and it was definitely hotter than specified.

'That was a good idea, Alice. So now we have identified a problem but we don't yet know if it's the cause of the trouble or the result of some other problem. If we run the motor for a short while we can watch, listen and test to see if we can work out if that's really what's wrong. We'll need to go round to Engine Control to set up a remote link.'

We both scrambled out of Engineering and it was a relief to be able to stand on a flat floor again. We walked round to Engine Control and found Ibo back sitting and watching the central projection and its surrounding screens.

'Hi, Mom,' Alice called out.

'Oh, hello dear, come and see what I'm up to.' Alice and I came over to have a look. Ibo gave Alice a hug and a kiss.

Nothing looked out of place. 'Looks good, Ibo. Anything amiss?'

'Not with the engine,' she replied. 'It's running real smooth. Alice, look and see how well the engine is running.' Ibo pointed at some graphs on the screen, which Alice studied.

'We're fixing the motor in Engineering,' Alice said, 'but I love this display. What are you doing if the engine is running smoothly?'

'Well the engine actually seems to be working better than it was before, just a little bit. I was wondering why. Menem, can you get figures for the unused material that we recovered from the broken tiles?'

'I can get you figures on the remaining mass from the tile recycler, and we can ask Agyei if she has any surplus material left over from the tile factory. I remember her talking about sludge accumulation that she cleared. I find it difficult to believe that the mass has changed significantly, other than the known fuel burn. A fuel tank leak seems highly unlikely and no sensors have reported losses. Perhaps we can do a seismic test of some sort to determine current ship mass. We could ask Minogue if he has any ideas on that and do a search in Archive for suggestions.'

'Interesting idea: I'll talk with Minogue and Agyei.' Ibo paused and then continued. 'So Alice, if you're fixing the rotation problem in eight, why did you come here?'

'We need to set up a remote link so we can try running the motor and test it at the same time. Isn't that right, Menem?'

'Yes, exactly. Let's have a look at the rotation display over here.' I pointed to the display I had been using earlier. 'You can see all the sections are in position except section eight. Let's set up the remote link and we can then go back to Engineering and operate it from there.' I authenticated my access code and talked Alice through how set up the remote link. 'Thanks Ibo, we're done here.' She gave us a wave.

Alice and I returned to Engineering, climbing back into the tilted room.

'We need to be very careful now, Alice. Once we start the motor the room should begin rotating again. We have to set up all the sensors we think we're going to need first. I would like you to fix them, OK?'

'Yup. If you tell me where to put them.'

'Good. Put this camera in the inspection port where we had it before, and then place these heat and vibration sensors on the gear housings: one at the back and one on the housing near the camera sensor.'

Alice crawled around in the void and fixed the sensors as I directed. It was so much easier for her to get them into good positions, given her small size and space-born agility. Once she had fixed the probes, I established a wireless link to each and set the test system to compare the sensor outputs with the specifications held in Archive.

After Alice had crawled back out, I asked: 'Are you ready? Remember the floor is going to tilt once the motor comes on.'

'Ready,' said Alice, staring intently into the equipment void.

I activated the remote control and the motor started to run. We began to feel the room slowly rotating. I watched the test screen. At first it all went smoothly, but very soon the vibration sensors showed than the gears in the final part of the chain were not meshing smoothly. Heat was rising in that area too and the power draw of the motor was increasing. The room had turned another five degrees and it had become clear where the problem lay, so I shut off the power and the motor stopped. Temperature readings continued to climb for a while but then plateaued and finally began falling again.

Alice pointed to the test screen and said: 'So it looks like a problem with that gear.'

'Yes, it does. Somehow one of those two gears has shifted and they are pressing too hard against each other. Next we need to try and find out what has shifted and why. The shift may be only a tiny amount. Let's look at the assembly manual and see how it was put together. Can you call that up on the screen?'

I gave instructions on how to bring up the structural diagrams from Archive. It didn't take Alice long to work out how to do it alone and she manipulated the images so we could compare the diagrams with the motor and gearbox in front of us. All the structural components to which they were mounted were ultra-lightweight honeycomb composite panels, with captive nuts moulded in. The motor and gearbox were of heavier construction, designed to contain the substantial forces they generated.

'Alice, can you take a camera probe and direct it at each of these four mounting points in turn?' I pointed to what I wanted on the diagram.

'You want me to crawl in the void and do that?'

'Yes. Are you happy to do that or would you rather I did?'

'No, I don't mind. Mommy told me not to get in the way when you're working.'

'You've been very helpful. I'll tell you if I need to do something undisturbed, so if you want to continue, then please do. I like your company.'

Alice looked cheered and grabbed the probe and crawled into the void.

I heard her muffled voice call out: 'Is this the right place?' I looked at the image on the screen and took a still and zoomed in and out on it, filming as I did so.

'That's one of them,' I called out. 'Now try another.' The picture swung wildly and another bolt and nut came in to view. I fixed another image and we repeated the process until all four were captured. 'Great, thanks Alice, come out now and let's look at the results.' She climbed out and we studied the four images. In each case we could see slight distortion of the structure around the bolts and that the bolts were no longer perfectly perpendicular to the panel. 'I think I can see what's happened. Somehow the motor and gearbox have shifted towards the gear fixed on the section. We can see that from the way all the bolts are bent over a tiny bit.'

'Can you fix them?'

'Yes, it's a relatively simple job, but messy. I'll have to take out those bolts, reposition the gearbox and somehow re-fix the nuts in the correct position. The old nuts were made as part of the panel, so it will be easier to cut them out, bond a new piece of panel underneath to reinforce it and then use longer bolts.'

'Will you do that now?'

'I need a break first. Let's pack up the test gear and then go back to the refectory. Can you retrieve all the test sensors for me?'

Alice dived into the void once again and peeled off all the sensors and handed them back to me.

'Is that it?' she asked.

'Yes, for now. Let's go.'

The refectory was empty when we got there. I ordered a coffee and Alice a fruit drink. We sat in companionable silence for a moment and then Alice asked: 'Do you have a girlfriend Menem?'

I almost choked on my coffee. 'There are lots of girls I like, Alice.'

'But no one special?'

'Yes there is, but she doesn't think I'm special.'

'Who is it?'

'I can't tell you that.'

'Is it Sahko?'

'Why do you think that?'

'Someone said that you two used to be together.'

'That's true. How about you Alice, do you have a boyfriend?'

'No. There isn't anyone my age.'

I wondered what it would be like to have got to ten years old and never met anyone your own age.

'In a couple of years the whole of Fleet will be together in our new home and then you'll be able to meet lots of children of your own age.'

'That will be weird.'

'Yes it will, but weird in a good way I think.'

'Do you think we'll get along or will we fight, like the big powers do back on Earth?'

'They don't all the time but, well, humans always fight a bit, sometimes even only two people. It's one way of resolving disagreements, letting the other side know how important something is to you. When Fleet has arrived we'll still be very few and there will be lots of space so I think we'll need to help each other and not fight very seriously. I hope we can have lots of parties and get to know one another.'

'It will be nice to meet some new people.' Alice looked wistfully up to the ceiling. 'When are you going to give us a class again, Menem? It's been ages.' I was grateful for the change of subject.

'Yes, it has. I've missed being with you but I've had to fix the ship, and as you've seen, there are still things to do. If I can fix the rotation problem today then I'll try to take a class tomorrow. Is Gunadi taking class now?'

'Yes.'

'Do you like Gunadi's classes?'

'Yes, I suppose so. She's, err, I'm not sure how to say it.'

'Different?'

'Yes, different, but everybody's different. She's great with virtual games, knows lots of tricks, so sometimes she's fun. She's the best at explaining maths too. Sometime she's a bit moody though.'

'Let's go back to the classroom and see what she's up to.'

We took our cups to the servery hatch and I held the door open for her as we left. 'Thanks for your help, Alice. It's nice to have someone to work with sometimes.'

'You're welcome,' she replied and gave me a little wave and disappeared into the classroom.

I continued on past Lifeboat Two to Engineering. It was going to be awkward working on a tilt, but I didn't want to further strain the machinery. The first thing was going to be to stop the motor and gearbox sliding away once I had removed the bolts. I found some webbing straps and a strap ratchet. It was a tedious job: undoing awkwardly placed bolts, gaining access to the underside of the mounting plate and cutting out the old nuts, finding a suitable secondary plate to go underneath, drilling it out, and temporarily gluing on some new nuts. The motor and gearbox then had to be repositioned following the recommended procedure for alignment, which didn't allow for working on a tilt of course, and finally tightening down the bolts and removing the webbing straps. I checked it all over carefully, put in some temperature and vibration sensors and activated the motor. It hummed quietly and the section rotated smoothly to completion. There was no excessive heating or vibration. I removed the sensors and replaced the equipment void access panel.

It was a relief to be able to work on the flat again, so I spent a minute wandering around Engineering, looking at all the stuff that filled the place: the big assembler machine, the finisher, the small assembler, all the storage for minor components, the test bench with its host of clamps, probes and read outs, and the design area with its big screen and control gloves. I carefully filed away in a secret drawer the papers I had made sketches on: caricatures of the crew, especially the women. While I was looking at all the kit I pondered on what had caused the rotation trouble in the first place. It might well be the same cause of failure in section five. At least I now had something to look for.

4024, 17:45

I went across the corridor to my apartment and had a refresh. Feeling tired, I lay down on the bed, briefly closing my eyes. The next thing my reminder alarm had gone off; it was time for the celebration meal. A particularly sharp ship-suit would mark the occasion; a copy of one Sahko had designed for me long ago.

Almost everyone was in the refectory already and most had made an effort to smarten themselves up. Ibo was wearing a bright green dress with colourful abstract flowers printed on it, with a scarf in a similar material wrapped around her hair, piling it up over her head. I went over and asked: 'Is everything still running smoothly?'

'Always does. You know me, citizen smooth.'

'Oh yes, always the smooth one, love the outfit. I meant with the engine.'

'Work, work, work, that's all it ever is with you, Menem. But since you asked, yes, the engine is running very smoothly right now, thank you: brake full on.'

'How is your lean, Menem?' asked Hyun who was standing nearby in a simple, grey, freshly-pressed ship-suit.

'All fixed now, thanks to my little helper. Alice gave me a hand.'

'Ah yes, Ibo said she was with you. I hope she was more help than hindrance.'

'Definitely more help and it was nice to have the company.'

'Have you found out what caused the trouble?' asked Bjorn who had joined us. He had on a collarless, golden-brown jacket, seamed up the front and tightly fitting. It emphasised his powerful physique.

'The motor overheated because it was overloaded, not from an internal fault. The motor and gearbox had shifted somchow, damaging their mounts and resulting in the final drive being pressed up much too hard against the gear on the section. Why remains a mystery at the moment.'

'Do you think the fault was recent?'

'Hard to tell. It might have been the result of the same event that caused the motor fire in five.'

'Don't want another fire in my section, so you better get that sorted soon,' said Ibo mock-sternly.

Gunadi came over, dressed simply in silky black jacket and trousers without any metalwork adornments, elegant for the first time I could remember. She said to me: 'Thanks for taking Alice off for a bit. She came back quite excited, and wanted to tell us all about what she'd been up to. She seemed to find it rather fun to have a room tilted over like that, so the children may ask you to rotate their room to see what it's like.'

'Oh dear, I don't want them getting too knowledgeable about the ship's systems or we'll find things being experimented on all over the place.'

'I think they know not to mess with my engine,' put in Ibo.

'Everyone knows that,' said Bjorn very seriously and to much laughter.

'I encourage them to play with the printers to a limited extent,' said Hyun. 'Sky, in particular, has got a great understanding of how they work and has come up with some very creative 'art' objects. Even Joko has mastered the basics and printed out a few things. It won't be long before she can have free-rein too, well perhaps not free-rein, but at least able to make things on her own.'

I saw Sahko arriving, wearing a rich, dark-blue suit, loosely cut and shortened to mid forearm and calf, and matching ankle boots with quite a heel on them. Massoud had a word with her and called us to order, asking us to sit. He had on a particularly brightly-striped galabeya. I found myself on the end of one side of the table, with Yingluq next to me. She wore a fetching short, tight, blue dress. The other chair beside me, at the end of the table, was empty. Gunadi sat opposite with Minogue next to her. Sahko was at the far end of the table and hardly visible. The children were also here, scattered amongst us. We were fifteen at table, plus the empty chair: Avalos's, the ghost at the feast.

The server bots placed a tray with a multitude of tiny plates in front of each of us. Each held a mouthful from a diverse range of strange looking foods. The bots added tall cups of oddly churning colourful drinks. It was another masterpiece of culinary creation.

I asked Yingluq if she had been involved with making the meal, seeing that she was Massoud's number two in bioengineering.

'Only a very little,' she replied. 'Massoud loves to do his own thing and is quite secretive about it. I helped with a suggestion regarding this crispy thing which he struggled to get exactly as he wanted. I hope the crew never have to rely solely on my talents in this department because it won't be feasts like this, unless Massoud has recorded what he came up with and the equipment can reproduce it without much intervention from me.'

'So we'd better make sure Massoud stays in good health then.'

'That I am trying to do. Perhaps he's a little too fond of experimenting on himself, but he should be good for a while longer.'

'I'm glad to hear that. You look healthy enough too, quite radiant in fact; anything up with you?'

'Nothing special. I had a league game with Bjorn before dinner.'

'Did you win?'

'Yes, in the end, but it was a hard fight.'

'You look very well toned.'

'Thank you, I can recommend exercise. You're behind in the games league, perhaps you should do more.'

'Is that doctor's orders or just a concerned friend?'

'More the latter than the former, but it's rarely bad medical advice.'

'I should, I should. Perhaps I'll take up jogging the corridor late at night.'

'That can be good exercise. I can recommend it, most pleasurable,' she smiled. Was there a twinkle in her eye? Was it an invitation?

Gunadi leaned over the table and said to me: 'The children were asking if you were going to take another lesson.'

'Are they hoping that I won't? Are my lessons so bad?' Gunadi seemed confused by my answer and drew back, I wasn't sure if I had been too abrupt. 'I was sort of joking. I was hoping that you were going to say that the children love my lessons so much that they can't wait for my return, or perhaps that I'm such a big softy that they know they can get away with almost anything in my classes.'

'I can't believe you're soft, Menem,' said Yingluq. 'Rather hard I seem to remember.'

Gunadi disagreed. 'No, no. The children seem to like Menem's lessons, most of the time. Sometimes they get a bit confused, I think, with rather more technical detail than they can understand, but they appreciate being expected to know things that they don't.'

'We're not a very well balanced bunch of teachers: far too much science, not enough arts,' I said.

'I try to talk about languages and give them examples of Thai,' said Yingluq. 'How about you, Gunadi, do you teach them any Indonesian?'

'Only a few words, usually when I can't think of the right word in English. I do try to get them to come up with stories and images for the games they write and play. I want them to have some idea of the basics of programming and systems of course, but maybe none of them will follow that line in the end.'

'I talk a bit about history and geography,' I said. 'Earth seems remote. Sometimes it's difficult to get them to engage with it. They may never see Earth so it seems irrelevant to them. I try to explain that, for better or worse, it's where we and our ancestors come from, and it has shaped us in every way. There is some importance to understanding our ancestral home. Some of them may even go back there one day. I try not to make it too heavy though. They're all still young, even Alice, although sometimes she seems so mature.'

'They have the virtual lessons for all the formal stuff, so they do get proper teaching,' said Gunadi. 'It helps to relate some of that to us so they can see that it's not entirely abstract. Also the crew being drawn from all over the non-aligned world gives them something tangible of Earth's diversity to relate to.'

'But without the big power arrogance,' said Yingluq.

'But with the little places bickering.'

'Do you think any of Fleet will try to make a break for it and get ahead?' I asked.

'Well the Indian ship is ahead anyway, so they simply have to mark the position and manoeuvres of the others. The Chinese are the ones to watch. I'm sure Captain Kirov won't let any of the others out-manoeuvre him,' answered Yingluq.

'I always wondered about Kirov: his doesn't sound a very Chinese name,' said Gunadi.

'He's from Vladivostok, which used to be part of Russia, but has been part of the Chinese empire since they absorbed most of Siberia long ago,' Minogue said, having joined our conversation.

'If anyone is going to make a break for it, it's likely to be the North American Federation. Captain Sanchez is a bit of a chancer, I had heard.' Hyun had joined our conversation too, a favourite ship-board topic.

'Well no one has their money on the Europeans, they took ages to agree who was going to do what and their ship is the smallest,' Yingluq said.

'I wouldn't rule them out completely, starting their build late allowed them to use the latest technology,' added Minogue.

'And Friedrich, their captain, is a wily old bird,' I said.

'But Andreotti would have been a more inspiring choice,' said Hyun.

'But the Hanseatics would never have allowed a southerner to be captain: he who has the gold rules,' I replied.

347

'But if the Europeans wanted to catch up then Andreotti should have been their captain.'

'Better to arrive last than have a smash along the way.'

'That European ship looks pretty sleek.'

'Maybe, but they left last,' Yingluq cut in again.

'So we conclude that Fleet will probably arrive in the agreed order, with an outside chance that the NAF will make a sneaky late stage charge,' I summarised.

'Not if we complete our contribution. We'll only be able to bring in one ship at a time.'

This discussion ended up at the same place it usually did. We didn't have any new information to go on, and any we got about Fleet ship conditions was no doubt heavily sanitised, most likely by Fleet but possibly by Bita and Sahko too.

The conversation split up and went several ways. There was talk of sports results, art of all sorts, children and relationships, all the topics of human interest, except perhaps the weather and house prices. They would no doubt be added back as soon as we set up home on a planet. The service bots removed empty plates and brought others with more exotic foods. Glasses were refilled. For a moment I was in a dead zone. Minogue was talking to Gunadi, and Hyun and Yingluq had joined a conversation down the table. I watched the animation of the crew and felt the relief. Now we had fixed our major problem we were in with a fighting chance again of completing our mission. I caught Alice's eye for a moment: she was sitting down the opposite side of the table. She smiled at me but was then drawn back into the conversation around her.

At the far end of the table Sahko too was out of a conversation for a moment. Massoud and Bjorn were on either side of her, with Kent and Sky next to them. Those four seemed to be laughing at something. Sahko was smiling as she looked around the table, appearing to be more relaxed than she had for a while. Hope must be rising in her too. She caught my eye and we gazed the length of the table at each other. I felt a smile on my face, but oddly my eyes started to moisten and I had to dab them with a pad. When I looked back, Sahko was walking around the table. She stopped part way along and leant between two people, I couldn't see who, it might have been Sky and Ibo, and joined in a conversation that I couldn't make out. She then broke off again and continued up the side of the table, occasionally reaching across to shake a proffered hand, or placing a hand on a shoulder and squeezing it, receiving a pat on her hand in response. Finally she arrived at the head of the table and sat down in the empty chair between Gunadi and myself. It was as if she had taken Avalos's place, absorbed his role, and pushed him out. I wondered if his ghost now occupied the chair she had vacated at the other end of the table and hoped not.

Gunadi was still deep in conversation with Minogue and she had hardly looked up as Sahko sat down. I watched Sahko as she observed the crew until she looked my way and gave me a friendly smile. I smiled back.

'Menem, thank you for all the work you've put in over the past week. It's a huge relief to have the engine back on.' I studied her face: her eyes were so beautiful and I noticed the tiny creases in the corners of her mouth.

'Ah, sorry, I was dreaming. Yes, great to have the engine back on, everyone has worked very hard on this.' I noticed a tiny lock of hair that had escaped and had fallen over her ear.

'You don't seem to be all that confident, Menem. Is something wrong?' I watched what a finely carved, petite nose she had, her perfectly smooth skin, and how it moved as she spoke.

'No, nothing wrong, well apart from all the things that you know about, like the mimic head. It's just that I'm always listening to the ship. I keep expecting an alarm to go off at any moment.'

'Why?'

'We were completely oblivious of the object field before we hit it, and we don't understand why it was there or how it was formed. I haven't heard that Bita, or anyone else, has come to any conclusions from its pattern. At any time we could run into another, or something else equally bizarre, that we're completely unaware of.'

'We have travelled for eleven years and that's the first time we've encountered anything other than a few grains of dust. As far as we know none of Fleet has encountered anything. On that basis it seems highly unlikely that we'll hit anything else. We were simply very unlucky.'

'It may be that such things aren't randomly distributed across the galaxy, but happen to be concentrated around the Alpha System. It does seem odd that the field is positioned exactly on the straight line path between the Solar and Alpha systems, a suspicious mind might think that it was placed there deliberately as a defensive measure.'

Sahko laughed. 'We've no reason to believe that. The Milner probes never reported anything of that sort.'

'They were tiny, and anyway not all got through: quite a lot failed somewhere along the way.'

'They were primitive technology, amazing really that any got there and were able to report back. The failure rate was consistent with what was expected, and not oddly concentrated between here and Alpha.'

'But what if their arrival triggered defensive measures?'

Sahko laughed, but then turned serious. 'Don't let one unexpected thing get to you. I need you to stay focused and not to go wandering inside that head of yours.' She looked me squarely in the eyes. 'I need you, Menem.'

I looked in to her eyes and wondered how she needed me: like I needed her? There seemed to be a softness in her gaze that I hadn't seen for some time. I felt the warmth of her hand reach for me under the table and she squeezed my knee. Gunadi was looking at us and I choked briefly, bringing my hand up to cover my mouth.

'I heard you talking about the object field pattern,' Gunadi said. 'Bita and I have done some further work on it and the distribution of objects does seem far from random. It's as though a crystal has been uniformly deconstructed. We can offer no explanation for why at the moment and we were hoping to share our findings with everyone else, once things had settled down again. Menem's triggered-defence theory is a new explanation. We will have to add it to the list.'

'Maybe that's going too far, Gunadi,' Sahko said, turning towards her. 'Somehow I had thought that the work on patterns had reached a dead end. When do you think you'll have something to share?' I looked at the two women.

'Anyone can see what we've done so far: it's in a public folder, but Bita wants to play around a little more before talking about it. She seems to think there's something there that she hasn't quite been able to grasp yet. We're also waiting for Agyei to analyse the sludge she collected in the tile factory and the leftovers from the tile recycling plant. We're hoping there will be material from the field objects that can be identified. '

'Do you think it will give us any insights?' Minogue asked, as he too had caught our conversation and become intrigued.

'It might, depending on the atomic weight of the particles' atoms,' said Gunadi. 'I'm mainly helping produce visualisations and can't even see half the things Bita talks about. It does look very strange, although it doesn't have to be unnatural. The objects are definitely not distributed in a random way, that's for sure. They are in some kind of turbulent motion, and highly charged, we think.'

'Very mysterious,' said Sahko. 'Keep pursuing this when you have the time, and let us know when you have anything you want to discuss.'

I wondered what the others were thinking. Had the mention of something 'unnatural' triggered the automatic connection to 'alien'. It was a notion that we all avoided because of the dark fears it might unleash. There was a tacit agreement to never voice the word and sometimes 'unnatural' became a substitute.

I decided we needed to change the subject. 'Talking of unnatural, what do you think this is?' I pointed to the latest set of plates that had been placed in front of each of us. They each held a small mountain of dark-purple translucent balls, about a centimetre across, that glittered with gold specs. They were interlaced with stiff golden-brown sheets about the size of a finger, but much thinner.

Gunadi stuck her spoon into her plate and scooped one of the balls into her mouth. We all watched as she ate. Her face glowed and she smiled and gave a thumbs-up.

'Wow,' she said, 'that's good. Like balls of cream with fresh fruit, mango perhaps, but they fizz in the mouth slightly as though carbonated.'

We all tried, tentatively at first, but after a bite, with great enthusiasm. The golden sheets were crisp and sweet with a ginger flavour, their crunch contrasting with the soft gelatinous fruit balls.

'Incredible Massoud,' called out Sahko, 'a masterpiece.'

She got up and clutching her unfinished bowl, walked around the table to Massoud and put her hand on his shoulder. He stood and gave her a big hug, almost lifting her from her feet. We broke into cheers and hoots and then splintered into a lot of animated conversations discussing the food and drink.

After that the children went out and the rest of us stood and cleared the table. I looked for Sahko but she had gone. Minogue and Bjorn were over in a corner watching a screen which was showing some Olympic sport. Bjorn cheered and I heard him say that some Quebecker had won a silver medal in a swimming competition, about the best the country could expect. Minogue was happy because Australia was outperforming for its relative population size as usual. I doubted if Uruguay would win anything, but if we added all the non-aligned countries represented by the crew, we expected to come fourth behind China, NAF and Europe, but ahead of India. Sahko's Japan, Hyun's Korea and Minogue's Australia making up nearly all the non-aligned successes. I watched briefly and then wandered off, noticing Gunadi looking at me, but she didn't come over. She was with Yingluq, Bita and Agyei discussing something. It was nice to see her being more sociable.

I felt I had had enough and left, making my way back to my apartment, intending to relax for a few hours before turning in. Maybe I'd do a bit of light reading or watch a film. I tried a book for a while but couldn't settle, so switched to a film. It absorbed my attention for a time, and certainly the leading actress was worth watching, although I was sure I missed a bit in the middle when I must have nodded off because the ending made no sense. I was going to go back and try to find the missing part but noticed that it had got late. I felt wide awake again and decided to go out to stretch my legs.

4024, 22:35

The passage was quiet as I walked around and there was no one in Recreation or the refectory. Even Massoud must have gone to bed. Yingluq was not in her door. On past Bjorn's, Gunadi's and Bita's apartments: all were silent. A light was on in Ops, but I didn't look in to see if Sahko was there. Next I passed Avalos's apartment and it was, of course, silent 'as the grave,' I thought. With a shudder I moved on. There was a light on in Science, so Minogue seemed to be at work. I stopped and turned around. If Sahko and Minogue were not in their apartments then Avalos's would be particularly isolated. I went quietly back around the corridor to Avalos's door, hesitated, touched the panel and the door opened. It was still unlocked as a result of my 'fix'. I quickly slipped in, closed the door and turned on a light. The refresher was still open, as were the panels which revealed pipes and wiring that I had left exposed as an excuse to return.

The closet on the other side of the entrance vestibule was first. The main clothes rack was completely empty. Massoud had been thorough in removing all his clothing to the storage boxes in the personal stores. Torchlight run over all the corners showed that nothing small had got left behind. Each of the drawers came out and was searched underneath, inside the drawer cavity and all around. There was nothing: no secrets taped up anywhere, no room for hidden compartments. If anything had ever been hidden here then someone had already got rid of it.

The furniture in the apartment was all standard-issue stuff, suitable for use in zero-'g'. My fingers explored the back of anything that couldn't be moved. There was nothing. Service bots had kept the apartment clean so there was no build up of dust and any tiny scraps would have been disposed of long ago. I felt that I was missing something. I was no expert in searching, I realised. Every stick of furniture would have to be broken up to be certain there were no concealed spaces. A close examination of all the seams in the wall panels to check if any looked as though they had been taken off and put back, perhaps repeatedly, also revealed nothing.

I looked up and studied the ceiling. There was discolouration on some of the panels, a slight yellowing, except in one large square placed directly over the bed. Four holes had been filled in, arranged in the corners of the clean area, and another pair of holes in its centre had also been repaired. It looked as though something had been attached to the ceiling which had since been removed. During the time whatever it was had been there, something had discoloured the rest of the ceiling, almost as though there had been a small fire in the apartment. I scraped a tiny part of the discoloured ceiling tile into a small sample bag and saved it in my waist tool-pack. Persuading either Agyei or Massoud to test it without my saying where I had got it or why I wanted it tested would be a challenge. I had another look at the pattern of discolouration on the ceiling and wondered if Avalos had had a view-screen above his bed where he could show films, display images from cameras or even set as a mirrored surface. Who knows what use Avalos might have made of that? As I hadn't known about it, it was likely that Gunadi had set it up and later removed it.

Sitting down in the chair by the desk, I tried to put myself in Avalos's place. What if I had something to hide, where would I put it? None of the wall, ceiling or floor panels gave the appearance of having been disturbed and they seemed a poor choice because there would always be the risk that someone from engineering or environmental services would have to remove them to get at equipment. Avalos might have a hiding place elsewhere in the ship, but the same applied. Even Navigation, which had been primarily his domain, would be frequented by others. How about the idea of hiding something in plain sight: making it so obvious that no one would look twice at it? Maybe there was nothing to find, but then there was still the locked box in Avalos's storage locker. There had to be a key for that somewhere, unless it had already been broken down in the recycler. Someone else might know where he had kept it because they had been present when he had opened the box: Gunadi perhaps.

Despairing of finding anything here, I tidied up so that it looked as though nothing had been disturbed. I took a last look around to make sure everywhere had been checked and went to the door. There it was, in plain sight, the one space not yet searched: the companion closet, certainly locked and only accessible to Avalos's face. Some people were very sensitive about their choice of companion, some of those with very good reason. Of course nothing mechanical was completely inaccessible to engineering: things went wrong and needed to be fixed. Those of us with curious minds learned how to get around security systems. In this case it was relatively simple, either an oversight by a designer somewhere or an over-zealous mass-saving measure. The clothes cupboard shared a wall with the companion closet and the covering panel between was easily removed. A nest of wires and pipes lay behind, but no unnecessary panel on the companion closet side of the wall. The companion standing there could just be made out, but more to the point the companion closet door lock was now accessible and was readily isolated from security and triggered. The door swung open and I stepped back to look Avalos's companion in the face.

It took the form of a handsome young man of quite slender build, dressed in some very old fashioned costume with an elaborately tailored jacket. It was clearly meant to be like a butler, straight out of one of those historic films, all "yes, sir, no, sir." It would no doubt have obliged Avalos in many ways, but its lifeless face and closed eyes did nothing for me.

I began to search it and almost immediately found a key in one of the pockets: a small finely carved metal object that looked the right size to fit the locked box. Through another pocket I could feel, but not reach, something. A pocket opposite it on the inside produced three pictures printed onto paper. The first showed what was presumably a young Avalos, aged perhaps twelve or thirteen, already very handsome, playing with a large brown dog on a beach, with a woman, perhaps thirty-five, wearing a bathing costume, looking on in the background. The second showed the same woman in close-up, slightly older: rather beautiful in a wide brimmed hat. The third was a picture of a small group of casually but smartly dressed men of various ages but of similar appearance. Avalos was among them. They had arms over each others' shoulders and were smiling and laughing together, facing the camera confidently. I didn't recognise any of the other people in the photographs but the resemblance to Avalos suggested that the woman might have been his mother and the men male relatives. There was nothing written on any of the pieces of paper, either front or reverse. I put the photographs back where I had found them.

All the other pockets of the jacket and trousers were empty. A check through the linings and seams of the companion's clothing for anything else produced nothing. I quickly shut up the closet door, put back the panel in the wardrobe, gave the room one last look around and turned out the light. I opened the apartment door carefully but drew back as a brief flash of colour shone out somewhere along the passage as someone went in or came out of another door. They didn't come my way, so I slipped out and shut Avalos's door behind me.

Once back in my apartment, I examined the key in some detail. Like the box that it probably belonged to, it was a fine piece of craftsmanship, but it told me nothing about what the box contained. On the handle end of the key was carved a portrait of a man with a receding hairline, long sideburns and a high collar, but that meant nothing to me. I weighed the key in my hand and knew I couldn't rest until I had opened the box.

I left my room once again and walked to the keel access tube, the door sealing shut behind me. As gravity was now provided by deceleration, the Habitat and Processes Rings were now directly connected, allowing me to make the quick climb up the link. At the top, I pulled on a pair of inspection gloves and went through another door back into Processes. I was slightly disoriented by the change of curvature of the passage and had to pause to work out which way round was the quickest to the storage lockers. Once through a couple of section doors I was again facing the row of named cupboards. I pulled down the table near Avalos's locker, set up a couple of full-spectrum inspection lights, and opened the cupboard. The crate with the elaborate box was where I had left it and no one had disturbed the hair placed on it. I lifted the crate down, took out the locked box and placed it on the table. Its polished surfaces glowed in the harsh light.

As before, it gave away no secrets. I took the key I had found and inserted it in the lock. It fitted perfectly and the lock opened smoothly and positively. Lifting the lid, I looked inside. The interior of the box was made of a light brown, wood-like material that gave off a faint, musty smell, like cedar. A sealed glass cover lay over the main portion of the box and its lid held three dials indicating pressure, temperature and humidity in some ancient measurement units. The dials were mechanical and had pointers that could be turned to select the desired conditions, but the indicators were nowhere near the pointers so the system regulating the atmosphere inside the box must have failed. If it had been removed from a charging plate when taken from the apartment any supplementary batteries would have run out long ago. Presumably no one had known that it was supposed to be kept near a power mat to maintain the interior atmosphere at the set point. Whatever lay inside had most likely deteriorated badly by now.

There was a cover to a compartment in the lid which I opened next. Behind, in a metal lined box, were three odd looking tools held in dedicated clips: one like a peculiar pipe cutter, another simply a long spike with a fancy handle, which rattled rather unexpectedly, the third looked like an archaic pistol.

I examined the spike tool first and found that I could unscrew the top of the handle. Inside was a short metal rod with one end threaded and the other formed into an odd shape. The spike tip on the tool could be unscrewed and the metal rod screwed in its place. Its purpose was obscure.

I took out the third instrument next, cautiously pointing the barrel at one of the boxes of clothing in the locker. If it was some kind of small gun I didn't want a projectile penetrating through the ship's outer skin. Nervously I pulled the trigger, and at first thought nothing had happened, but then noticed that a small flame emerged from the tip while I held the trigger in. It seemed to be a device for setting light to something, forbidden on the ship the risk from fire being so great. No wonder Avalos had kept this locked up securely. I hastily returned the tools to their storage compartment and shut its cover.

I stood back and cautiously opened the sealed glass plate to the main part of the box and then a wood-style cover to one of the pair of compartments below. This space was divided in to ten sections, each about twelve centimetres long and two wide, but it was empty. It gave off a sweet, acrid odour, mixing with the cedar-like smell of the box. It wasn't unpleasant, but it might be toxic. I wasn't wearing any kind of mask and perhaps that was a mistake. Lifting the cover on the second compartment showed it too was divided into ten sections, two of which were empty, but the other eight held strange, brown cylinders, that on close examination looked like tightly wrapped leaves. I thought of Avalos supplying Bita with drugs and realised this could be something both ancient and potent. I took an image of the contents, noting that each of the brown cylinders had a paper wrap around it, part way along its length. Each wrap had a picture on it of the same man carved on the key. I hastily closed the lid

I did a search on the image and got a warning that it was restricted content. There was only a simple child restriction on the information which was easily bypassed. The database told me that the cylinders were "Bolivar Royal Corona Cigars", a classified drug that was consumed by setting light to the leaves and inhaling the smoke, a mixture of addictive nicotine and other chemicals, including tars: known carcinogens. These drugs were sourced from Avalos's home island of Cuba. Three centuries ago it had apparently been highly fashionable amongst very wealthy men to inhale these drugs, usually after all male dinners and in combination with potent alcoholic drinks. It all sounded very primitive.

It seemed sensible to put on a filter mask and gloves before investigating the contents of the box any further. Around a section was a fire point which held several breathing masks with self-contained air cylinders. I put one on and adjusted the mask and airflow, also adding a pair of vapour-impermeable gloves in case I was allergic to any of the toxic products in Avalos's drug box.

I went back and opened it again, rather more carefully this time, and lifted one of the cylinders of compacted leaves from its resting place. It started to crumble in my hand so I returned it to its rack. There were handles on either side of the two compartments which unfolded and could be lifted, bringing out the whole top section. The box was all beautifully fitted. Below there was a further glass lid that was also well sealed but opened easily. Beneath that there was another thin wooden lid which, when lifted off, revealed many more of the leaf cylinders closely packed together. I estimated there were well over a hundred in there. If Avalos had been consuming one a month then they would have lasted him the whole voyage.

There was a notice on the inside of the lower lid explaining how the box was supposed to be used: it called itself a 'humidor' and had been specially made for the type of cigar it contained. Its two levels were designed to hold the cigars at slightly different temperatures and humidities: the upper one for immediate consumption, the lower for long-term storage. It explained that the batteries would last a year away from a charging mat, but after that the cigars would deteriorate, depending on the temperature and humidity of the environment in which the box was kept. The box also circulated a small volume of air through itself to prevent the interior becoming stale. Presumably it had to go through some impressive filter to prevent any odour escaping and being detected. All this incredible workmanship must have been done in great secrecy, considering how illegal it was. And somehow Avalos had managed to smuggle the box aboard.

Lifting out the lower container, in which the bulk of the cigars were stored, revealed the machinery for maintaining the correct atmosphere in the box. Tucked in a corner, almost hidden behind an air circulation fan, was a small booklet. I pulled it out and looked through it. A hand-written table had been drawn up. Each page had a series of letters down one side and numbers across the top. There were ticks against some of the letters in most of the columns, particularly at the start, although they seemed to get less as the numbers increased. Only in the row labelled 'G' did the ticks continue at regular intervals. The letters corresponded to the names of the crew. I had a nasty feeling it was a sex-encounter diary. I put the book down and studied the box itself.

Why had someone attached the clumsy base? It didn't match the level of craftsmanship of the box. It appeared to be simple solid block, perhaps of wood, attached by four screws, the heads of which were visible near the corners, inside the bottom of the box. The screws required a tool of a pattern unknown to me but reminiscent of the spike's oddly shaped replacement tip. It fitted perfectly in the screw heads.

The base had been crudely hollowed out and there was a package inside, wrapped in foam. This contained a circuit board, about thirty by fifteen by two centimetres, densely populated with blocks of stack-ICs. It looked like the standard size boards used all over the ship. I photographed it, including its serial numbers, and uploaded them to Archive, which immediately identified it. It was a spare board that should have been in the electronics rack in the main antenna transmission sentinel. The transmitter required sixteen similar boards, and also carried two spares, of which this should have been one. What could Avalos possibly have been doing with it? Why remove a spare and then hide it away in this elaborate manner? Removing it wouldn't affect the equipment in any way. He must have wanted it for some purpose, but it was simply stored here and not connected to anything. What had he been planning to do with it?

I reassembled the box, making sure each layer was sealed properly, and was about to close the lid when I realised I had forgotten to put the notebook back. I picked it up and flicked through the blank pages again. Something caught my eye: the paper was strangely patterned. I adjusted the lighting, having it scan through its spectrum to see if the pattern was clearer in a narrower frequency band. Suddenly the pages popped as the light came up through the ultraviolet range. I set the light and took another look at the book. The pattern seemed to be random numbers but on one page, near the back, the numbers were clearly arranged into two columns, one of which was a count up from one to five thousand, and the other a random number between one and four hundred or so. It looked to me like a code reference table. Perhaps the first column referred to the days of our voyage and the second to the pages of another book, allowing the generation of a form of coding that varied for each day of the voyage. Avalos could have used it to encrypt messages somehow, perhaps hiding them inside innocuous personal communications? Maybe it was time to inform others of my findings. But who? Avalos might not have been acting alone.

I put the notebook back where I had found it, repacked the box, closed the lid, locked the box and returned it to the crate and the crate to the locker. The key went into a space where the table would hide it. My tell-tale hair went back in place and the locker was shut. After packing up the table, returning the head mask, gloves and air cylinder to the fire station and ensuring the cylinder was on recharge, I started to make my way back to the Habitat Ring.

A sudden thought occurred to me as I reached the door. Why hadn't someone notice the missing circuit board from the transmitter sentinel? They would expect to see a full rack. And wasn't that the sentinel that contained the power electronics for the main transmitter, the one that had caused Avalos's death?

I changed direction and made my way to the equipment room behind the main aerial. It felt cold there and the lighting seemed harsh. The room lacked the brightening of Bita's presence. The four black sentinels stood guard over the space, rising from floor to ceiling as though massive pillars supporting an immense weight above.

I opened the outer door of the transmitter sentinel using the panel handle from my tool kit and was about to open the inner screen when I stopped. I didn't want the same thing to happen to me as had happened to Avalos. I connected to Control and set a voice key to prevent the transmitter powering up. Had Avalos done the same? It would have left a record in Archive if he had and perhaps he hadn't wanted anyone to know he'd been here. He must have been aware of the risk because of all the safety notices on the inner screen.

I swung the screen door open, imaged the interior and had Archive check it with the reference image. They matched. There was no missing spare circuit board.

Archive showed me the location of the two spare boards in the rack and identified the slot where it thought the board Avalos had removed was. The edge of the board looked identical to the one in the humidor. I unlatched the board and tried to pull it out. It shifted but somewhat reluctantly because there were some fibres attached to it along the top. I swung the whole rack out and saw that the board was the only one with cables attached. The cables unplugged, allowing me to pull the board out and disconnect it from the back-plane of the rack. It looked quite different from the one I had seen earlier: much simpler. I imaged it and asked Archive to identify it. There was no record and the board had no serial numbers or any other form of identifying marks.

Why had it been attached with extra connections, and where did they go? I began tracing the fibres, which disappeared behind the safety cover over the high power part of the transmitter. I removed the cover, exposing the high-power bus-bars, and discovered one fibre tapped in to the power feed controller, the part that supplied the massive power to the final stage of the transmitter. The other fibre was connected to the primary stage of the receiver circuit, right after the initial amplification of the incoming signal, but before any signal processing was applied. Judging by its design, the circuit board only contained a simple wireless interface and a processing unit. It looked as though Avalos was intending to be able to interfere with both the outgoing transmissions and incoming messages. I was beginning to see how this might work, how Avalos could communicate with someone in Fleet with a similar setup. By tapping into the final stage, anything he added wouldn't be noticed by us. It would be picked up by the Fleet, including by the ships he wasn't interested in, unless they were all in it together which seemed unlikely. But what if his equipment modified the signal in someway that no one else was looking for, such as a mild amplitude-modulation? The data rate would be slow but that might not matter. Avalos's could inject his messages by slightly modulating the power output of our transmitter. An accomplice, on one of the Fleet ships equipped with the same kit, could pick the message out while everyone else remained oblivious. Avalos could receive messages from his accomplice in the same way, by tapping in to their unprocessed incoming signal.

Was it simply bad luck that Avalos had been fiddling with the power circuitry at the moment when the transmitter had been turned on, or had someone known what he was up to and wanted to stop him? They could have confronted him with the evidence: surely there was a security camera in here that would have filmed what he was doing. But then what would have happened? Realistically it would have been impossible to imprison him for the remainder of the voyage. The mission would never have survived the disruption. His death had been very convenient for the mission. Either a tragic accident or suicide. No one had questioned it. I was now regretting my investigation. If his death hadn't been entirely accidental then maybe mine could be arranged too, if it was felt to be jeopardising the mission. Poor old Menem, he was under such strain recently…

Carefully closing up the sentinel and deactivating my safety key, I left the room as I had found it, cold and inhospitable, and made my way back to the Habitat Ring.

4024, 23:50

Emerging through the door from the keel access tube into the dimly lit corridor, I turned towards my apartment.

A soft voice behind me asked: 'Working late, Menem?'

I jumped in surprise and turned to see someone standing there, a small figure leaning against the wall, looking straight at me: it was Sahko.

'Gosh, I nearly had a heart-attack.'

'Guilty conscience?'

There was a twinkle in her eye and I noticed that she was dressed like a cat-burglar, wearing black gloves to go with her soft black polo-neck pullover, black jog pants and black running shoes.

'No, not at all.' I thought it was best to say as little as possible. I should have thought up an alibi before I had gone. It was too late now to invent a good one.

She came towards me into the light. 'Let's go to Engineering and have chat, better than out here.' I felt a trickle of sweat down my spine. If she had disposed of Avalos then she probably knew how to do the same to me.

'Look, Sahko, I'm rather tired, couldn't it wait?'

She gave me one of her steely stares: 'No, Menem, it can't anymore.'

I was trapped, unable to stall, sighed and led the way to Engineering. She sat down in a chair and invited me to sit in the one beside her. It didn't feel like a choice.

'You've been in Avalos's apartment and in his locker in storage.' She might be guessing and I could bluff a denial, but I was too slow, too obvious. 'What did you find?'

I decided to lay all, well nearly all, my cards on the table. 'Did you know Avalos was a smoker?'

'No, but I'm not altogether surprised. Tell me more.'

'There's a beautiful box in his storage locker that was locked when I looked in there before. Today I found a key in his apartment which opened it. A label inside describes it as something called a humidor, designed specially to preserve an organic leaf based drug in the form of tightly rolled cylinders which, I discovered, are called cigars: addictive, toxic, carcinogenic. Judging by how many are left and how many consumed, my guess is that Avalos planned to take one a month for the duration of the voyage.'

'Well done. No-one else had managed to find that key. As I said, I'm not surprised. I had found out that he consumed milder drugs. No big deal. Those 'cigars' you found aren't quite as toxic as you imagine, although they certainly increase the risk of cancer. If he was only consuming one a month then he would be very unlucky to die from them. He was a spacer and a risk taker anyway and he volunteered for a highly speculative, and therefore exceptionally dangerous, mission. A few cigars were a long way down the list of risks he took.'

'He was also a sadist,' I said quietly.

Sahko looked directly at me for a long time, searching for something and then said: 'When did you find that out?'

'A week or so ago.'

'So is that what suddenly rekindled your interest in Avalos's death?'

'Partly. I thought the two might be connected.'

Sahko sat back and continued to look intently at me. It was unnerving. I asked: 'So you knew?'

'Yes, I knew. Long ago, before he died, only a couple of months after we left.'

'One of Gunadi's "accidents"?'

'Yingluq and I worked out what was going on. It wasn't difficult: Yingluq had some firsthand experience of his taste.'

'You weren't happy about his manoeuvre around Jupiter either, were you?'

'No, I wasn't. That was completely different: unprofessional.'

'It saved us a lot of fuel and some time.'

'Bullshit.' I was startled by the strength of her reaction. 'That's what Avalos put about, but it wasn't true. We were being pulled by the solar tug at that stage, if you remember, out to the edge of the Solar System. We didn't need a gravity assist from Jupiter: it only added about twelve kilometres per second to our velocity, which as you know maxed out at a hundred and twenty thousand and a mission delta-vee of more than twice that, so we saved less than a tonne of fuel out of a total of eighteen-thousand. More to the point, we didn't need to go anywhere near as close as that to change direction, which we did need to do. Going so close was sheer recklessness. It might make some sense in a racer when you're trying to maximise the Oberth effect, but not for us under steady tug. He might have torn the whole ship apart under the strain.'

A sudden thought crossed my mind. 'The problem with the rotation motors. The one in here had shifted on its mountings. I didn't see what forces could have done that. You've just given me an idea.'

'The Jupiter flyby, the point of maximum 'g'?'

'The motors and gearboxes are heavy and they're mounted on not very strong composite floor panels.'

'Hell. I feared there would be trouble but it had seemed as though we had got away with it. The fire in Engine Control when Main went out?'

'Probably the same cause, although there was something extra there because the motor should have shut down when it overheated. The structural faults might have been caused much later after we hit the object field, by the vibration and shocks from the fuel leakage annihilation and sudden Main shut down. Compounding all that is a manufacturing fault I've found in the two motors I've taken apart so far. Whatever the cause, I need to check all the rotation motors, their mountings and heat sensors.' I was laying it on so that Sahko would have more use for me alive than dead.

'Do that, Menem, and check anything else heavy.'

'I'll ask Ibo if she can take a look around the engine room: there are some big heavy things there. Thinking about it, trouble is more likely to come from odd little masses tucked away that aren't well fixed to the structure and could have shifted: perhaps tanks of liquid, stores or something in the payload. I think we would have noticed any service liquids missing. The risk remains from something on the edge of safety. If we're forced to do some similar manoeuvre on arrival, it might finally tear loose.'

Sahko seemed to sag for a moment, as though she had lost her confidence. 'Please, Menem, do what you can. Heaven knows what we're going to have to do when we get close. I need to have confidence that the ship will hold together when making navigation decisions, it will be hard enough anyway. We might even end up being grateful to Avalos for that extra tonne of fuel.'

'I'll do a thorough check. The ship has sensors everywhere on the structure. We'll look through the strain gauge data for anything that has stretched or moved, and vibration data to see if there are any cracks. The ship will be only one third of the mass when we arrive compared to what we were when we flew by Jupiter with all the fuel consumed since, so the strain on the basic structure will be much less even if we have to execute a high 'g' turn.'

She was still gloomy. 'Yes, a lot lighter in the fuel tanks, but not elsewhere, and also ten years older, bombarded by cosmic rays all that time. No one knows what effect that might have had on the structure.'

'A lot of thought went in to that problem. The outer skin, including the coolant system and surface hydrogen tanks is quite resistant and protects the structure.'

She brightened a bit and stood up. 'Thanks, Menem. I worry.'

'We had best check all the small stuff very carefully. I'll work with Bjorn on it. We'll do a complete review of the structure and all the loaded masses.'

I stood too and looked at her. In that moment she was not the dragon lady but vulnerable, with a temporary crisis of confidence. I took a step towards her and put my arms around her, hugging her. She rested her head against my shoulder and I smelt her fine black hair. We stood for a while like that, supported by each others' warmth. At last I felt her head draw back and she looked up at my face.

'You mentioned something odd on the motor in Engine Control. What did you find?'

I took a step back. Her eyes were hard again.

'The overheat cut out controller was a non-standard device, although it looked similar. I haven't been able to work out why because it melted in the fire. The wire from the overheat sensor on the motor didn't look as though it had been connected inside. The unit did have connections into the engine control system though, and I can't see any reason for those and there is nothing in Archive about anything non-standard there. Possibly the shipyard fitted a piece of test kit and it never got taken out again because it looked so similar to what should have been there.'

'Or someone was planning to seize control of the engines.'

'Wow. That's the sort of thing I usually come up with.'

'Tell me what you found in the antenna control room, Menem.'

'The antenna room?'

'Yes, where you've just spent some time.'

I sat back down again. I had no idea how much she knew. If there was danger to me it was probably most likely to come from being on the wrong side of Sahko. Surely she couldn't be an Avalos accomplice.

There were two other things inside Avalos's humidor. A notebook and a piece of electronics from the transmitter: one of the spare signal-processor boards, simply wrapped up and stored away. I'd no idea why, so I went to have a look to see where it had come from. It had been replaced by another board. Superficially the machine looked untouched.'

'No wonder we couldn't find what he'd been up to. The equipment checked out against the reference images. We assumed he'd been in there for a reason, but we ended up concluding that he hadn't had time to mess with it, or he was checking it out so that he could do something to it later. We thought that he might have wanted to cut our communications link with Fleet at some point. I was worried that he'd planted some kind of bomb in there, but we didn't detect anything when we did a sniffer check. What do you think this other board did?'

'It's connected to the final-stage power supply of the transmitter and the primary-amplification stage of the receiver. It also has a wireless link that would allow anyone with the right access code to load a message into it or read one out. I suspect that the device allowed a signal to be added on top of our communications with Fleet using amplitude modulation. It would be low data rate, but neither we nor anyone in Fleet who wasn't looking for it, would be aware that it had been added. In addition, the notebook I found contained what looks to me like a primitive encryption system.'

'Wow. Well done. I don't suppose you know who in Fleet he was trying to communicate with or for what purpose?'

'No to both of those. We could take a very close look at the components used in his board and the manufacturing technique used, but I expect that would be fruitless, given the sophistication of the operation.

Gunadi would have the most expertise in that area. We wouldn't have any record of his incoming or outgoing messages because they would have been extracted before or inserted after our recording process.'

'I don't think we should involve anyone else just yet,' said Sahko quietly but firmly. 'We cannot be entirely confident where loyalties lie.'

'Come on, I would trust everyone on board. After eleven years, surely anyone who started out with divided loyalties will have gone native by now. We've all pulled together recently.'

'We have, but that was necessary to get us to our destination. What happens when we have arrived concerns me.'

'OK. Clearly I don't know what's really going on. I thought we were on a simple mission to set up residence in a new star system. "De-risking humankind", as someone put it, or "reaching for the stars as our manifest destiny". Or simply going on the most exciting adventure imaginable, which is what I thought I had signed up to.'

'We need to be careful, Menem. Others are certainly looking to take advantage. We must keep our eyes open. Avalos was up to something. At the very least he was privately communicating with someone in Fleet. It seems likely that attempts to cheat the game are going on.'

'I'll keep my mouth shut. I voice printed a safety key for the transmitter because I didn't want to be fried like Avalos. Won't Gunadi notice that?'

'Only if she looks for it. That will be interesting in itself. I'll be watching to see if anyone does a search.'

'Didn't Avalos print a safety key?'

'No. We checked that. Presumably he didn't want it to show up in the system. He can't have expected the transmitter to come on at that time of day.'

'Why did it?' I asked innocently.

'We had recently passed the first relay satellite and were beginning to conduct communication tests with it.'

Her answer was glib, as though well prepared. It was not entirely convincing: why use full power in the transmitter when we were so close to the satellite?

'It is possible he had already sent or received a test message as he'd finished wiring up his board. He might have used his personal communicator to interact with the board. I haven't seen his communicator, but maybe I could check it.'

'Ibo had a good look at it and found nothing.'

'Ibo? Why not Gunadi?'

'Gunadi would have been at least as competent but her loyalties were in question. Ibo's weren't.'

'You knew Ibo was an Avalos sceptic then?'

'You aren't the only one who talks with the crew.'

'Of course. Although it might be a cover: being a sceptic.' The conversation paused. 'Oh, and another thing,' I continued, 'surely there's a security camera down there. Didn't the footage show Avalos at work on the sentinel?'

'Unfortunately it wasn't aimed in the right direction. He had altered it himself, apparently to record a practical joke he was playing. I can show you.'

Sahko activated a screen and searched through Archive. She found what she wanted remarkably quickly. The screen showed a recording from a security camera pointed at the sentinels. Nothing changed for a while then lights switched on and Avalos came in, dressed in an extraordinary outfit: a long tailcoat, a gold jock-strap and high-heeled shoes. His face was made up like a clown and he had a bow tie, with a rolled up plastic shirt front under it. He mugged for the camera as he swam towards it in zero-gravity and reached out a hand as he came close. The camera image swung wildly and then refocused on the hatch up to the observatory. Avalos swam back and positioned himself beside the hatch and put a finger to his lips to give an exaggerated hush signal to us, the viewers.

Nothing happened for a few minutes except that Avalos gave a few hand gestures to indicate 'hurry up'. Finally the hatch swung open and Bita and Yingluq swam through together, holding hands. Avalos swam behind them, placed a blowout whistle to his lips and blew a blast. Bita and Yingluq leapt apart like a pair of scalded cats, and I had to suppress a laugh. Avalos cracked up and dived around blowing his whistle. Bita and Yingluq turned on him and began beating him with their fists, which he easily warded off. The three disappeared from the camera's view but we continued to hear what was happening. Suddenly Avalos's laughter cut off and he let out a scream. One of the women said: 'Well done' and the other replied: 'That'll teach him'. Sahko stopped the recording.

'I'm guessing he never repositioned the camera,' I said.

'No he didn't. This happened less than six hours before his accident.'

'I'm glad he used some of that time to get changed. I wouldn't want to be seen dead in a costume like that.'

'Shut up, Menem.'

'Sorry.' After a pause, I asked: 'Do you think he played that whole stunt simply to provide an explanation for why the camera wasn't positioned correctly, allowing him to mess with the transmitter without being observed?'

'I assume so.'

'And the camera didn't trigger an alarm when it found it was looking at something other than the reference image.'

'No. He had disabled that function earlier in the day. Quite legitimate while he was working on the navigation equipment down there.'

'It also means that if someone helped him on his way to the next life, they also weren't observed.'

'No one could have used images from that camera to time when to turn on the transmitter.' Sahko's response was fluent, rehearsed one might think.

'Indeed not. They would have needed to set up their own surveillance system, and removed it discretely afterwards, assuming it's not still there.'

'Bit far-fetched, isn't it, Menem? What do you think really happened?'

'He was cheerfully playing practical jokes only six hours before his death, but that could have been a cover to prevent the camera recording his suicide. Possibly someone rumbled what he was up to in the intervening time, and he decided on suicide to prevent his secrets being revealed. But that doesn't seem to fit the character of the man: his only loyalty was to himself. The official line, of an accident due to his foolish playing about with dangerous equipment, seems the most plausible explanation, don't you think? Perhaps he intended it to be part of another prank, as he seemed to be in that mood.'

'I've always thought that.'

'And after all, it's very unlikely that anyone from Fleet is going to come knocking on our door asking how their spy so inconveniently died.'

'I think that's unlikely.'

'It might be unhealthy for me to take matters further or to spread speculation.'

'Indeed.'

'It must be much too late to listen in using Avalos's kit. We let Fleet know almost immediately that Avalos had died so his contact would have stopped sending long ago.'

Sahko nodded in agreement. 'If Avalos had a second here they are unlikely to use that means of communications. They would surely have assumed it was compromised on his death.'

'Perhaps you could leave it to me to tidy up a few loose ends: swap back Avalos's board for the transmitter's spare and put the security camera in the transmission room back in to position, if someone didn't do that long ago.'

'That would be kind. Good to keep the ship in order.'

'You've had help from Massoud I gather. He led me to Avalos's locker on your instructions.'

'He and I go back a long way. I once helped him out of a jam and he has been loyal to me ever since. We served together on previous ships. He was Egyptian Special Forces at one time. Did you know that?'

'No I didn't. I have a lot of time for Massoud myself.' I wondered if that was true about the Special Forces, or was she trying to intimidate me?

'Good. We'll leave it there then?'

'Yes. If anyone asks, an accident is the only possible explanation.'

'That is the interest of the mission.'

'The mission comes first with me.'

We fell silent and I studied Sahko. Bold and vulnerable. It was a powerful combination. We both stood and looked at each other, wary, assessing. Awkwardly, I went over, looked down at her, brought my head close to hers and kissed her lightly on the lips. We breathed together and she pecked my lips with hers, then brought her hand up and, leaning back, wiped my lips with her fingers as though removing a trace of something. She smiled softly up at me.

'Thank you, Menem.'

'For you, Sahko,' and I hugged her tightly, but she gently pushed me away. She stepped back and walked to the door, turning there as she opened it to look at me once again. Her face was radiant and there was a halo of light from the corridor around it. She smiled, victorious, and disappeared.

I stood still for a long time, hanging on to what had happened, trying to work out if I was the mark in some deeper game, and if so what the game was. Ultimately it must be about who ends up controlling this star system. It seems as though the mission might be hardball, and not the cooperative venture it was billed as. I might be an instrument, being manipulated by Sahko. Actually, I decided, I didn't care, as long as it kept me in her orbit. Perhaps she hadn't been aware of this deeper level when we had set out, and had only begun to piece it together later. Gunadi was now in play, but was she pawn, pawn promoted to queen or always a queen, and of what colour?

I went slowly out of Engineering, across to my apartment and to bed.

Mission Day 4025

4025, 08:00

I had slept badly: disturbed by nightmares dominated by a close up of Avalos's clown face, leering at me. Awake I was able to focus on the good: the certainty that my relationship with Sahko had at last moved on, with luck in a positive direction. Jazz wasn't there, she must have sensed that her companionship wasn't needed. I stretched lazily, got up and went to the refresher, even briefly taking the cold needle shower treatment for a change, which woke me properly and left my skin glowing.

Bjorn and Agyei were in the refectory when I arrived, eating silently together. I ordered breakfast and they beckoned me to come over and sit with them.

'Sleep well?' Bjorn asked.

'Fair to middling,' I replied and then glanced up at the screen showing the speed clicking down at its steady pace.

'You seem cheerful this morning,' said Agyei. 'Any special reason? Have a special night?'

'I am in a good mood. The ship seems to have held together overnight, which is always encouraging. You both look well too.'

'We're both fine, thank you. I slept easily, but Agyei was a bit disturbed.'

'Bit early for something to be moving around isn't it?'

'I had a touch of morning sickness, but it wasn't bad. Oh, as you're here: I've done some analysis of the dust that was in the equipment bay here. It's almost certainly composite, and it most likely was created by panels or structural elements rubbing against one another.'

'That would be consistent. I'll have a more detailed look in that bay sometime today.'

'What do you mean by 'consistent'?' Bjorn asked.

'The trouble with the rotation motor in Engineering was caused by the motor and gearbox shifting, actually tearing away from the panel on which they're mounted. It would take a lot of force to do that. The damage might have been a result of the fuel leak explosion and related vibration, but the time the ship was subject to the most serious force was the nice little turn we made around Jupiter. That might have disturbed quite a few things. It's possible that machinery mounts in here got distorted by the same means. Two parts of the ship might now be grinding against each other, producing the dust.'

'Phew,' said Agyei. 'It makes sense as a hypothesis, but the implications are rather alarming. Other things may have been torn adrift that we haven't noticed.'

'Come on, that turn was over ten years ago and we've survived so far,' said Bjorn, but clearly he too was disturbed by the implications. 'Wouldn't the structural sensors have shown up anything wrong by now?'

'We would certainly expect so and we need to check that out. I'll ask Gunadi to run a sensor check. After the trouble we had with the water tank sensors not even being switched on, I've lost a bit of faith in them. Why don't we see if Gunadi is around and can join this conversation?' I activated comms, and seeing that Gunadi was up, called and invited her over. 'She's on her way. What is most concerning is not the structure of the ship but how small, concentrated loads are attached.'

'Payload,' said Bjorn. 'I'll need to check that nothing has shifted. There are a lot of small masses in the machinery. Goodness knows how to start looking for trouble amongst that lot.'

'I think I would like to check out the lifeboats first,' said Agyei. 'What if one of the launchers has become detached or distorted?'

'OK, before we start getting too panicked about this, let's think it through. Who do we need on this problem?' I asked.

'We've the right people here I think, plus Gunadi. Others will need to be included like Ibo for the engines, Hyun and Massoud for their bits,' said Agyei.

'We need to let Sahko know,' added Bjorn.

'Sahko knows about this issue. I thought of it while having a conversation with her last night.'

Bjorn and Agyei looked at each other and Bjorn said: 'You had a conversation with Sahko last night?'

'No wonder you looked so cheerful this morning,' laughed Agyei.

'Don't get the wrong idea people. It was strictly business.'

'Oh yeah?'

'Yeah. Strictly.'

'Business makes you happy does it?'

'We had a polite, normal, adult, business discussion. I was happy that we were able to do so.'

'Right.'

'Adult?'

'I got that too.'

'Shut up you two. Ah, here's Gunadi.'

She looked cheerful as she came in. 'Hi, everyone.'

'Have you had breakfast?' I asked.

'Don't usually have any, but coffee would be good. So what can I help with?'

Bjorn smirked. 'Menem had an "adult" conversation with Sahko last night.' Agyei smiled, Gunadi did not.

I hastily leapt in. 'What he means is that I had a discussion with Sahko last night about the state of the ship.' Gunadi stopped frowning but still looked serious. 'I've developed a hypothesis that our close encounter with Jupiter on the way out may have over-strained some parts of the ship, added to by our recent engine trouble. In particular, this may have resulted in some of the rotation motors shifting on their mounts.'

'Jupiter was a long time ago and we haven't seen any other problems,' said Gunadi. The other two kept silent and watched us. Gunadi's coffee arrived.

'True, but we had done only one, controlled, gentle rotation each way since then, before our most recent mishap. You no doubt remember we had some quite severe vibrations when the fuel pipe got hit and Main went out and spin-up was at maximum speed. I found that the rotation motor and gearbox in Engineering had broken away from the structure and I've had trouble detaching two other motors from their mounts. The motor in Engine Control overheated which could have been caused by overloading if it had shifted. The other motor I've dealt with is the one in here and the void contains a lot of dust. Agyei says it is composite and may be created by two parts of the structure grinding together.'

'OK, three data points looks bad, though not necessarily anything to do with our close encounter with Jupiter, which, as I said, was a long time ago.'

'It was when the ship came under greatest stress: the highest 'g' we've done, way above normal for freighters like this, and we were fully loaded with fuel at the time and being pulled by a solar tug.'

'It's possible. So what?'

'Well I'm concerned that other heavy bits of equipment may have strained their attachment points.'

'Especially in the payload,' put in Bjorn.

'But we don't have any immediate cause for alarm: none of the structure sensors has indicated trouble,' said Agyei.

'We did find that the clean water load sensors had never been activated,' I said.

'OK, so you want me to do a structural sensor check? I could see if everything is working and look for any anomalies, even if they haven't yet triggered an alarm.'

'Yes, please, Gunadi.'

'OK, but it won't tell you anything about some small scale stuff, such as a motor in the payload coming loose.'

'No,' said Bjorn. 'We'll have to set up a review of the ship loading, but before trying anything we were thinking of ways to prioritise, to find the things that are most likely to be near their limits.'

'Patterns?'

'Yes,' said Agyei. 'Would it be possible to devise an algorithm to look through the entire ship's plans, including the payload, and see which items are most likely to have come under excessive strain during the Jupiter encounter and our recent trouble?'

'I would need much more to go on than that. A search algorithm could be set up to go through all the loadings, but a much more specific task would need to be defined to be able to tell it what to look out for.'

I thought for a moment. 'We'll do some work to specify the conditions we're concerned about such as objects masses and structural attachment specifications. For example, the system could look up the mass of the rotation motors and gearboxes, the method of attachment to the structure and the strength of the materials used for the fixings. It could then calculate what force would be required to do damage and see how that would compare with the forces they have experienced. We could look at all the rotation motors and see if they were equally stressed or if only some of them were, maybe because of their different positions relative to the forces involved. Archive will have a record of how the Ring was positioned during the Jupiter manoeuvre and the engine shut down. It wasn't spinning on either occasion because we were accelerating or decelerating at those times. All this might give an algorithm some parameters to use to assess whether something might have become overloaded or not. The motors didn't come adrift completely, so that must set something of a suitable starting point: the position and force vectors for each. Anything that experienced more overloading than they did should be checked first.'

'That might be a start. I can set up a pattern recognition algorithm if you can give me the detailed search criteria. I'll need to search the literature to see if anyone has tried such a thing before. Otherwise there may be a lot of trial and error.'

'I don't see a huge hurry on this. What I'm most concerned about, and Sahko is too, is that everything is solidly fixed when we begin serious manoeuvring and entering orbit.' Gunadi frowned at the mention of Sahko's name. 'We've no idea at the moment what manoeuvres we'll have to execute. The ship could come under a lot of strain if we have to do anything sharp. If something came loose it could tear a hole in its side.'

'We need to have time to fix any problems before we get to that point,' said Bjorn.

'Definitely,' I said. 'How about we aim to get this done in the next seven days?'

'That should be possible, if you can get me the initial data on the rotation motors in the next couple of days to set the parameters for the search. You'll also need to help me with the structural engineering aspects.'

'Either Menem or I can help you with that,' said Agyei. 'We have to inspect all the rotation motors first, today if at all possible.'

'I haven't reviewed my priority task list for today,' I said. 'There's the mimic head to fix, but I assume Hyun can do most of that. I need to talk to Ibo about the engines and inspecting the structure in the engine room. That's where a lot of the biggest masses are concentrated.'

'The fuel tanks are fairly empty now,' said Bjorn. 'We could shift fuel around if that would help. Rearranging payload wouldn't be so easy.'

'Gunadi, presumably you've quite a lot on with navigation modelling.'

'Minogue and Sahko prepare the model designs and the datasets, but occasionally they call on me to implement a new version, restructure the existing models, add some new piece of analysis, or create a new visualisation. It's all simple stuff. However, they're talking of creating a whole new model of the system which might need a different design of analytics core. There's also the stuff I'm doing with Bita on the object field pattern, but that's low priority. Bita will be disappointed if it slides too far.'

'Can you at least take a look at this today, set up the literature search you talked of, and see if you think a week is a realistic timescale to get a result?'

'I'll take a look and let you know later today. Anything else?'

'No, I think that's about it. Thanks for coming over, Gunadi.'

'Sure.' She got up and smiled shyly at me, nodded to the other two and left.

Agyei and Bjorn looked at each other. 'I think she's fond of you, Menem,' Agyei said.

'I thought everyone was.'

'Not like that. Be careful, Menem.'

'Oh dear. Seriously?'

'Seriously.'

'Surely not.'

'Indeed. So you're not fond of her?'

'Well sort of, yes, I like her. I think she has had a hard life, a troubled life. I only learned that recently.'

'A bit slow.'

'You knew?'

'Well I know a bit at least. I thought everyone did.'

'Even I've heard enough to know she's troubled, and we all know she can be obsessive,' said Bjorn quietly.

'You think she's fond of me?' I asked.

'Oh yes,' said Agyei firmly.

'What do you think I should do?'

'Run away,' suggested Bjorn.

'Ha, ha.'

'Don't encourage her.' said Agyei. 'Try not to be alone with her, especially not in an apartment. Speak to Bita if it becomes a problem.'

'What about Sahko?'

'Tell her at the first opportunity. It wouldn't be good for you if she finds out some other way.'

'Couldn't you do it for me? You could say I asked you to.'

'No.'

'Bjorn?'

'No.'

'Oh dear.' I sat in silence for a while. 'It started out as such a good day.'

'Bad luck, Menem.'

'You're laughing, both of you.'

'No we're not. Well not much. Hardly at all.' They were both definitely laughing now.

'Fine friends you two are.'

'Who is this chap, do you know him?' Agyei asked Bjorn.

'No, not at all. I might have seen his feet sticking out from under a piece of machinery once, but that's it. Nothing to do with us, officer.' They both giggled. What had started as a glorious sunny day had suddenly turned into yet another heavy overcast.

'You two seem to have nothing better to do than laugh at me. I have work to do.' I stood up.

'Come on, Menem. Poor old you, just when things were getting better. Bjorn and I will help.'

'Sure buddy, we'll do what we can. No idea what though.'

'Maybe you could divert Gunadi's attention.'

'Careful Bjorn,' said Agyei. 'There are limits to what I'll allow.'

'I wasn't suggesting that, although it is an idea.'

'No.'

'OK, I won't ask you to involve her in a ménage. Trouble is there aren't many spare men floating around. Minogue? Massoud?'

'Minogue is multitalented.'

'I don't want to manipulate Gunadi, I only want her to cool off, if what you say is true.'

'It's true all right.'

'Can we keep her busy with work and could you guys do most of the communicating with her? It might be best if I avoided being alone with her for a while, as you suggested.'

'That's a bit more sensible,' said Agyei. 'We'll do what we can. No, I'll do what I can. What if I take on the communication role for our little investigation into the damage done by our close encounter with Jupiter or whatever?'

'You don't trust me then?' said Bjorn sweetly.

'Nope,' said Agyei firmly, but they smiled at each other. She let Bjorn kiss her on the cheek and she patted his face.

'Careful, Bjorn,' I said. 'Maybe Gunadi prefers girls.'

'I think we all know what Gunadi prefers,' said Agyei.

'And he's dead.' I said. 'Maybe that was when it started.'

'What?' asked Bjorn.

'I went to thank Gunadi for some kit she had given me for the Wayclear repair. We got talking about her story, and I found out about her and Avalos. I'd no idea. When she told me something of her history I was sympathetic.'

'Sympathetic? You didn't?' said Agyei.

'No, no, I, err, I expressed my sympathy for what had happened to her. Her life story, not good.'

'I knew that asking around about Avalos was going to cause trouble, but I didn't expect that it would be this sort. You're an idiot Menem, why didn't you let sleeping dogs?'

'I was worried.'

'A bit late,' said Agyei.

'What about?' said Bjorn.

'I might be next.' Agyei and Bjorn looked at each with incredulity and then started laughing.

'I knew you were an idiot, Menem, a lovely idiot of course, but I didn't realise how big an idiot you are,' said Agyei.

'Killer on the loose, out to get you, Menem?' Bjorn asked. 'Taken their time to hunt you down haven't they?'

'I wanted to know, that's all.' They shook their heads. 'Enough. If you think I'm an idiot then I probably am. Don't laugh too hard when you find me in a pool of blood with a knife sticking out my back.'

'They would be Sahko's fingerprints on the knife, I should think,' said Agyei.

'Or they could be Gunadi's,' added Bjorn.

'Maybe the whole crew enjoyed taking a turn with the knife.'

I looked up at the ceiling and around the walls. The velocity meter was still counting down steadily. There was also a clock ticking away my life. I noticed the time. 'Gosh, I've got to go. I'm supposed to be teaching the children this morning.'

'Paranoia classes?' suggested Agyei.

'Ha, ha. Can we sort out who is doing what later, on the rotation motor business?'

'I'll start on that and post any findings in a project log page, so you can see what I've done when you finish your stint with the children,' said Agyei.

'I'll dig up the records on our Jupiter flyby and get the data on the ship's orientation and stress loads,' said Bjorn. 'I want to review the payload to see if there's anything obvious that should be checked first.'

4025, 09:05

I went round to the children's room. Ibo was telling them some story from her home in Kenya. Perhaps Alice had heard it before because she was sketching, but Kent and Sky were fully engaged. Joko was sitting beside Ibo and seemed to be paying attention too. It was a challenge, if not impossible, to find anything that would engage all four of them at once. Often I got them to split up and do something each at their own pace and level. There were a huge amount of teaching resources available, but I tried to vary my sessions by going on tours to Engineering or some other part of the ship, to add some real-world relevance to what they were learning. Once again I wondered about how real-world anything was in this highly restricted environment. They had known nothing else, of course.

Ibo pointedly looked at the clock to tell me that I was late, handed Joko to me and left. I asked the children what they had been doing with Ibo and if they remembered what I had been teaching, last time I was with them. We had done a bit of geography and history, they told me, and I remembered discussing where all the crew came from. We had used a globe of the Earth to find the countries and discuss their differences and similarities. Sometimes I had talked of my childhood: my parents home where I had been born, in Uruguay, what it had been like growing up in the high Andes of Chile, while my father worked at the Atacama telescope complex, and how that had inspired me to go into space.

I often brought along a piece of equipment I was working on, to explain something of its function or to use it as a starting point for a problem-solving session. Part of the time I spent with them was supervising their formal lessons: sitting with each in turn as they were taken through something on a private screen, each child working at their own level and pace. We talked afterwards and tried to relate what they were learning to each other, the crew, the ship and our mission. Their life experience was so confined it was always a struggle to get them to think of anything beyond the ship.

Today, I decided to use the help that they had provide to solve the missing water problem as a starting point to talk about water and its importance to life. It was a subject that easily filled the two hours I spent with them, and would provide many branching topics for discussion and interesting experiments that could keep us going for many more sessions.

Yingluq came in long before I had exhausted the subject. I tried not to notice how well toned she was and how well her clothes fitted. I was having enough trouble with women for the moment. Yingluq was going to do sport, exercise being another important aspect of ship life. How easy it was to sit and do nothing for much of the time and let our bodies waste away. She liked to mix it up and try every type of sport. She talked about the Olympic Games going on, showing them some extracts, and about how the athletes trained both physically and psychologically. I know that at least once Yingluq had taken them into some zero-'g' environment and had shown its effect on trying to play familiar games. It had resulted in a lot of laughs and a few bruises, I had gathered.

I returned to the refectory for a coffee. Only Massoud was there, studying a screen. He looked up and waved me over. I took a look, reappraising him in the light of recent revelations. Maybe his un-athletic and uncomplicated demeanour was something of an act: he moved with a certain grace. I was glad we were on the same team.

My coffee arrived quickly and Massoud finished what he was reading.

'Come in for refreshment?' he asked.

'I've been with the children for the past couple of hours. We were talking about water.'

'A subject you know something about.'

'Don't you start. Yes, I did begin with talking about the leak, mainly because it was something the children had helped with. It led in to a discussion of the importance of water on the ship, and then broadened out to the importance of water to life.'

'I do something similar sometimes: start with a simple food like bread, get them to help me make some and in the process talk about the ingredients and where they used to come from, progressing on to all sorts of topics like fermentation, protein synthesis and agriculture, leading in to geography and history.'

'Keeping Joko occupied is a challenge still: she's too young yet to engage with academic subjects.'

'She seems to enjoy making things in the kitchen, and has come on a long way in the past year. Anyway, tell me about you. You seem to have sorted out the rotation problem.'

'All the sections are currently rotated properly, but we think there may be a systemic structural issue with the rotation motor and gearbox mounts. It seems likely that they couldn't really cope with the sharp turn around Jupiter.'

'That was long ago. The trouble could be due to the vibration when we got hit by the object field.'

'That's possible too. Something caused at least one of the motors to shift and the Jupiter encounter was when they were under greatest stress.'

'So once again Avalos takes the fall.'

'He might actually have done us a favour. We may have to pull even sharper turns than that when we manoeuvre into orbit. At least we're now aware of potential trouble, making plans to identify vulnerable components, and fix any weaknesses.'

'Ah, so that was presumably what Agyei was investigating in here a while ago. She had her head in one of the voids for quite a while. It would be good to check the rest of the ship too if it turns out that this is a problem. Some of the fermentation vats in Processes are heavy for example, and it would get very messy if one of them came adrift, as well as spoiling dinner.'

'Bjorn is worried about the payload.'

'Lots of massive machinery there too, I imagine. You certainly don't want to get into more trouble, do you Menem?'

'No, not more trouble.'

'I heard.'

'News travels fast. What have you heard?'

'That someone may have got a bit of a crush on you.'

'News does travel fast, but in this case it doesn't seem likely.'

'Likely: no. True: yes.'

'You think so?'

'I've seen her looking at you.'

'Really.'

'I'm afraid that it is true. It complicates matters for you, I gather, because you do not quite reciprocate the lady's feelings.'

'I like Gunadi, but I've no passion for her. I have feelings only for Sahko.'

'Also not reciprocated.'

'May not be true.'

'Really? Hope springs eternal. Has there been a breakthrough, a thawing?'

'A little thawing. I have hope.'

'Well congratulations, my friend, that's great news. However, this other matter definitely complicates things.'

'Yes, indeed. Any advice you may have to untangle this "complication" would be appreciated. You don't fancy Gunadi by any chance?'

'Sadly no. She is intriguing and I like her, although that's not always easy to do. She's often not very communicative but clearly very clever with the analytics. She has helped me with protein synthesis many times and we've spent much time discussing ways of modelling biochemical reactions and such like. Also, we both are fond of abstract games and have spent many happy hours battling each other remotely. She can get a bit over-enthusiastic, obsessive one might say.'

'Oh dear. Well any advice you can offer would be greatly received. How did I get in to this mess?'

'You've many talents it seems. I'll think on your problem. My only advice at this time is to talk to Sahko before she finds out from some other source. Maybe she can help you overcome this little difficulty. I do not want to see any one of you hurt by these things. It will not help the ship or our mission.'

'Thanks, Massoud. You're right; I must talk to Sahko as soon as possible. I need to think what I'm going to say first. I'm going to spend a bit of time clearing my head by doing what I'm supposed to be doing: fixing the ship.' I got up to go.

'Don't spend too long thinking, my friend. Bita is someone else you could call on for help.' I felt another pang of guilt. I mumbled an acknowledgement and left, wondering how much Massoud talked to Sahko. I called up Agyei on my way back to Engineering to find out how she had got on.

'I started by investigating in the refectory,' she said. 'It was a devil to find the source of the dust problem, but I'm now convinced that the frame on which the gearbox panel sits is binding on the non-rotating part, generating the dust. Even someone walking around in the refectory is enough to create rubbing there. I've found one fractured joint in the structure, but the rest must have only creased slightly. Ideally, we should do an X-ray investigation in there to look for micro-cracks in the composite panels. I've appended a suggested fix to the file. Take a look and let me know if you've any other ideas. '

'OK. I'll have a look at what you suggest. I doubt this is a life threatening problem, but it would be good to secure the motor mount better. If that dust escapes it's unlikely to be healthy eating or breathing.'

'We need to stop it being created at the very least. I've also had a look at the rotation motor and gearbox in Engine Control. That one has a similar problem to what you found in Engineering. The gearbox mounts are worse if anything, although oddly the motor seems not to have become displaced which would explain why you didn't notice a problem with the mount when you swapped over the motors. That motor must have come under massive load from the displaced gearbox and if it was a bit marginal itself it would explain why it overheated so badly.'

'So now three of the rotation motor mounts are definitely faulty.'

'I've also checked the one in Chemistry and there are noticeable signs of the panel buckling where the motor is bolted to it. It's less bad than the others, but still needs fixing. That's as far as I have got. I was going to look in Science next, but Minogue is in conference with Sahko and Bita, so I won't disturb them for now. I'll go on to Navigation.'

'Thanks Agyei. I'll start in Robotics and then Printers and then work back the other way. Do you have time to continue with this?'

'Yes, for another hour or so. I've some things to do early in the afternoon and then can get back to it. We really need to work out how bad this is to be able to give Gunadi parameters for the whole ship review. That could take time in itself, and the more I think about it the more difficult it seems. If we can get anything out of it, we'll have to check everything it identifies and fix any problems, or potential problems. Do you think we need to ask Sahko what maximum 'g' she thinks we might pull when coming in to the system? It will be her call.'

'It may come down to us telling her what maximum 'g' the ship is able to withstand, and she can then plot a course accordingly.'

'I hope we have that luxury.'

'Me too. OK, thanks, Agyei. Back to work for me.'

'Before you go, what about the Processes Ring?'

'Grief. Let's concentrate on the Habitat Ring for now and see what we get.'

'Agreed. Talk later, Menem.'

I called Hyun to tell him I wanted to check the rotation motors in Robotics and Printers, and asked when would be convenient. He told me that he was working on the mimic head in Printers, but that I could go ahead anytime provided I didn't create any dust. I picked up a containment tent and some other gear from Engineering and went next door to Robotics. It took only a moment to see that there was clearly a problem with the motor mounts in this section too. The motor hadn't shifted but there was considerable tearing of the composite panel to which it was attached. At some point the motor must have wrenched the panel and torn it but then fallen back in to position again. Another bang might tear the motor away completely.

After taking some pictures, I made a note in the project log and went back to Engineering. I decided to have lunch alone to avoid having any more embarrassing conversations, or running the risk of encountering Gunadi or Sahko before I was prepared.

A note appeared on the project log from Agyei showing that she had found the motor mountings stressed but not broken in Navigation. It looked as though we would have to reinforce all the motor mounts. I messaged Agyei asking if she agreed.

Hyun messaged about the mimic head, suggesting I drop by to discuss the best way to do the rebuild. I messaged back to say that I would come by in fifteen minutes after I had finished a few things.

Hyun was still in Printing when I went round, bent over one of the machines.

'I'm going to need your help with this printer too, I think,' said Hyun, pointing at one of his machines. 'Something went wrong and the print head overheated. Now it's solid with burnt thermoplastic. There's a spare and so I'll swap it out, but this one will need taking to pieces. I don't know how it happened and I'm worried that the same thing will happen to the replacement. We don't carry any more spares, and they have a lot of fine parts which take a long time to print.'

'Before you set that printer going again, I'll take a look at it. Maybe something got out of alignment and jammed. It shouldn't overheat though. How are you getting on with the mimic head?'

'I've made all the parts for it, except the cameras. They are the problem, as we discussed before. We don't have any spare sensors of that quality and we don't have the capability to make them.'

'If we don't, we don't. We'll just have to go with something less good. Operating the mimic with the bot-net cameras was quite serviceable.'

Hyun looked miserable. 'I don't like it. It may not be so easy when we are in sunlight. The original sensors gave it tremendous capabilities. They are incredibly broad-spectrum and have the ability to cope with a huge range of light levels: from looking directly at a star at close range to almost pitch-dark. The camera sensors are integrated with the lights too, enabling additional illumination to be automatically provided if the sensors say the scene requires it. Different sensors will require retuning that bit of control software as well. I don't like a sub-optimal solution.'

'Nor do I, but we have to get something to work. We're going to need the second mimic when deploying the payload, and, come to think about it, for setting up the telescope before that. What do we have in the way of spare cameras, and could we use multiple sensors to give the range of capabilities we think we'll actually need?'

'Multiple sensors would be awkward. I suppose we could have some way of switching the sensors behind the optics package, on a carousel for example, but the optics and sensor are usually designed together. There isn't room for multiple optics in each eye position.'

'Let's have a look at what sensors we do have available, or can take from some less important function.'

A search in Archive found thousands of image sensors of all types on the ship, mostly of simple human-eye capability used for monitoring and control, either in fixed positions or embedded in such devices as the service bots and transport carts. There weren't many that had true broad-spectrum capability: a few in the engine section that were part of the safety system and a few embedded in payload equipment. It didn't seem a good idea to raid either. Admittedly the payload ones were not needed for a while, but they would be essential later and it would jeopardise the mission if they got damaged in the mimic. There were some quite similar ones incorporated in equipment used in the chemistry lab: they had the right sensitivity but their spectrum capability was limited to the optical range.

'They look the best we might reasonably use,' said Hyun. 'I'll leave it to you to prise them off Agyei though.'

'She's not usually unreasonable about lending equipment, but I don't know if she's using them at the moment. She could have them back if she needed them later.'

'She'll know that's not true.'

'If she gives them up, do you think we could fit them? The optics would have to be changed.'

'We could print what we need. There are lots of recipes on file for artificial eye optics. Let me check to see if we have something to match those sensors.' Hyun searched in the printer database in Archive. 'Yes, I think we can do that… Checking we have the materials in stock…. Yes, nothing really special… Only small quantities required… They need some fancy polishing and coating, but I should think either you or Agyei have the kit to do that. I'll send you the links to what's needed.'

I pulled up the machine requirements that he had sent me. The finisher would be able to handle the polishing, but the coating had to be done in a vacuum sputtering chamber, which Agyei would have.

'It looks possible, but we're also going to need Agyei's help with the coating process. I better start by talking to her about it. She's been helping me determine the extent of the trouble with the rotation motors.'

'Is it a bigger problem than just a couple of bad motors?'

'We're increasingly certain that all the motor and gearbox mounts aren't very strong and couldn't stand the maximum forces they have encountered. This whole Habitat section was a bit of a last minute thing, lifted from a personnel carrier.'

'My understanding was that the mission was originally going to be robotic, but then someone worked out that random failures would accumulate and not necessarily be fixable by general purpose robots.'

'That and political considerations.'

'None of the four powers wanting to let any of the others be first in the Alpha System.'

'Quite.'

'So going back to the rotation motors, you're saying that at some point their fixings got over stressed.'

'Right.'

'And that would have been? Don't tell me, it had to be when we did that turn around Jupiter.'

'That's our hypothesis, perhaps compounded by the vibrations caused by our encounter with the object field.'

'I'm surprised we haven't noticed something wrong before now.'

'We had only done two gentle changes of spin since Jupiter, acceleration to cruise and cruise to deceleration, until we did the emergency rotation recently. That and the severe vibration may have been enough to break the mounts on at least six of the motors, which is what we've found so far.'

'If it broke those, might other things be damaged too?'

'That thought has occurred to some of us and we're trying to design a way of evaluating where the risk of damage might lie. We've asked Gunadi to see if she can come up with a way of systematically going through every component of the ship and assessing which are at risk.'

'Phew, that sounds like a big task.'

'The difficulty is in structuring the question. We're trying to narrow it down by analysing all the rotation motors, assess the level of damage to each, and review that against the exact position of the ship at the time of the Jupiter fly-by and recent vibrations.'

'Will you assume the vibration affected the whole ship equally?'

'Interesting thought, which I haven't considered. We could review all the strain-gauge and vibration sensor information that Status will have collected at the time. I assume that the vibration would have affected all the motors equally because the forces would have been transmitted via the keel to the Habitat Ring. We do need to check that though. I suppose there could have been some harmonic vibration in the Ring that affected some more than others. In a way I'm less concerned about that than the risk from another high-'g' fly-by. The navigator needs to know how much acceleration the ship can stand before it starts to fall apart. The more room she has for tight turns the better, particularly seeing that we're coming in faster than we had planned.'

'We would all rather the ship didn't come apart on arrival. That would be disappointing.'

'It would.' We paused, contemplating that outcome. 'Back to the mimic head: let me call Agyei and see if we can use her optical sensors.'

I got Agyei on the comms link and talked her through the mimic vision problem and why we thought the most suitable sensors might be in Chemistry. She said that she would have to check what they were used for. I also described the problem of coating the lenses we were proposing making, and she said she was happy to help with that and had the kit for the process. She filled me in on her latest findings with the rotation motors and that she hadn't found any signs of damage in Ops. She signed off saying that she was planning to go on to Comms next and then Analytics.

'What do you think we should do now?' asked Hyun.

'Oh, I should go ahead with making all the parts you can on the basis that she'll agree, after all it will be harder for her to refuse if everything else is made.'

'I'll blame you if she complains.'

'Why not? Everyone else does. If she finds those camera sensors are vital for something we'll just have to go with some lower quality ones. We've plenty of service-bot type spares and they're as good as the bot-net ones we've already used. With more refined optics they'll be serviceable. We can use the other mimic for anything that requires better vision.'

'As we discussed before, I'm most concerned that they don't burn out when we're deploying the payload in bright light. Looking directly at the star from close range could be damaging.'

'There are a couple more mimics packed away in the payload somewhere. We can keep this one for those few occasions when we need all four in action. Anyway, surely we can come up with something to react to light intensity and shield the sensors if it gets too bright and it would have to work over the whole spectrum of both Alpha stars' high energy output.'

'I'll look and see what we have on file. It would also have to be completely transparent in low-light conditions. Maybe that's not such a big deal. There must be lots of designs for such things used in bots, in welding applications for example. OK, I'm coming round to this, we can make it work. I'll do some research and start making parts.'

'I'll leave it to you. By the way, how is Ibo, now that the engine is running smoothly?'

'Oh, she's very happy at the moment. It's quite a relief in some ways that she's cheerful again.'

'But not in everyway?'

'Well she can be demanding.' Hyun seemed to be searching for the right word. 'Exhausting even, when she's so cheerful.'

'That sounds not so bad.'

'I need a rest sometimes, so I come to work.'

'Better than being miserable and, err, cold.'

'Yes, yes, true. May I ask you something in confidence?'

'Of course.' I was agog: Hyun never asked anything related to private matters.

'This business with Agyei and Bjorn.' He hesitated.

'Expecting a baby?'

'It has got Ibo thinking.'

'Ah.'

'What do you think?'

I paused for a while and then said: 'If you both want to, why not? We should be arriving in system long before the baby is due. Once we get there, all being well, we can quickly rearrange things in the Habitat Ring. The children need gravity so if we can't land on a big rock to provide it they will have to live in the spinning rings, but the rest of us don't need to. Humanity needs to expand its population rapidly out here if it is to survive. We have no idea what sort of world these children will be born to, but then that was true of Alice and the other children we already have. Come to think of it, none of us chooses what world we're born in. We simply have to make the most of whatever we find. Who knows how the children of the Alpha System will turn out?'

'You didn't seem very keen when the Agyei announcement came out.'

'I over reacted. But as it was against ship's rules we should have discussed it first and not been bounced in to it.'

'Unlike you bouncing Agyei into letting us have sensors for the mimic head.'

'That's quite different: it's not a ship's rule.' Hyun chuckled sceptically but I continued: 'It also shouldn't have been up to Sahko to make a unilateral decision. I thought that was outside her area of competence as captain.'

'But you've changed your mind?'

'Not about the ship's rules business, although it became clear in the meeting and in conversations I had afterwards that I was in a minority about that.'

'A minority of one.'

I pressed on. 'I was never against Agyei having a child. It's a personal matter for her. But we all have to live within the ship's capabilities, and that doesn't include an unlimited number of children. We couldn't feed, house, educate and otherwise take care of many more on the ship.'

'The ship has a designed capacity for six children and twelve adults.'

'Exactly so, but it's not for one or a few to grab all the child spaces. The rule was one child for each couple.'

'What about Minogue? I don't remember you complaining about the ship's rules when we found out he was the father of Bita's child.'

'No I didn't. I hadn't thought through the consequences at the time and with Avalos gone, well... Actually the rule was framed badly. It should have been one child per woman.'

'That might have left some men out in the cold. I'm sorry, Menem; we all feel for you, especially Ibo. She knows how good you are with Alice and the other children.'

'Good of her to say that. Maybe I am a bit too sensitive on this. I would be delighted if you two decide to have another child. And as you say, I'm very fond of Alice.'

I turned away and examined one of the printers which had a fascinating pattern on its assembly deck.

'Thanks, Menem. It will mean a lot to Ibo not to have to fight you on this, and to me too.'

I talked to the wall. 'You won't have to fight me. You both have my full support. Sorry, must be going now. I'll be back later to look at the broken printer.'

I hastened to the door and went out into the corridor which seemed cold after the heat of the printer room.

After I had left I remembered that I hadn't checked the rotation motor in there. It would have to wait until Hyun had gone. I went back the other way. The children were in their room so I decided not to disturb them either. Next door was Recreation where Bita was working out. I waited and watched while she finished an intense session on an aerobic-trainer machine. Her shoulders flexed in rhythm, her skin glistened, her long legs flowed and her calf muscles stood clearly defined. She had earpieces in so presumably was listening to some music or a motivation coach, but she had noticed me enter in the mirror opposite us.

After a minute she started to wind-down and eventually came to a stop. She took a towel and wiped her face and neck. Her exercise gear was skimpy and skin-tight. She raised one leg straight out, higher than her waist, and placed it on a wall bar. She lifted her arms over her head and folded her torso along her out-stretched leg like a ballerina.

'Come to admire the view, Menem?'

'Magnificent. Such grace, such power, such beauty.'

'Shut up, Menem. What do you want?'

'I came because I need to check the rotation motor in this section. Agyei and I are inspecting them all round the Ring.'

'That's why I came here. Agyei wanted to check out the one in Comms so I decided it was a good moment to exercise.'

'Sorry, I don't want to stop you. Do continue.'

'Won't you find that a bit distracting?' She came over to me, quite close so I could smell her sweat.

'Yes. I mean no.'

'It seems to be a bit of a problem for you, doesn't it?'

'What do you mean?'

'When to say "yes" and when to say "no".'

'I, err, I don't follow.'

'Gunadi.'

'Oh, dear.'

'Oh dear indeed. You've been playing with fire.'

'I, err, I need to get on and fix the motors. I'll come back another time. Don't want to disturb you now. No need.'

I backed towards the door, but she put a hand on my shoulder and dug her fingers in.

'Look me in the face, Menem.'

I did fleetingly and there was real anger there.

'What have I done?'

'You don't love Gunadi do you?'

'Eh? No. I like her, respect her. I really do. I know she's a damaged person and I have been trying to help. Agyei and Bjorn seem to have constructed something on the basis of a single look she gave me. She just admires me, or is grateful that I've taken an interest in her.'

'Agyei and Bjorn aren't the only ones to have noticed the looks she has been giving you recently.'

'Really? Who else? When?'

'Why did you take a sudden interest in Gunadi, Menem? Why has she got the wrong idea about you?'

'I didn't just take a sudden interest in her. I went to thank her for finding some parts for me and we ended up talking about Avalos. That set me thinking about how little I knew about him. I decided to find out what others thought.'

'You wouldn't leave it alone, would you? Now look were it has got you.'

I sighed. 'Maybe I could use some advice on how to get out of this trouble you seem to think I'm in.'

'You certainly could. You need to have a direct conversation with Gunadi. Explain exactly what you do and do not feel for her. Be very clear, Menem. No beating about the bush. Then listen to her response, listen properly. She may shout or cry, but hear what she's saying; she's not as irrational or unstable as you might think. She does get hooked on a line of thought and the only way to break that is to talk directly, calmly, and rationally about whatever that is and explain how others see the situation.'

'OK, yes, I'll… umm, yes.'

'Do it soon, Menem, before a bad situation gets out of hand. If you haven't by midday tomorrow I'll ask both of you to come to a counselling session with me. Actually I think that would be a good idea anyway. Tomorrow at two p.m., be there. I'll invite Gunadi. Better if you talk to her alone first.'

'Oh dear, all right, I'll be there.'

I put my hand on the door pad, ready to make my escape.

'One more thing: talk to Sahko about this, before she finds out from someone else.'

I nodded and pressed the pad, the door slid open and I backed out, Bita's eyes burning me as the door slid closed. Again I felt the cool and quiet of the corridor.

I tried Food Prep next and found Massoud studying intently some samples under a powerful magnifier. He looked as though he didn't want to be disturbed so I pointed to the wall panel and held up my tools. He waved me on. I set up a containment tent around the area and went inside, glad that Massoud didn't want to talk. I'd had enough advice for one day, and I needed to think what I would say to Gunadi. I knelt down and removed the access panel. There were some signs of distress where two of the motor bolt mountings were fixed. It had survived so far but would need reinforcing. Definitely all the motor fixings would need repairs. I took some images and then packed up my gear and disassembled the tent.

Massoud was still engrossed with analysing his samples but looked up briefly as I went to the door. He waved his thumb up and down enquiringly and I gave a hand wave with a bit of a thumbs-down. He shrugged his shoulders and bent to his research.

Next was Medical and I dreaded a similar conversation with Yingluq to the one I'd just had with Bita. Fortunately Yingluq wasn't there but unfortunately the door was locked. I messaged Yingluq to tell her I what wanted to do and she immediately messaged back, granting me access. I let myself in and glanced around. I was already in too much trouble so decided not to look through her system or raid the pharmacy. Not that I had the capability to do either without Yingluq's authorisation. I wondered whether Gunadi could. No system was likely to be safe from her. She could probably look through the medical and personnel files without anyone knowing. Only Ibo had the same skills to set up alarms and false trails in the systems, but I suspected Gunadi would know everything that Ibo could do to try to stop her. Besides Ibo was usually too preoccupied with the engines to be playing games with systems' security. Who knew what games those two might be playing with or against each other? Sahko was almost certainly right to trust Ibo first.

I repeated the setup and test on the motor and found a similar story to the others so made a record and packed up. No one was in Payload so I inspected that one with similar results. I messaged Agyei with my current findings and she messaged back to say that Comms and Analytics were similarly damaged. I let her know that I was going round to the children's room next because they should be in the refectory about now.

Agyei asked about Recreation and I realised that I had made my escape before doing any investigating there. I said I would look at it after doing the children's section. Agyei said she was about to have a break and would do Printers either after supper or first thing tomorrow. I said I would do Science when it was empty. That would cover them all and we could then review our findings.

I went round to the children's room and nobody was there. After moving a few boxes, I examined the motor and gearbox mounts. They were badly torn here too, and it was surprising that they hadn't broken loose. Checking in Recreation, I found Bita had left and no one else was there. A layer of dust covered everything behind the panel, as there had been in the refectory, and the motor and gearbox mounts were torn. I felt tired and not inclined to go back to Science for now. There could well be someone there and I didn't need any more advice.

I decided to eat in my apartment and was making my way when a message arrived from Sahko, asking me to come around to Ops at about eight that evening. That buoyed me up: she wanted to see me. She hadn't said why, but she probably wanted an update on our investigations which she had almost certainly picked up on by now. Of course she could read the project file on Status to know the basics, so she no doubt wanted to get the feelings behind the facts. Perhaps she wanted further discussion of my Avalos discoveries. It could be that she simply wanted to see me. Take it slow, Menem, take it slow.

I thought that it would be best if I had completed the investigation of the motors before then. I checked and found that Minogue was still in Science. We messaged and he replied that he would use it as a good time to go off to the refectory for a meal.

There was some distortion of the motor mounts in Science too, but it didn't look as though the panel had torn. I packed up and was about to go around to Printers when I got a message from Agyei saying that she had checked in there. She had found that she was getting faster at the investigations, now that she knew what to look for and wanted to complete her part today. I messaged back to say that I had found the same, and had completed my half too. That would be something positive I could report to Sahko, if she wanted to discuss the state of the ship.

Back in my apartment, I ordered supper, had a refresh and changed clothes which made me feel less weary. My meal arrived and I sat down to eat, pondering on what I should say, if anything, to Sahko about Gunadi. I wasn't sure if the others were right about what Gunadi thought of me. Sure, I had become more friendly with her over the past week, but that was because she had only recently opened up her history to me. Anyone's sympathies would have been aroused by that. After that, it was not surprising that she had been friendlier towards me in response, as she had, now I came to think about it. As to things going any further between us, well, I had rejected her sort-of advances made in the heat of the moment. A temporary misunderstanding, that's all, soon smoothed over. Now we had a good professional relationship, colleagues. That was it, I could say that to Sahko, would say it, in case any unfounded rumours reached her that there was anything more to my relationship with Gunadi.

Talking with Gunadi seemed like a good idea, to let her know that there was some gossip going around linking us, and it would be helpful if we both could honestly deny it, to stop any further tittle-tattle. Open and honest. I would speak to Gunadi soon. Perhaps not tonight because I was going to see Sahko in a short while, but tomorrow morning at the latest, provided there were no emergencies.

At a quarter to eight, I got up and cleaned my teeth, brushed my hair, checked myself over in the mirror and clipped a few stray hairs. I practiced smiling sweetly. Not good: it always ended up looking forced. I checked my nails were clean and thought about aftershave but decided that was a bit too obvious. One final check in the mirror: no food stains or crumbs? No. Time to go then. Bit early still, it only takes one minute to walk around to Ops. Might get delayed on route so better set out early. OK, hair still in order?

I walked slowly, trying not to skip or trip. There was no one about so I got to Ops early. I kept going and realised I was about to pass Gunadi's apartment so turned around and went back. It was still too early as I passed Sahko's door again. I walked on past Avalos's door, the source of many of my and others troubles, now safely disposed of, to trouble us no more, except in our nightmares. Past Minogue's door, the ship-father, I thought bitterly, then Agyei's door, mother and soon to be double-mother, then Ibo's door, mother and intending to be double-mother. I looked at the time and realised I had gone too far. It was already eight. Turning around, I hurried back.

Ops' door slid open as I came up to it. Sahko was facing away looking at a screen, standing in a pool of light in an otherwise dark room. Unusually she was dressed in red, a rich blood-red. A military-cut coat came down to the middle of her thighs, with a high collar fitted tightly round her neck and brilliantly shiny ruby studs gleaming around the coat's belt and on the epaulets. Her hair, short and straight, revealed a little band of neck exposed as she bent forward to examine some detail. Below the coat she had tight leggings that emphasised her slender legs, disappearing into highly polished boots, heavier than her usual style.

'Come in, Menem,' she said in a neutral voice without looking round. The door closed behind me and a light came on above. I watched her long delicate hands reach out and manipulate some information display.

'Hello, Sahko,' I said warmly.

'Tell me about the problems you've found today,' she said to her screen.

I gave a brief summary of what we had found regarding the rotation motors and our plan for identifying any other poorly supported items.

'Thank you for your report.' Sahko stood straight upright but had still not turned towards me. I was a bit disappointed that she was not being more welcoming, but perhaps she wanted to get the professional stuff out the way first. After a minute's silence I started to shift uncomfortably on my feet. Finally she turned round. Her face was devoid of expression, ghostly in the down-light. She stepped out of her illumination and came towards me. I could see the gleam of her eyes: a panther in the darkness.

She arrived close by, under my pool of light. Her face was a mask of stone, her long alabaster neck rising out of the crimson jacket. She fixed me with her eyes, pinning me. She slowly raised one arm and drew it back. My cheek burst with pain and my head recoiled from the blow. I staggered a little, stunned, shocked. My cheek was on fire and I could taste blood from where it had been cut on my teeth.

'You bastard, Menem,' she hissed into my face as she came up close to me.

'What have I done?'

'Gunadi, you bastard.'

My mouth felt as if it was dribbling and I shook my head, which made the ache in my cheek worse.

'I haven't done anything to her. I asked her to help with the structural analysis.'

'Don't play with me, Menem. I know you too well. You've been taking advantage of her, haven't you? You know how vulnerable she is and you've been using her. How contemptible you are, you piece of shit. I'm thinking of throwing you out of an airlock. How could you do it, Menem? Did you think you could get away with this? All your high principles about ship's rules. I'll give you ship's rules, you prick.'

'Wait, I'm sorry, I didn't realise. It was only this morning someone said she had a crush on me. I didn't think it was true. I didn't encourage her.'

'Didn't encourage her? You fucked her didn't you? You dirty, sneaky, lowlife shit.'

'No I didn't, I...'

'Did what? What did you do? Let me tell you something. She came here this afternoon asking if I minded if she had your baby. That's what you wanted isn't it? Don't care who the mother is, just want to keep up in the fatherhood stakes, don't you? That's what you've always wanted isn't it? So you pick on the most vulnerable woman on the ship and talk her in to having your child. You're the lowest form of worm.'

I thought she was going to kick or knee me, but then I noticed her eyes had watered and she turned walked away and sat down again.

'I haven't had intercourse with Gunadi,' I pleaded. 'She can't have my baby. I don't want that, you know I don't. I want a family with you.'

'Too late.'

'It's not too late, Sahko.'

'Yes it is, you bloody liar. She already has a sample.'

'A what?'

'A sample, a phial of your sperm which you kindly donated and which is now safely locked away in Yingluq's freezer awaiting sorting and making ready to fertilise a selected one of Gunadi's eggs. Good luck, Menem, with becoming a father.'

Tears flowed down Sahko's cheeks.

'I didn't give her a sample, I swear it. I don't know how she got that if it's really mine. Maybe she hacked my companion to collect it. She's quite capable.'

A black cloud hove in to view and I thought of the incident a week or so ago in my refresher. Perhaps it hadn't been Jazz.

'You're telling me that you never had sex with her and never gave her a sample of your sperm for fertilisation?'

'I never gave her a sample during sex or at any other time.'

'She says you suggested having a child.'

'Wilful misinterpretation. It might have been after we had fixed the laser. I went to thank Gunadi for very promptly supplying some parts we had needed. We talked and she opened up about her troubled past and about Avalos. She told me what had happened between them and about all the earlier abuse she had suffered. You knew about that I assume?'

'Yes, I knew.'

'Well I hadn't known. Naturally I was horrified and felt sympathetic.'

'So you comforted her?'

'Yes. No, not sexually. We chatted for quite a while. We talked about families and in passing I asked Gunadi if she had ever wanted a child. That's all, I swear.'

'Don't swear, Menem. People who say that always lying.'

'Why did Gunadi come to you? What did she say?'

'Gunadi asked to see me. She was clearly nervous but excited. She said she wanted to have a child and wanted my permission. People think they now have to ask me, so perhaps you were right and we should have had a formal amendment to the rules. We're less than six months away from arriving so I don't see any problem any more.'

'We may have to live on this ship for sometime after we arrive and we've a job of work to do then. The children will have to remain confined to the Habitat Ring for quite a while, until Fleet can take them down to a planet's surface, if that's ever possible.'

'We will have to rearrange things. We can make more space to live in. We should be able to cope before Fleet start to arrive a year later. Stop distracting me, Menem.'

'Sorry.'

'I asked Gunadi why she was seeking my permission. Was it simply about the ship's rules? After all, she hadn't had a child before so was entitled to one place at the very least. She said that she appreciated that, but she wanted to make sure I was all right with it. I suspected there was something more, and I realised I didn't know who the father was, or even who he was likely to be, so I asked.'

'And she said it was me?'

'Yes.'

'Wow.'

'I asked her if she was in a formal relationship with you and she said not. She wasn't concerned about that. She said that she thought you cared for her and would make a good father for her child. She wanted to check that I wouldn't be upset. She said of course she knew that you and I had been together a long time ago but she thought that the relationship had been cold for years. She thought it courteous to ask me.'

'What did you say?'

'I was stunned. It was a bolt from the blue. A hidden object-field we might say, with the potential to leave mayhem in its wake. I tried to get a grip and put the mission first. I said that I was fine with her having a child and that the whole crew were her family. I said I would speak to you to make sure everything was clear between us.'

'You've made things clear between us.'

'I haven't finished with you yet.'

'Did you finish off Avalos?'

'Don't even start on that Menem or you'll end up as a pile of dust too. What do you want, Menem? Last night I thought... well I thought... you were nice. I thought you still wanted me.'

'I did. I do. Why do we make it so hard, Sahko?'

'Over the last week or so, Menem, since we ran into the object-field and the engine went off, I've watched you gradually putting the ship back together. When we found out about the damage to the nozzle, I thought we were done for, as did most of the others. But you didn't. You got on with it. First fix this and then fix that. Gradually the others all realised it could be done and they joined in. Everyone made a significant contribution. We stand a fighting chance now, thanks to you. I came to realise how much I needed you by my side, not only as our engineer but more than that: as a friend, as an inspiration. As I realised that, love returned. I had started to look to the future, to beyond the journey and I realised I wanted to be with you then, in the promised land.'

I put my head in my hands. 'What should I do, Sahko? Tell me what I should do.'

'Speak to Gunadi, sort things out one way or another, Menem. No more trying to be nice to everyone. You have to choose, decide which team you're on. You're going to hurt someone. Get it over with, get over it. When you've spoken to her and sorted things out, come and tell me. I can cope with what ever you decide on.'

I held on to the door frame. Sahko stood and looked at me, there was still determination in her eyes: she was strong.

'I will, Sahko. I will sort things out with Gunadi and then I'll come back to you. I don't know what I'm going to say. I don't want to push her over the edge, I don't want her on my conscience, and besides we need her skills. Bita has fixed up a meeting with Gunadi and me for tomorrow afternoon.'

'Speak to Gunadi before then. I think that you'll be able to work something out.'

Sahko came close to me and looked up in to my face. She brought a hand up and touched my bruised cheek and I flinched.

'Don't look away, look at me, Menem. This is something you have to face.' She came very close. 'Don't forget the hurt you've caused.'

She held my gaze for some time; her eyes were like infinite pools.

'If you come back to me, just remember that if you put that where you shouldn't, I'll damage you so much next time that you won't be able to have children, ever, with anyone. Now get out.'

I felt the door open behind me. She gave me a shove and I staggered and fell outside. The door shut with a hiss.

4025, 20:25

I lay for a few seconds, then slowly stood and made my weary way back to my apartment, collapsing on my bed. My cheek was screaming, it must have been split because there was blood in my mouth. I needed some pain relief so messaged Yingluq to ask if I could come and see her for a few minutes because I had tripped and hurt myself. She agreed to call round. I lay back on my bed and gritted my teeth, trying not to stretch my cheek in the process, thinking about what Sahko had done to me. I hadn't seen the blow coming; somehow she had managed to divert my attention. A story was needed quickly: what had I tripped on? There was a knock on the door and Yingluq arrived dressed in seamed-up doctor's white jacket and trousers.

'So what's the problem?'

'It's my cheek,' I said in a quiet voice that only too realistically conveyed the pain. 'I caught my foot under a machine, fell and caught my cheek. Very careless.'

Yingluq looked at me sceptically. 'Let's see that cheek.' She bent over me and studied my face, a half-smile on her mouth, her beautiful eyes twinkling close to mine. 'That's quite nasty. Looks like you hit it quite hard. Let me look inside your mouth. Ah yes, some bleeding, but that will soon stop. It might be a little painful to eat on that side of your face for a day or so. You really have suffered. Quite a remarkable injury from a fall, very bad luck. You really were very careless.' She fiddled in her case a moment. 'Here's some cream for your cheek. It will sting when I apply it but then you'll feel much better and the swelling will go down quickly.'

She was right about the stinging-when-applying bit. I nearly screamed. It was almost as bad as the initial damage.

'That's a very impressive injury. I couldn't have done better myself without inflicting lasting mutilation. You really should be more careful.' She was smirking and might have guessed what had happened.

'Thanks, Yingluq, for coming around so quickly. The pain has lessened already. I feel as though I might live. That thing must be sorted so no one trips on it again.'

'You need to do that very soon, before someone else gets hurt.' She put away her medical kit and stood up. 'Is there anything else I can do for you at the moment: a drink, or something to eat?'

'No, nothing, thanks.'

'A good night's rest might be best. You'll feel better tomorrow. Be careful in the refresher; you might want to hand-wash your face.' I watched her tall athletic figure walk away. She turned around and saw me looking at her. 'Not dead yet are you, Menem?'

I lay back on the bed and looked at the ceiling. What had Sahko said? Whatever it was, it conflicted with her actions. One thing I was sure of was that she had told me about Gunadi going to see her. Talking with Gunadi had become urgent and yet had to be done very carefully. There was a risk of turning a bad situation into something much worse. How fragile was she? Perhaps it would better to leave it to Bita; she was a professional after all.

There was a knock at the door. Presumably Yingluq had forgotten something and had come back. The door opened but it was Gunadi, dressed in black, and she seemed nervous.

'Sorry to come around like this, but I saw Yingluq coming out of here with her medical bag. I thought you might be injured.'

'Nothing serious. I tripped on something and bashed myself rather badly. Yingluq was fixing me up.'

'Oh gosh yes, you've injured your cheek. It looks as though someone slapped you really hard, you poor thing.'

Of course Gunadi was an expert on such things. She would know what a slap would look like.

'Really? My toe caught under something and I came crashing down, hitting my face.'

Gunadi came closer and sat on the edge of the bed and looked down at me.

'It looks like a very hard slap. You've had a rough time.' I may have been mistaken, but there was a gleam in her eye. 'Can I do anything for you? Do you need anything? Something to eat perhaps?'

'No thanks. I ate before I went to see Sahko.' Suddenly Gunadi was very still, looking down at me.

'You went to see Sahko? Did you talk with her?' Gunadi's voice was calm, almost monotonal.

'Yes. We talked.'

'What about?' I was silent. 'Did she tell you that I had been to see her earlier?'

'She did.'

'And that I had decided I wanted a child?'

'Yes.'

'And that it could be your child?'

'Yes.'

'What did you say to her? I can see what happened to you.'

I turned my head away and stared at the wall.

'You don't want to have child with me, do you? You're still in love with Sahko, aren't you?' She sighed. 'I've known that all along. You know you may never have child with her, that she might not want one with you, that she might not be capable of having one, at least with you? Look at me, Menem.' I turned back. Her voice was strong, she seemed calm.

'Yes, I know that,' I whispered.

'And she's not prepared to share you?'

'I didn't ask. I'm sorry, Gunadi. I wish it were otherwise.'

'I can see how it is.' She was amazingly calm. 'Well that worked anyway, my going to see Sahko certainly triggered action.'

'You did it deliberately?'

'Maybe it wasn't a good idea, but for a while I thought you did want a child with me. You suggested it in a kind of way, and I thought it a nice idea, but I always wondered if I had misunderstood. Massoud warned me.'

'Massoud?'

'Yes, we talked. We work together sometimes. We play games together.'

'You do? He said something, but I didn't think he was in to that kind of stuff.'

Gunadi laughed. 'What a mind you have, Menem. Virtual games. Massoud and I write games for each other, kind of puzzles.'

'Ah yes, he told me that. What did he say about me?'

'He said that you were still in love with Sahko. He warned me.'

'I'm sorry, Gunadi.'

'That's the way things are. Can't be helped. It might be for the best. At least we are all clear now, perhaps even Sahko, about what we want. You know what? Massoud said that if I decided not to go with you that he would like to father my child. Provide a sample, you know, and help bring up the child. He said he had long wanted to do that but thought that it wasn't to be.'

'Do you like him enough? You know his tastes?'

'We both have uncommon tastes so perhaps we'll be well suited. We can have our companions satisfy our 'tastes', as you call them, and then be good friends. It might work out well.'

'Are you sure, Gunadi?'

'Sure? No. But it seems like a reasonable plan at the moment. I'm not going to rush in to things. Who know what I'll think in the morning?'

'Gunadi, if things get bad, come and talk to me, please.'

'Thanks, Menem, but I doubt that's a good idea. You're sweet though, that's one of the things I like about you, always trying to help. Trying.' She smiled down at me, looking calm and confident. 'I'm not quite as fragile as some people seem to think. Sure, I have my moods, but I've survived this long and I'm damn well going to see it through.'

'Good for you. I don't want to be a burden to you, but if you need me, I'm here. I need all the support I can get as well.'

'Maybe you're not as strong as people sometimes think, not quite so robust, but you do seem to be able to get up again when you've been knocked down. We'll be here for each other, won't we?'

'Yes, we will. Thank you, Gunadi.'

She put her hand up to her cheek and said: 'Maybe we don't have such different tastes after all. Maybe that's the problem, we have the same taste.' She laughed rather hollowly: 'Not a good taste, Menem.' She got up, smiled and said quietly and a little sadly: 'Take care, Menem,' and then she left.

Lying back on my bed, I was too tired and sore to move. What had I done, or had had done to me? The pieces didn't fit together, perhaps they never would. As usual something was missing, something not understood. Had Gunadi orchestrated the whole thing? Had I done the right thing? How does one ever know? Alone on my bed, I stared at the blank ceiling.

Mission Day 4026

4026, 07:20

I had a headache and my cheek was on fire. Other than that, all was fine. Well, apart from the fears racing around in my head and that I had slept very badly. I was still in the yesterday's clothes and lying on top of my bed rather than in it. Reaching over to a drawer beside the bed, I pulled out a strip of painkillers, took a couple and sat still for a few minutes while they got to work.

Peeling off my top went OK as long as my damaged cheek was avoided. The refresher misted and sponged me gently and then dried me. Shaving seemed like a bad idea. I cleaned my teeth myself, very carefully, to avoid the damaged cheek.

The pills were having their full effect, allowing me to move a little more freely. I dressed and ordered some fruit juice, yogurt and coffee: foods that could be consumed while avoiding the damaged side of my mouth.

A message was waiting from Sahko that read "Sorry." That was it: sorry. No kidding. The woman had practically killed me and all she could say was sorry. Ah well, could be worse.

There was also a message from Gunadi: "Sorry I've caused you so much pain!?"

Everyone was sorry today. I used to be sorry for Gunadi and now she was sorry for me: how the world turns, or the galaxy in our case.

Agyei had sent a message too. At least she wasn't saying sorry. It was just as well that we had finished checking the rotation motors before my seeing Sahko. Crawling around in cramped voids didn't seem very appealing at the moment. Agyei was asking where we should meet to review what we had found and to agree the way forward. I messaged her back to let her know that I had tripped and injured myself last night and suggested we meet in twenty minutes in Engineering.

My breakfast arrived and after a tentative start, I managed by using only the right side of my mouth. Trying not to drool down my clean shirt proved tricky; my cheek was still a bit numb from Yingluq's anaesthetic.

Easing myself into a chair in front of the main screen in Engineering, I pulled up images of all sixteen motor mounts, ordering them in the circular sequence of the sections. There was no clear pattern. The most severely damaged were all in one half of the ring, but all had some form of problem. I was studying these images when Agyei arrived.

'Ah, so you've got them all set up together,' she said, drawing up a chair and sitting beside me. 'Any conclusions?'

'Not really. There's slightly more damage to the ones on this side, from four to eleven, than on the other, but it's not a large difference.'

'Wow, what have you done to your face? That's quite a mark.'

'I tripped.'

'Gosh, what did you trip on?'

'I caught my foot on something.'

'You poor thing.'

'These things happen.'

'Very nasty. So how did it happen? Was it in here?' She looked around but there were no convincing trip hazards present.

'I wasn't looking, my foot caught under something and I fell forward and seem to have hit face. But I'm all right, Yingluq fixed me up and she thinks I'll live, so don't go sizing up my quarters just yet.'

'But where did it happen?'

I waved my arms around vaguely. 'I was a bit stunned afterwards so I'm not sure.'

'You don't know? It must be a serious trip hazard to cause injuries like that. We should do something about it. I don't want it to happen to me, particularly in my condition.'

'I'm sorry, I can't remember the details. I'll make sure it's cleared up.'

'You must remember where it happened.'

There was the trace of a smile on her face. 'Leave it, Agyei, please.'

She was quiet for a moment and then whispered: 'Oh I get it: on an assignation, you naughty man. You seem to have paid a high price this time.' She was definitely smiling now.

I groaned. 'No, it wasn't what you're thinking.' That didn't sound convincing even to me. This wasn't going to be the last I heard on this subject. Being a recluse for the next few days, if not months, was a possibility. 'Let's deal with the ship's problems. They're a lot easier to fix.'

Agyei seemed to have got enough value out of my troubles for the moment so turned back to the screen. We worked out the direction and forces required to do the damage in each section based on the masses and the strength of the materials involved. We got all that plotted up and then worked on a process for remediation that used as little new material as possible. Agyei sent our suggestions to Bjorn, to get an independent check, and the results of our analysis to Gunadi, to see if she could use that information in the virtual structural survey. It was a long morning's work and by the end I was stiff and sore and needed another painkiller. Agyei suggested a lunch break. I declined joining her in the refectory, claiming some routine work needed catching up on. She smiled and took the hint.

When she was gone, I messaged Massoud and asked if we could meet, perhaps late-afternoon. He messaged back to say that he would come around to Engineering at four, as he had heard about the trip. That reminded me of the session with Bita; was it still happening? Presumably it was. I messaged both Bita and Gunadi, asking if the meeting could be moved to Engineering because I needed to watch a machine. It looked as though I might get away with spending the whole day in Engineering which had the distinct advantage of avoiding any more jokers.

For lunch, managing something a bit more substantial than my breakfast seemed possible, but it still mustn't need much chewing. A soft pasta type dish would be the thing. I ate carefully and alone, thinking about my predicament. My boats with Gunadi were burned and I might regret that. Sahko was probably done with me for good too, which I definitely would regret.

Status pinged and there was a message saying that a document had been added to the object-field file. Intrigued, I opened it and saw it titled "On the structure and origin of a previously unknown type of interstellar object", and the authors were Bita, Gunadi, Agyei and Minogue. I read the abstract and learned that they had determined that the field was made up of grains of pure crystalline silicon, with a very low concentration of aluminium diffused through it. They had calculated that the object field was stable because the force of gravity trying to collapse it was counteracted by the objects in the field being highly charged, and therefore repelled one another. The shape of the field had to be a spherical shell, as we had experienced. The team had been able to create a model that showed it could be stable for millions of years if it was undisturbed. The grains in the eggshell swirled around in an ever-changing pattern of vortices, a complex of multiple harmonic patterns. It was the angular momentum of the grains within the vortices, driven by their electrical repulsion, which prevented the field's collapse.

The team speculated that the object had formed when a single massive crystal had encountered an interstellar gas cloud, causing it to heat up and become highly charged. The heat build-up must have been very slow, penetrating to its depths, but eventually had become so great that the crystal exploded into almost uniform tiny particles, thrown outwards until they stabilised into their current structure.

I flicked through the main document and looked at the very pretty patterns in a few of the diagrams. It seemed to me all rather speculative, but very impressive.

There was already a comment attached from Sahko: "Fascinating. Please set up a time to present this to anyone interested and for us to ask questions – I have a few. At least it doesn't seem to be a defence device."

I added another. "Congratulations, this explains a lot. I should like to attend a presentation too. There are some things I don't quite understand here. Not sure it entirely rules a defence device: after all how did such a massive (how big?) crystal of that particular composition form in the first place and where? Also, I don't recall any large, charged, dust clouds in the vicinity."

Regretting my comment as soon as it was posted, I was about to recall it for editing when another comment popped up: this one from Yingluq. It read "Fantastic that you could make sense of the O.F., looking forward to a presentation. Comments so far suggest it's going to be another Jude and Punchy show – should be fun!!!" That comment raised doubts about Yingluq's commitment to medical confidentiality.

I swung my chair back to the screen and started to review the ship's vital statistics to keep my mind from wandering off on unwanted byways. The engine was running smoothly, Wayclear hadn't detected any incoming for some days now and all the ship's services seemed to be functioning. It was a rare lull, with no impending disasters for me to get my teeth stuck in to. I had a look at other open projects: the mimic head, the printer trouble, rearranging some food-prep kit, the sensor survey, the power surge. Oh dear.

Hyun was working on the mimic head and again I had forgotten to ask Agyei about the camera sensors. As Hyun was busily making all the optics for them she must have agreed to give them up. Putting all the parts together would keep me busy for a while. Checking all the motor mounts in Processes and repairing all of the broken mounts was another big job that shouldn't be left long. That would inevitably mean encountering most of the crew somewhere along the line, something that would have to be faced eventually. The motors would have to be brought in for checking for the same fault as the one from the refectory.

There was a knock and Bita came in with Gunadi. Bita was an innocent fairy, flamboyantly dressed in colourful flowers and birds on a sky blue ground; clothes that had been made from the fabric Massoud and I had seen being woven on our visit to the Processes Ring. Gunadi was a dangerous pixy in a light green and brown with remarkable delicate pumps.

No one said anything for a while. I was starting to wonder who was going to crack first. Then Bita started to laugh.

'You're in a mess, Menem, aren't you?'

I sat up a bit straighter and adjusted my shirt. 'I tripped and damaged myself,' I said with dignity. Gunadi smiled and looked away.

'That must have been quite painful. I hope the other party, sorry, thing you tripped on, didn't get hurt.'

'I don't think any damage was done, except to me, but I haven't had a chance to check since it happened.'

'Yingluq sorted you out, or was it Sahko?'

'Yingluq treated my injuries.' I wished she would get off the topic so I changed the subject. 'Gunadi and I have already had a talk, as you probably know.'

Gunadi looked back at me. She seemed to have collected herself and appeared confident. It was though a weight had been lifted off her.

'Yes, Gunadi has filled me in.'

Gunadi immediately added: 'I hope you don't mind, Menem. I wanted to put Bita in the picture as soon as possible, to limit any awkwardness.'

'Do we really need this meeting?' I asked. 'We seemed to reach a good understanding last night, unless you've changed your mind.'

'I haven't, but I wanted to be sure that you don't regret your choice. I thought it would be good to have Bita here to listen to us and to offer advice.'

I was amazed at her confidence. She suddenly seemed adult, no longer a child to be sheltered and protected. I noticed that she had brushed her hair and it was held by some clips away from her eyes. She sat upright, as though no longer embarrassed by her breasts.

'Good,' I said rather feebly and looked at Bita who was smiling encouragingly, trying to get a small child to join in the party. It was disorienting and I was not at all sure I wanted to be here, or where I wanted to be. No, it certainly wasn't here, confessing my sins to these two women.

'Go on, Menem,' said Bita. 'Tell me what you want.'

Don't ask that Bita, I thought. I don't know. There are several "me"s here, fighting for preference: the me that wants to spend eternity with you, naked in the viewing dome, the me that wants to explore the darker side with Gunadi, or the me that wants to settle down with the woman I love and have a family and live happily ever after, or just the me that likes fixing the ship and doesn't want the messy complication of human relationships, or even the me that's the hero of the hour that leads the crew to triumph and glory. Which me?

Instead I said: 'I'm sorry, I'm not sure what to say. I don't feel all that together at the moment.' I felt myself squirming in my chair and studied the floor.

'Are you in pain? Shall I call Yingluq?' asked Gunadi.

'No, no, thanks, it's getting better.'

'Why did you get hurt, Menem?' asked Bita kindly. At least it sounded kind until I noticed that she had asked 'why?' and not 'how?'

'I tripped on something and hit my head.'

'That won't do.'

'I'm sorry?'

'I asked 'why?' Why did you get hurt?'

'I was careless I suppose.'

'You were careless. Somebody beat you up because you were careless. It wasn't Gunadi who hit you was it?'

I saw Gunadi suddenly sit upright in her chair and stare at me, startled. I wondered if, for a moment, she thought she had done it, whether she had actually physically assaulted me.

'No, no, Gunadi didn't do anything. She didn't touch me, she wasn't there. It wasn't her fault.'

'Gunadi, did you assault Menem?' Bita asked in her teachers' voice.

'No. I didn't physically assault him. It could be that some of the things I did or didn't do led to this result. Who knows, maybe it was something you did, Bita, or didn't do?'

The two women stared at each other.

'It looks to me like a jealous lover attack or defence,' said Bita. 'I don't think that it was a man, although some may have concerns about Menem sniffing around. Those injuries don't look like those a man would inflict in such a situation. Men are more likely to punch in the face, stomach or kidneys and then boot when the victim is on the floor. Menem's injury looks more like those inflicted by a woman, the sort of thing Yingluq teaches in her self-defence classes: the classic shock slap to the face, stamp on the foot and knee to the groin. Very well executed it seems, although fortunately for you, only the first of those. There are six women on board; who is the most likely to want to do that to him? I've enjoyed time with the man here recently and possibly Yingluq has as well, but neither of us is the jealous type. I would rule out Agyei and Ibo for now, although I might revise that view if either of their babies end up looking like Menem. Gunadi, you deny it, and Menem has said it wasn't you, so I think we can conclude who it was. Always dangerous, investigative work, isn't it, Menem? You never know what awkward conclusions you might reach.'

I gulped. 'Yes, no. I tripped...' My voice faded.

'Perhaps we had better all agree on that for now. It might be career limiting to do otherwise. I'll therefore swiftly move on to the point of this meeting which I called to try to help resolve some feelings. Gunadi tells me that you two have managed to sort out those problems by yourselves. Makes me feel a bit useless: can't have my clients sorting out their own problems or I should be out of a job. So tell me, Menem, what you think the situation is?'

'I think I made a mistake. I had misinterpreted some things that Gunadi had said to me. I thought that she might be interested in me as a, a, possible partner, as a, a, possible father for her child. Last night she was able, very kindly and gently, to put me straight. She told me that she has reached an understanding with Massoud that he should be the father of her, err, prospective child. I had been flattered by what I thought was her interest in me and of course a bit upset and jealous when she made clear to me that her intentions lie elsewhere.'

'How sweet. Very gentlemanly of you, very old fashioned sentiments. It even sort of accords with what Gunadi said, although she was a bit clearer.'

'Thank you, Menem,' added Gunadi. 'You really are decent. It took a while for me to realise that it wouldn't work between us. As I said, in some ways we're too alike.'

Bita looked amused, which was dangerous. 'So all that remains is that we resolve the other thing.'

'What other thing?' I foolishly asked.

'Well the trip hazard. We don't want you falling and hurting yourself again. If it doesn't get you it might get someone else, and we don't want that.'

'It's one of those things that are hard to shift. I'll try to take better care in future and, as far as I know, no one else is in imminent danger of tripping on it.'

'I think I may have been at least partly responsible for Menem's fall,' added Gunadi. 'Maybe it was dodging me that precipitated it. I'll make sure I don't get in the way again. Perhaps others should be warned too.'

Gunadi was staring at Bita. Bita looked down at her notepad on which nothing had been recorded.

'Life is full of hazards. We can't avoid them all,' I put in brightly. 'It would be very dull if everything was too safe.'

'I think I'm done here,' said Bita. 'Anything either of you two wants to add?'

'I think we're done, Menem, don't you?' said Gunadi.

'I'm done, for the time being at least, perhaps permanently.'

'Well if either of you want to talk to me more, either privately or together, you know where to find me,' said Bita.

I couldn't help wondering what sort of invitation that was. I watched as the two women stood up and left together, both lean, like cats on the prowl looking for small creatures to slaughter. I shuddered as a black hand of pleasurable anticipation and consequent pain passed over me.

4026, 15:25

I messaged Agyei about the camera sensors for the mimic head and she confirmed that she had agreed to give up a couple and would send them over. I messaged Hyun and said I was ready to start work on assembling the mimic head. He replied to say that the parts had almost all been printed; there were only a couple of lenses left to do. He would send the completed parts over but reminded me that the optics would need polishing and then sending to Agyei for coating before assembly.

I reviewed Hyun's redesign of the mimic head. He had refined a couple of details which should allow smoother, more natural control. It was also smaller than the original, which I thought might look a little odd, but which had saved significantly on materials. He had added a light activated screen on the front which would protect the optics if the head was suddenly pointed at an intense source of light. That gave the eyes a slightly protruding appearance, adding to the inhuman look of the head. My priority now was to get the polishing of the lenses sorted out. I started searching Archive for recommendations on how to do that with the limited equipment we had with us. There were a lot of helpful suggestions as usual, and a few that might actually work.

Massoud knocked and tentatively came in looking more reserved than his usual ebullient self. The galabeya he was wearing was in dark and light vertical stripes. I observed how it smoothed out his physical shape, obscuring his strength. Neither of us spoke and I wondered how awkward this was going to be. I should have thought about it more beforehand and, at the very least, prepared to be hospitable. Massoud had anticipated my inadequacy and produced a flagon with a rather elegant spout. He pulled up a chair, found a crate to serve as a small table and from the top of his pot he unclipped a pair of very small cups and poured two strong black coffees. We faced each other across the crate and drank down the coffee. He refilled our cups.

'Tell me my friend,' Massoud began, 'to satisfy my curiosity, who killed Avalos?'

I paused before answering and looked at him, wondering how serious he was. 'We all did.'

'How so?'

'He joined us late, substituting for the well-liked Frousch, and never really bonded into the team. It was always going to be an uphill struggle, and after a couple of months it was clear he had no friends here, and quite a lot of the crew were actively avoiding him. He must have felt increasingly isolated. The other crew members didn't want to play his games any more, except perhaps Gunadi, but that was more out of addiction that desire. He was a proud man and despised weakness in others. If any one of us had made more of an effort to befriend him early on, to see past his strutting, we might have found the human being, with the usual mix of problems we all have. But none of us did. We might have recruited him properly to our mission. Instead he remained an outsider.'

'Everyone is to blame and no-one.'

'The usual story.'

'Do you think he died as a result of an accident, or was it suicide?'

'We will never really know. I find it hard to see how it could have been an accident. It would have been a series of very unfortunate events for that to be the case. I am inclined to believe that he realised that his game was up, and the party over.'

'That seems to be a reasonable conclusion.' Massoud seemed satisfied. He now knew I wouldn't denounce him for what he had done. He knew I had sold my soul to Sahko and therefore we were on the same side.

'He may not have been acting alone,' I said.

'Do you have any evidence of that?' he asked. I saw him come alert.

'There was the oddity in Engine Control. Unfortunately it got too damaged in the fire to determine what it was for. It may have been some kind of divert device to allow someone else to take control of the engines.'

'I understood that you thought it was another shipyard mistake.'

'It might have been, but I have never heard of such a thing, and why disguise it to look like the motor safety controller? Also Ibo had once found him in Engine Control without authorisation. It might have been one of his practical jokes as he had claimed.'

'So what is your theory?'

'I don't have one, other than it might have been part of a plan to seize control of the ship.'

'What purpose would that serve?'

'I can only speculate.'

'Go on, speculate.'

'What if we complete our mission and start to bring Fleet in. We are going to do this one at a time, at about three month intervals. But what if either we were delayed setting up or our equipment went wrong part way through that time? Bad news for some.'

'It would. But how would that be achieved?'

'If someone wished to disrupt the later arrivals they could use this ship to destroy what we plan to build. There will still be anti-matter in the fuel tanks, quite enough for that.'

'Fantastic. If that was Avalos's plan then it has been averted.'

'Unless he wasn't alone.'

'He was the only one who joined our mission at the last minute.'

'Maybe his people had already successfully placed someone amongst the crew, but they decided they needed more than one and so got Avalos added. Or it could be they found out a plant was already aboard from another team and wished to interfere with their plans. Another possibility is that Avalos recruited one or more members of the crew to his cause.'

'Any idea who?'

'Two possibilities spring to mind.'

'Only two?'

'It comes down to the type of person and their expertise: someone who knew what to do to get control of the ship and someone who trained in covert operations, perhaps with a Special Forces background.'

Massoud didn't blink, merely smiled slightly and nodded. 'You know Sahko and I go back a long way,' he said.

'I do. You are completely loyal to her and she trusts you.'

'That is so.'

'Yingluq is a possibility but Gunadi seems the most likely recruit to Avalos's cause.'

'She is, but she isn't. She hated him in a way, for his control over her, but he never recruited her, so she says. I believe her, and even if I am wrong I have neutralised her and she is now at one with me.'

'So the conspiracy, if there ever was one, has died.'

'We must always remain alert. Others may have other plans.'

We stared directly at each other, allies now. I wondered if he and Sahko would compare my inconsistent responses and what the consequences of that might be. We lapsed into silence, drinking our second cup in small sips to stretch out the time.

'On to other matters.' He paused and looked around. 'This is awkward is it not?'

'I don't know what to say.' I shifted uncomfortably. 'I'm afraid of insulting you in some way when I want to thank you. But thanks doesn't seem right either. I really want to find out if you're happy with the situation we find ourselves in, and if not, what we can do about it. I want to know if you're simply being very kind.'

'This is a complicated matter and it doesn't seem possible to isolate simple motivations for any of the parties involved. Let me say that I'm delighted with the solution. From the beginning I was very concerned, mainly about Gunadi, but also about you and about Sahko. I became worried when Gunadi started to pay attention to you because I know that you're indiscriminately attracted to women. It seemed unlikely that you were interested in her as a prospective partner because you've been fairly consistently obsessed by Sahko, despite all your playing around. However, it was conceivable that you might use Gunadi in some misguided way to try to make Sahko jealous. You might be playing with Gunadi and not realising the havoc you could cause. I was wrong about that in this case and apologise for thinking that way. You are not the type of person to deliberately use Gunadi for such ends, but sometimes love makes us do things that we aren't even aware of or that have consequences that we didn't look for. I didn't know why Gunadi had suddenly, as it appeared to me, taken an interest in you. Had she discovered that you could meet some of her needs, as Avalos had? It was unlikely because I had never seen that in your character or heard the slightest rumour to that effect. Am I making sense to you?'

'Please go on.'

'We've all become unsettled. We're in the final phase of our marathon voyage: the last few months. Then we ran in to the object field and the engine went out, and it looked as though disaster had overtaken us. I've never seen Sahko so worried. You set to work fixing things. You got us all involved, hope returned. Agyei announced that she was pregnant and we all started to think about the future. You were going round talking to everyone. You seemed to have created an excuse to do so, actually two excuses: the apology for your outburst after Agyei's announcement and also your investigation into Avalos's death. These conversations sparked chatter amongst the crew: what was Menem up to? It helped divert attention. We all had something to talk about that was not to do with the ship falling apart.'

'I didn't have that motive in mind. I never thought of it.'

'That is entirely believable. Sometimes we do things that turn out right by happenstance. Sahko might have gone around talking to everyone, but it would have been seen as forced: an attempt by the captain to jolly us along, whereas your enquiries seemed, sorry my friend, a bit delusional. Poor old Menem is under such pressure. You can imagine the things that were said. It was hugely helpful. Our only concern was that you really would find something out about Avalos's death that would blow apart the unity of the crew.'

'I don't know what to say.'

'However, I and others started to notice a change in Gunadi's behaviour. It was obvious to me because she and I play those virtual games. The puzzles she created tended to have very dark themes and they suddenly switched to being light and humorous. She was like a billiard ball that had been moving in a straight line and had suddenly changed direction because it had encountered something solid. This change was a puzzle in itself but it didn't take me long to work out its cause. It seems that you had said something to her that had struck a chord. She was looking at you, paying attention in a public way that I had never seen her do with anyone before, even with Avalos. We never really knew if Avalos had recruited her to his team. The more I saw, the more concerned I became that she had become obsessed with you, had perhaps fallen in love with you. I tried to talk with her obliquely about it. At first she denied everything, but gradually it became too obvious and I confronted her more directly. She talked of her life slipping away and what would happen to us once our mission was over. There would be no glory in it for her and there's no going home. She didn't want the voyage to end. I thought that might be dangerous.'

'We all feel some of that don't we?'

'Not everyone. Hyun and Ibo would like a little more distance, a little less sharing, Agyei and Bjorn maybe also. Yingluq would like to stretch her talents rather more, be part of a bigger medical team perhaps. It is quite a responsibility and not terribly rewarding to be in sole charge of the health of a small number of people over a long period of time. She would like to share the responsibility and have some more challenges. Maybe she wants to escape the shadows of Avalos and Mo.'

'We'll have only each other for at least another year, before Fleet arrives. Who knows how things will work out then? It will be different certainly: we'll be part of almost a thousand people rather than fifteen.'

'That's so. We all sense things about to change, and so Gunadi started to think about the future. You asked her whether she had thought about having a child, and she hadn't really up to that point, she told me. Your question came in immediately ahead of Agyei's announcement. We're all getting older. Everyone knows that you would like children of your own. Gunadi began to think that maybe you didn't care who the mother was, or that you might even be interested in her, having been so rejected by Sahko. She began to observe you as a potential father and liked what she saw. She began to dream.'

'You never know, you never know.'

'Quite, my friend. But I too have dreams, I too grow old and think of the future. I too think of children, children I never thought I would have and never thought I wanted. As you know, I couldn't take a woman to my bed, but that's not necessary of course. A plan began to form, a plot. I've sought to replace you in Gunadi's womb. I've conspired against you my friend.'

'I think you've played well, Massoud, very well. You've been a true friend: a friend to me and to Gunadi, and also to Sahko and the mission.'

'Thank you, Menem. I was concerned that you would think that I've stabbed you in the back. You may think so. Nothing is yet set in stone. We all have time to change our minds but I don't think any of us will. The die may not yet be cast but everyone concerned seems content that it be so.'

Massoud got up and walked slowly round the room, looking carefully at some of the machines. With his back to me he said: 'There was even the possibility that you were the third person.'

'What? A conspirator? With Avalos?'

'That thought has occurred.'

'Why? How could you think that?'

'You have toyed with Sahko for years, unsettling her. And recently you have been paying attention to Gunadi. Perhaps you wanted to know what happened to Avalos because you didn't want the same to happen to you.'

'But I have been sweating my guts out trying to fix the ship.'

'Everyone needs the ship to survive.'

'I have been consistently loyal to Sahko. I love her.'

'So you have posed, although "consistently" may not be the right word.'

'You can't seriously believe I'm plotting to seize control of the ship, can you?'

'No, I don't. You needn't worry; your loyalty is not in doubt. But you see how easy it is to twist the facts to make up some fantastic tale.'

'My goodness me, I don't know what to say.'

Massoud came over and put a powerful hand on my shoulder, squeezing it slightly. 'I'll leave you now. We all have things to think over. I hope we'll enjoy coffee together again.'

'I'm sure we will. Many coffees I hope.'

Massoud gathered up the cups, re-fixed them to his coffee pot, and stood.

'You should talk with Sahko.' He said, so quietly that I wasn't sure I had heard him.

'It didn't go so well last time I did that.'

'You know why she was so angry with you, don't you?'

'Yes.'

'Well you are both a little wiser now. She is waiting for you.'

'Are you being her messenger again?' I asked.

'No. But I see things from a little distance. Sometimes that gives clarity.'

'Thank you, Massoud.'

He left without a sound. How much was he the puppet-master? Or had we all been played by Gunadi? I sat awhile and stared at a blank wall. A few minutes later parts arrived for the new mimic head from Printing. I loaded them into the finisher and pressed "reset".

The ship sailed on into the trackless void and the stars directly ahead grew imperceptibly brighter.

Look out for

RIVAL ARRIVAL

Choosing a destination (and other trouble) on arrival in Alpha Centauri part 2 of the Alpha System series (due Spring 2021) See www.williamjohngraham.com for more info.

Acknowledgements

My very grateful thanks to readers of early drafts of this book. Your constructive criticism, typo spotting, technical discussions and even sometimes silence have been a huge help: Will Dawson (U.K.), Marcus Macrae (Canada), Mike Butterfield (U.K.), Calum Chace (U.K.), Gary Gibson (Taiwan) and Bridget Schafer (Germany). Also to my wife, Masako Ishii, who repeatedly gave me the sensible advice to do something more useful with my time.

Thanks to all the writers and editors of Wikipedia: such a fantastic resource, and to many others who have published information on the internet from NASA on down.

If you have any comments or questions or spot any mistakes (surely not?) then please get in touch: www.williamjohngraham.com

About the Author

Previously: farm hand, ice cream salesman, perpetual student (B.Sc., M.B.A., D.Phil.), computer designer, management consultant, entrepreneur (failedx3).

Presently: writer and spaceship designer.

Currently living in Wiltshire, U.K., with a wonderful wife, a cute cat and some curious chickens.